PARAGAEA

PARAGAEA
A Planetary Romance

CHRIS ROBERSON

an imprint of **Prometheus Books**
Amherst, NY

Published 2006 by Pyr®, an imprint of Prometheus Books

Paragaea: A Planetary Romance. Copyright © 2006 by MonkeyBrain, Inc. Paragaea map by Ellisa Mitchell. All rights reserved. No part of this publication may be reproduced, stored in a retrieval system, or transmitted in any form or by any means, digital, electronic, mechanical, photocopying, recording, or otherwise, or conveyed via the Internet or a Web site without prior written permission of the publisher, except in the case of brief quotations embodied in critical articles and reviews.

Inquiries should be addressed to
Pyr
59 John Glenn Drive
Amherst, New York 14228–2197
VOICE: 716–691–0133, ext. 207
FAX: 716–564–2711
WWW.PYRSF.COM

10 09 08 07 06   5 4 3 2 1

Library of Congress Cataloging-in-Publication Data

Roberson, Chris.
    Paragaea : a planetary romance / Chris Roberson.
        p. cm.
    ISBN 1–59102–440–4 (hardcover : alk. paper)
    ISBN 1–59102–444–7 (paperback : alk. paper)
    I. Title.

PS3618.O3165P37 2006
813'.6—dc22

2006003360

Printed in the United States on acid-free paper

For Edgar Rice Burroughs, Alex Raymond, and David Gerrold

Acknowledgments

This book would not have been possible without the patronage of Lou Anders; the encouragement and support of Alan Beatts, Jude Feldman, Jennifer Heddle, Karen Jones, and John Picacio; the assistance of Jenny Lewin, who keeps my daughter Georgia entertained so I can work; the careful eye of Deanna Hoak, who makes me look better than I deserve; and the love of the long-suffering Allison Baker, wife, partner, and friend.

PARAGAEA

Pentexoire

Azuria

Lisbia

Hausr

TAURED

Theman

EASTERN
DESERT

OGANSA
VALLEY

SAKRIA

Bacharia

Masjid Empor

ALTRUSIA

Elvera

CROATOAN

Benu's Temple

Inner
Sea

PAROUSIA

Patala

Laxaria

Keir-Leystall

RIM MOUNTAINS

Drift

Masjid Logos

WESTERN
JUNGLE

Masjid
Kirkos

LATHE MOUNTAINS

Outer
Ocean

Hele

Outer
Ocean

ESCHAR

Atla

Hieronymus Bonaventure

CHAPTER 1

Sparrow, Dawning, Seven

As the first-stage rockets ignited, a low-frequency rumbling somewhere far below her like the voice of the Earth's discontent, it first occurred to Leena that she might die. At this hour, on this day, caught up in a fiery holocaust as the liquid chemical engines overtook their processes and burned all of Baikonur down to ashes. Fire had licked at her heels all her life, and this was the moment it would finally outpace her.

"Pjat', pjat', pjat'," came the voice of the technician in the control bunker, calling the all-clear. *Five, five, five.* His voice buzzed in her ears, the sound from the speakers rebounding around her visored helmet like a shouted echo in a hangar.

Leena rechecked the seal on her gloves, squinting in the low light of the red bulb burning. Any minute now, she was sure. The technician would call out the warning—*Three, three, three*—and the flames that had burned at her footsteps since Stalingrad would finally be upon her. Her parents, and Sergei, and now Leena herself, all fuel for the fire.

The engines below her entered their primary stage, the low rumbling intensifying into the roar of approaching thunder that set her teeth on edge. Smoke and steam would be billowing out now from the base of the launchpad, Leena knew, though she could see none of it, the viewport blocked by the heavy nose fairing covering the module. She thought of the others in the barracks, listening in on radios wired to the walls, and the select few dignitaries joining Korolev and the technicians in the bunker. Yuri would be there, weighted down with medals, as would Gherman and Andrian, Pavel and Valeri. And Valentina, of course.

Valentina Leonidovna Ponomaryova would be nearby, sealed into her bright orange pressure suit, ready to take Leena's seat in the event that a replacement was needed, determination burning beneath her thick brows. Leena couldn't help but pity her. Twice a second, first for Tereshkova and now for Leena, at this rate Ponomaryova would never reach the stars.

"Pjat', pjat', pjat'," buzzed the voice of control in her ears.

Leena could stand the anticipation no longer. Either she would launch, and serve the Soviet as few before her had, or she would die in a fiery conflagration, there on the pad. There were no other options. Let the technician buzz *Five, five, five* until his lungs bled out all their air, damn him. Leena would not wait.

"Poyekali!" Leena shouted, not to the technicians, or to Korolev, but to the spirit of flame that had haunted her days. *Let's go!* Not an eager cry for adventure, as it had been when Yuri had shouted it three years before, but a challenge to her pursuer to finally face her.

"Vorobyey," came the voice of the technician in her ear, as the timbre of the engine's roar crescendoed. "Zapuskat'."

Sparrow. Launch.

Slowly, like dawn stealing softly over a wide plain, the rocket began to rise. So light was the transition from Earth to flight that Leena at first didn't recognize it. There followed a slight shiver, and then the vibrations rippling through the metal sphere module shifting up the spectrum, becoming a high-frequency whine like a kettle gone to boil.

The pressure of acceleration pulled at Leena's face, the g-load slowly climbing from Earth normal to roughly five times that. She tried to speak into the microphone fixed to the base of her helmet, to respond to control's calls for status, but she found it difficult to talk, the muscles of her face drawn back taut against the bones of her skull.

All three stages of the rocket were firing now, pushing against the bonds of gravity, shooting towards the far horizon, and the curve of space beyond. Leena felt pinned to the seat like a butterfly on cork, unable to move even if the heavy straps were not still in place.

Without warning the strain eased, and Leena felt herself grow lighter. The pressure pushing her against the seat dropped suddenly, and it seemed to her as if something had separated from the rocket. Creeping silence followed, the high-pitched shrill of the engines growing ever and ever softer. The fairing, a heavy plating covering the module to protect against air friction during the steep climb, fell away. The viewport finally unobstructed, Leena could see outside.

Looking up through the circular window, Leena saw hanging above her the curve of the Earth, a kind of aura around the horizon bleeding from light blue into violet into the black of space beyond. The stars, hanging on the curtain of deepest black, were larger and brighter than Leena ever could have imagined possible. The Earth's seas, passing overhead, were of a uniform gray from this perspective, the surface rippled and uneven like windblown sand dunes.

Only a handful of people before Leena had seen their planetary home from this height, the half-dozen cosmonauts who'd preceded her and a handful of Americans, if the reports from overseas were to be believed. They had all come for only brief stays, though, the longest of them no longer than five days. Leena, the second woman to come this far, would outlast them all: ten days spent orbiting the Earth as high as the lower Van Allen belt in the belly of Vostok 7.

Ten days, and then she'd return to the bosom of the Earth, Hero of
the State, welcomed into the Party with open arms, and perhaps even
given an honorary promotion in rank. Senior lieutenant, perhaps, or
even commander, but never major. That was for Yuri and the others.
The men. Poor Valentina Vladimirovna Tereshkova, on her return, had
not even been granted the slight honor of a senior lieutenant's commission, still holding only the junior lieutenant's grade that all of the
members of the Female Cosmonaut Group had been awarded years
before. Though she'd never risen higher than the rank of private in the
Red Army, with her previous military service record Leena hoped for
something better.

Senior Lieutenant Akilina Mikhailovna Chirikova, Female Cosmonaut Group. It had a certain ring to it.

Pulling a pencil and tablet from a zippered pocket at her side, she
intended to take the requisite notes but became too engrossed in the
slow ballet of the pencil spinning end over end in zero gravity. Leena
smiled, muscles moving strangely without resistance, and laughed at
her early fears. She'd come this far, this high, because the fire had never
caught her, after all. She'd been silly to think that it ever would.

✦

The mission plan of Vostok 7 was simple: a high-altitude flight into
the lower Van Allen radiation belt for radiological-biological studies,
lasting ten days, at the end of which the craft's orbit would be allowed
to decay naturally to reentry. That the studies were concerned primarily with what would happen to the human organism if exposed to the
radiation of the lower Van Allen for ten days was a factor of the mission upon which Leena chose not to dwell. Having been obsessed with
flight for so many years, she would now be flying higher and longer
than any human before her. And after the first few hours of the flight,

she was feeling no ill effects of the radiation exposure. The interior of the craft was holding steady at a reasonable 20 degrees centigrade, and though she'd not yet released the harness holding her into the launch chair, in the low-gravity environment neither the tight straps nor her cumbersome pressure suit were especially noisome.

Bykovsky was originally scheduled to make this flight, but in March of the past year the decision had been made to have him fly Vostok 5 in the place of Ponomaryova. She was certainly the most qualified, both technically and emotionally, of any in the Female Cosmonaut Group, more qualified than many of the men; but Ponomaryova was an agitator, always complaining about the treatment the women received, always saying that they were the equal to the men and should be treated as such. And she was not an ideologue, causing many to doubt her loyalty to the principles of the Soviet. Instead of women flying both Vostok flights 5 and 6, as planned, only Tereshkova was allowed to go, with Bykovsky pulled forward out of Vostok 7 to take Ponomaryova's place. Initially, it was suggested that this was for safety purposes, and that Ponomaryova would be going aloft in Vostok 7, but in November when the flight crews for the next seven Vostok missions were announced, the task had instead fallen to Leena. Ponomaryova was on the list, but only as Leena's second. Worse, when news arrived a few weeks later of the American president's assassination, and with the chief designer making plans to begin Soyuz launch the following year, there were already talks about canceling any future Vostok missions, and going to the multicrew Voskhod configuration for all future flights, to compete with the American's two-manned Gemini missions. Any three-manned Voskhod mission would be precisely that—three men. Korolev would never agree to send up three women in the same capsule, and decorum would not allow one woman to accompany two men. And so the chances were increasingly slim that Ponomaryova would get her chance at glory. And chances were good that Leena might be the last woman into space for some time to come.

Leena didn't spare time to worry about such hypothetical eventualities. She had mission operations to consider; so far, however, the flight had been far easier on her than anticipated. Leaving aside any radiological fears, it seemed to Leena that the potential hazard of low gravity, too, had been overestimated. Once the initial stress of launch was passed, the flight hadn't been nearly as bad as Leena had feared. The rumor was that Tereshkova had been so ill and nauseated from turbulence and the subsequent low-gee that she was virtually incoherent for much of her seventy-one hours in orbit, and it was whispered that even Gagarin had been unable to control his rioting stomach on initial launch. Leena thought the orbit itself was much easier to endure than the interminable training that had preceded this day. Hot mock-up—whole days and nights spent in full pressurized space suit in the ground spacecraft simulator—had been more grueling than this by far. Yerkina, who was to have been Ponomaryova's backup on Vostok 6, had been excluded from the mission after removing her boots one day into the hot mock-up simulation, having eaten only three rations in the three days of her test. It had reflected badly on all the Female Cosmonaut Group that Yerkina had failed so miserably . . . though Leena could not help but notice that similar failings by the male cosmonauts did not cast a shadow over *their* entire groups.

The orbital path of Vostok 7 would carry the module over the northern reaches of the Soviet Union, across the Pacific Ocean and the southern Atlantic, then over the length of Africa, over the Atlantic, Turkey, the Black Sea, and then back over the Soviet Union.

The orbital period was just under two hours, and the module had nearly completed one complete orbit, passing over northern Africa, the Mediterranean just coming into view. Leena knew that, in the coming days, it was a sight that she would see countless times again.

From the radio came a sudden burst of static. The module was approaching the broadcast range of Star City itself, and the operator at the Baikonur ground station might be trying to contact her. Leena adjusted the gain and frequency, trying to regain the signal.

"Povtorjat', pozhalujsta," Leena said, confirming that the tells on her transmitter showed active. *Repeat, please.*

Just then, the interior of the module was filled with a blinding white light, and squinting against the glare Leena leaned up to the viewport to look outside. There, just before her, hung an object that shone like the sun. It was impossible to judge size or distance, but it seemed small and close enough that she might reach out and snatch it up in her hands. A sphere, it glinted like a mirror, reflecting back the light of the sun behind her.

Could it be another satellite, some early Sputnik prototype the authorities had not publicized? Or an American counterpart, positioned over Russia for the purposes of espionage? Whatever it was, it was directly in the path of Leena's module, the distance between them closing with every heartbeat.

"Centr upravlenija?" Leena whispered into the helmet microphone. *Control center?* Before she could go on, before the ground crew in the Baikonur facilities could answer, the module was upon the object, only bare meters away.

Leena gritted her teeth, anticipating a jarring impact. She closed her eyes and felt a wave of unease flood over her. There came no jolt or bang, nothing to indicate the object had struck her craft.

Tentatively, Leena opened her eyes. Through the viewport, the mirrored sphere was nowhere to be seen. What she did see, however, was impossible.

Where before there'd been only the gray sand dunes of the Mediterranean with the southern edge of Turkey just visible on the horizon, she now saw mountains surrounded by lush green forests, blue ribbons of rivers slipping down to the seas, tan deserts stretching out across the far distance.

Leena knew her geography. She'd studied the projected path of Vostok 7 in its orbits until she could have drawn maps of the continents from memory, had pored over the photos snapped by the earlier cosmonauts until they painted her dreams, and at no point, in all of those months and years of work, had she ever seen anything like the vista stretching out before her.

Wherever she was, whatever had just happened, she was no longer orbiting the Earth she knew.

CHAPTER 2
Falling Star

The whisper of static bled from the speakers in her helmet, no voice from the ground station calling alarms or the all-clear, but Leena hardly noticed. She didn't have the luxury of confusion, no time to stop and reflect on the impossible situation in which she found herself. With unfamiliar vistas stretching out below, the Vostok module began slowly to rotate out of true, falling out of orbit toward the strange planet below.

Below her on the cabin floor, just visible past the edge of her helmet's visor, the eight ports of the Vzor periscope device flashed the story of Leena's coming doom. When the craft's attitude was positioned correctly, the module centered perfectly with respect to the planet's horizon, all eight ports would be lit, the sun's light reflected through an elaborate mechanism worked into the hull of the sphere.

As Leena watched in growing horror, the ports began to wink out and go dark: first one, then three, then six. Then, as the rotational force dragged at her insides like a fist, the ports lit again, then grew dark, then lit, strobing in increasing frequency as the module began to spin faster and faster.

There followed a faint tolling, like distant bells, the automated onboard systems indicating a rapid increase in velocity and drop in altitude. A high-pitched scream began, at the edge of hearing, the upper reaches of the atmosphere clawing at the surface of the module as the craft dipped ever lower towards the planet's surface.

The temperature within the cabin started to climb, and even nestled within her insulated SK-1 pressure suit Leena began to feel the heat.

Leena would have cursed if she'd had the chance, would have screamed herself red with rage at the injustice of it, but this was another luxury she could not afford herself. She would have to do something, there being no one now who could help her, or in very short order she would be dead.

The controls of the Vostok module were all set to automatic by default, any necessary course changes controlled remotely by technicians on the ground in Baikonur. The chief designer had been concerned since the beginning about the fallibility of those chosen for service in the Cosmonaut Corps, and had put as many safeguards between the effectiveness of an operation and the potential breakdown of the cosmonaut as possible. The authorities had relented, though, in the face of continued opposition from the cosmonauts themselves, by allowing manual control in emergency situations.

This situation was an emergency, if any could be, so Leena had no compunctions against initiating the appropriate protocols.

Unfortunate, then, that the combination needed to unlock the manual controls was transcribed on a slip of paper in an envelope kept safely in a zippered pocket on her left thigh. Unfortunate in that the rotational forces whipping the module ever faster had left Leena feeling too sick even to blink, her arms pinioned against the walls of the cabin as securely as if they'd been glued there.

The manual controls, just centimeters away, would allow Leena to fire the attitude rockets, stop the maddening spinning of the craft, and eject the service module in preparation of ballistic reentry. With too much longer a delay, the craft would descend too far into the atmosphere for the rockets to be of any use, and with the service module still attached to the reentry sphere the whole of the craft would burn to a cinder in the resulting friction.

The fire would finally have her, at long last.

Unable to move, vision swimming and stomach in revolt, Leena plummeted to her doom.

She was going to die; she was dying; she would be dead, her life ended —burned down to particulate matter at the heart of a cold steel sphere, to rain down as dust and ash on the surface of an unknown world. She would die with questions left unanswered, left even unasked, mysteries she would never solve: Where was she, and what had brought her here?

The curiosity that had led her from Stalingrad to Moscow to university, then sustained her through years in military service, then driven her to excel when first selected for the cosmonaut program, burned within her hotter than the red tongues that now licked the outer surface of the module. In a sense, Leena had been an explorer since childhood, blazing a trail alone through a strange and hostile world since the day the firebomb had taken away her parents. Now, a whole new world of discovery before her, the thought of surrendering to the doom that had dogged her heels was unacceptable. Whatever the cost, whatever the risk, she would survive. She simply had to know.

The module was now spinning on three axes, the rotational forces pinning Leena to the inner surface of the module. Her hands and arms were unable to move more than a few centimeters; her head was forced to one side with her ear pressing hard against the helmet's lining.

Metal clamps on the floor of the cabin held her booted feet in place, but Leena felt the centrifugal pull working against them, dragging her knees up and towards her chest.

If her left boot could be worked free, the force of the rotation would be enough to bring her left knee up almost to her breast, the zippered pocket on her thigh only centimeters from her left hand. The inside of the module was growing hotter still, hazing like the air over hot desert sands. If Leena was going to act, she would have do it now.

To release the clamps on her boots, without her hands free to aid in the process, Leena had to force her feet down and forward, and then pull up at her heel. Opposite the forces pulling her body the other direction, with her weight feeling as though it doubled with every centimeter she moved, she inched her painful way towards her goal. Drawing on her last reserves of energy, Leena managed to work her booted foot fractionally forward in the clamp. Centimeters like kilometers, eyes closed against the maddening gyrations of the craft, she crossed the small distance.

Leena's skin began to prickle, an instant sunburn spreading over her like scalding water. With teeth gritted she managed to angle her heel up the slightest fraction of a centimeter. That centimeter was all it took. As soon as the grip of the clamp was loosened, the rotational forces pulled her foot away from the cabin floor like a rocket, her knee forced up and slamming into her sternum with a thud.

Knocked breathless, Leena could not afford elation. With every passing second the craft spun faster, hotter, and nearer disintegration.

The fingers of her left hand were bare centimeters from the pocket on her thigh, now forced against her abdomen. Once the envelope was free, she'd have to mangle the contents out, read the combination, reach nearly thirty centimeters along the wall to her right and unlock the emergency controls, then manually fire the braking and attitude rockets.

Seconds to go, and she'd only come a fraction of the way.

Straining, her mind and will almost to the breaking point, Leena fell into a kind of fugue. With one portion of her being concentrating on the task at hand to the exclusion of all else, another smaller part of her conscious mind walled itself away, seeing events unfold as a detached observer. Like watching an actress in a play, Leena saw herself struggle against the bonds of force to wrest the envelope from her pocket, watched the mad fumble as she brought hands together from left and right to tear and claw at the envelope's seal, watched herself fighting to lift her head forward far enough to read the combination typewritten on the paper clutched in a vise grip in her hands.

Throughout it all, watching herself slowly dying, Leena could only think how sad it was that there would be no one back at home to mourn her. A plaque somewhere, perhaps, if she was lucky; a cryptic and official notation in the government files back in Moscow if she was not. But no statues, no parades to the glorious dead. Those back in Baikonur would not know how she had died, only that she was dead, and the grand work would continue, the march into the future of the Soviet Man continuing without her.

As Leena watched herself batter at the combination tumbler, spinning the last number into place, she was strangely disappointed. She had been quite involved with imagining her own funeral in absentia, and now plans would have to be delayed.

Her last erg of motivation draining, Leena stabbed at the switch that initiated the braking procedure.

She slammed forward in her harness, thrown towards the center of the module, as the braking rocket fired. The g-load reversed, then increased, the straps biting into the fabric of her pressure suit, bruising her skin. The rotations of the module increased, and then after forty seconds of thrust the rockets petered out. With a resounding bang, the service module broke free, and the reentry module continued its descent.

The module began again to spin, this time back and forth, ninety degrees to the left and to the right. Leena felt herself being tossed back and forth in her harness like a rag doll, the g-load steadily increasing as the craft dipped farther and farther into the atmosphere.

Leena caught a glimpse of the instruments, the hand of the altitude dial spinning like a propeller, and then everything began to grow fuzzy. A blanket of gray falling over her, Leena could only trust in the automated systems to take over for her.

There came a whistling of air, and flashes of red from the viewport overhead, stars dimly visible through the burning curtain of sky.

At seven thousand meters, the first explosive bolt on the hatch blew like a shot, then another. Leena blinked, her eyes for the moment sightless, unsure whether she was yet free of the craft or not. The forces on her relaxed, and she lifted her head, hoping to make out her position through the haze that blurred her vision. At that moment, her chair shot up through the hatch with such force that she bit down hard on her lip, blood streaming out onto the helmet's visor. She and the module, now separated, fell on parallel courses towards the planet below, the service module burning up somewhere in the atmosphere above them.

The ejection chair, Leena strapped firmly in place, spun end over end, tumbling like a falling leaf through the cold blue sky. A cannon fired, jarring Leena with the shock of it, and the stabilizing chute shot out from the top of the chair, dragging behind and straightening her descent.

Leena rotated slowly to the right in the chair, blinking back tears of panic and exhilaration, trying to see something of the land below her. To the south there were mountains, purple and tall, to the east an endless expanse of oceans, and below her a carpet of forest stretching out to the western horizon, a wide river ribboning through it.

The next parachute opened, blossoming orange and huge above her, then the next, both dwarfing the miniature stabilizer that had opened first, hanging small and white above them, a moon to their twin suns. The chair's rate of descent slowed, and looking down past her feet Leena saw the river and dense foliage below her. Unable to direct the motion of the chair, she could only watch as touchdown grew nearer.

Fluttering down beneath orange canopies as if on a slight breeze, Leena's chair dropped slowly and directly towards the wide river below.

As the chair touched down, Leena's feet disappeared below the surface of the water. The water burbled up to her waist, the weight of the steel chair dragging her down, and Leena couldn't help but think that she might have her funeral in absentia after all.

With a splash of finality, the chair disappeared beneath the swift currents, the three parachutes floating on the surface like fallen leaves until they, too, were drawn under.

The ejection chair sank like a stone into the murky depths of the river, drifting slightly with the strong undercurrents. Strapped securely in place, Leena experienced something very near a state of shock while breathing up the last of the oxygen reserves left in the pressure suit. The air hose, which should have sealed off when separated from the life-support systems of the Vostok module, had failed to close completely, and a hiss of water spilled with slow but relentless finality into the helmet. The silty water had filled up to the level of Leena's chin, and it would be a close race whether the helmet filled first with water or with exhaled carbon dioxide.

The chair touched down on the soft bed of the river, kicking up clouds of silt that were drawn away downriver by the current like smoke in a strong wind. Leena, head tilting ever farther back to escape the rising level of the inflow, moved her stiff fingers in slow motion through the water to reach the strap releases.

The straps ran across her shoulders, chest, and waist, and she had the first of them released when the riverbed drew up slowly to embrace her. The three parachutes, still attached to the chair, floated on the river's surface, and were being dragged downstream by the strength of the current. Tethered like an anchor on the riverbed, the chair was being towed along behind, but the chair's weight was too great for it to move far. In the tug-of-war between gravity and river flow a balance was struck, and the base of the chair remained firm on the silty bed while the top end was dragged forward and down, swinging like a door closing shut, face-first into the ground.

Leena found herself trapped under the heavy chair, the faceplate of her helmet pressed into the loam of the riverbed, mouth and nose trapped in a growing pool of water with the last pocket of air trapped behind her head. The design of the chair, pressed into the riverbed, left her hands and arms free to move, but she had only her last gasp of air to sustain her.

Eyes stinging and nearly blinded by the murky water, she hammered at the catches on the remaining straps, releasing first one, then another, her pulse pounding in her ears and her lungs feeling as though they would at any second explode. Drifting on the edge of unconsciousness, exhaustion threatening to overtake her, Leena slammed open the last of the strap releases. Pushing forward with arms thrashing, she frantically attempted to get free of the chair, beating arms and hands and head into the soft surface of the riverbed, sending up massive clouds of silt. Free from the waist up, though, she found that her legs below the knees were still trapped below the heavy weight of the chair.

Turning on her side, twisting painfully from the knees, she managed to angle her head far enough to let out a sputtering cough and take in another lungful of air. Then she turned her attention back to the chair, trying to push it up off the riverbed far enough to pull her legs free. The surface of the riverbed was soft and yielding, though, and the harder she pushed, the farther her hands sank down into the soil. The chair had not moved a centimeter.

The air pocket was shrinking fast, the helmet filling faster and faster, and unless she was able to extricate herself from the chair and reach the surface, Leena had only minutes left. She was trapped, and drowning.

If she could not lift the chair, and lacked the strength to pull her legs loose, her only option was to shovel away the silt beneath her, freeing her legs from below. The air remaining in the helmet slipped out in a steady stream of bubbles through the partially sealed hose, replaced by cold and murky water. The pounding of her heartbeat in Leena's ears increased, until she was sure her eardrums would burst. She had very little time to act.

Forcing herself to remain calm, Leena pressed back into the semblance of a sitting position on the overturned chair. This provided her space to move, with less than a meter between her head and torso and the soft floor of the riverbed. Then, tucking her head down, she bent at the waist, reaching down to her knees. She began to scrape furiously at the soft loam beneath her legs, like a dog digging to hide a bone, sending up flurries of silt.

It was like trying to dig a hole in wet beachsand as the tide rolled in. As soon as Leena scooped away a handful of the soil, the water pressure would push more in from all sides. Alternately scooping away with her hands, and pulling with all her strength at her legs, she managed to work her legs centimeter by centimeter out from under the heavy chair. After the first few seconds, she rose back into an inverted sitting position, tilting her head back and to one side to catch a quick breath, but there was so little air left in the helmet that she drew in as much water as oxygen. Racked by coughs, she steeled herself and returned to the task at hand.

It couldn't have taken more than a handful of seconds, far less than a full minute at any rate, but it seemed to Leena like an eternity before the ground gave way sufficiently for her to work her feet free.

Survival training winning a war of attrition with her mounting panic, Leena remembered the survival kit strapped to the side of the chair before pushing away to the surface. The clouds of dirt and silt she'd kicked up with her digging still hung around the area like a low, black fog, but Leena was able to feel her way to the airtight metal case clipped to the chair's side. Her hand closing over the handle, Leena began to feel a glimmer of hope. The kit's contents—emergency rations, signal flares, compass, medical supplies, knife, pistol and rounds—made her feel equipped to handle whatever challenges this strange world might present. She'd survived the siege of Stalingrad, the state orphanages, several years of military service and cosmonaut training; she could survive anything.

Pushing away from the riverbed, Leena's vision was almost completely obscured. A combination of exhaustion, lack of oxygen, and the current-borne silt clouded her view. Fortunately for her, the designers of her pressure suit had anticipated the possibility of a water landing, if perhaps not the possibility of being trapped by the chair. Around the base of the helmet, which could not be detached from the suit, was a rubber collar. Leena pulled the release tab, and the collar inflated, pulling pressurized gas from a small reserve tank fixed to the back of the suit. Floating blind, Leena let the collar drag her to the surface, the current pulling her downstream from the chair.

Before reaching the surface something brushed past her, almost knocking the heavy metal case from her grip. Her limited vision couldn't make out many details of what the thing had been, but she'd gotten the impression of something huge, something with massive teeth and a thick, leathery hide. Clutching the survival kit protectively to her chest, she thrashed the waters with her legs violently, desperate to reach the surface and air.

It wasn't until she'd kicked her legs twice against hard, unforgiving rock that she realized that she'd reached the shores of the river. Scrambling over the stones, seconds from passing out due to oxygen deprivation, she splashed her noisy way to the surface.

Throwing the metal case onto the ground, lying from the waist up in dry air with her legs and feet still resting underwater and painfully on the rocks, Leena worked frantically to open the helmet's visor. Encased in wet leather-palmed gloves, her fingers fumbled at the latch, useless. There was some irony in this, a small part of Leena noted, to drown only after safely reaching the shore. And after everything else that had happened to her.

In the last instants before losing consciousness, Leena managed to slide the visor open, and the water trapped inside spilled out in a rush. She collapsed forward onto the rocky shore, sputtering coughs shaking her, drawing in ragged breaths until her pulse slowed to something approaching normal. Rolling onto her back, she drew her knees up, feet dragged out of the water, as though afraid the current might take revenge and drag her once more under. The strange sun was high overhead, and Leena closed her eyes, lying in red-lidded darkness while the rays of light warmed and soothed her. She was still alive, and grateful for it.

A shadow fell across Leena's face, the backsides of her eyelids going from red to black. She opened her eyes, and immediately wished she hadn't.

It stood upright on two legs, with two arms and a head, and in a dim light might have been mistaken for a human being, but with the bright sunlight behind it there could be no question. It was some sort of cat-thing, standing some more than two meters tall, spotted like a leopard or jaguar. Black lips curled back over wicked teeth under its pronounced snout, and while its hands were shaped like those of a man, the fingers were tipped with curved black claws that glinted like obsidian in the bright light. A collection of straps and belts criss-crossed its chest, arms, and legs, and an abbreviated loincloth hung at its waist. Otherwise it was naked, the golden-yellow fur with the black and white spots its only covering.

"Mat'ata'rrom," the thing snarled, pointing a clawed finger at Leena's nose. "Mat'ata'das'ul."

There came from all sides the sound of low growling, and angling her head from one side to the other Leena could see another half dozen or more of the creatures approaching, encircling her.

CHAPTER 3

Captured

Leena felt less the jaguar men's prisoner than their fallen prey. Remembering their long curved incisors, and the long tongues that unfurled to lick black lips between guttural grunts, it was not too hard to imagine them feasting on her remains.

She was bound hands and feet, and hoisted on a long pole carried on the shoulders of two of the creatures, one on each end. If she relaxed her back and neck, her head lolled back, seeing only the ground passing beneath. By tensing, and pulling herself up a fraction against the rough wood of the pole, she could see a bit from side to side, though the position was too much a strain to hold for long.

One of the creatures had retrieved her survival kit, and carried it in a mesh bag slung over its wide and muscled back. This creature walked directly in front of the foremost of Leena's bearers, and from time to time she would catch a glimpse of the sunlight glinting off the polished metal of the case.

Any one of a number of items in the case would be sufficient, Leena knew. Had she believed in any higher power besides the State, she might have prayed; as it was, she only hoped that the universe herself might be watching, and would be willing to lend a hand.

With the chrome-plated Makarov semiautomatic pistol, snugged in its nylon holster inside the kit, Leena might have held the creatures at bay long enough to make her escape, back at the banks of the river.

With the signal flare, she might have been able to call for some assistance, or else set fire to one of the creatures, for all the good it would have done her.

With the kit's folding knife, she might now be able to cut her bonds and free herself, possibly even making into the forest's wilds far enough and fast enough to elude her captors.

With the emergency rations, she might not be as damnably hungry as she now found herself. When her stomach had first growled, hours before, she'd thought for a moment it was the call of the strange creatures.

But the survival kit was carried on the back of one of the monsters, and Leena saw no clear way to freedom.

They were taking her somewhere; that much was certain. If they intended to eat her, whether alive or cooked and prepared after her death, it appeared they didn't plan to do so immediately. From time to time one of the jaguar men would growl a few syllables, curt orders to the others Leena assumed, but for the most part the group traveled in silence. They padded along the forest track single-file, making hardly a sound. With her eyes closed, Leena found she could scarcely hear even the breathing of the creatures at her head and feet. The jaguar men moved through the forest like ghosts.

Leena could not say with any certainty how long they'd been traveling. Her awkward position, hanging uncomfortably by bruised numb ankles and wrists from the pole, and the pounding of her pulse in her ears as the blood rushed up each time her head fell backwards, left her oblivious to the passage of time.

There was only Now: this moment, with the pain, and the anxiety, and the fear of her imminent and unknown death, surrounded by the silent figures of the strange catlike creatures.

After an eternity of that moment, something happened, and the tenor of her pain changed key. Leena had been on the edge of consciousness, straddling the border between delirium and sleep. Something changed, and she struggled to clear her thoughts enough to understand what.

She had stopped moving, no longer gently rocking back and forth with each silent step of her bearers. The party had come to a halt.

"Tar'elmok," she heard the creature in front say.

It was dark, the bare moonlight painting the forest in indistinct grays. Some hours had passed then, at least, if not more. Was it still the same day? How long ago had Leena first glimpsed this strange world of monsters? How long since she'd lifted off from Baikonur towards the heavens and glory?

"Alal'kasen'lak," answered the creature behind, barely above a silent breath.

The creature in the lead, who carried Leena's survival kit in the bag at its back, held up one hand, palm forward. Leena strained to see in the low light, and could just make out the glints of the retractable claws extending up and out from each fingertip.

"Tar'tamedt," shouted the lead creature, and in an instant the configuration of the party shifted. The two creatures at Leena's head and feet released their hold on the pole, jumping one to the left, the other to the right, letting their captured prey fall unceremoniously to the cold ground. Leena struck the ground spine first, the breath punched from her lungs in a painful sigh, and looked up dazzled to see the strange creatures circle around her.

Eight muscled backs of black-and-white-spotted golden fur confronted her, dimly seen in the gray light. The party's full complement faced outward, hands raised defensively, some holding long staffs, some knives, but most with their hands empty, their only weapons their extended claws and bared fangs.

Leena could hear the jaguar men now. They were no longer silent
ghosts slipping through the forest. There was a low rumbling noise, like
distant thunder, climbing slightly in pitch and volume with each
passing second, that sounded from somewhere deep inside the creatures'
chests. Their breathing was louder, too, sounding closer to panting.

Above these rising sounds, Leena heard the noise of some movement from the dark forests beyond the circle. Still bound hand and
feet, still crippled by pain-numbed limbs, she tried to lift up on one
elbow to see farther through the legs of her captors.

The sounds of movement from the trees increased, and were joined
by similar noises from the opposite side of the circle. The creatures
tensed, and began to roar.

Leena understood at last. Her captors, somehow, were afraid.

Just then a figure, white in the moon's low light, burst from the
trees and rushed towards the circle, metal glinting cruel and long in
his hand.

The jaguar men were under attack.

✦

The attack was swift, concentrated, and confusing. Leena, lying hands
and feet bound on the unforgiving ground, perceived it only as a series
of sounds and obscured images. Metal on metal, metal on flesh, flesh
on flesh, and the quick ballet of shadows and shapes dancing fatally
over her were all Leena managed to follow.

The pole from which she'd been suspended lay across her, pinned
between her legs, pressing down into her stomach, and resting against
one side of her helmet. Her hands were tied together, but only looped
over the pole, so as she flinched away from the sounds of battle first on
one side, then the other, she found herself inadvertently working her
hands up and over the pole's end.

The attacker, a blur of white and metal in the moonlight, was joined by another from the clearing's far side, a hulking shadowy figure who plowed the leader of the jaguar men to the ground, snarling and bloodthirsty.

While the jaguar men's leader and his shadowy foe thrashed across the rough forest floor, the other attacker moved like a shot from one end of the clearing to another, shouting and laughing by turns.

The first of the jaguar men to fall collapsed backwards over Leena, a gruesome rent opened across one side of his neck and down his chest, a black bubbling ribbon in the moon's low light. Leena's breath was knocked from her, the pole pressed harder against her chest, the helmet forced to one side, with her legs from the waist down trapped beneath the insensate hulk of her captor.

Leena struggled to free herself, working her shoulders and hips from side to side and reaching her hands back and over her head for any hold. Snaking her way out from under the jaguar man's bulk, her hands slipped loose over the top of the pole without warning. Pausing for breath, the fierce struggles continuing all around her, Leena brought her bound hands down and against the fur and muscle of the jaguar man's side and pushed for all she was worth.

The fallen form would not budge. Leena fell back, the jaguar man immobile, and took a deep breath. Gritting her teeth, her parched dry lips splitting from the effort, she pushed again, harder and longer, and slowly the jaguar man began to move. Angled slowly up on one arm, rolling up on his side and pressing into her knees, the senseless form lifted off her waist and stomach.

Leena paused in her exertions, unable to continue without rest. A glint of moonlight caught her eye, from below. Dazed from hunger, exhaustion, and the shock of her present circumstance, Leena looked with slow-blinking eyes to the unconscious jaguar man's back and saw the mesh bag still hung over his shoulders. The mesh bag, and the metal glint of her survival kit within.

Her hands, bound and encased in their thick insulated gloves, lunged for the kit. Leena's first thought was just to retrieve the kit, to take back that which had been taken from her. It was only as her hands brushed against the hard metal corners of the case, and brought to mind the contents and their uses, that she saw a more immediate purpose.

With gruesome luck, the strap holding the mesh bag in place had been almost completely severed by the blow that had felled the jaguar man, so it was a matter of relative ease to pull the bag away from its back, and the kit away from the bag. It remained, then, to open the kit.

A dark figure flashed before Leena's eyes as one of the combatants leapt over her, whether jaguar man or attacker she couldn't say. Leena ignored their threat, and concentrated on the kit.

She battered at the simple metal latch, her fingers useless in the thick fabric of the gloves. She dragged the kit up onto her chest, angling her head up within the helmet for a clearer view, trying for finesse. It was like threading a needle with a plumber's wrench. The sturdy catches on either side of the case's lid both had to be opened, but in opening one her exertions seemed always to shut the other.

The melee continued, and someone kicked Leena's side, almost knocking the survival kit from her grasp. As she scrambled to maintain her hold on the kit, inspiration struck, and she turned the case on its end, leaving the two catches positioned one above the other. Holding the kit in place with one hand, she could angle the other up far enough to flip open the latch. Sliding her hands carefully down the case, she then repeated the procedure, and the lid flipped open with a snap.

There was a shout and an accompanying groan from somewhere to Leena's right, but she ignored the sounds. Pushing the kit back onto its base and down onto her thighs, careful that the lid not close again, Leena pulled herself painfully into a sitting position, the deadweight of the jaguar man still lying across her knees. Breathless, she pawed with bound hands through the contents of the kit, finally closing her thick-gloved hands on a piece of nylon-wrapped chrome and steel.

She lifted it to her mouth, and unsnapped and pulled loose the nylon holster with her teeth. Then, carefully, she worked one gloved finger into the trigger guard, and thumbed off the safety.

Her wrists and ankles were still bound, her hands still encased in insulated leather and an unconscious monster still pinned her to the ground. With the chrome-plated Makarov semiautomatic in her grip, though, Leena suddenly felt more in control of the situation.

Leena looked up, and her grip on the Makarov tightened.

A man stood over her, breathing heavy with exertion, naked to the waist and gored black with the blood of fallen jaguar men. In one hand he held a curved sword, in the other some kind of pistol.

Leena aimed the Makarov at his chest.

"Maht elmok," he said, smiling, and Leena pulled the trigger.

CHAPTER 4

Traveling Companions

The pistol's hammer fell on the empty chamber, hitting only air, and Leena was out of options.

Her instructors in the Red Army had drilled into her the three basic laws of small arms care: always keep the safety on when holstered, keep the clip fully loaded whenever possible, and leave a round chambered at all times. It seemed that whatever support technician at Baikonur had provisioned the survival kit had not had the same instructors.

With her wrists bound, Leena could not position her hands to pull back the slider, was unable to rotate a cartridge into the chamber. The Makarov was useless, deadweight.

The man standing over her slid his own pistol into an ornate holster at his waist, and angled his sword away and to the ground. He seemed to smile, through the grime and sweat and splattered blood freckles across his cheeks, and chuckled slightly. Leena tightened her grip on the Makarov, hoping he might bend close enough that she could slam the barrel against his grin.

"Kestra," he said in surprisingly tender tones, reaching his free hand to her, palm up and tentative. "Mitra," he added after a short pause. "Kare. Caraid. Amicus."

He kept on, slowly repeating one set of syllables after another, watching her closely in the low light. Leena narrowed her eyes, suspicious.

"Amiko. Ami. Amigo."

Was this madness, or some sort of test?

"Freund. Friend."

The syllables were resolving themselves into words, familiar but certainly not Russian. English, perhaps? It had been years since she'd heard it spoken, not since her days in the army at the listening post in Berlin.

"Drug," the man said. *Friend.*

Leena's eyes widened.

"Vy . . ." she began, uneasily. "Vy govorite po-russkij?"

Do you speak Russian?

The man nodded slowly, and smiled sheepishly.

"No, I'm afraid not," he said, and Leena struggled to bring her rusty English up to speed. "Not very well, at least."

Leena relaxed her grip on the pistol, her arms lowering. Was he American? Where precisely was she?

"Kto?" she began, and then shook her head violently as though to loosen long-dormant skills. "Wh-who?" she finally managed, snaring the appropriate pronoun as it raced through her thoughts. "And where this?" she added uncertainly. She inclined her head to one side in the dome of the helmet, indicating the mysterious surroundings.

"So you're a new one, as I'd assumed," the man answered, cleaning his sword's blade on the fur of one of the fallen foes, then slipping it with a steel whisper into a hanging scabbard opposite the holstered pistol. "Did you hear that, Balam?" he shouted to one side, out of Leena's line of sight. "She is new after all. You owe me a drink at my earliest convenience."

There came only a growl in response, but from her awkward position, pinned beneath the insensate form of the fallen jaguar man, she could not make out the source. She was able to follow the man's English better and better with each passing moment, the ancient engines of her forgotten training slowly revving to life.

"I'm sorry we don't have time for formal introductions," the man said, leaning down and grabbing the unconscious jaguar man by his harness and hauling him bodily off of Leena's legs. "But more of the Sinaa will be on us in numbers shortly, if we're not quickly away."

Leena's lower body unencumbered, the man stepped forward and, reaching down, slipped his hands under the pits of her arms and drew Leena to her feet.

"We'll have enough time for questions and answers soon enough," the man said, gingerly pulling the Makarov from her grip and snugging it into his belt, "but for now, it's enough for you to know that this is Paragaea, and that you are far, far from home."

Leena looked on, still dazed, as the man untied her wrists and then ankles with a few deft movements.

"Are who . . . ?" she began, struggling with the syntax. "Who . . ." She paused, moving her arms in glorious freedom, shifting painfully from leg to leg. "Who are you?" she managed.

"My apologies," the man answered with a slight smile, giving her a shadow of a bow. "My name is Hieronymus. Hieronymus Bonaventure."

He stepped to her side, taking her elbow, and steered her towards the far side of the clearing.

"And this is my friend, Prince Balam."

Leena looked up, and before her towered the hulking, shadowy figure she'd glimpsed tussling with the leader of the jaguar men before. It was another of the jaguar men, but with black fur instead of golden. His clawed hands and the lower half of his broad jaws were spattered with shining red blood, shimmering like strings of rubies in the faint moonlight. He wore a leather harness with gold fittings, a loincloth of deep forest green draped between muscular thighs, and one of his ears was deeply notched, an emerald dangling from the other.

The black-furred jaguar man smiled, teeth like sabers glinting wickedly in the low light, and Leena was not sure whether she'd been rescued, or had fallen into the hands of an even darker threat.

✦

They traveled through the darkened jungle tracks not making a sound, the English-speaking man in front of Leena and the black-furred jaguar man following behind. The going was difficult, with Leena still swaddled in her pressure suit with its helmet and heavy boots and gloves, but they pressed on without pause. Only when they had gone several kilometers did the man and his jaguar companion seem to lower their guards, and they drew finally to a halt.

Minutes later, Leena sat near a fresh-kindled campfire, soaking up its warmth, her eyes fixed on the two figures sitting on the far side of the flickering flames. Neither she nor they spoke, though a strange smile peeked from the corners of the man's mouth.

Her shoulders and neck ached from the long hours spent wearing the heavy visored helmet, but to rid herself of the weight she had no choice but to remove the whole suit. The helmet on the SK-1 pressure suit could not be removed, another safeguard on the part of the chief designer, out of fears his cosmonauts would panic in their capsules and remove them while still in flight.

Leena removed the heavy gloves, awkwardly loosening the clasps holding them connected to the oversuit and then shaking them to the ground, her bare hands luxuriating in the free air for the first time in hours, if not days. With her hands free, she began working at the fasteners and fixtures holding the oversuit in place. In theory, the suit was designed for a cosmonaut to remove without aid, since the Vostok capsules were intended to land across a broad and sometimes unpredictable range of terrain. Even so, Leena had never removed a suit on her own before, always able to call on the Star City technicians when necessary.

Now, as she bent and twisted into uncomfortable contortions to reach inaccessible fasteners, she wished she had a few of those technicians on hand now.

"Do you need any assistance?" asked the man from across the fire.

It took Leena a moment to sift through her long-disused English vocabulary and parse out the man's meaning.

"Net," she answered, and then quickly translated, "No."

The man replied with a shrug, and sat back to watch. The black-furred jaguar man at his side made a noise back in his throat that might have been a growl, or a chuckle, Leena could not say which.

Finally, Leena managed to strip off the orange nylon oversuit and attached helmet, and the heavy leather boots, and was left standing in the grey-checked pressure liner. It was form-fitting and warm, too warm for the humid night air, but it was lightweight, and that at least was some small comfort.

Suddenly, the black-furred jaguar man was on his feet, bounding to Leena's side. She shrank back, raising her arms defensively, wishing her Makarov was in her hands and not still snugged at the waist of the other man. The jaguar man's attention was not on Leena, though, but on her discarded oversuit. He grabbed it up in one claw-tipped hand, removed a wicked-looking knife from a sheath at his hip, and with three sure moves cut loose the helmet from the material of the suit.

The jaguar man tossed the helmet to the ground by the fire, and proffered the orange nylon oversuit to Leena.

"It is warm," the large figure said in his baritone grumble, his English laced with an indefinable accent. "Wear this instead; it will be cooler."

Warily, Leena reached out and accepted the oversuit.

"Spasibo," she said, thanking him. The jaguar man nodded, solemnly, and then padded back to the far side of the fire.

All modesty forgotten, she stripped out of the pressure liner, naked for the briefest moment, shivering even in the humid air, and then put back on the orange nylon oversuit and the heavy leather boots. When she had done, she sat back cross-legged on the ground, and opened up the case of her survival kit.

As she inventoried the contents, working out what was useful, what was damaged and what wasn't, the English-speaking man on the far side of the fire kept watching her, that strange half-smile peaking the corner of his mouth. He wore a loose-fitting white shirt, a pair of dark trousers, and high boots that came almost to his knees. Across his lap lay his scabbarded sword, while at his side rested a satchel.

And still he didn't speak.

Finally, Leena could stand it no longer.

"Kto . . . ?" she began, then stopped herself, dredging up the necessary vocabulary. "Who are, and . . . how you here come?"

"I already told you," the man said with a smile, his teeth flashing white in the firelight. "My name is Hieronymus Bonaventure."

"Hyr-ronn-eye-mush," Leena repeated, taking each syllable in turn, with some difficulty.

"Call him Hero," growled the jaguar man. "Trust me, it's just easier."

"Hero," Leena said, trying out the sound. Much better. "But why? Come you here how, to what place is this?"

The man called Hieronymus tilted his head to one side, trying to work out the meat of her question. Then he nodded, and crossed his arms over his chest, his eyes on the middle distance.

"I was an officer in His Britannic Majesty's Navy during the recent troubles, the war against the French and later against their Emperor Napoleon, and through misadventure I was thrown overboard in a squall on the South Pacific Seas. I thought myself dead for certain, my sins caught up with me at last, but in the midst of a surging wave I found myself falling through a mirrored hole. It was a hole in the midst of the air itself, and through it I fell into other waters. I found myself in the

Inner Sea of Paragaea, and was taken onboard one of the cities of Drift."
He paused, and smiled wistfully. "I was lucky to be taken in as a member
of their community, as among the people of Drift, everything found
floating on the waves is either Food, Fuel, Furniture, or Family. Nothing
escapes categorization into one of those four classes."

Leena looked at him, her eyes narrowed. She'd been able to absorb only
parts of the man's narrative, but those small parts had made little sense.

"Chto? The year, it is 1964," Leena said sharply. "You are madman,
think you battle Napoleon, buried last century?"

The man shook his head.

"No, I am not mad, or if I am, it is on other grounds entirely. Time
moves differently between the two worlds, Earth and Paragaea, and not
all doors open onto the same era."

Leena kept her gaze steady, considering what he'd said.

"And he?" she said, pointing to the jaguar man. "How is such
thing possible? Such man?"

"What? Balam?" the man answered. "He's a native to this land,
one of the nation of the Sinaa, the jaguar people of the Western Jungle.
Once coregent of the nation, he was cruelly . . ." The man stopped, and
looked to his companion apologetically. "I'm sorry, Balam, perhaps
you'd prefer to tell your own tale?"

The jaguar man shrugged.

"No, you go ahead," he said, through a saber-toothed smile. "I'm
not the one in love with the sound of my own voice."

The man seemed not to notice the jibe, but continued on, unabated.

"Balam, as I said, was once one of the rulers of the jaguar nation of
the Western Jungle. His sisters, his former coregents over the nation of
the Sinaa, ousted Balam and replaced him with his cousin, Gerjis, who
had poisoned their minds against their brother with his twisted reli-
giosity. The coregents of the Sinaa now argue for an alliance of some
kind with the wizard-kings of the Black Sun Empire. Balam's cousin is
a follower of Per, the leader of the Black Sun Genesis, a religion among

the metamen that preaches that the wizard-kings in their Diamond Citadel of Atla, with their science and ancient machines, are not just mortal men, but are in fact the creators and gods of metamankind."

Leena's English was growing stronger with each passing moment, like a long-dormant muscle coming back into use, but she still understood little of what the man said, and what little she comprehended she refused to believe.

"You say . . . I think you say, this some Sargasso Sea," she said, hotly, "into which fall men and ships, to return never. Some Fairyland, with animal men and wizards and kings? Bessmyslica!" She spat in the dust at her feet. "Nonsense!"

"Fair enough," the man said with an infuriating smile. "I leave it to you, then, to explain him."

The man pointed at his animalistic companion, whose feline face split in an alarmingly toothy grin.

CHAPTER 5

Maps and Territories

The next morning, they dined on a meager meal of wild berries and some sort of rodent roasted on a spit over the embers of the campfire. When she had finished, Leena tied her pressure liner into a makeshift pack, and loaded it with the remains of her survival kit. All except the Makarov, which still glinted in the belt of the man sitting a few meters off.

"Hero," Leena called out, grateful for the diminutive. "Pistolet moj?"

The man glanced over, confused.

"Come again?" he said.

"Pistol mine," Leena translated, and pointed at the man's waist. "My pistol." She pointed again, and then at herself. "I want."

"Oh," the man said, glancing down at the Makarov as though he'd forgotten it was there. "Well, if you promise not to go pointing it in friendly faces anymore, I don't suppose it would hurt."

The man tugged the gun from his belt, and glanced at the jaguar man, who looked on warily with amber eyes. With a shrug, the man tossed the pistol to Leena, sending it arcing end over end through the air, glinting silvery in the morning light.

Leena caught it neatly by the handgrip, and checked the chamber and the action carefully before tucking it into a zipper pocket on her right thigh.

The man and his jaguar companion left off eating, and began to gather their things. In bare moments, they had fully packed, and began to head away from the clearing.

"Where you go?" Leena said, snatching up her makeshift pack and jumping to her feet.

"We are heading to relative safety in the north, away from the country of the Sinaa," the man answered, pausing and glancing over his shoulder. "We have business in the city of Laxaria, and had we not encountered you and your furry fellows along the way, we'd be some hours nearer our destination." He paused, and then added, "You are welcome to accompany us. However, remember that you are not our prisoner, nor are we yours, and if you want to strike out on your own, we won't stop you."

Leena was silent for a moment, considering her options. Her first duty was to return home, to report to her superiors her discovery of this strange otherworld. The successful launch of the Vostok 7 would pale in comparison to newfound worlds for the Soviet to explore and improve. There was no question now she'd be invited into the Party and given a rank, though now she had visions of a major's insignia on her lapels, not merely those of a lowly lieutenant.

"Who knows way?" she asked at length. "Between worlds? Who knows way to travel between?"

The man and his jaguar companion glanced at each other, and turned to smile at her patiently.

"That is a large question," the jaguar man said, his black lips curled back in a full grin.

"Most in Paragaea don't even accept the existence of Earth,"

Hieronymus explained apologetically. "How many in your country still believe in Fairyland as adults? It is no different here."

Leena shook her head, determined.

"Net," she said fiercely. "No. Someone in authority, I think, there must be. Someone knows this thing." Leena was a firm believer in the power of authority, and in the wisdom of those in high places. A lifetime serving the greater good of the Soviet could lead her to no other opinion. "There must be place of study," she went on, "a university, a school, where men and women of learning, they gather together?"

The man and his jaguar companion looked to each other, and consulted in a strange tongue, sounding a little like that of her jaguar men captors. They spoke for a few moments, smiling and nodding, occasionally casting quick glances Leena's way. Finally, the man turned, and addressed her, his tone apologetic.

"Well, my colleague and I agree that the nearest place that meets that description would be the Scholarium in Laxaria, which city is luckily our destination. But I warn you now: you won't like the answers they'll give you."

Leena shouldered her makeshift pack, and headed towards the track leading to the north, the way the two had started.

"For me to decide, I think, that is," Leena said, passing them and heading back into the jungle.

✦

The trio passed the rest of the day moving through the jungle, heading ever northwards, making tracks as best they could in that trackless wilderness. Hieronymus and Balam kept silent, the one taking the lead and the other bringing up the rear, ever vigilant, watching all sides, above and below, for any sign of danger. Whether they feared that the jaguar men would trace their steps and attempt some reprisal, or wor-

ried that some other jungle denizen lurked in the shadows, waiting to
pounce, Leena could not tell.

As they walked, Leena busied herself in the attempt to reacquaint
herself with English. She'd scarcely used the language at all since she
was transferred from the East Berlin listening post to the flight training
program of the Air Defense Forces. And even then she'd been primarily
a passive receptor, listening to the language for endless hours, clammy
headphones to her ears, pencil and paper in hand, but she'd rarely had
occasion to speak the language. Not since the linguistic courses she'd
taken at the Red Army facility outside of Moscow had she been forced
to generate words and phrases in the convoluted English tongue. Now,
seeing the vital urgency of complex communication with this
Hieronymus and his jaguar man companion, she dredged up her every
memory of the language as best she could. She recited old poems to
herself, dimly recalled from copy-book pages. She conjugated verbs: *He
kills, he killed, he will kill*. She strained her memory to recall the nouns
and names for every creature and object that came into view. "Tree."
"Man." "Stream." "Monster." "Mystery."

And still on they walked.

$$\diamond$$

As the sun set, they stopped for the night. Hieronymus set about
starting a fire, gathering branches and dried bracken to use as tinder,
setting them ablaze with a flint-and-steel from his pack. Balam slipped
into the darkening woods for a few short minutes, soundlessly, and
then returned with a bloodied coney in either hand. The rabbits were
feral, and somewhat lean, but when Hieronymus objected that they'd
present a poor repast, Balam insisted that with proper seasoning they'd
be more than filling. Hieronymus, as though it had been his intention
all along, dusted off his hands and stepped away from the cook-fire,

wagering Balam that he couldn't make the coneys palatable. The jaguar man, it seemed, could not resist a challenge, and so fell to preparing their rustic evening meal with abandon.

Hieronymus came to sit beside Leena, where she warmed her hands in the heat of the flickering fire. He kept a respectful distance between them, but when Leena glanced over favored her with a companionable smile.

"You look confused," Hieronymus said pleasantly. "It's hardly surprising. I could scarcely credit the evidence of my senses when first I arrived on Paragaea."

Leena scowled, tilted her head to one side thoughtfully, and then nodded in reply, almost as an afterthought.

"This world," she said, carefully arranging her words and meanings. "What you called it?"

"Paragaea."

"Pair-ah-gee-uh." Leena repeated each syllable slowly, shaping the word in her thoughts. "Paragaea."

"That's it." Hieronymus nodded, like a headmaster pleased with the progress of a student.

"What is this Paragaea? How it comes to be?"

Hieronymus took a deep breath through his nose, and then sighed contemplatively. "Would that I could tell you, little sister," he said. "All I know is that, in some regards, it seems that Paragaea is a more ancient twin to the Earth you and I once called home. Where civilization's recorded history on our world dates back only a few thousand years at best, going no further than the earliest days of the pyramid builders and the flowering of the Euphrates, Paragaean history goes back many hundreds of times further. There are beings in these lands" —he indicated the jaguar man with a jerk of his head—"who can measure their family's lineage back many thousands of years, and whose cultural records and writings go back countless millennia further."

Hieronymus glanced from Leena to Balam, and then to the stars just beginning to wink in the darkening skies overhead. When he spoke again, it was as though a hint of fear and wonder had crept into his voice. "And there are still older races, who linger at the edges of the known world, stranger and more ancient still."

Leena mulled over what he had said.

"But twin?" she asked, and then paused, restructuring the sentence in her thought. "Why you say twin?"

Hieronymus reached into his shirt, and pulled out a necklace of solid metal links, from which depended a small round pendant. The pendant was spherical, a little over two centimeters in diameter, and covered in dyed-blue sharkskin. Around the circumference of the sphere ran a line of brass, like an equator, with a sickle-shaped latch on one side and brass hinges on the antipodes.

"Observe," he said. With a practiced maneuver, he unlatched and opened the sphere, revealing within an ivory ball, covered in engraved and stained representations of familiar continents. Tipping the open hemisphere carefully to one side, he caught the ivory globe in his out-stretched hand, and proffered it for Leena's inspection. "Recognize this?"

Leena took the tiny globe, and turned it over in her hands. The craftsmanship was evident, the lines and curves of the continents remarkably accurate, given the small size. Its only principal errors were the lack of some detail in the western shore of South America, and the complete absence of the Antarctican continent. Leena glanced from the miniature globe to Hieronymus. If he was truly from the early nine-teenth century, as he claimed, his conception of the world's geography would not include Antarctica, not discovered until long decades later. His madness, if madness it was, could be said to be self-consistent, at the very least.

"Earth," Leena said. "It is Earth."

Hieronymus nodded, a wistful expression passing fleetingly across his features. "It was a gift from my mother. A long . . . very long time ago. My grandfather had been a cartographer, employed by Dutch traders to chart the passages to Japan, and my mother grew up in his household as something of an amateur cartographer herself. Before she died, while I was still a student at Oxford, she commissioned the London firm of James Newton to produce this diminutive globe, that I might be able to carry it with me always." Hieronymus's voice trailed off as he stared into the middle distance.

Leena smiled uneasily, not sure how to respond.

"In any event," he went on, reaching into his pack and pulling out a metal tube capped with some sort of rubberized plug on either end, "finding myself here, in this strange land, I eventually felt called to pursue this ancestral avocation of mine, and set about measuring the limits of my newfound world."

Unstopping one end of the tube, he slid out a curled sheaf of papers, and laid them before Leena, careful to position them out of the range of sparks popping from the cook-fire.

"This," he said, not without a hint of pride at his workmanship, "is Paragaea."

Leena looked over the map in the flickering firelight. It was an unusual projection, all of the landmass of the planet enclosed inside one ellipse, the lines of longitude curved rather than straight. An equal-area projection, of the Mollweide or Sinusoidal varieties, instead of the more typical Mercator projection.

"Chert voz'mi," Leena muttered under her breath. *Damn it.*

She shook her head. Back at TsPK in Star City, when they'd studied maps and cartography as part of the regular cosmonaut training regime, Leena had often found herself more involved in the mathematics that created the map than with the territory it described. Now, here she was looking at a map of an alien world, and her thoughts raced over which projection the strange man at her side had used in calculating its dimensions.

"Note the shape of the continent," Hieronymus said, pointing at the large landmass dominating the map's center.

There was but a single continent on the Paragaean map, ringed on
the north, east, and west by tiny islands and archipelagos. In the
middle of the continent was a body of water labeled "Inner Sea," and
bordering the landmass on all four sides a vast body labeled "Outer
Ocean."

"At first blush," Hieronymus went on, "this world bears no especial resemblance to the Earth you and I know." He reached over,
plucked the globe from Leena's hands, and held it just above the map's
surface. "But regard how the western coast of the continent resembles
in gross detail the western extremity of the North American continent
on Earth. And how the jutting peninsula of Parousia shares a remarkable similarity to the shape of India on terrestrial seas. A few short
years before I myself was translated here to Paragaea, I chanced to reach
a monograph by a German naturalist named Alexander von Hum-
boldt, who noted a congruence between the bulging shape of South
America's eastern shore and the bight of Africa, and conjectured that
the lands had once been joined. But now, if the continents of the Earth
are mobile upon the planet's surface, and can move about like ice floes
in a melting lake, then so too might they continue to migrate, moving
out of their familiar arrangements into ever stranger configurations.
And if they did, mightn't the resulting globe resemble in large part
the shape of this Paragaean continent?"

Before Leena could answer, Balam called from the other side of
their campsite.

"The rabbits are as palatable as they'll ever be, Hero, and I fully
expect that you'll concede our wager with the first bite."

Leena did not have the opportunity to answer Hieronymus's theo-
ries on continental drift, nor Hieronymus to sample the jaguar man's
culinary treatment, for at that precise moment the trees to their immediate south exploded with a thunderous sound, and some massive
shape thudded to the jungle floor only a few short meters away.

Hieronymus was on his feet at once, expertly stowing his map back in its tube and his globe back in its case in a matter of heartbeats, his hands then flying to the saber at his side, all before he'd even had a chance to register what the danger might be. By the time Leena had reached a standing position, Balam was at her side, knife drawn, and fangs and claws bared.

It took Leena's eyes a brief moment to adjust to the gloom, having stared so long in the direction of the firelight, but the dim illumination cast by the still-flickering cook-fire aided somewhat.

There, only a few meters before them, hulked the massive form of a sloth, but not like any sloth Leena had ever seen, in life or in photograph. Laying supine on the ground, its muzzle pointed towards them, eyes blazing in the flickering firelight, this sloth was easily two meters from belly to back.

"What is?" Leena said, almost unable to breathe.

The sloth climbed slowly to its hind legs, standing almost as high as the surrounding trees, and brandished claws almost as long as Leena was tall.

"Trouble," Hieronymus said simply, and tightened his grip on the saber.

CHAPTER 6
Attacked

The giant sloth towered over them, standing six meters or more from nose to tail, covered in long, shaggy brown hair. Lumbering forward on its thick hind legs, its enormous weight counterbalanced by a massive tail, it swatted at the air before it with long claws and lifted its deceptively docile-looking snout to emit a fearsome, rumbling bellow.

"Sloth eat plants!" Leena objected, scrambling backwards, keeping as far from the reach of the enraged creature as possible.

"This one doesn't appear to be particular," Hieronymus said out of the side of his mouth, sidling to the left while Balam slid to the right, flanking the beast.

"Mad beast," Balam shouted back, his tone as clipped and to the point as his choice of words. "Bloodlust."

The giant sloth's black eyes followed Hieronymus and Balam as they circled around to either side, its snout pointing first at one, then at the other.

The sloth chose Balam, lunging forward and sweeping towards the jaguar man with both of its forelegs, its claws splayed out like a deadly fan. The jaguar man, with a lithe agility that brought to Leena's mind the wild cat he resembled, leapt a meter straight up in the air, high enough that the vicious claws of the maddened beast sailed unimpeded beneath him. Landing nimbly, he slashed out at the sloth's forearms with his knife, and though the blade did not bite deep, it drew blood, the pain serving only to make the beast more enraged still.

The sloth bellowed again, its maddened bloodlust increased. Its torments, though, were not through. With the beast's concentration on Balam, Hieronymus dashed forward and slashed at its left hind leg with his saber, cutting far deeper than Balam's knife had done. Hieronymus's blade came away slippery and gored, and the giant beast bellowed with rage. But, pricked on one side and sliced on the other, the sloth showed no signs of retreating, no indication that it was losing its balance or inertia.

The sloth now turned its attention to Hieronymus, the most noisome of the two pests prodding it. As it had done before, it lunged forward, and swatted at Hieronymus with the claws of both forepaws outstretched and deadly. Lacking the jaguar man's dexterity, Hieronymus danced back out of reach as quickly as he could, but not quickly enough. The leading edge of the claws ripped his shirt to ribbons and carved wicked gashes across his chest. Hissing with pain, Hieronymus swung his saber in an ineffective attempt to parry the beast's attack, and staggered backwards.

Without wasting a breath to speak, Balam rushed forward, sinking knife and talons into the thick tail of the giant beast, his fangs bared, eyes wild and flashing.

The giant sloth reared up, mouth wide and howling with insensate rage, twisting to one side and the other, trying unsuccessfully to dislodge the jaguar man from its tail. Hieronymus shouted, trying to get the great beast's attention, and Balam, digging deeper with knife and claw, began to roar.

The deafening din was brought silent by a single sound.

BLAM.

One of the sloth's black eyes blossomed into a red bloom, and the beast's horrible bellow was immediately silenced. The sloth jerked upright for a moment, twitching slightly, and then crashed forward, its massive form falling to the jungle floor with a sound like distant thunder.

Hieronymus, his saber still held high, and Balam, fangs bared, both turned to regard Leena, who stood holding her still-smoking Makarov pistol in a two-handed grip, her legs wide in a firing stance.

"Trouble solved," Leena said.

✦

"What was the meaning of *that*?!"

Hieronymus, grip white-knuckled on the hilt of his saber, advanced on Leena, his eyes flashing.

"What mean you?" Leena slowly lowered the barrel of the chrome-plated semiautomatic, her expression confused.

"A needless waste," Balam said from the other side of the fallen creature's ponderous bulk, cleaning his knife and claws on the sloth's shaggy fur.

"You mourn beast's death?" Leena asked, disbelieving. She'd hardly taken the two for sentimentalists, to weep and wail when an animal met its just demise.

"Of course not!" Hieronymus snapped, slicing at the air with his saber to sluice the blood and gore from the blade, and then slamming it into its sheath in one smooth motion. "But you've wasted valuable ammunition when Balam and I had very nearly driven the beast away."

Leena tilted her head to one side, and regarded the parallel wounds on Hieronymus's chest quizzically.

"This is nothing," he said, following her gaze and prodding at the gashes with an outstretched finger. He stepped forward, closing the distance between them. The volume of his voice dropped, but lost none of the fire in his tone. "A bit of bandaging and a little time and they'll be nothing more than scars."

Without warning, Hieronymus reached out and snatched the Makarov from Leena's loosened grip, and shook the firearm barrel-first in her face.

"But once you fire the last of your rounds from this"—he gestured with the pistol—"you are that much nearer to never firing another round again."

Leena, her expression hard, held out her hand palm up.

"Pistol mine," she said.

"It might be better for all if you kept it, Hero," Balam said, stepping up behind his companion.

"Look," Hieronymus said with a shake of his head, laying the Makarov on Leena's outstretched hand. "Firearms are thin on the ground in this world, and ammunition hard to come by. Metal is a scarce commodity here, and there are few willing to spare even the basest lead in the manufacture of bullets, slugs, and shot. Most of what ammunition we have, we find ready-made, having fallen to Paragaea through the gates from Earth." He took a deep breath, forcing himself to calm. "Shoot, but only if your life depends upon it."

"And sometimes," the jaguar man interjected, "not even then."

"But in fight with his people"—Leena pointed at Balam, her eyes on Hieronymus—"you had pistol in hand. Not to shoot?"

Hieronymus smiled slyly. He drew his pistol from the leather holster at his side, and regarded it with an expression bordering on love.

"Sometimes the signifier of a thing serves the same purpose as the thing itself," he explained. "And by brandishing a pistol I introduce into my opponents' calculations the thought that I might have occasion to fire it. Usually the threat itself serves my purposes well enough that I need not often pull the trigger."

"Mauser," Leena said, looking at the pistol in the flickering fire-light. "C96."

"Why, yes it is," Hieronymus said, somewhat surprised. "When last I sailed the oceans of Earth, single-shot muzzle-loaded firearms were the pinnacle of human achievement, but I have seen such wonders in my years in Paragaea. This pistol was a spoil of war, taken off a brigand on the city of Drift, just as my saber was won during the Battle of Calabria back on Earth, taken from one of the French general Massena's fallen hussars." He held up his pistol, looking it over admiringly, and then slid it back in its holster. "So I take it you're familiar with this brand of weapon?"

"First saw one, Battle of Stalingrad." Leena's face darkened, and she drew up straight. "First firearm I shoot. Then, I only five years old."

Hieronymus's face took on a quizzical expression, and he made as though to speak, but anything he'd been about to say was interrupted by the rumbling death rattle of the giant sloth. Although its brain had stilled a few moments past, it seemed as though it had taken the rest of the body a short while to catch up.

With Balam in the lead, and Leena bringing up the rear, the trio drew near the felled beast to investigate.

"You were right," the jaguar man called back to Leena, over his shoulder. "The great beasts typically eat only plants and leaves, scavenging meat from carrion rarely if ever, but they will not attack if they do not feel threatened."

"Any animal will fight to defend itself," Hieronymus said, pointing to the sloth's shaggy back. During most of the encounter, the bulk of the great beast had hidden its rear quarters, and only now as the trio approached its prone form were they able to see the knives and spears bristling in its hide. The wounds were somewhat fresh, from the looks of them, no more than a day or two old.

"Those are the hunting implements of the Sinaa," Balam said, disgusted.

"Balam's own people," Hieronymus said in an aside to Leena.

"I remember," she answered, shuddering.

"These Sinaa were foolish indeed," Hieronymus said. "Everyone knows that a full-grown giant sloth is virtually indestructible."

"These the same Sinaa who capture Leena?"

Balam nodded. "Most likely."

"Why, then?" Leena looked from the countless spears and knives in the beast's hide, to the jaguar man at her side. "Why males of your kind hunt beast, if it cannot be killed?"

Hieronymus and Balam both turned to her and, after a long second's pause, burst into laughter.

"The hunting party would not be flattered to hear you say that," Balam said, leonine laughter rumbling deep in his chest, a somewhat unsettling sound.

"Or perhaps, my friend," Hieronymus said, clapping the jaguar man on the shoulder, "it is you who should be offended."

Balam looked at him, and for a moment Leena thought they might come to blows, but then their peals of laughter rippled out again, even more boisterous.

"What?" Leena said, looking from one to the other. "What is funny?"

"Little sister," Hieronymus said, laying a companionable hand on Leena's shoulder. "I'm afraid to say that Balam is the only *male* of his kind that you have seen."

Leena, confused, crossed her arms over her chest, scowling.

"In my culture," Balam said, trying to control his laughter, "it is the females who are the principal hunters, with the role of warrior falling to the males."

Leena's eyes widened with understanding.

"But if we should happen upon any of your captors again," Hieronymus said, unsuccessfully trying to stifle his chuckling, "I should be obliged if you pointed out to them that, in your eyes, any one of them could pass for a male."

"It would serve the bitches right," Balam said, and exploded into laughter again.

$$\bf \text{✦}$$

Not wasting the opportunity at fresh meat, Balam and Hieronymus worked half the night to hack hunks from the giant sloth's fleshy tail, and then cleaned and dressed it. Hieronymus pointed out to Leena that in perfect circumstances he'd have preferred to smoke the meat, but that in view of the need to reach their destination in short order, salts and spices would have to serve as the necessary preservatives.

When morning came, Balam had treated several kilograms of the marbled meat, wrapped it in broad leaves, and stowed it in his pack. They were able to break their fast, though, with fresh strips of sloth meat, grilled over their cook-fire until the juices flowed. The resulting flavor was strange and somewhat rangy on Leena's tongue, but no less a welcome diversion from the meaner fare of the past days, for all of that.

In the daylight, they were able better to see the extent of Hieronymus's wounds, and having finished with the morning meal, Balam set about cleaning and dressing the gashes dug into his companion's chest.

Sitting by the cooling embers of the cook-fire, Leena saw that this was hardly the first injury, or even the hundredth, that Hieronymus had suffered. His back was a crisscrossed nest of scar tissue, lines and curves of scars spelled out strange sigils on his chest and arms, and on his lower abdomen was what appeared to be the remaining marks of a gunshot or puncture wound. She'd seen the faint white scar that ran in a line from his right eye, across his temple to his left ear, but had entertained no notions that that was just the figurative tip of an iceberg of ancient wounds.

The tracks of time, though, had left other traces on his flesh. On his left bicep was a spiraling black tattoo, similar to that Leena had seen in photographs of South Pacific islanders.

"There's another one," Hieronymus said, startling her. He'd seen her gaze lingering on his tattoo, and was smiling slightly. His smile faded to a wince at Balam's less-than-gentle ministrations, but his eyes still twinkled. "The other indicates my status as Family in the nation of Drift. But I'm afraid I'm not quite comfortable enough in your presence yet to show you *that* one."

"Trust me, woman," Balam snarled, not looking up from his labors. "You *don't* want to know where he's got it hidden."

They struck camp and set out, continuing along in their roughly northern direction for all the daylight hours, their every attention on the path ahead.

By nightfall, through the breaks in the tree line, they could see the sky glowing dimly red to the north and east of their position, the lights of some large city. Hieronymus smiled, and pointed ahead.

"Laxaria."

The next morning, after a simple breakfast and a few short hours' trek through the final stretches of jungle, they reached the main road. It was hard-packed dirt, and ran from east to west.

They continued on to the east, following the main road, and near midday came upon a company of half-sized humans driving aurochs along before them. The small beings, with arms reaching down to their knees and wide mouths across their small heads, wielded S-shaped boomerangs, and bristled at the trio's approach.

Hieronymus approached the small beings with his hands held

palm forward before him, and said, "Ebvul das letdak." He paused, and then added, "Mat odat Sakrian?"

One of the diminutive creatures stepped forward. Standing just over a meter high, he was the tallest of them, and seemed to be the leader. He shook his head, and in halting syllables answered, "Elum odat Sakria."

"Dakuta," Hieronymus said, smiling beneficently. "Elar ata uk etvam. Erre kad mat, at Laxaria."

The little creature turned and exchanged a few words with his fellows in a language of long vowels and halting consonants. At length, he turned back to Hieronymus and nodded.

"Dakuta. Uk etvam. Erre."

The small creatures, waving their long arms to drive their aurochs ahead of them, moved to one side of the road, giving the trio a wide berth as Leena and Balam followed Hieronymus down the road and past them.

When they had gone a few hundred meters, safely out of earshot of the small creatures, to say nothing of the range of their S-shaped boomerangs, Leena grabbed Hieronymus's elbow.

"What those short men?" she asked.

"There are many races of men on Paragaea," Hieronymus answered, glancing back over his shoulder at the small creatures following a safe distance behind, driving their aurochs before them in a cloud of dust. "Even leaving out the number of metamen like the Sinaa, and other sentient beings. The half-sized men behind us are the Sheeog, who are rarely seen out of sight of their mound homes in the deep forests, but come to town only to sell their domesticated aurochs at market."

As Hieronymus spoke, they came about a slight curve in the road, and the forest gave way to wide, flat plains. There before them lay a grand city, stretched for wide kilometers in every direction, encircled completely by high walls. The road upon which they walked joined with several others just beyond the walls, indistinct masses of people and vehicles coming into and out of the high gates.

As they drew near the city walls, Leena could scarcely believe the types of beings streaming in and out of the city gates. The jaguar people and half-sized men were the least of them. There were beings walking on two legs like men, but who had the characteristics of lizards and birds, dogs and birds, and more combinations than Leena could comprehend. Beings that looked like humans in every respect, except that they towered almost a full foot over Leena. Strange beasts, too, and vehicles and conveyances the likes of which she had never seen. All jostling for position as a half-dozen roads converged at the city gates, all hurrying either to enter the city, or leave it behind.

Into this confusion of creatures and cultures Leena walked, her head spinning.

CHAPTER 7

Laxaria

A s they made their final approach to the city walls, Hieronymus took Leena by the arm, helping guide her through the
ever-increasing crush of bodies.

"This," he said, "as I have said, is the city-state of Laxaria. We are
now at the southern edge of the plains of Sakria. The Sakrian princi-
palities—Laxaria, Lisbia, Hausr, Azuria, and so on—are among the
youngest civilizations on Paragaea, going back only a handful of centuries at most. The majority of the Sakrian city-states were founded by
humans of the type with which you're familiar from Earth, but in
recent decades more and more of the older races have begun to migrate
to the cities, leaving behind their hidden places in jungle, mountain,
and desert, leaving the old ones to dream of lost days of empire while
they, in their youth, try to better their situation."

"This is a human age," Balam said at her other ear. "Before the humans,
the Metamankind Empires divided the globe amongst them, and before
them ruled the martial Nonae, and before them the Black Sun Empire."

"And now," Hieronymus went on, "at the edges of this new-minted human world, still linger the older powers, in decline but not yet dead. Perhaps they bide their times, looking for a moment to return to power. The wizard-kings of the Black Sun Empire have retreated into their citadel city in the cold southern wastes; the Nonae patrol the eastern deserts in their small numbers, raising their children up tough and hard-edged, weaned on adversity. The metamen fight their internecine wars, race against race, tribe against tribe."

"Those that have not chosen to follow the banner of Per and the Black Sun Genesis, that is," Balam noted with evident scorn.

A heavy silence hung over the trio as they passed beneath the arches of the main gate, entering the city proper. A city guardsman, some sort of air-powered rifle slung at his shoulder, gave them a long glance as they passed by, but made no move to stop them.

"Be that as it may," Hieronymus said, trying to brighten the mood, "Laxaria is one of the more welcoming of the Sakrian cultures, and is a pleasant change from the forest primeval." He paused, and then added, his voice low, "But you should still watch yourself."

✦

For the man Hieronymus and his jaguar companion Balam this was a brief respite, a momentary return to civilization; for Leena, it was like stepping once more into another world.

To Leena's eyes, the city seemed like something out of the days of the czars. Hieronymus explained the surroundings as best he could—the people, the buildings, the conveyances—but after the green monotony of the jungle trails, she found it difficult to take it all in at once.

The honor guards of the Laxarian Hegemon marched in their rank and file through the wide avenues, escorting some minor princeling on his business, pneumatic rifles slung on their shoulders. Airships passed overhead, bound for the northern reaches of the Sakrian plains, or to the far shores of the Inner Sea. Caravans gathered in large squares, heading out across the flat lands to the other Cities of the Plains, bearing passengers and goods. Presbyters, cenobites, and mendicants wandered the streets, each preaching their own flavor of salvation, each ignoring the others. Temples, money houses, stables, and inns lined the avenues and byways. Near the city center stood a large theater, a sporting arena, a library—each larger than the last. There were mounted police on their patrols, and cutpurses and sneak thieves skulking in the shadows. There were men and women in every hue of skin imaginable, and small scatterings of dog men, laughing raucously. A figure with the body of a woman and the head and paws of a cat caught Balam's eye, but hissed with her shoulders arched as he walked past. In the shadow of a nameless temple, a bent figure with scaled, hairless skin, large eyes, and a double slit for a nose recited strange poetry, perched on one leg, while at his feet a smaller snake-creature with scales of yellow flecked with violet caught the coins tossed by passersby.

Leena, threading her bewildered way through this swirling insanity, had no choice but to accept it all. No longer could she question the reality of her situation. However she had come here, she was in a world not her own, and it was her most pressing duty to return home and report what she had learned.

"Shall we pause for victuals?" Hieronymus asked, pointing out a row of food stalls along a narrow promenade.

"No," Leena barked, eager to press ahead. "Answers first, eating after."

"Fair enough," Hieronymus answered, and guided her by the elbow on through the crowds. "Don't forget, Balam," he said to the jaguar man following close behind, "that you owe me a drink."

The outlaw prince of the jaguars growled, low in his throat, but did not answer.

In the eastern quarter of the city, they came to the Scholarium, a large edifice surmounted by three domes. They passed through an immense oaken door, with bronze cladding, engraved with astronomical symbols and mathematical formulas. The air within was heavy with age, dust lanced in the air by shafts of sunlight.

Beyond the doors was a long arcade, hung on both sides with ancient banners. On each banner was embroidered an intricate symbol of angles and curves, a different one for each. Their meaning escaped Leena, though they reminded her somewhat of atomic notations, somewhat of circuit diagrams.

"My earliest tutor was an alumnus of the Laxarian Scholarium," Balam said, his voice rumbling softly near her ear. "The Scholarium is given over to the study of thaumaturgy, the art of effecting change in the surrounding world."

"What my heathen friend means," Hieronymus added, at her other ear, "is that this place is dedicated to natural philosophy, what you might term science, though its practice and execution here might differ from that which you would recognize."

An ancient, bent man wearing heavy robes and an unlikely hat ambled across the timeworn floor towards them, a look of inquisitiveness etched on his open face. His skin was the color of ebony, and what little hair he had was stark white, the shade of new-fallen snow. The ancient man spoke to them in a language Leena could not follow, sounding much like that which Hieronymus and Balam whispered to each other when they didn't want her to hear.

"This is the magister of the institution," Hieronymus explained, after exchanging brief words with the old man. "The head man. He says he's happy to answer any question put to him."

"Ask him, how it is you get to Earth," Leena said while the old man looked on, smiling uncomprehendingly.

Hieronymus translated, her sentence reduced to a few brief syllables, and the old man held forth for what seemed an eternity. Hieronymus listened carefully, nodding and making polite noises when appropriate, while Leena waited impatiently for the translation.

"The magister explains," Hieronymus translated at length, "that Earth is a quaint belief among the indigenous peoples of the mountains and jungles to the south and west, and that many view it as a kind of otherworldly paradise, to which the beneficent will go upon their deaths. The crude peoples of the city of Drift . . ." At this, Hieronymus paused, and shot a harsh glance at the ancient man, who smiled beatif-ically. "The people of Drift in the Inner Sea speak of 'The Other Ocean,' a supernatural abode which parallels in many ways the mythical Earth, from which bounty flows from wave and sky. Among the Pakunari of the Ogansa Valley there is a religious doctrine which—"

"No," Leena said, shaking her head in annoyance. "Tell him I am from Earth, and that my desire only is to return."

Hieronymus shrugged, and translated. When he had finished, the magister looked at her with something like pity clouding his features. He made a sign in the air, muttered a few words, turned, and walked away.

Leena looked from the retreating magister to Hieronymus and back again.

"Chto? What? What did he said?"

Hieronymus looked on her with an expression torn between sym-pathy and amusement.

"Well, you see, the magister has decided that you are insane, and said a quick prayer for your psychic well-being before departing."

That evening found the trio at a pub near the commercial district, where Hieronymus and Balam conducted a secretive meeting at a back table while Leena languished at the bar. The cheap spirits the barmaid poured out reminded her of the worst vodka she'd ever had, but it was slowly ushering her into a sense of numb oblivion, so Leena wordlessly motioned for a refill whenever her mug emptied.

She was trapped on a mad world full of mad people, with no way to return. Those back in Baikonur would never know that she still lived, nor know to mourn her if she died, her life reduced to a cryptic reference hidden in a file somewhere in the cold heart of Russia. Failures were not proclaimed, as they were not conducive to the general spirit of the Soviet peoples; so the populace would never know that Vostok 7 had ever launched, much less failed. It hadn't failed, of course, but succeeded beyond the chief designer's wildest imaginings; but only Leena would ever know it.

She slammed her fist down on the pitted wood of the bar, shouting a wordless howl of rage.

"What troubles you, little sister?" Hieronymus asked, sliding onto the stool at her left.

"She does seem agitated, doesn't she?" Balam said, easing onto the stool at her right. He motioned for a pair of drinks.

"And why should not I be, I think?" Leena snarled. "I am here, in this crazy place, with no way home, and no one knows the way home, so I am stuck. Should I not seem the agitated?"

Balam took a long quaff of the mug the barmaid sat before him, and swallowed hard before erupting with a roar of laughter.

"You give up too easily," the jaguar man said, and took another long pull of his drink.

Leena, annoyed, looked from the large jaguar man to the slyly smiling man on her right, and back again.

"What is it you say?" she demanded.

"Well," Hieronymus began sheepishly, "we never said that *no one* knew the way back to Earth. Only that most people don't believe in its existence, and that you'd find no answers among the learned men and women of the cities."

"Chto?"

"I mean, in all the world, there must be *someone* with that knowledge," Hieronymus went on. "There are whispers and rumors aplenty, out on the fringes, of those who know the secret ways. One of them *must* be true, it only stands to reason."

Leena looked into the depths of her mug, the fumes from the spirit stinging her eyes.

"But how will I find them with this knowledge?"

Hieronymus and Balam exchanged glances over her head. The jaguar prince laid a clawed hand on her forearm, gingerly.

"We have no pressing business, at the moment," Balam rumbled.

"Yes, things have been getting a little dull, of late," Hieronymus said. "A proper quest would give my life a bit of shape, a sense of purpose. What do you say, Balam? Shall we help the little sister in her hour of need?"

Leena looked up, not willing to trust to hope.

"We've taken on harder tasks for less reason before," Balam answered. "Which is not to say it will be easy."

"Easy?" Hieronymus said, pushing off the stool and jumping to his feet. He mimed a martial pose, like a comic opera hero. "And where would be the fun if it were easy? If we have to storm the walls of the Diamond Citadel of Atla, if we have to scale the fire mountain of Ignis itself, well . . ." He tapered off, looking around the pub and realizing his drink had gone empty. "Well," he went on, sudden inspiration striking, "isn't that better than hanging around here till death takes us in our sleep?"

"If you say so," the jaguar man rumbled with an easy shrug, and turned his attention back to his drink.

Hieronymus dropped back onto the stool, and laid a comradely hand on Leena's shoulder.

"Little sister, tomorrow we will set off in search of safe passage back to Earth, so that you may fulfill your duty. For now though, if you please, will you stop looking so damnably depressed, and have another drink with us?"

Leena looked at the pair, one a time-lost officer from a capitalist navy, the other an impossible animal man straight out of her childhood fairy tales, and offered a weary smile. Perhaps it was the cheap spirits, but she was beginning to feel something not unlike hope.

"Another," Leena said, motioning for the barmaid with her empty mug. "If there is a single thing the Russian understands, besides their duty," she explained with resigned humor, laying an arm across Hieronymus's shoulder and another across Balam's, "it is the value of a drink."

CHAPTER 8
Acclimation

The next morning, with Hieronymus leading the way, Leena was dragged through innumerable market stalls and upscale shops and boutiques. Her ragged orange nylon oversuit was quite the worse for wear, and her two companions had insisted that she be outfitted with clothes and supplies immediately.

Leena was less interested in fashion than in function, saying that she could make do with Hieronymus's castoffs, but Hieronymus had urged that she should be able to blend in as much as possible with the populace. Not all of the Sakrian cultures were as cosmopolitan and welcoming of outsiders as Laxaria, and it would be useful to learn now how to blend in unnoticed with a crowd.

Leena was unused to the range of choices presented to her, and even more unused to being followed around each stall and outlet by a sales clerk, eager to meet her every desire. Even in the days before she wore nothing but uniforms—and she'd worn nothing but the standard issue for the Cosmonaut Corps, the Air Defense Forces, and the Red Army since she was in her teenage years—her clothes had been provided for her by the state orphanage, and they'd simply supplied whatever the markets had in approximately her size, usually shapeless dresses of browns and grays, and roughly made leather shoes that never quite seemed to fit. The dizzying array of styles and colors presented to her in the shops of Laxaria were almost more difficult to accept than the inhuman creatures walking the city's streets.

In the end, they found a tailor who dealt in functional items with only minor concession to the fashions of the day, and Leena was loaded up with a few pairs of sturdy trousers, a few long-sleeved shirts, a sleeveless vest outfitted with pockets and hidden pouches, a waist-length jacket of some sort of softened animal hide, a heavier lined coat reaching to midcalf, sturdy walking boots, and a pack in which to carry it all. Into the pack Leena transferred what remained of her survival kit, the heavy boots she'd cut from her SK-1 pressure suit, and her extra ammunition for the Makarov. She discarded the orange nylon oversuit, the gray-checked pressure liner, and the helmet. Connecting the Makarov's nylon holster to her new leather belt, she hung the pistol at her waist, and was ready for anything that might come her way.

Almost anything.

Hieronymus demurred initially, but at Leena's insistence he also helped her locate an apothecary, where she was relieved to discover that Laxarian society had developed sufficiently to have the equivalent of tampons on the shelf, so that she wouldn't be forced to make do with jerry-rigged sanitary napkins when next she menstruated. She bought the apothec's entire stock, and that of several other vendors they found, and loaded them in her pack.

Finally, grateful to have left matters feminine behind, Hieronymus took Leena to an armory, and with the help of the armorer selected a short sword the correct heft and length for her.

"You will wear this at all times," Hieronymus said, sliding the blade into a sheath of leather and wood, and handing it to Leena. "And you will practice with it as often as circumstances allow."

Leena accepted the sword reluctantly, and drew it experimentally from its sheath.

"I would sooner use Makarov," she said distastefully, "if there is more trouble."

Hieronymus went to pay the armorer a few coins, and then crossed the floor to stand beside Leena. "I have explained about the scarcity of ammunition," he began, his tone cross.

"Da, da." Leena cut him off with a wave of her hand. "Not to shoot the pistol unless in emergency." She pointed with the tip of the short sword to a rack of long-barreled rifles hanging on the armory's wall, tagged with prices in Sakrian numerals. "But why not carry those, instead? They are rifles, net, erm, no?"

"No rifles," Hieronymus answered, nodding. "Which is to say, yes, they are rifles, and no, we won't be carrying them. Sakrian pneumatic rifles, powered by canisters of compressed air, fire slugs of compressed carbon, which are effective at short range, but which tend to be overly burdensome to carry for long distances, and are expensive to recharge and maintain. Good for riot control, but not a campaigner's weapon."

Leena nodded. Sheathing the short sword again, she hooked it onto her belt, opposite her nylon holster.

"Understood. But if again I face a six-meter, clawed monster, I reach for this"—she touched the holster—"and not this." She touched the sheathed sword. "No question."

Hieronymus held up his hands in a sign of surrender.

✦

Balam had secured rooms for the three of them at a tavern in the shadow of the city's northern wall, and near the tavern there was a periodic street market, where Laxarians and outlanders of all shapes and sizes jostled around closely spaced market stalls. To one side, in a small plaza, space had been set aside for street theater, and mummers and mimes plied their trade for the passersby. There were also dumb shows and puppetry for the children, to keep them entertained and not underfoot while their parents haggled with the stall vendors.

While Hieronymus and Balam shopped for supplies, looking for bargains in the market stalls, Leena joined the children in front of the puppet stall, paying careful attention to the simple stories and allegories, trying to learn more of the Sakrian dialect. She'd not had to learn a new language since Berlin, all those years ago, but Hieronymus insisted that she would find the language of the plains of Sakria surprisingly easy to learn. Simple, almost mathematical syntactical structure, the words composed of only a handful of phonemes.

After listening for endless hours to the chattering voices of the puppeteers pitched high and screeching, trying unsuccessfully to absorb the vocabulary and follow the confusing plotlines, Leena had come to the conclusion that Hieronymus was a far more skilled linguist than she. Or that he was having a joke at her expense.

She leaned towards the latter, in the absence of any other evidence.

$$\text{✦}$$

Past sunset, Leena joined Balam and Hieronymus in the tavern, sharing a simple meal and a few rounds of cheap spirits before retiring for the night. The menu, which Hieronymus said was prepared in the style of Masjid Empor, consisted of flat breads, some sort of cracked grains cooked into a paste, and spiced strips of grilled meat. Balam and Hieronymus fell to eating with gusto, while Leena approached her servings with more trepidation, but after a few exploratory bites, she found the savory flavors to her liking. After a short while on the tongue, the spices began to sear, and if the only liquid she had on hand to wash her palate clean was the vodka-like liquor she'd had the night before, Leena hardly had cause to complain.

When the meal was done, the three of them sat around the table, sipping their mugs, feeling the warmth of the spirits slowly suffuse to the tips of their fingers and toes. Leena was reminded of other meals, and other nights whiled away in company with a bottle to hand, with her fellow soldiers in Berlin, or with the other cosmonaut candidates at the training grounds of TsPK. The only difference between now and then, Leena realized, was that in those instances, she'd known precisely with whom she was drinking, the type of men and women they were, and what she could expect of them. Sitting across from the time-lost naval officer and the jaguar man, she had no such assurances.

"Excuse me, please," she said, leaning forward, her words slurring only slightly. "I wonder to know. When we were in pub, last night, you met with men. Some business, you said."

Hieronymus took a sip from his mug, and nodded absently.

"What of it?" Balam asked, leaning back casually in his chair, his mug held daintily between thumb and finger.

"What business was?" she asked. "What kind work do you two do?"

Balam and Hieronymus looked at each other thoughtfully, and shrugged.

"Whatever work comes to hand, little sister," Hieronymus answered with a sly smile.

"As for me," the jaguar man said expansively, "I'm just keeping myself occupied, and my skills honed, until the day I can reclaim the throne of Sinaa from my cousin Gerjis, and drive the blight of Per from my home."

"But what purpose do you serve? What goal?"

"Even when I served under the flag of His Britannic Majesty," Hieronymus answered, "my one true master was the call to adventure. I left home to escape a studious life of boredom, and I will gladly accept any task that comes my way, so long as it means a bit of excitement."

"So you serve nothing greater than yourself? Not objective or moral?" Leena shook her head, unable to mask her expression of disgust. "So you are mercenary, only."

A cloud passed across Hieronymus's features.

"I have done things," he said, his voice low and brows knitted, "in the past, of which I am not proud. But I will take no job that offends my sensibilities, as rugged and roughshod as they may be."

Leena made to reply, but Balam held up a silencing hand, shaking his head sadly, so she stared into the bottom of her mug, instead. On reflection, perhaps those nights drinking in Berlin and Star City had not been so different than this, after all, each person carrying old wounds beneath the skin that might never heal, scars that the eye could not see but the heart could not help but feel. Leena thought back on those last days in Stalingrad, long after her parents had died in the incendiary attack, when Leena was forced to do terrible things to survive, and the child she'd once been had died forever.

Leena knew what it meant to have done shameful things. Who was she to judge another who knew the same shame?

✦

Having failed to find any answers at the Scholarium, once Balam and Hieronymus had resupplied and concluded their outstanding business, Leena insisted that one or the other of them accompany her to other centers of learning in the city, such as might be available. There were other centers of learning in the city, surely, to be found.

Balam, stretched out full length on the floor like a cat sunning on a porch, scratched at his belly with an outstretched claw and pleaded with Hieronymus to take the first shift. The jaguar man insisted that he'd not had a good few days' rest in months, and that if he was not allowed to nap for at least a few days, he would be useless when next they were on the march.

Hieronymus, chiding his leonine companion for his laziness, offered Leena his arm and agreed to usher her around the city, as she liked. Leena declined the proffered arm, but thanked him for his services.

The educational facilities of Laxaria were easy to dispense with, taking no more than the morning and part of the afternoon. What academies and salons there were could all be found clustered in the shadow of the Scholarium, and each in its own way looked to the larger institution for direction. In none, whether the training ground for officers of the militia, or an academy catering to those who could not afford the Scholarium's tuition, or a salon housing those instructors whose teachings were considered too outré or offensive for the more staid institution, did they find anyone who disagreed in substance or detail with what the magister had told them. Earth was a myth, a legend, and anyone claiming otherwise was deluded, or a fool, or both.

If the academics of this strange, backwards world were benighted and shortsighted, Leena concluded, then perhaps other sources, less credible in Leena's own world, might still be of use here. And so the following day, she and Hieronymus went about to the various temples and tabernacles that dotted the Laxarian streets, to ask the patriarchs and matriarchs if they had any knowledge of Earth. But none had anything of use to share, just the tortured logic and platitudes Leena knew from Earthly religions, promising punishment and reward in some eternal hereafter for one's behavior in life. None, not the frater of the Great God Ta'o, or the high soror of Odir, or menester of the Holy Catoptric Church, or even the head missionary of the Order of St. Kaspar of Hausr, had any answers for her.

In the days that followed, Leena searched on, with Hieronymus or Balam as her guide, among the mystics, the madmen, the seekers after mysteries, but none had any answers for her, and as the days blended into weeks, Leena felt no closer to home.

CHAPTER 9

Employment

Leena readied herself for her habitual foray out into the city, the sun streaming in through the slats of her window shades. She performed her morning ablutions, heated water carried by ceramic pipes to a large basin in one corner, separated by a high curtain from the rest of the room. Pulling on a pair of trousers and a long-sleeved shirt, she buttoned up her sleeveless vest and stomped into her boots. In a mirror so ancient it had lost almost all reflective capacity, her image ghostly and indistinct in the dim glass, she appraised her reflection as best she could. Her hair, worn short for so many years, was beginning to grow longer than it had been since she was a child, and as she strapped her holster and short sword to her belt, she considered briefly drawing the blade and hacking her bangs back to a respectable length with the cutting edge. But the thought of what might happen if she should swing too far in her eagerness for shorn locks drove the idea from her mind; not just the injury itself, but the mocking response from Hieronymus and Balam that would surely follow, once they'd tended to her wound.

Securing her room behind her, Leena climbed down the stairs, to the tavern hall where Balam was to meet her, it being the jaguar man's turn to serve as her guide and interpreter in her daily expedition. She was surprised, then, to find Hieronymus waiting there, as well. Usually, when one of the two was accompanying Leena through the streets of Laxaria, the other would be off skulking in the shadowy corners of the city's warrens, or napping, or propping up a tavern's bar.

"I have news, little sister," Hieronymus said, seeing her confused expression. He climbed to his feet, and made for the door. "I'll explain as we walk."

Balam followed close behind, leaving Leena to catch up. The trio walked out of the tavern into a bright Laxarian morning, the streets crowded with vehicles, beasts, and foot traffic.

"I have heard intelligence," Hieronymus went on, "of an expert in natural philosophy in the northern city-state of Lisbia who might well prove your salvation. This man is said to specialize in the hermetic and the occult, those areas of knowledge which few admit exist and fewer still claim to understand. And it is just possible that this man might know how to track and predict the location of doorways between Paragaea and Earth."

"What are we waiting for?" Leena shouted, squealing with an embarrassingly girlish glee.

"The journey to the far north is long," Balam said, shaking his head, "and the broad plains of Sakria harsh and unforgiving."

"We have no horses, little sister, and no means of procuring them short of horse thievery, which is one task to which I'll *not* turn my hand. Besides"—he glanced at Balam with a twinkle in his eye—"rare is the horse that would suffer a full-grown jaguar man as a rider, and Balam is as good a horseman as he is a swimmer."

The jaguar man growled good-naturedly.

"We could try to wheedle our way onto a merchant wagon train," the jaguar man answered, "making the slow trek from caravanserai to caravanserai across the plains, but the journey could take long weeks, even months, and I doubt we could rely upon the goodwill of strange merchants holding out that long."

"So we need only find a way to get there quicker than traveling by foot."

"I not care!" Leena objected. She stopped short, and only Hieronymus's gentle insistence, his hand on her elbow, kept her moving forward through the street. "I do not care how long it take. Better to be moving, following answers, than sitting here in *okajannyj* Laxaria with nothing but ignorance on all sides!"

Balam laughed, shaking his head merrily as he turned a corner, and headed up a broad avenue.

"What funny?" Leena demanded. "Why do you laugh?"

"What a stroke of luck," the jaguar man said, his fangs showing in a wide grin, "that I caught word just last night of a traveler needing personal protection. The word in the taverns was that Tahth the Broker is looking to hire a few pairs of strong arms, to accompany a merchant of some kind who is bound for Lisbia."

Leena looked from the smiling face of Balam to Hieronymus's wide grin and back again, and shook her fists in exasperation.

"So we go, yes? We go meet this broker? Right away!"

Hieronymus stopped, placing one hand on Leena's shoulder and pointing with the other at a large structure looming ahead of them. Standing higher than any of the buildings around, it was an arena of some sort, cylindrical and roofless like the Roman Coliseum. A crowd could be heard cheering over the walls, already caught up in some sport, with the sun only now climbing up the eastern sky.

"What is that?" Leena asked.

"That's the Spectaclum," Hieronymus answered, guiding her towards the arena's entrance. "And it is here that we will find the broker."

✦

They entered the Spectaclum, paying a few coins at a small pavilion, and made their way through the crowd to the upper deck, which at this hour of the day was only sparsely populated. The lower decks, though, were already crowded with Laxarians, eager for the sight of first blood. The sport of the day was gladiatorial events with wild animals, and the current match involved a pair of giant armadillos with spiked tails pitted against a juvenile *Tyrannosaurus rex*. The armadillos had the advantage of numbers, and together slightly outweighed the dinosaur, but Leena's money, had she any to bet, would have been on the tyrannosaur.

On the highest point of the upper deck, far from any other arena-goers, they found a tall, thin creature with the arms and legs of a man but the thin skull and beak of a bird. On each hand he had three talonlike fingers opposite a curved thumb, and he was covered head to foot in a soft down of yellow feathers, with a simple red tunic belted at his waist and hanging down to his knees. On their approach, the bird creature regarded them with cold, round eyes, his expression alien and unreadable.

"Tahth," Balam said as he and Hieronymus approached, their hands held up, palms forward, the customary Sakrian greeting. "Ebvul das letdak."

Leena hung back, the bird creature unnerving her.

The bird creature held up one hand, like the talon of a great raptor, and muttered distractedly, "Das letdak."

"Leena," Hieronymus said, calling over his shoulder and motioning for her to step forward. She held her ground, regarding the bird man. "This is Tahth the Broker."

"He is of the nation of Struthio," Balam said in an aside, "one of the more ancient races of metamankind."

"Let elum, Balam?" the Struthio said.

"Elar odat Anglis," Hieronymus interrupted, stepping forward. He glanced over at Leena. "Ta utok suvas."

Leena could pick out the words for "say" and "woman," but had trouble following the rest.

The Struthio looked at Leena inquisitively.

"Enum ata let mat?" the bird man asked.

Hieronymus waved Leena to come stand beside him, and nodded slightly.

"We speak the English," the Struthio agreed, nodding.

Hieronymus saw Leena's confused expression, and chuckled. "A few years ago," he said, "Tahth here overheard me and Balam speaking in English during one of our negotiations, and when I explained to him that only a handful of beings on Paragaea spoke the language, he insisted that I teach him the rudiments of the tongue, so that he might use it when communicating sensitive matters to his agents and subordinates."

"And those lessons, they cost me greatly," the bird man said, his words sounding sibilant and strange through his vicious beak. "Still convinced you gouged me in the price, Hero"—he waved a talon absently at Hieronymus—"but I find use enough for the secret language, from the time to the time, that I do not bear the grudge."

"So gracious," Hieronymus said mockingly. The crowd in the stands below them howled as one of the giant armadillos landed a solid blow with its spiked tail on the tyrannosaur's flank. "Tell me, Tahth," he went on, his eyes narrowed, "do you never tire of blood sports?"

Tahth looked down his curved beak at Hieronymus and smoothed the feathers of his narrow head with an outstretched hand. "I it is not me who seems to derive the endless pleasure from watching other the species batter themselves to death for the purposes of the entertainment." He pointed towards the lower deck, where the Laxarians cheered as the vicious teeth of the tyrannosaur cut red ribbons on the armored back of one of the giant armadillos. "Are these not your kind, the human?"

"These are still a young people, Struthio," Balam said, leaning casually against a pillar. "Even our peoples, in ancient days, went through barbarous period, did they not?"

"All the cultures are cruel in the youth, is that what you say, Sinaa?" Tahth steepled his talonlike fingers before him. "Perhaps. But does their youth excuse the barbarities? If the adult is murdered by the child, is he any less murdered for his assassin's age?"

"You traffic in arms and those that bear them, Tahth," Hieronymus said, his tone even but his expression dark, "conducting your business here, the smell of blood and sawdust ever present in the air. I admit that I find it somewhat ironic that you would choose to criticize another species for its violent tendencies."

"Not surprised at inability to appreciate the true irony," Tahth answered, tilting his head to one side in an expression that suggested smugness to Leena. "You are only the human. The rationality is the province of the older species."

"You mean rationality like that practiced by Per, and his thugs of the Black Sun Genesis?" Balam countered, his amber eyes flashing. "Who burn sin from the penitent's flesh, and cast out any who don't adopt their simpleminded creed?"

Eyelids flicked closed and open across the Struthio's round eyes, and he hung his head, a momentary silence falling over him.

"The Black Sun Genesis," the bird man repeated, shuddering slightly. "It is the . . ." He broke off, shaking his head from side to side, as though to knock loose some unpleasant memory.

"There is a job, no?" Leena stepped forward, exasperated, unable to keep silent any longer. "Enough of these other matters. Now we talk about job!"

Tahth sighed, as though Leena's words were just the proof he required of everything he'd said about humans. "Yes, I am looking for a pair of the bodyguards, for the businessman heading north to Lisbia. Hazard pay, regular rates and contract."

"We'll take the job," Hieronymus said, stepping forward and holding out his hand. "You've contracted out to us before, and despite our differences, you know full well that we are capable of doing the job, no question."

"Yes," the Struthio said, the word hissing through his beak. He regarded Hieronymus's hand coolly, unmoving. "But there are the three of you, not the two."

"It's all three or none," Balam said, crossing his arms over his chest. "But I suspect you don't have any choice in the matter, if you're driven to using the rumor mills and tavern talk to drive potential applications to your perch here. There are more than enough able candidates in Laxaria, but I suspect that there are few who wish to be stranded in Lisbia without work at the completion of the contract. Especially given the Lisbian khanate's dim view of mercenaries and hired arms. I don't imagine that the distant city of Lisbia is looked upon as a vacation spot by many in our line of work."

"And yet," Hieronymus added, "Balam, Leena, and I *are* willing, and so everything works out in everyone's favor."

Tahth reached up and tapped his beak with an outstretched talon. "The fee calls only for two pairs of the arms," he said finally, his head cocked to one side, "and if the client accepts, each of you paid a third less than if only the two."

"Agreed," Balam said.

Tahth and Balam clasped hands, and the deal was sealed.

✦

The client, it transpired, was a Laxarian businessman named Jophar Vorin, and was to transport some valuable item or information to the far north province of Lisbia. Better yet, he intended to travel by airship, which could make the passage in a matter of days, and not weeks.

Airship travel was expensive, the lighter-than-air gases used to inflate
the envelopes a dear resource, but Vorin was in some considerable
hurry, and damn the expense.

The three companions could hardly believe their good fortune. The
job took care of two birds with a single stone. It would pay each of
them ready cash, enough that they'd not need to worry about their
finances for some months to come, and would provide quick transportation to the location they wanted to go anyway. They had no idea
what it was that Vorin was transporting, just that it was confidential,
intended only for the eyes of the ruling zamurin of Lisbia. Vorin carried a leather case with him always, bound to his wrist, and the only
task given to his bodyguards was that one of them be with him at all
times to ensure that the case did not leave his possession.

Once past the security pickets at the airdocks, and with the *Rukh*
safely in the air, it seemed that they had little more to do than relax in
relative luxury for a handful of days, until they reached the airdocks of
Lisbia and their responsibilities were discharged. There were only a few
dozen passengers onboard the *Rukh*, most of them merchants or government diplomats, with a few artisans and missionaries among them.

Balam and Hieronymus were convinced these would be the easiest
wages they had ever earned.

CHAPTER 10

Aboard the 'Rukh'

L eena stood by the windows in the observation lounge of the passenger gondola, watching the airdocks of Laxaria fall away as the
Cloud Cutter *Rukh* cast off from the mooring post and began its slow
ascent. The skies were overcast with a solid blanket of low clouds, as
dull and flinty as lead, an inauspicious beginning to their journey. Still,
as it always had, liftoff gave her a momentary frisson, her pulse quick-
ening and her temperature rising. This must be, Leena knew, what
other people meant when they spoke of love at first sight. Not for her
the tawdry pleasures of a messy embrace, though, of furtive tumblings
in darkened rooms; Leena's passions were reserved for piercing the
heavens above.

She turned from the window as the *Rukh* crested the cloudbank,
and the crowded streets of Laxaria disappeared behind a haze of gauzy
clouds. Weaving through the travelers and merchants scattered around
the lounge, she made her way to the aft passageway, and to the suite of
cabins she shared with the others.

That it was good fortune and not ill that she'd encountered Hieronymus Bonaventure was something that Leena had been forced to remind herself time and again, in the days and weeks since. At times the only thing keeping Leena from throttling him, or shooting him, or walking out, or some combination of the three, was the fact that Hieronymus was her best chance of returning to Earth.

This was proving to be one of those occasions.

"Little sister!" Hieronymus called out in English, as Leena stood in the open doorway. "Pray close the hatch! There are unshuttered ports in the passageway, and I can't stomach yet to look down."

"You are not yet accustomed to flying?" Leena asked with a sly smile, leaning on the open door. Hieronymus sat on a chair riveted to the deckplates, his hands white-knuckled on the chair's arms.

"With my eyes closed, I fancy that we are on a ship at sea, and then I am at peace, but when confronted with our altitude, my blood runs cold."

Hieronymus Bonaventure was the product of an earlier era than Leena, and though he'd spent the last years making his way across the face of Paragaea, learning its customs and languages, and making a life for himself, in one respect, at least, he was still a man of a different age, and the notion of sailing through the air rather than on waves had never sat well with him.

"Perhaps Hero just needs to be held, like a swaddled infant," came the rumbling voice of their companion, from the far side of the common area.

Leena turned, and smiled, but the smile was empty and forced. She'd traveled with Balam for some time, but even now, on seeing him, she still felt deep within a brief thrill of terror. Seated just a meter away in another bolted-down chair, the large black-furred jaguar man, outlaw prince of the nation of the Sinaa, idly tapped the emerald dangling from one ear, baring his saber-teeth in a knowing grin. He wrinkled his catlike snout in Hieronymus's direction, laughter rumbling faintly in his barrel chest.

"I'll remind you of the time we took a spill in the Inner Sea, Balam," Hieronymus shot back, with dark humor. "What was it you cried out, when first your precious fur touched water? 'Save me, mommy, I'm wet!' or something like that, wasn't it?"

The toothy grin froze on the jaguar man's face, and he narrowed his amber eyes.

"That was different," Balam answered, his voice lowered. "We could have drowned."

"We were so near the shore that the water was only knee deep!" Hieronymus shot back, punctuating the statement with a bark of laughter.

The jaguar man crossed his thick arms over his chest, and lowered his eyes.

"I don't like water," he said sullenly, refusing to meet Hieronymus's gaze.

Leena closed the door, and stood in the middle of the room with her hands on her hips. She'd not had to deal with any such nonsense back in Baikonur. The flight engineers, technicians, even her fellow cosmonauts had all taken their tone from the chief designer, who'd not had much patience for fun and games. Here in Paragaea, where the stakes so often seemed so much higher, one's life so often on the line, her new companions seemed instead to treat *everything* as a game. It was not an easy transition to make.

"Where is our employer?" Leena asked, looking from Hieronymus to Balam and back again. "I thought it our charter that he was never to leave our sight?"

There came the sounds of suction and gurgling plumbing from beyond the bulkhead, and Hieronymus pointed to the privy door.

"He's in the head," he answered, "and we're not paid enough for me to follow him in *there*."

The door handle rattled, and a heavyset, red-faced man entered the room, drying his hands on a cloth. He was dressed in the high fashion of Laxaria: waistcoat, cravat, and piped trousers, with the medallion of his guild membership hanging from his breast pocket like a pendant. Tucked under his arm was a brass-reinforced leather case, the hasps locked and the handle chained to his left wrist.

The red-faced man looked at Leena with a broad, toothy grin and spoke a few words in the dialect of the Sakrian plains. Leena caught her name, and the word that suggested successful completion, but little else.

"His Lordship wants to know if we're safely away," Hieronymus translated into English, the only language he and Leena shared.

"Tell him yes," Leena answered, addressing Hieronymus but keeping her eyes on the heavyset man, her face a polite mask. "We are airborne, and should be clear of the city in moments, and on our way to Lisbia."

Hieronymus spoke a few short syllables in Sakrian to their employer, who seemed immediately to deflate with relief. The red-faced man crossed the cabin, gave Leena an avuncular pat on the shoulder, and then arranged himself on a low couch set along the bulkhead, laying the case gingerly across his ample lap. He reached up and drew back the shutters covering the port, and looked out as the airship rose towards the blanketing gray clouds above.

Hieronymus blanched, averting his eyes from the view.

"Man was not meant for such heights," he said, his voice quiet and strained.

Balam laughed again, a leonine rumble deep within his chest, and Leena was tempted to join in.

That afternoon, once Laxaria had disappeared in a haze of clouds and fog behind them, and the *Rukh* had climbed above the cloud line, Vorin insisted that the quartet leave the cabin together, to share a meal in the dining compartments in the rear of the passenger gondola. Hieronymus was reluctant to leave behind the security of his chair, safely bolted to the deckplates, and Balam made some minor noises about the potential security risks, but in the end Vorin was dead set on going, and his were the purse strings.

The dining compartment commanded the rear of the gondola, three walls dominated by large reinforced-glass windows. Steps led down from the passageway to the floor of the dining area, so that the ceilings were twice as high as elsewhere in the passenger sections. Tables and chairs were secured to the deck, here as everywhere through the ship, but aside from this minor concession to air safety all else was just as it would have been in the finest of restaurants on firm ground. Every table was covered in linens imported from the far east, across the Inner Sea, and each place setting had cutlery of the finest ceramics, fired in the Rim Mountains, and delicate porcelain plates and mugs hand painted by the craftsmen of Hele.

The menu was sturdy fare with slight cosmopolitan flourishes. The standard meat and vegetable dishes of the Sakrian plains, but with a scattering of clay-baked items borrowed from the Roaming Empire, and even a few piscine dishes prepared in the manner of the city of Drift.

Vorin and the three companions were seated by the far aft windows, and after they had placed their orders, they sat sipping mugs of mulled wine, looking down on the crenulated landscape of clouds below.

The jolly businessman raised his mug, looking amongst the three companions, and said a few rhyming syllables, the meat of which Leena was unable to follow.

"He wishes us good fortune on the journey," Balam translated, as Hieronymus was still looking uneasily out on the curtain of clouds below them.

"Schast'e," Leena answered in her native Russian, raising her own mug and downing the contents in a single pull.

The next morning, after a simple meal served by the ship's stewards in their suite of cabins, Vorin insisted that they repair to the open-air deck.

Leena was well rested and relaxed, perhaps more so than she'd been since Vostok 7 took off from the launchpad in Baikonur. They'd passed the night in shifts, each taking watch for a span of hours while the other two slept, but she'd taken the first shift, which meant that she'd gotten more uninterrupted sleep in the comforts of the cabin's bunk than she'd gotten in weeks. If on rising their employer wanted to take in the morning air, it was all one to her.

Hieronymus was less enthused about the open-air deck. He'd slowly gotten his air-legs under him the previous night, with the distant ground safely masked by a blanket of clouds, but the morning sun had burned the clouds away, and now the view from the *Rukh* was of the Sakrian plains, hundreds of meters below.

The open-air deck was situated at the forwardmost point in the passenger gondola, just before the control gondola at the prow of the ship. The control gondola held the flight deck, access panels leading into the body of the gas-filled envelope, and the quarters of the captain and crew, and was connected to the passenger gondola by an umbilicus of a passageway, airtight and sealed against the elements. Between the two depended the platform of the open-air deck, which afforded a full circumference view typically enjoyed only by the stoutest of passengers.

The air was cold and sharp outside the safety of the gondola, and even through their thick, layered coats the quartet shivered in the stiff breeze. Above them curved the envelope of the airship's main body, its shape held rigid by the pressure of the ballonets within and the curved spine of the rigid keel. At this pressure height, the majority of the envelope was filled with helium, the air-filled ballonets normally used to control trim now deflated to their smallest circumference. The engine nacelles on either side of the passenger gondola hummed away, their screws turning, propelling the *Rukh* ahead as fast as a horse at gallop.

Stretched out below them like an immense quilt were cultivated farms, the rotated crops alternating green, tan, and brown like the game board for some unknown variant of chess. Vorin pointed to starboard, where the Inner Sea was just visible over the eastern horizon, and said a few words. Leena recognized the word for "water" in the Sakrian dialect. When Vorin pointed to the port side, and the Rim Mountains barely visible in the far distant west, Leena understood the word for "majesty" or one of its cognates, and something that sounded like the term for "wings." She was surprised, not having imagined the well-fed businessman as a poetic soul.

Balam began to growl, and Vorin backed away, becoming alarmed. Leena realized it was not poesy that gripped him, but fear.

Approaching from the west were large creatures on leathery wings, with long vicious beaks, and bony crests atop their narrow heads. Each was nearly twelve meters from wing tip to wing tip, and carried on its back one or two men, wearing goggles and wide-brimmed hats, with heavy scarves wrapped around their heads from neck to nose.

"Sky Raiders," Balam rumbled, unsheathing his claws, amber eyes narrowing.

"Dragons," Hieronymus said, hands tightening into white-knuckled fists at his side.

Leena had heard tavern talk about the men and women called Sky Raiders, but had dismissed it as the kind of stories one shared over spirits and wine. Evidently they were real, but she knew these were no dragons. These were pterosaurs, extinct on Earth since the age of the dinosaurs, but through ill fortune still surviving here on Paragaea into the age of man. She'd never imagined they could grow so large, but she'd learned that few things in this place were as she would have imagined.

Hieronymus turned from the railing, all his acrophobia forgotten.

"We'll need our weapons," he said, his tone clipped.

"Locked in a secured locker in the control gondola," Balam answered, his eyes fixed on the approaching pterosaurs. They were drawing nearer, perhaps just minutes away.

"I'll take care of that," Hieronymus said. "Little sister, get our employer to safety."

Leena nodded, and took Vorin by the right hand, his left clutching the leather case. She didn't bother to mutter soothing words or platitudes. There simply wasn't time.

✦

Leena led Jophar Vorin into the control gondola, past crewmen who bustled past them, their attention solely focused on their duties. Vorin would not be safe in the passenger gondola or the crew areas. The ship would simply be too dangerous once the Sky Raider boarding party had come aboard, even if the crew were ultimately successful in repelling the attack. Vorin's best chance was to safely wait out the attack, hidden away and secure.

Leena had paid careful attention as they'd boarded the *Rukh* the previous morning. She'd lost too many friends on launchpads and in flight to ever climb aboard any sort of plane, rocket, or aerostat without knowing all the contingencies. She led Vorin in a beeline to a side room off the main passageway, and opened the hatch overhead. A rope ladder unspooled, from the ceiling to their feet.

"Vlezt'," Leena said in Russian, then quickly added in English, "Climb!"

Vorin looked at her, nervous and confused.

Leena pointed up towards the hatchway, then grabbed Vorin's shoulder and shoved him towards the rope ladder. Understanding dawned in his small eyes, and he clambered inelegantly up the ladder. Leena followed.

Within the envelope of the airship, things were much as Leena had anticipated, which was some small blessing. The curve of the keel overhead like the spine of a cathedral, the large lunglike shapes of the helium-filled containers pressing against either side of the envelope, and at either side the deflated air-filled ballonets. These last, small bladders that would fill with air from outside the ship when the *Rukh* descended, were used to help maintain pressure on the envelope when the helium bags were deflated. At full pressure height, with the helium at near-full expansion, the ballonets were little more than partially inflated sacks of breathable air.

Leena took Vorin by the elbow and dragged him to the nearest of the ballonets. There was an airtight access panel near the seam that held the ballonet in place, and it was the work of only a few quick moments to wrest the panel open. It was only a meter or so square, just large enough for a grown man to climb through.

"Inside," Leena said, pointing. "We'll come back when it is safe."

Vorin looked from her to the limp air sack, and back again.

"Ka utok," Leena said, struggling, trying to piece together what little Sakrian she knew. *Through this.* She paused, then added, "Uksalke." *Safe.*

Vorin at last nodded, understanding. Clutching the leather case to his chest, he wriggled his ponderous bulk through the access panel, and looked out forlornly as Leena closed it up behind him.

"Just wait," she said, trying to sound reassuring. "You'll be fine. Uksalke. I promise."

✦

Leena rejoined Hieronymus and Balam on the platform of the open-air deck. They were surrounded by crewmen armed with poleaxes, clubs, and bayonets, half a dozen men ready to repel the boarders.

Hieronymus had his heavy cavalry saber hanging from his belt, his holstered Mauser C96 pistol at his hip. He handed Balam his knives and sling, and Leena her chrome-plated Makarov semiautomatic pistol, snugged in its nylon holster, and the short sword he'd insisted she start carrying. She tucked the blade into her belt, distastefully, and checked that the magazine on the Makarov was full.

"Take care with your firearm," Hieronymus warned, eyeing Leena's grip on her pistol. "We've precious little ammunition as it is, and besides, I've no desire to go plummeting down to our doom if you start shooting holes in this thing." He jerked a thumb at the curve of the envelope overhead.

"Not to worry," Leena answered. "Pressure inside the envelope is low, only a fraction of kilogram per square centimeter. If we were to punch hole in the fabric, it could take hours, even days before we noticed any change."

"I think we'll have more pressing matters to engage us, in the meantime," rumbled Balam, baring his teeth.

Leena and Hieronymus followed his gaze to the west.

The Sky Raiders were almost upon them.

CHAPTER 11
Sky Attack

The first wave of the Raiders was intended to disorient their prey, the pterosaurs sweeping in close, the Raiders riding pillion letting fly with spears and crossbow bolts at the defenders on the platform.

Leena was glad that firearms were so scarce in Paragaea, or their resistance might have proven futile. As it was, between her pistol and Hieronymus's, they were able to pick off three of the pterosaurs and their riders in the first two passes. But Leena's marksmanship had never been anything but journeyman at best, and Hieronymus had only limited ammunition for his Mauser, so by the time the Raiders began their boarding run, their best hope lay in fist, and club, and blade.

The Sky Raiders drew near the *Rukh*, just beyond the reach of the crew's poleaxes, matching the airship's speed. The pillion riders unfastened themselves from the saddle harness, drew a cutlass in one hand and a war-axe in the other, and with a bloodcurdling whoop leapt across the open air, crashing headfirst into the serried defenders on the platform of the open-air deck.

Balam met the boarders with tooth and claw, Hieronymus with a fierce grin and his cavalry saber in hand. Leena tried to draw a bead on one with her Makarov, but in the melee her shot went wide, and she came near to shooting one of the defending crewmen in the back, the shot instead ricocheting off the deckplates, sent zinging up and into the fabric of the envelope. With great reluctance, she holstered her pistol, and drew the short sword tucked in her belt, better suited for close quarters.

Leena watched as one of the crewmen went over the side, pitched head over heels by a Raider. That same Raider was an instant later brained by a heavy club, his teeth crunching together with a sickening crack, his eyes rolling up sightless in his skull as he fell insensate to the deck. Another Raider surged into the breach, and was caught up in the arms of the outlaw prince of the Sinaa, Balam, whose claws drew red rills of blood across the Raider's chest as the jaguar man threw the Raider overboard. Hieronymus's saber flashed in his hand, and Leena took up position at his back, handling the short blade as best she could, covering his rear while he mowed through the attackers.

The crew and the three companions made a valiant show of defending the ship from the boarders, but in the end, the Raiders' numbers were simply too great. Wave after wave of pterosaurs and riders came at the airship, another and another and another, until the defenders were near buried under attackers. In the end, the odds were simply too overwhelming, and the defenders had no choice but to lay down their arms and surrender.

The Raiders howled in celebration. The ship was theirs.

✦

The Raiders left a prize crew onboard as the pterosaurs wheeled off back to the west. A dozen men were enough to hold the ship, with the defenders left dead, injured, or merely disarmed. They were under the command of an old Raider with a long scar running along the left side of his face from forehead to chin, his nose broken and bent out of true. On his orders, the ship was steered off course towards the western Rim Mountains, and the secret hideaway of the Raiders. The surviving passengers would no doubt be sold off into slavery, the ship's cargo parceled out and fenced, and the *Rukh* itself broken down into constituent elements and sold at the best price, the metal components not least of which.

Hieronymus, Balam, and Leena bided their time. They were gathered in a mass along with the rest of the passengers and the surviving crew in the observation lounge, under the watchful eye of three Raiders armed with swords and crossbows loaded and primed. The Bent Nose leader of the Raiders and the rest of the prize crew were busy steering the ship, or rummaging through the cargo holds and cabins looking for plunder.

Leaning in close, the three companions whispered together in English, a language no one else onboard shared.

"We can take these three," Balam purred low. "They are cautious, but we have speed and strength on our side."

"And what of the nine more beyond the passageway?" Hieronymus asked quietly. "They've taken our arms away, and we're left with only our bare hands to defend ourselves."

"Not all of our hands are quite so bare," Balam answered, popping one of his claws out and grinning mercilessly.

"I think we have other things to worry about," Leena said, glancing over nervously at the three guards.

"Yes, you're right, of course," Hieronymus said apologetically. "Our first priority must be to secure the safety of Jophar Vorin."

"Well," Leena said, nodding slowly, "that's certainly correct, and something we should definitely look after, but that's not what I was thinking of."

Balam and Hieronymus looked at her, their expressions confused.

"During the attack, I fired a shot that went wide, and punched a hole in the envelope."

"Do the Raiders know?" Balam asked.

"No," Leena answered. "I don't think anyone else has noticed. It will be some time before the ship is affected, but sooner or later we will begin to lose altitude, and if that should come on quickly enough, we could all be in for a shorter trip than we had intended."

Hieronymus glanced behind them, to the wide reinforced-glass windows of the observation lounge, the purple mountains in the distant west and the hint of patchwork farmlands far below them.

"I hate flying," he said, closing his eyes tightly against the view.

✦

They continued to the west, the Raiders in the flight deck of the control gondola laying on speed, the hum of the engine nacelles rising to a piercing wail as the screws turned faster and faster.

In their whispered conference, hidden from the guards' attentions by the terrified masses of huddled businessmen, missionaries, and artisans, the three companions worked out their most likely plan for success. They would wait until the ship neared the Raiders' hideaway, just before reaching the foothills of the western Rim Mountains. By that point, the *Rukh* should have dropped low enough that they could descend safely to the ground below. They would overpower the prize crew, and drop lines off the side of the gondola to lower themselves, Vorin, and whatever other passengers had the nerve down to the ground. They could lose the Raiders in the thick forests of Altrusia, which spread out like a carpet all along the eastern slope of the Rim Mountains, and make a clear getaway.

Their plan hinged on the slim hope that the prize crew would become overconfident as they drew near their journey's end, with their home clearly in view. Hieronymus had been in similar situations on sailing vessels during the Napoleonic War, though, and he assured the other two that he was convinced of success. They had only to bide their time, and all would work out to their best advantage.

Still, timing would be crucial, and there was the constant threat that the *Rukh*'s envelope would lose pressure too quickly, and send them crashing to earth. If they made their move too soon, the chances of the Raiders repelling their insurrection was far, far greater; if they waited until too late, though, the airship might reach the Raiders' base before the companions could effect their escape, and they'd have the amassed might of the Raiders against them. They'd be sold into slavery, or tortured for sport, or worse.

The three companions huddled together, their watchful eyes on their captors, their thoughts on the actions before them.

✦

The forest of towering conifers spread beneath them, as far as the eye could see to the north, east, and south, while to the west the snow-capped peaks of the Rim Mountains grew ever larger. They had just hours to go before it would be time to make their move, and the three companions were tensed and ready.

The sound of the fat man wailing from the passageway signaled the end of all their plans.

Bent Nose, the leader of the Raiders, came into the observation lounge dragging Jophar Vorin by the scruff of the neck, a half-dozen Raiders crowding the passageway behind him.

"Damn," Hieronymus breathed, his hands tightening to fists.

Leena had almost risen to her feet when Balam laid a heavy hand on her shoulder.

"Not now, little sister," the jaguar man whispered, holding a finger up before his black lips. "Bide awhile."

Bent Nose threw Vorin to the deckplates, the heavyset Laxarian businessman still clutching the leather case chained to his wrist. The Raider commander then turned his scarred face to the assembled prisoners, and began to spit a steady stream of invective. His words, strained through the skein of his mountain accent, were impossible for Leena to follow.

"What is he saying?" Leena whispered to Hieronymus.

The passengers and crew looked to one another nervously as Bent Nose raged on.

"They found Vorin in the ballonet, while they were looking for hidden treasures," Hieronymus explained. "With the case chained to his wrist, the Raiders suspect him of being some kind of intelligencer for the Hegemon of Laxaria. They are going to cut off his wrist if he doesn't unlock the case for them. They are calling for his coconspirators to present themselves."

None of the prisoners spoke, but one by one their gazes began to turn towards the three companions, crouched together against the far windows.

"I don't like this," Balam rumbled.

Bent Nose left off ranting, and followed the gaze of the dozen or so passengers and crew who had looked at the three companions they'd all seen with the man trembling on the deckplates.

"Be ready," Hieronymus said in a harsh whisper.

"Ready for what?" Leena began to ask, but then it was too late, and her answer was before her.

Before Bent Nose could signal to the Raiders behind him in the passageway to come forward and take the three companions in hand, Hieronymus leapt to his feet and, with a wild cry, rushed at the Raider commander with his arms flung wide. Balam was just steps behind, his claws unsheathed, an unsettling roar bellowing from between his vicious jaws.

Leena didn't hesitate, but jumped up and followed after, running low with her arms held in a ready stance, her military training coming back to her like high water just beginning to seep over a low dam.

While Hieronymus grappled hand to hand with Bent Nose, and Balam took on the Raiders still crowded back in the passageway, Leena turned her attentions to the three guards who had stood watch over them these last hours. They had been standing on their feet without rest or respite for much of the day, and their energy must have started to flag as time wore on.

Leena plowed into the first of the guards, knocking his crossbow unfired from his hands and sending him stumbling back into the nearest of the other two. The guards went down in a confusion of arms and legs, while Leena managed to keep her feet below her, though her head rung with the impact.

The third guard, to her good fortune, did not carry a crossbow but only a short club. Precisely the thing her military instructors had trained her to defend against. At the time, she'd harbored bitter thoughts about the uselessness of such training, sure that no one would ever attack her with a two-foot length of wood. As the guard swung the club down at her overhand, Leena reacted instinctively, and silently asked forgiveness of every drill instructor she'd cursed in her thoughts. She sidestepped, grabbed the guard's elbow, and then pinioned his arm against his side. Then, sliding her leg out and shifting the guard's weight forward, she succeeded in flipping him head first over her hip, sending him crashing into the unforgiving deckplates.

By the time she looked up, Hieronymus had knocked Bent Nose unconscious, and Balam was entertaining himself with the Raiders who remained standing in the corner of the observation lounge.

"Quickly," Leena shouted. "It won't take long before the rest of them come to investigate."

Hieronymus nodded a quick reply, and then bolted towards the passageway. Balam held off the rest of the Raiders, who tried to surge out of the observation lounge, while Hieronymus went aft and retrieved their arms from the closet where Bent Nose had stowed them earlier, along with their packs from their quarters and a length of stout line. His Mauser tucked into his belt, and his cavalry saber in hand, Hieronymus stood a little straighter. Leena was forced to admit that, with her short sword in one hand and her Makarov in the other, she too felt that she stood a little taller.

With Vorin supported on Leena's arm, Balam in the lead, and Hieronymus bringing up the rear, the company made their way through the forward passageway, their packs slung on their backs. They encountered two more Raiders along the way. The first went down under Balam's claws, the second with one of Leena's bullets in his chest.

At length, they reached the open-air deck. Hieronymus unslung the coil of line from his shoulder, and went to work securing one end to the heavy, wrought-iron railing of the platform.

Balam kept his eyes on the steps leading down from the passageway, while Vorin stood gripping the leather case tightly in his arms. Leena walked to the railing and looked down. The ground was much closer than it should have been, the tops of the trees only bare meters below the gondolas.

"Chto?" Leena muttered, and then looked up to the envelope overhead.

The entry point of her errant shot had widened from a single puncture to a long fissure that ran at least a meter long. The surface of the *Rukh*'s envelope looked shrunken and withered, like the skin of an old prune. The ship was losing pressure far faster than she'd anticipated.

"Bozhe moj," Leena swore. She wheeled to face the other three. "We must hurry!"

Hieronymus nodded a silent reply, and tested the heft of the line.

"We are ready," he shouted back. "Vorin! You are first!"

The Laxarian businessman hung back, hesitant, standing on his tiptoes to peer over the platform's edge.

"Now, damn your eyes, or we'll leave you to *their* tender mercies!" Hieronymus snapped, his expression hard.

The businessman took a heavy breath, and then crossed the platform to Hieronymus's side. Leena stepped forward, and together she and Hieronymus helped Vorin to swing one leg over the railing.

"Lower yourself with care and speed," Leena said. "You may end up bruised and scraped, but at least you'll keep both your hands."

Vorin glanced from Leena to Hieronymus, confused. It was only then that the two realized he'd not understood a word of the English they'd spoken.

Leena pointed down towards the ground, and said the only word of Sakrian that came to mind. "Uksalke."

Safe.

Vorin nodded, reluctantly, and swung his other leg over the railing. He crested the railing, his hands fastened tight on the stout rope. Vorin paused, glancing with terrified eyes at the treetops whistling by just beneath him, and back up at Leena and the others waiting to follow. A Raider with a crossbow appeared at the top of the steps from the passageway, and before Balam could react the bowstring snapped and the bolt had thudded into Vorin's shoulder.

Vorin opened his eyes wide, his mouth a perfect circle of shock, and then he fell over backwards into open space as his hands lost their strength, like a tall tree felled by a lumberjack, and was gone.

With a roar, Balam took hold of the Raider before he was able to reload his crossbow. Carrying him overhead, the jaguar man crossed the platform to the railing, and then unceremoniously threw the Raider overboard, his screams torn away by the high winds.

"Bastard," Hieronymus spat.

More Raiders appeared at the top of the steps, and from the direction of the Rim Mountains Leena could see an advance party of pterosaur-riding Sky Raiders come out to escort them in.

"I think we should be going," Balam said, laying his clawed hands on the railing and looking over.

"You first, you great pillock," Hieronymus said darkly. "So far as we're concerned, I think our journey is completed, successfully or no. Let's away before the bill comes due."

Balam snarled, and then vaulted over the railing, catching the rope only after dropping nearly a meter in midair. He slid down, the rope held loosely between his hands and feet, and soon disappeared beyond the green foliage below.

"Now you, little sister," Hieronymus said, moving between Leena and the Raiders advancing from the passageway.

Leena wanted to object, but a quick glance at the Raiders approaching on pterosaur-back was enough to convince her the odds were not in their favor. Tucking her short sword in her belt, and securing the Makarov in its holster, she slipped over the railing and began to descend hand over hand towards the forest below. The tree-tops rose up to meet her faster than she was climbing down. The air-ship had only seconds before it crashed into the trees.

The branches and trunks lashed at her, raising welts and cuts on her face and arms, stinging her eyes, filling her mouth with pine nee-dles. She felt the line tug away hard in her hands, and she lost her grip, falling down three or more meters to the ground. She landed with a sickening thud that drove all the air from her lungs and left her dazed and unable to move on a bed of fine fallen needles, the sunlight filter-ing green through the canopy of trees above.

From overhead came a horrific sound, of metal screeching against metal, of trunks and branches snapping like dry bones, and Leena knew the *Rukh* was no more. But what had become of her two com-panions?

CHAPTER 12
The Forest of Altrusia

Through the sort of small miracle that seemed strangely common on Paragaea, neither Balam nor Leena was seriously injured in their descent, and they were able to locate one another with relative ease. They searched the surrounding area for Hieronymus, but by nearly nightfall they'd not yet found sign of him. Above the treetops, the pterosaurs of the Sky Raiders wheeled and turned, intent on revenge.

Leena and Balam were nearly set to break off their search, giving up their companion for lost, when a shadow split from the darkness surrounding them, and Hieronymus Bonaventure stood before them again.

"Don't you two have anything better to do than stand around in the dark?" Hieronymus said, walking past them and continuing towards the east. His clothes were torn to tatters, caked with dirt and stained green.

Leena and Balam glanced at one another, and then hurried to follow after him.

"We failed in our commission," Hieronymus said, without a word of explanation. "Vorin hired us to protect him, and his body now lies scattered some miles away in this forest, possibly lost forever."

"To be fair," Balam said, in a dark humor, "Vorin hired us to ensure that no one removed the case from his wrist." He paused, and then added with a mournful chuckle, "That, at least, we accomplished."

Hero shot him a black look, and kept walking.

"What happened?" Leena asked, exasperated. "How did you escape?"

"Well," Hieronymus answered, "once you'd shimmied down the line, the platform had dipped too near the trees for me to safely descend, and I had the remaining handful of Raiders to contend with."

"And the escort flying in from the west," Leena added.

"Did I? I don't think I noticed them. In any case, my sword was quick enough to keep the Raiders off me, but not enough to give me room to breathe, so in the end I had to wait until the *Rukh* was about to crash into the forest's canopy, and then I just jumped overboard onto a tree. It was touch and go, but I managed it, and climbed down to safety without breaking any important bones. Of the passengers and crew, I know nothing."

Leena gaped, and looked over to Balam, who only treated her with a knowing and weary smile.

"You mean that you leapt from a crashing airship and caught hold of a tree on the way down?" she asked, disbelieving.

"Yes," Hieronymus answered impatiently. "I said I didn't like heights. That doesn't mean I'm going to curl into a ball and whimper. Now come along, both of you. We're still bound for Lisbia in the north, and thanks to these damnable dragon-riders we're so far west that we've nearly twice as far to travel. Whatever Vorin carried, I damn well hope it was worth it to him."

Leena glanced back towards the Rim Mountains, hidden by the thick forests, and the hideaway of the Sky Raiders beyond.

"There are those who perhaps should not choose to travel. Vorin seemed the sort to be happier in his own home than he ever could be anywhere else."

"And there are those of us whose homes are denied us," Hieronymus answered, thoughtful. "So let's get to Lisbia, and see what we can do about that, too."

Leena took a deep breath, and sighed. She followed Hieronymus towards the east, Balam at her heels. In the forests behind them were strewn the remains of the Cloud Cutter *Rukh*, and they had long kilometers ahead before they slept.

✦

Hieronymus, Leena, and Balam made their way through the rain forest of Altrusia. They headed roughly east, trending north, making for Lisbia, though it was now farther from them than ever before. And as far distant as they were, that the going was so slow and ponderous was all the more noisome. Leena had thought that the trees of the Western Jungle into the midst of which the Vostok 7 module had crashed were enormous, but compared to the towering giants of the Altrusian rain forest they were little more than scrub and bush.

There was very little light on the ground level. The canopy of the top branches of the massive trees, dozens of meters off the ground, blocked out virtually all sunlight, so that even at midday the trio found themselves in a gloomy, twilight world. Birds called from overhead, raucous, near-deafening calls, and monkeys chattered and hooted from the lower branches. Strange predators prowled the dark underbrush, just out of sight, rumbling low.

Some of the trees were so large that their diameter was wider than Balam was tall. Others were so encased in constricting vines, each as wide as a man's leg, that no sign of the tree itself could be seen.

Having little else to do but walk, Leena insisted that Hieronymus and Balam drill her on the Sakrian dialect. She'd very nearly come to a bad end on the *Rukh* because she could not communicate effectively with Vorin, and since she could not reasonably expect all the sentient beings of Paragaea to learn English—or, better yet, Russian, though she longed to hear again her native tongue—she would have to learn the lingua franca.

So, as they walked, Hieronymus and Balam would point out items that they passed, asking Leena to repeat the name for each in Sakrian. After the first day of traveling, Leena had said the words "barad" and "sedet" and "kenet"—or *tree* and *plant* and *rock*—more times than she could count; and while she sorely wished that she'd had occasion to say "kones"—*sky*—they'd had no hint of blue above them since the *Rukh* went down.

Several days into the Altrusian forest, they came upon a small dinosaur lying at the top of a slight rise, its brains dashed out. It was no bigger than a large dog, with small grasping hands and a long neck, and from its relatively diminutive size and its physiology, Leena assumed it was some sort of plant eater. It was laid out on the forest floor, arms and legs splayed, neck stretched out before it, pointing downwards on the slight slope. But where the head should have been, the neck instead flattened out and terminated in a large, spreading pool of red and gray gore, dotted with tiny flakes of bone fragments. Otherwise, the body was untouched.

The company was immediately put on the defensive. From the looks of the red ruin that had once been the dinosaur's head, they could see the kill was very fresh. It didn't look like the work of another animal. A predator would not have left a kill uneaten, if it could somehow contrive to demolish its prey's skull in this fashion; more-over, the trees were too closely placed for an animal large enough to crush the dinosaur's head underfoot to pass by, and there was no sign that a beast of sufficient size to cause the damage had come this way.

Without warning, they heard a crashing, branches snapping, fol-lowed quickly by a sudden thunderous thud from a few meters away, as though a cannonball had been fired directly at the ground. Leaving the ruined form of the dinosaur behind, they rushed towards the sound. Lying in a slight cavity in the leafy mold underfoot was a large, spherical shape, the size of a cannonball but made of wood or some other type of vegetable matter.

"Another airship?" Leena said, looking up with trepidation. "Some kind of bombardment?"

"No airship could possibly detect our presence, or that of any other target," Hieronymus said, shaking his head. "Not this far beneath the thick canopy overhead."

Balam prodded the round object with an outstretched claw, and then straightened up, bristling. "It is a seedpod."

Hieronymus and Leena looked up at the towering treetops overhead.

"Another like it must have fallen from the tree back there," Hieronymus said, jerking a thumb over his shoulder, "and struck the dinosaur. Because of the slight rise, the seedpod must have rolled downhill and out of sight by the time we arrived."

From a short distance off came the sound of more crashing, more branches snapping and breaking, and the thunderous sound of another seedpod cannoning into the ground.

Leena shivered, her hands tightening into fists. "I don't want to be beneath the next one of those to fall."

"I agree," Hieronymus said hurriedly, as Balam nodded his assent.

Doubling their speed, they hurried their way through the forest, heading always north and east, Lisbia somewhere in the far, unthink-able distance.

A week further on, having luckily moved out of the zone of the seeding giants into another region of the forest, Leena's command of Sakrian language improving by leaps and bounds, they finally came to the edge of the twilit world.

The company approached a break in the rain forest, clear sky visible overhead, and the tallest trees in the near vicinity a much more manageable height, no more than a dozen meters. Leena luxuriated in the warm sunlight, glad to leave behind the twilight, if only for a short while.

After walking between the copses of trees for the better part of an hour, through the sun-dappled clearings, they came upon a small stream, a tributary of one of the greater rivers that divided the Altrusian forests. When fording the stream, Leena was surprised to discover that it was paved, the streambed lined with ancient cobblestones.

"What culture would have paved such a thing?" Leena asked, pointing out the neatly fitted stones to Hieronymus and Balam. "And for what purpose?"

"Paragaea is a much more ancient world than Earth," Hieronymus reminded her, regarding the paved stream. "And its landscape is littered with things of unbelievable antiquity, whose origins no man can guess. What is more, the very ground beneath our feet often holds hidden secrets: the ruins of civilizations, peoples, and cities long forgotten." Hieronymus looked up and down the course of the stream, rubbing his hands together thoughtfully. "I doubt there is any untrammeled wilderness on the face of Paragaea. Every stretch of jungle and forest is just what the wilderness has been able to reclaim from civilization."

"The struggle is not yet through." Balam pointed ahead, to the far side of the narrow stream. "It would appear the wilderness has not yet swallowed whole whatever culture once thrived here."

A few hundred meters from the far bank of the stream, its edges and details obscured by centuries' growth of vine and lichens, stood the ruined sculpture of a coiled serpent. It was easily hundreds of meters from side to side, standing a dozen meters tall, and before closer examination Leena had initially taken it for a hill rising before them, not something fashioned by hands.

"It must have been the same culture that paved the stream," Leena said as they approached the sculpture. "But why make such a thing, and how?"

"Well," Hieronymus said, a philosophical tone creeping into his voice, "it could well be that the beings who constructed this enormous snake idol were all dead and gone when the world was new, before man ever trod a foot upon Paragaea."

"No, perhaps not," Balam objected. They were now within arm's reach of the sculpture, standing entirely within its sharp-edged shadow. "There is every chance the idol-makers are very much alive."

Balam directed their attention to the figures emerging from the shadows all around them. There were nearly a dozen beings in all, looking like the products of a union between man and snake, scaled and hairless, with large round eyes, double slits for noses, and only abbreviated holes on either side of their head for ears. Their scaly skins were ranged from hues of deep russet-gold to red to green, iridescent and shimmering slightly like oil on water. Each stood nearly two and a half meters tall, but walked hunched over, the two massive fingers and thumb of each hand reaching out and grasping, a kind of hissing sounding deep in their chests.

CHAPTER 13

The Temple-City of Patala

Leena didn't waste a single thought, but immediately reached for her short sword, falling into a martial stance.

"Peace, little sister," Hieronymus said, laying a hand on her arm. "These are Nagas."

"Despite their sometimes fearsome mien," Balam said, "the snake men are by and large peaceful creatures."

Reluctantly, Leena let the blade slide back into its sheath, but her hand remained near the hilt.

One of the snake men stepped forward, and bowed slightly from the waist, his large round eyes glistening in the shadows like polished glass.

"I am Oshunmare," the Naga said, in perfectly accented Sakrian. "Whom do I have the pleasure of addressing?"

"I am Hieronymus Bonaventure, and these are my companions, Balam, prince of the Sinaa, and Akilina Mikhailovna Chirikova."

"You are most welcome to the lands of the Nagas, Hieronymus

Bonaventure." Oshunmare bowed again, dipping more deeply, and his fellow snake men followed suit.

Hieronymus and Balam bowed in return. Leena felt awkward, but had been raised to bow to no man, and so instead snapped off a crisp salute. She hoped it would not give offense.

"You are invited to be our guests in the temple-city of Patala"— Oshunmare pointed towards the east—"if you are willing only to be interrogated by the interlocutors, to help us increase our conception of the All. In return for this courtesy, you will be provided housing and sustenance for as long as you might require."

Leena bridled at the mention of "interrogation," thinking back on her Red Army training in anti-interrogation techniques, but from the responses of Hieronymus and Bonaventure, she assumed the meaning carried different connotations in Sakrian.

"We would be delighted," Hieronymus said, answering for the group.

"This way, then, to Patala." Oshunmare turned and, without further ceremony, led the party on a path to the east, around the massive carved serpent and back into the forests.

✦

As they walked, with the dozen snake men a short distance ahead of them, Leena spoke in low tones to her companions, asking them what they knew of this strange race. Were they another race of metamen, like the jaguarlike Sinaa and the birdlike Struthio, or something else besides?

"They are not among the kingdoms of metamankind," Balam answered in a quiet voice. "Not so far as I have always been told. As children, my sisters and I were taught that the culture of the snake men is one of the most ancient in all of Paragaea. I'm not sure anyone knows their origins, perhaps not even the Nagas themselves."

"If that is the case," Leena said, "and they are so ancient a culture, perhaps they will have some arcane knowledge of Earth lost to the rest of the world."

"Perhaps," Hieronymus said, rubbing his lower lip between thumb and forefinger. "I can't admit to much knowledge of the Nagas. I've seen snake men in the streets of the Sakrian cities, of course, and in the port towns of the Inner Sea, but those are typically snake men who have left their own ways behind, to better assimilate, their cultural traditions reduced to mummery performed on street corners for coins from passersby."

Leena, whose mother's people had been Russian gypsies, knew what it meant to have traditions degraded to the level of street performance.

After a short journey through the forests, they reached the city of Patala. Though not large for a city or township, as the whole city was one large complex of buildings and temples, in terms of single standing structures it was enormous. The temple-city first impressed itself on the senses as being unimaginably ancient. Its high, gray stone walls were in places completely obscured by climbing vines, in other places stained by mosses a deep greenish black. The temple-city rose in seven tiers, like a layered cake or step pyramid. As they climbed the wide, deep steps carved into the stone structures, they passed open-air plazas and pavilions, dotting the upper reaches of the complex, where Nagas young and old gathered to recite strange poetry, or dance, or debate, or produce haunting tones from vibrating crystals.

Oshunmare led the trio to the third tier of the temple-city, where waited for them three Nagas, each wearing a simple copper-colored tunic and, around their necks like a sort of badge of office, a crystal pendant.

"These three," the snake man explained, pointing to each in turn,

"Kalseru, Vasuki, and Manasa, are the designated interlocutors for this cycle, selected from all the population of Patala for this honor. They will have the rare opportunity to interview all outsiders who visit our temple-city until the next turn of the seasons, when the honor will fall on other fortunate Nagas."

The three Nagas stepped forward, each extending a two-fingered hand to one of the trio.

"If you would each follow one of the interlocutors," Oshunmare said, "the interrogations should be complete in short order."

Leena was anxious at the notion of being separated from her companions in a strange place, surrounded by inhuman beings, however placid or unthreatening they might initially seem. Hieronymus saw the concern etched across her face, and turned to address the interlocutors.

"We will be allowed to keep our weapons, of course."

"Of course," Oshunmare answered. "And no doors will bar your way. You may leave at any time during the interrogation, though in doing so, you would perforce be refusing our continued hospitality."

"Understood," Hieronymus said, and cast a glance at Leena.

Reluctantly, her hand staying near the hilt of her short sword, Leena nodded.

"I am Kalseru," one of the interlocutors said in perfect Sakrian, stepping towards Lena and bowing reverently. From the tenor of Kalseru's voice, she was evidently a female of the Naga species. "If you would accompany me, please, we may begin."

✦

In a private interview chamber, little more than a semicircular room open to the plaza, Kalseru explained to Leena that it was the custom of the Nagas to welcome outsiders with reverence and respect, seeing each encounter as a possible opportunity to expand their understanding of Ananta, a concept that most easily translates into other tongues as "the All." Kalseru would ask Leena a series of questions about her people's views on religion, cosmology, and existence, and Leena should answer as truthfully as she was able, with as much or as little detail as she felt comfortable providing.

Leena responded to all of Kalseru's questions—somewhat surprised her Sakrian had improved sufficient to the purpose—explaining about Marxist dialects, historical imperatives, and the inevitable rise of the proletariat. Leena explained in no uncertain terms that any belief in the supernatural, whether the occult or the divine, is simply a sop for the masses in decadent capitalist countries, to keep the workers' thoughts on the illusory rewards of the hereafter, and not on their miserable condition in the here and now.

"So," Kalseru asked, lazily drawing symbols in the sands of the chamber's floor, legs folded beneath her, "can we then assume that your conception of the All does not allow for the possibility of other planes of existence, of other realms of being?"

Leena was brought up short. Until a few weeks ago, her answer to that question would have come as easily and unbidden as her other answers, but now she wasn't so sure. Did the superstitions and fairy tales of the unenlightened have their origins in the other-dimensional realm of Paragaea? Was this the Fairyland of her grandmother's stories?

Leena began now to question Kalseru, asking her what knowledge the Nagas had of other worlds.

Kalseru was unable to answer her questions, and excusing herself for a moment, called in Oshunmare. The older Naga joined them, but after listening to Leena's inquiries about Earth, he, too, was unable to answer her questions. A number of other interlocutors, debaters, poets, and thinkers were brought into the chamber in the hours that followed, all of them listening respectfully to Leena's questions, and then disagreeing one with another over how little the Nagas' conception of the All was able to account for her questions.

The Nagas agreed on one point, at least. They had, of course, heard of the existence of portals between Paragaea and the plane known as Earth—no culture of their great age could have avoided the knowledge—but they knew of no way to predict where and when such portals would occur

Finally, Oshunmare called for silence. It was clear that none of those present had a sufficiently advanced conception to address Leena's questions. Their only option was to take her before the Aevum.

"I was promised food and rest after all those damnable questions," Balam rumbled as they climbed the steps to the upper reaches of the temple-city. "And now I have to go along and listen to you ask even more?"

Leena did not answer, but continued to mount the deep steps to the summit.

"I've not talked so much about the great god Thun since I was a cub taking my maturation examinations," Balam said, "and perhaps not even then."

"I quite enjoyed the interview, actually," Hieronymus said, smiling. "I confess that I'm scarcely qualified to speak to the religion of my own people, since while I was ostensibly raised in the Church of England, I only attended service a handful of times in my whole childhood. Instead, I spoke with Vasuki at length about Greek myths and legends, which I learned from my mother, who, if nominally a Dutch Protestant, would more likely have worshipped at the altar of Zeus, or at least of Homer, had she been able."

With Oshunmare guiding them, the three were led to a wide, open-air pavilion at the top of the temple-city, with stone pillars surmounted by carved representations of the sun, moon, planets, and stars.

Seated cross-legged on a low, wide pillar at the center of the stone floor was an ancient snake man. The sun's last rays bore down from the west, and the snake man's head was tilted back, a look of quiet contentment on his alien features.

"Here, please." Oshunmare motioned the trio to sit, indicating the sandy ground at the base of the pillar.

Leena, Hieronymus, and Balam sat in the sand at the feet of the Aevum. His mottled scales, once the brilliant green of the young snake men, had faded in hue until they were nearly gray, and they hung loose and flaking upon his slender frame. He drew a heavy breath through his double-slit nose, lids drawing shut over his enormous, yellow eyes, and then he began to speak.

"I like to spend my days here in the uppermost pavilion of Patala," the Aevum said, in a voice as ancient as the stone walls of the temple-city, "soaking in as much of the sun's life-giving rays as I am able in my final hours." He prodded at the dry, sagging scales on his rib cage with an outstretched claw. "I will likely not live to molt again, but will return to the dust which birthed me, to rejoin the All until the cycle of creation turns again, and it is my time once more to be instantiated." He turned his attention to the trio. "I am Sesha, the Aevum, leader of the Nagas."

"These outsiders," Oshunmare explained, "having been fully interrogated by the interlocutors, have questions of their own which the assembled wisdom of Patala cannot address. It is hoped that the Aevum will have answers for their ears to hear."

"Repeat your questions," the Aevum said, his huge eyes on the trio.

Hieronymus and Balam turned towards Leena, and after taking a deep breath, she answered.

"Like Hero, my companion"—Leena indicated Hieronymus with a wave of her hand—"I am originally from Earth, another world. I need to learn how to locate the gates that periodically open between the worlds, and further how to locate one that will return me to my own place and time."

The Aevum was silent for a span, his alien expression unreadable, and at length he slowly shook his head.

"Our conception of the All allows for other worlds besides our own, and we have from time to time interrogated those who claimed to originate on worlds other than this, but our conception, I'm afraid, does not include the knowledge of how to move from one world to another."

Leena deflated visibly, a feeling of despair flooding the pit of her stomach. If this most ancient of cultures did not have the answers she sought, what hope was there?

The Aevum, though, was not yet done speaking.

"The wizard-kings of the citadel city of Atla, perhaps, might have had the answers you seek, had they not sealed themselves away behind an impenetrable barrier in the far, frigid south. Or the heresiarch of Pentexoire, who was whispered to hold all of nature's secrets, before vanishing centuries ago into the annals of history. There is another, though. Our legends tell of an ancient man, a human, who once every thousand years comes to the temple of the forgotten god in the dense jungle. A year later, a young man emerges, and goes off into the world. There are legends that this man is the forgotten god of the temple himself, who survived long past the death of his last worshipper. He makes his weary way around the whole circuit of lands, stopping once every millennium to be rejuvenated at the seat of his former glory. The man is said to wear a rare jewel around his neck that is the source of his knowledge and power. If one were to wrest this jewel from him at his weakest moment, one could force him to reveal his secrets, and to answer any question or riddle put to him." The Aevum paused, and leaned forward on his perch, his gaze bearing down on Leena. "The time of this ancient man's return to the jungle is upon us, and if the legends are true, he can even now be found in the forgotten god's temple. If any on the face of this world has the answers you seek, it would be this man."

CHAPTER 14

Journey

Leena, Hero, and Balam passed one night in the city of Patala, which was more than enough for Balam. With the morning's first light, they were back in the forests heading to the east, in the direction in which the Aevum had told them that they would find the temple of the forgotten god. They found themselves in much the same twilit world through which they'd passed in the stretches south of Patala, the canopy overhead blocking out the sun and sky.

"The food and drink of the Nagas is not fit for a Sinaa to consume," Balam insisted as they struggled through the undergrowth. "I do not know if humans of your variety can stomach such weak fare, but the more delicate, sophisticated palate of the jaguar men could not abide it for another meal."

"I was surprised," Leena answered, "that beings descended from reptiles, themselves meat-eaters, would have evolved into strict vegetarians."

Hieronymus hacked at thick brambles with his saber. "The diet of the Nagas is one of culture, one inculcated by nurturing, not by nature. My interlocutor told me a bit about it, during our interview. The Nagas view every living creature as an embodiment of the All, seeing consciousness as the means through which the universe deigns to experience itself. To interfere with the experiential journeys of any consciousness, whether the elevated mind of a jaguar man"—he prodded Balam jokingly—"or the minor, flickering intellect of a hummingbird, is to offend the All itself."

"But they eat plants, yes?" Leena said. "Isn't it true that some hold that plants themselves have some level of mind? Don't they turn towards the sun's rays as it moves across the sky, suggesting some rudimentary level of awareness?"

"I asked the Naga interlocutor Vasuki the same question myself," Hieronymus said.

"And what did he say?" Balam asked.

"The interlocutor allowed that they might be giving some small offense to the All by consuming roots and tubers, but he responded by asking whether it wouldn't be a greater offense to allow the collective minds of the Nagas to be extinguished by failing to properly nourish their bodies?"

Balam shrugged, and growled appreciatively. "Well, perhaps there's hope for them, yet."

✦

A day into their journey from Patala to the hidden temple, the three travelers crouched around a flickering fire in a small clearing, sharing their meal and their thoughts.

"So what question will you ask, Balam," Hieronymus asked, "if this figure out of legends should prove real? What one answer do you cherish?"

Balam scratched the underside of his leonine chin with a half-sheathed claw and rumbled thoughtfully.

"I suppose, if I could have any answer, I would want to know whether I will ever regain my throne, and again lead the nation of the Sinaa." He paused, taking a leisurely bite of the piece of grilled meat skewered on his knife, checking the progress of the other portions sizzling on a spit above the flames. "Yes, that would be it, I think. And you?"

Hieronymus chewed his lip in contemplation.

"To be entirely honest, I don't know," he said. "You've known me long enough to realize I have little curiosity at all. All I want from life is a comfortable bed; clean, dry clothes; a little coin in my pocket; and a bit of excitement from time to time. All that I can secure for myself without terrible difficulty without peeling back the secrets of the universe. Why should I meddle with perfection?"

Leena snorted, and shook her head.

"You never cease to amaze me, Bonaventure," she said, a mocking smile on her lips.

Hieronymus shrugged, and turned his attention back to the meat and the fire. Neither he nor Balam asked the cosmonaut what question she would ask.

Silence fell over their little camp, and the night wore on.

✦

The trio passed the night, sleeping fitfully, and in the morning pressed on. They traveled throughout the day, swatting away flies the size of hummingbirds, and enormous spiders that depended from webs stretching several meters on a side. They passed skeletons picked clean, the molds and lichens of the forest floor reclaiming what was left of the bones. Though the trees here were not as high as those under which they'd passed before reaching Patala, they were even more closely packed together, and so the light at the forest floor was even darker than before, closer to midnight than twilight.

At one point they encountered a group of apelike men, or menlike apes, who stood on the other side of a snaking river from them and hooted and jeered. But the hairy creatures had no means to cross the river, and the trio had no reason to do so, and so the encounter ended as it began, with the trio continuing on through the trackless jungle.

That night they reached a small clearing and decided to stop for the night. They huddled around another campfire, but their journey through the thick undergrowth of the forest had tired them, and conversation was limited to the essentials: asking for food, for drink, for quiet. The closest they came to exchanging thoughts was when Balam expressed a longing for his home in the Western Jungles. There was something to the deeply forested Altrusian woods that unsettled him. Leena, having spent only a short while in either place, was forced to agree.

They slept, the stars overhead just visible through the boughs of the trees, and dreamt uneasy dreams.

✦

They were off at dawn, and after a short while, found daylight. They had at last reached the edge of the deep forest, and though the undergrowth was still as thick as iron grating, the trees stood fractionally farther apart, so that more light reached the ground. In a few steps they passed from midnight, to twilight, to full daylight, the clear blue skies overhead tantalizingly close as they tore their way through the clinging vines and barbed branches. They continued on, trying to shake the funereal sense that had clung to them throughout the midnight woods.

They reached the ruined temple by midmorning, hacking their way through the thick undergrowth with sword, knife, and claw. The ancient structure was almost completely obscured by the dense foliage, the stones of the walls stained a deep green by the centuries' accumulation of lichens and mosses growing on them. This was a temple

without a name, dedicated to some forgotten god, raised by some forgotten race, to which no road, track, or path led.

Over the archway into the temple was a statue representing a beast
raised on its hind legs with its head thrown back, but time and the elements had erased any distinguishing characteristics. The three wayfarers rested in the hazy shadow of the statue, their backs against the
cool, damp stones of the temple wall, catching their breath before
venturing inwards.

"What do you suppose it is, Balam?" Hieronymus asked, wiping his
forehead with his sleeve and indicating the statue with a jerk of his head.

The jaguar man rumbled contemplatively, deep in his chest, his
amber eyes narrowed at the indistinct figure above them.

"A tiger, I would think," Balam answered, trying to smooth the
matted fur of his shoulders and chest with his hands, his claws safely
retracted.

"Then you would think wrong," Hieronymus said with a sly grin,
"because it is obviously a horse."

"A horse?" the jaguar man replied, black lips curling back over
saber-teeth in a wicked smile. "This jungle heat has gotten to you.
You've lost all sense of reason."

"Budet!" Leena snapped in Russian, and then quickly translated
into English. "Enough! We came here for answers, not to indulge your
appetites for foolish games."

She turned to the arched entrance, which was skeined with
creeping vines, and began hacking at the vegetation with her short
sword. Within a few moments she'd carved an opening large enough
to squeeze through. Then she tucked the sword back into her belt,
drew her chrome-plated Makarov semiautomatic pistol from its nylon
holster, and slipped through the curtain of severed vines into the cool
darkness of the temple beyond.

Hieronymus and Balam glanced at each other, shrugged, and followed
her in, drawing unlit torches and flints from their packs as they went.

CHAPTER 15

Temple of the Forgotten God

Though outside it was broad daylight, inside the dank, cool interior of the temple it was dark as night. The three travelers carried torches, which sputtered and popped in the still air, and made their way through the labyrinthine corridors of the temple.

The Aevum had mentioned that the legends spoke of perils, and of guardians in the temple of the forgotten god. After an hour of making slow progress through the temple passageways, sometimes reaching dead-ends or switchbacks, forced to retrace their steps and choose other branching paths, the trio had nearly decided that any such perils were the province of legends alone.

When they first heard the skittering, like the sound of hundreds of claws striking stone, again and again, they realized they had been entirely too quick to dismiss the stuff of myths. Hieronymus drew his heavy cavalry saber from his belt, leaving his Mauser C96 pistol holstered at his hip. His torch held high in one hand, the saber at the ready in his other, he slowly advanced forward. Balam drew his knives from their sheaths on the leather harness crisscrossing his broad chest, while Leena tightened her grip on her chrome-plated Makarov.

"Don't waste ammunition, little sister," Hieronymus reminded her, motioning to the short sword in her belt. "Use the blade if possible."

Leena shook her head, her expression taut.

"I'll use what seems appropriate," she said, "and from the sounds of whatever's coming, I'd rather be in firing range than at arm's reach."

In the next instant, a sickly white wave surged around the bend in the passageway. Dozens, perhaps hundreds of strange creatures, all rushing towards the three wayfarers. A horde of lizard-rats, an unnatural amalgam, they were each about a foot long, with four limbs terminating in vicious claws. Their red eyes glinted evilly in the flickering torchlight, and their pale, hairless hides shimmered sickly like oil on water. Each had a wide mouth lined with double rows of serrated teeth, and a spiny ridge ran from the base of their triangular skulls to the tip of their whiplike tails.

"Der'mo!" Leena swore, swinging the pistol up.

"Wait," Balam said, raising a hand to stop her.

The jaguar man stepped forward, and held his torch out to Leena. The lizard-rats were almost upon them.

"To train the royal children in the arts of defense, the warmasters of the Sinaa drop them into pits full of creatures like these," Balam explained casually, taking a long, wicked knife in each hand, their blades pointed at the ground. "It's been a while since I had any real exercise."

Hieronymus gave a slight bow, and then stepped out of the way as the jaguar man rushed forward, roaring a blood-chilling war-cry, teeth bared. Balam threw himself into the midst of the creatures, laying about on all sides with his twin knives, meeting the seemingly endless waves as they came. In a rain of gore, the foul creatures began to pile at his feet, some twitching their last, some already lifeless, as the jaguar man dealt with their remaining brethren, a vicious smile curling his black lips.

Once Balam had seen to the last of the lizard-rats, they came to a gallery of bronze statues made viridescent with age, easily a dozen of them. Each was of a warrior, each from a different culture or time period. They were tall, the shortest of them easily a foot taller than Balam, who himself towered over Leena. Some of the statues wielded swords, some spears, some war-axes, but all were armed.

The three wayfarers had made it halfway through the gallery, their torchlights casting shifting shadows on the statues, when Leena drew up short.

"Did you hear that?" she asked.

Her two companions stopped in their tracks, their attention sharpened.

"A kind of creaking?" Balam said, his ears twitching.

"Yes," Leena answered.

"Then no," Balam said unconvincingly. "I didn't hear a thing."

All around them, the statues began to move, slowly at first, and then with more speed and grace.

"Brilliant!" Hieronymus said with a laugh. "Clockwork soldiers. This is going to be fun." As he brought his saber to the en garde position, he glanced over at Leena. "Promise me, little sister, that the next time you two are inflicted by curiosity, I'm not to talk you out of it!"

✦

In the end, it was Hieronymus who dealt with the majority of the clockwork soldiers. He was much more adept at swordplay than Leena, and his saber was of a sufficient length to keep the animated statues at bay. Balam, with his claws and knives, was forced to get in too close in the melee, allowing one of the statues nearly to crush him between bronze arms at one stage.

The three advanced up the passageway as quickly as they were able,

Leena in the lead, Balam following closely behind, and Hieronymus bringing up the rear, fending off the pursuing clockwork soldiers. As strong as the statues were, the trio were lucky that they moved so relatively slow. Finally, the three wayfarers reached a point where the passageway narrowed before a junction, a space just wide enough for one to pass.

Hieronymus, holding his saber in a two-handed grip, rained blows against the bronze bodies of their pursuers, sounding like ringing gongs. He found, through sheer luck, that they were weakest at the joints between their torsos and legs and that by pounding continually at that juncture, he was able to sever the lower limbs from the body. Cut and bruised from the lunges that made it past his parries, Hieronymus finally succeeded in immobilizing a half dozen or so of the statues, their arms and heads still thrashing as they clattered to the cold stone floor. Packed in tightly together in the small space, they could not drag themselves any farther with their hands, and they were wedged in securely enough that those behind could not push or pull them out with ease. From the safety of this bronze wall of fallen attackers, Hieronymus was able to make quick work of the remaining mechanical foes, and in a short time all lay helpless on the passage floor.

Leaving behind the clockwork soldiers, the three wayfarers found themselves nearer the center of the temple labyrinth. Their path had taken them in a wide spiral, tracking several times around the circumference of the ruined temple, drawing inexorably nearer the center with every revolution. They entered a broad arcade and heard loud noises from the darkness in front of them. A giant scorpion emerged from a side passageway. It towered above them, easily ten meters long. If they managed to escape its wicked pincers, they would leave themselves vulnerable to its barbed tail. If they managed to survive being impaled by the thorny tip of the tail, the poison would claim them in a matter of minutes.

"I am tired of this nonsense," Leena said, and raising her chrome-plated semiautomatic, put three bullets one after another into the skull of the scorpion.

The monster danced awkwardly from side to side for a moment, its tail waving drunkenly in the air above it, and then it crashed to the ground, lifeless and still.

"*That*," Leena said to Hieronymus, "merited a little bit of ammunition, don't you think?"

She turned and, without another word, skirted around the scorpion's giant bulk into the passageway beyond.

✦

They reached at last the center of the labyrinth, the heart of the temple. Coming out of the darkened passageway, they found themselves at a circular amphitheater, open to the sky. The day had come and gone since they'd first entered the temple, and the sun had long set. The thin light of the gibbous moon overhead filled the chamber, everything painted in shades of gray.

At the center of the space was a stone platform, as long and as wide as a coffin, upon which lay a young man, insensate, naked, and unmoving, eyes shut tightly. Where his generative organs should have been, the skin was smooth and unbroken, but otherwise he seemed a typical specimen of humanity. Over him stood an ancient, hairless man, dressed in white robes, with an opalescent gem the size of a man's palm in his hands. Ringing the room were strange twists and curves of metal tubing, carved stone shapes, bits of crystal and glass, a maddening assemblage of shapes and substances, though whether they constituted some sort of machinery, or sculpture, or something else entirely, none of the wayfarers could say.

Hieronymus was across the room in the blink of an eye, snatching the gem from the old man's withered hands. Before the old man could react, before he could even speak, Hieronymus tossed the gem to Balam, and pinned the old man's arms behind him.

"Return the gem!" the ancient man wailed in the language of the Sakrian plains, without bothering to ask who his attackers were, or what they wanted. He turned milky white, sightless eyes towards the entrance, his expression pained. "You must return the gem to my keeping! My life depends upon it!"

Leena, her Makarov pointed to the stone floor, drew near the young man on the platform.

"What goes on here?" Leena said, prodding the still form with her pistol's barrel. She spoke in the same dialect the old man had used, the Paragaean lingua franca. Her skill with Sakrian was even less sure than her command of English, but she knew enough to get her point across.

The figure on the table did not respond to Leena's prodding, not stirring a centimeter. He was completely hairless, head to foot, without eyelash, brow, or body hair of any kind, his skin the color of polished marble.

"Please, I implore you," the old man continued, shifting tactics to pleading. "I must have the gem, and immediately, or all is lost!"

"This," Balam said, sauntering to Leena's side, tossing the gem lightly in the air and catching it, "is unexpected. Is this one the old man's patient, or his dinner?"

Leena's mouth drew into a moue of distaste, and she shivered.

"Look," she said, pointing at the young man's chest. There, where his breastbone should have been, was a large cavity, big enough that Leena could just barely cover it with her outstretched hand. It was not a wound, but a perfect concavity, the skin smooth and unmarred.

"Perhaps his meal has already begun," Balam said, glancing up at the old man.

"Well, Balam," Hieronymus said, "I wasn't quite sure *what* to expect, myself. But I'll admit surprise."

With a casual air, Hieronymus turned his attentions back to the old man, who struggled without effect against his bonds.

"Now, ancient one, let's exchange words. From the snake men, to the west of here, we have heard the legend of an undying man who returns to this temple to be rejuvenated once every thousand years. Can we safely assume that you are he?"

"Please," the old man wailed piteously. In the moonlight, his milky eyes looked almost opalescent, twins to the bauble in Balam's hands. "The gem."

"We'll return the gem to you," Leena answered from across the chamber, not without compassion, "but only if you answer our questions."

"Why must you torture an old man?" their prisoner wheezed. "Return my gem to me, ere it is too late."

"Answer our questions, and it will be returned to you," Hieronymus repeated.

"I don't know," Balam said. He absently tapped at the emerald pendant hanging from his ear. "I quite like it, actually. It could make for a fine bit of jewelry."

"Balam," Hieronymus warned, eyes narrowed.

"All right, all right," the old man consented, bitter but resigned. "If I hear and answer your questions, you will return my property to me?"

"You have our solemn word," Hieronymus said, without a trace of humor.

The old man's mouth drew into a tight line, and he nodded sharply.

"For each of you, I will answer a single question," he said. "Begin."

CHAPTER 16
Questions and Answers

Leena's question was first, her need for the answer judged to be the greatest.

"My question is about Earth," she began, guardedly hopeful, "which many in this strange land claim to be mythical, but from which I myself came."

"Yes," the old man answered, nodding slowly, his sightless eyes on eternity. "I have seen innumerable portals to Earth in my many years. I have seen ships at sea disappear into them, never to return. I have seen, too, all manner of strange men and creatures issue forth from them. Great lizards that stand taller than trees, their teeth long and sharp as cutlasses; men and women in strange fabric which nature never knew, speaking unknown tongues; rains of fish and frogs falling from the sky; vehicles of glass and steel which soar through the air; great flocks of birds . . ."

"Budet!" Leena snapped, excitedly, cutting him off. Remembering herself, she continued in Sakrian. "My question is this: Can you predict where and when the portals between Paragaea and Earth will open?"

The old man considered his answer for the briefest instant, and then shook his head.

"This skill is not mine," he said, "but I have encountered those in my travels who claim to have that knowledge. Whether they do or not, I cannot say."

"Who are they?" Leena asked excitedly, her hands in white-knuckled fists at her sides.

The old man simply said, "From each of you, a single question I will answer."

Balam was next to ask his question.

"If I return to my home in the Western Jungle," he said, "will I be able to oust my former coregents from the throne, and retake my place as leader of the Sinaa nation?"

The old man thought for a moment before answering, weighing his response.

"You overestimate my skills. I am not prescient, merely knowledgeable. That said, with a proper study of the facts I *could* make an educated guess. The facts, however, are not known to me, beyond the mere generalities. I was last in the lands of the Sinaa during the reign of the coregents Onca and Penitigri, when they went to war against the dog men of the Canid."

Balam's mouth hung open in surprise, and his amber eyes widened.

"Onca was my grandsire, six generations removed," he said, disbelieving but still not convinced the ancient man wasn't telling the truth. "Just how old do you claim to be?"

The old man simply said, "From each of you, a single question I will answer."

It was now Hieronymus's turn. He looked through narrowed eyes at the ancient man.

"Leena," he called over his shoulder, "I hope that you'll forgive me not repeating your question, but I find that I *do* possess curiosity, at last. I simply must know." He turned his attention back to the old man. "Who are you, and what is this gem you cherish so dearly?"

"Benu," the old man said simply.

"Which do you mean?" Hieronymus said. "Is Benu your name, or that of the gem?"

"Benu," the old man repeated.

"Answer me, curse your sightless eyes, or you'll never lay hands on the gem again."

The old man hung his head, and drew a heavy breath.

"I am Benu, the reborn one."

"And what is the gem?" Hieronymus asked.

"Benu," the old man answered.

"You speak in riddles," Hieronymus said, growing agitated. His cavalry saber slid from its scabbard with the whisper of steel on steel, and he prodded the old man in the chest with the blade's tip. "Speak clearer, or I'll not warn you again."

"The gem is Benu," the old man answered in a faraway voice. "The gem is me, in every way that counts."

Hieronymus prodded the old man in the chest once more.

"Very well," the old man said, and drew himself up straighter. He shrugged his shoulders out of his robes, and stood naked before them. In the middle of his sunken chest was a fist-sized hole, twin to that in the chest of the young man lying unconscious on the platform. He was as hairless as the young man, and likewise sexless, but his skin was wrinkled and spotted, and hung loosely on his skeletal frame.

"I am an artificial being, not born of woman," the old man went on. "I was forged hundreds of centuries ago, by a race of beings whom I can no longer clearly recall, and whom I have not seen in many long millennia. I was constructed to collect knowledge for those who created me, to walk the wide world until I had learned everything that could be learned. My bodies, though, last only a short span of years, even with the periodic repairs I am able to make, so that they are worn out and beyond use after no more than a thousand years. Once in every millennium, then, I construct a new body, and transfer my mind and memories to my new incarnation. The gem you hold in your hands"—the old man gestured to Balam with his chin—"contains all that I am, and all that I ever have been. If it is not seated in my new body before this old shell expires from age and exhaustion, then all I have learned in my long years will be lost."

"Assuming we believe you," Hieronymus said. "Why, with all that you have learned, can you not better answer our questions?"

The old man simply said, "From each of you, a single question I will answer."

Leena, who'd remained silent since receiving her unhelpful response from the old man, surged forward, her hand flying to the Makarov pistol at her hip

"If he knows the way to Earth," she shouted, "he will tell me, or I will kill him!"

Hieronymus leapt in front of her, blocking her path and pinning her arms to her sides before she was able to draw her pistol.

"We gave our word," he said apologetically. "We've little else to call our own in this strange world, to trade it away so callously."

Hieronymus led her to the far side of the chamber, trying to soothe her rage.

"Balam," he called over his shoulder, "return the gem to him."

The jaguar man, with a casual shrug, did as he'd been told, dropping the opalescent gem into the old man's withered hands. The old man immediately groped his way to the still form on the slab, touched the gem for the briefest instant to his forehead, and then placed the gem in the cavity in the young man's chest.

A heartbeat passed, and the young man on the table opened his eyes, the lids drawn back on opalescent irises that seemed cousins to the gem now secured to his chest. At the same instant, the old man's sightless eyes shut one last time, and he fell straight to the ground, like a marionette with its strings cut.

The naked, hairless man on the slab sat up, swung his legs out over the side of the platform, and jumped lightly to his feet. He reached down, and effortlessly picked up the still form of the old man in his arms. He turned to the three travelers, who had drawn together on the far side of the chamber, and gave a slight smile.

"If you will help me bury the remains of my former incarnation," he said, his voice clear and strong, "to keep it safe from thieves and predators, we can be on our way."

"On our way? Where?" Balam asked.

"The questions put to my previous incarnation excited my curiosity," the new Benu said thoughtfully. "I am somewhat curious to know whether you will be able to retake your throne, jaguar man, but I'm profoundly intrigued by the notion of traversing a portal to Earth. In my long years of roaming the wide world, I have learned nearly everything there is to learn, having to suffice these last few millennia on minutiae about the reigns of kings, trivia surrounding the dogmas of the world's various religions, and working out the final answer to the riddle of the meaning of existence. On Earth, however, there is an entire world of new information to gather. I'd have millennia of work before me, an unwritten book of knowledge to fill."

The three looked at one another, not sure how to respond. It was Leena who finally broke the silence.

"Come along then, if you're coming," she said, turning back to the passageway from which they'd come. "If the road ahead of us leads back to Earth, I'd just as soon be on our way."

"I should lead the way, I should think," the new Benu said, glancing towards the passageway, "so that I may disarm the temple guards as we pass."

"Oh, those nuisances?" Leena said distractedly. "Already taken care of."

Leena relit her torch from her flint-and-steel, and stood at the entrance to the passageway, waiting impatiently for the others to follow. Balam, with a shrug, moved to stand beside her.

The new Benu, naked and strong, followed after, his former body held in his arms. Halfway to the passageway he paused, and glanced back at Hieronymus, who still lingered on the far side of the chamber.

"Are you in some distress?" the artificial man asked, a hint of concern in his clear voice.

"No, it's simply that . . ." He paused, shaking his head. "I'm just . . ." Hieronymus laughed reluctantly. "I'm just curious. Who constructed you? How do you function? Why trust yourself into the hands of strangers, and join us on our possibly fruitless quest? Why . . . ?" He broke off, and glanced around the room. "We won our way into this room for answers, and leave only with more questions."

"And with me," Benu corrected.

"But if you aren't a walking question in your own self, then nothing is."

Benu smiled, an expression of ancient wisdom drifting across his fresh, young features.

"In my few years of existence, walking the wide world and gathering knowledge, I have found that answers are rarely what we need. It is the questions that we live for."

CHAPTER 17
A Change of Direction

Their company was now expanded by one, their trio become a quartet, and with the change in their number came also a new destination.

"I have traveled throughout the city-states of Sakria in these years past," Benu said as they made their steady way east, heading towards the eastern extremity of the Altrusian forests, where the trees gave way to the high plains of Sakria. "And I was most recently in the self-same Lisbia of which you speak. And I can assure you, in no uncertain terms, that no one in any Sakrian culture, leastwise Lisbia, holds the knowledge you seek."

Leena, following close behind the strange artificial man, felt a sense of vertigo deep inside, as though she were standing at the edge of some metaphorical chasm, teetering on the brink.

"So we are back where we started, then?" she said, dispirited. "Figuratively, if not literally, mired in ignorance and with no idea where to go for answers?"

"But making good time." Balam laughed mirthlessly, following a few paces behind. And he was right. In addition to knowing the hidden tracks and paths through the thick forests, Benu's strength and reserves of energy belied his slight frame, and with him at their head, tearing through the undergrowth, blazing a trail before them, they moved at a pace far faster than any they had managed on their own.

"Heading nowhere fast," Hieronymus said, bringing up the rear. "So if we're not now bound for Lisbia, are we to wander aimlessly for answers?"

"I did not say that." Benu glanced back over his shoulder, his opalescent eyes glittering in the slanting rays of the afternoon sun. Leena was still disconcerted that he chose to walk unclothed and unadorned, as naked as he had been when lying on the slab in the ruined temple. Benu had explained that he had no need of clothes, but that if it bothered her to see him in such a state, he would endeavor to procure suitable clothing at the first opportunity. He explained that he usually adopted the fashions and customs of the culture in which he happened to find himself, but that when he traveled through the unpeopled wilds, he rarely maintained such affectations. "I said that no Sakrian cultures held the answers. Some, though, are aware of the questions, which might serve us as clues."

"What do you mean?" Leena asked.

"In the city of Hausr, there is the sect of Kasparites, for example."

"I know of them," Hieronymus said. "Their missionaries infest the other Sakrian cities like weevils, spreading the good word of their savior. What of them?"

"They cleave to a most peculiar doctrine," the artificial man went on, not turning around, but raising the volume of his voice that they might hear over the snapping and tearing of the undergrowth in his wake. "The central figure in their religion is a boy named Kaspar who dwelt in Hausr some centuries ago. This otherwise unremarkable young man is said to have disappeared in a flash of light in full view of many witnesses. As so often happens with matters difficult to explain, in time complex exegeses and cosmologies built up around this singular incident, like the layers of a pearl slowly accreting around an irritant, and in time matured into a full-blown belief system. Kaspar was eventually looked upon as a kind of holy vessel, one which walked among men for a time before being taken up into communion with the godhead. In light of your questions, Leena Chirikova, I can't escape the conclusion that this Kaspar at the heart of the mystery was the victim of another similar aperture between worlds, though this one translating him away from Paragaea rather than into this world from elsewhere."

Leena, for her part, could not escape the conclusion that Benu liked to lecture almost as much as Hieronymus did, if not more. Perhaps it was the long centuries spent gathering data that he was never able to deliver, an unimaginable store of knowledge packed into the gem that was the core of his personality.

"Of course," Benu went on, his lecture continuing, "the obverse is also true, and there are religions and creeds found on Paragaea which arguably have their origins in incidents of travelers from other worlds arriving unexpected in this world. The Pakunari of Ogansa Valley, as a perfect example, are a separate species of humanity who worship sibling deities, Wira and Ahari, whom myth contends came to the cradle of Pakunari civilization from another world at the beginning of time. While the doctrine does not record the specifics of their arrival, the broad strokes would certainly indicate a resemblance to your own story."

"Your examples serve to illustrate that it is possible to move from one world to the other," Hieronymus called from the rear of the train, sounding out of breath and somewhat frustrated. "But this is a point which all present have already accepted as fact. What we require is the ability to predict where such points of transfer can be found, and to know where and when the resulting gates will lead."

"Fair enough," Benu said, raising his hand and glancing back over his shoulder, something like a contrite expression written on his unmarred features. "Centuries ago, I once passed a few long days amongst the hive mind of Croatoan island in the company of a wayfarer who had visited the oracular forest of Keir-Leystall."

"And survived to tell the tale?" Balam's voice dropped to a whisper.

"So he reported," Benu answered.

"What is this forest?" Leena asked.

"A grove of talking trees of metal," Hieronymus said, disbelieving, "who are said to know unplumbed secrets no other being can know. But I had always thought Keir-Leystall to be nothing more than a myth, a traveler's tale for the fireside."

"No," Benu said absently, "it is quite real. I have visited there myself, from time to time, though I can't recommend the experience. In any event, this wayfarer claimed to have exchanged secrets with the oracular trees, and that one of the provinces over which the trees claimed mastery was the knowledge of moving between the worlds. Given that the trees are quite mad, I'm not sure how well to credit their testimony, but based on the available data, my contention is that if the answers to Leena's questions are held anywhere on the face of Paragaea, it would be there."

"So it's settled," Leena said. She could not escape feeling a glimmer of hope, serving somewhat to balance her earlier despair. "So how far a journey is it to this . . . Keir-Leystall."

"Far," Benu said simply. "Very far."

That night, around a crackling fire in a small clearing, strange hoots and calls ringing back forth from the copses of trees around them, the company consulted Hieronymus's maps. Benu allowed that they were fairly accurate, giving the current configurations of landmass and terrain on the Paragaean continent, though there were some irregularities to the placement of some of the townships and cities in the northwest reaches of Taured, and that to the best of his recollection the citadel city of Atla, atop Mount Ignis, was farther to the north and east than Hieronymus had placed it, nearer the edge of the burned steppes of Eschar.

"I will want to discuss this further," Hieronymus said, a gleam in his eyes, reluctant to change the topic of conversation away from matters cartographical. "But for the moment, I'm more concerned with the exact positioning of the fabled oracular forest of Keir-Leystall."

Benu leaned forward, and with a smooth-tipped, nailless finger pointed at the peninsula of Parousia, which dominated the eastern shore of the Inner Sea.

"There, several days inland from the southern inlet of Parousia, beyond the mangrove swamps."

Balam growled, shaking his head discontentedly.

"And we are where?" Leena asked, scanning the map for recognizable terrain.

"Here," Hieronymus said. He pointed to the forests that ran north and south between the high plains of Sakria in the east and the Rim Mountains in the west. Nearly half of the breadth of the continent separated their position from the location Benu had indicated.

Leena rubbed her feet, for the moment mercifully free of her heavy boots, and sighed a ragged sigh.

✦

Days passed—bone-wearing days of traveling through the undergrowth, Benu ever driving them onwards farther and faster, seeming never to tire.

It seemed to Leena as though they would never leave the woods behind, and every clearing they passed was just a momentary tease, a tantalizing hint of clear skies and open spaces, before the next stand of trees plunged them once again into the forest deeps. So it was that, stepping through a break in the tree line and walking into the broad sunshine, it took her a few blinking moments to realize what it was she saw. The tree line behind her continued in an unbroken line to the left and right, a forested wall running from the northwest to the southeast, but the broad, open plains before her continued as far as the eye could see, dotted here and there with little copses of trees that were completely dominated by the high plains around them.

They stood at the edge of the Sakrian plains, the darkened forests of Altrusia behind them.

"There," Leena said, pointing ahead. "What's that?" Smoke curled on the far horizon, rising above a gray smudge that seemed to darken the landscape from the far north to the far south. "A city?"

"With no buildings rising above the horizon?" Balam said, shaking his head. "Not likely."

"It is a city, of a sort," Benu, whose opalescent eyes could see farther and more keenly than any of theirs, said. "But there are no buildings."

Leena was confused, but Hieronymus and Balam seemed immediately to take his meaning.

"It's a city such as you've never seen, little sister," Hieronymus said, smiling somewhat wistfully. "One which picks up stakes and moves with each turn of the season, migrating from one corner of the globe to another."

"The Roaming Empire," Balam said, licking his black lips, and Leena fancied she could hear his stomach rumbling. "And while their cuisine is hardly without parallel, it would no doubt far overshadow the meager fire-roasted offerings of this damnable forest."

"More to the point," Hieronymus said, "they traffic in knowledge, so mayhap we can find someone willing to trade a secret or two for transportation."

"It seems our most likely course." Benu nodded. "And with my stores of knowledge full to the brim, with my long years of wandering, I'll have ample coin with which to barter."

"It is decided, then," Balam said, heading out across the grassy plains towards the horizon. "We make for Roam."

CHAPTER 18

Roam

It took them most of a day to cross the grasslands, during which time Leena insisted that Benu be outfitted with clothing. Their choices were few, and in the end Benu was forced to make do with one of Leena's shirts and Hieronymus's spare set of trousers, cinched at the waist with a belt from Balam's harnesses. Benu assured all involved that he would procure his own supplies once they reached the city, and return their articles undamaged. As ungainly as his costuming was, though, Leena preferred it to the sight of his hairless, sexless nudity.

Leena was curious about their destination, this place called Roam, but neither Balam nor Hieronymus could offer much insight. Each had been visitors in the city, at least once, but while they could wax nostalgic about food tents or tavern wagons they had visited, and could make broad guesses about the economic and social forces that had created such a strange nomadic civilization, they could not address with certainty any of her precise questions. Benu, however, with his encyclopedic knowledge ready at hand, was only too eager to synthesize the facts at his dis-

posal to provide the answers she sought, though their exchange was perhaps more soliloquy than colloquy, her first question—"What is Roam?"
—enough to solicit an hour's worth of responses.

✦

"Roam," Benu began, "or the Travelers' Nation, is more properly
known as Forjus Vardo, or 'Wagon City' in Roamish, though few know
the name and fewer still choose to use it. Most simply call it Roam,
and there is no reason why we shouldn't, as well. Roam is a nation
always in motion, relocating in some years two or three times, and in
other years with every turn of seasons. The laws of Roam dictate that
only pure-blooded Roamish can enjoy the pleasures and burdens of citizenship; however, they have relaxed the requirements of what consti-
tutes a Roamish over the generations, so that now anyone who is able-
bodied and honest—honest enough, one supposes—can apply to the
family of travelers.

"When in motion, the caravan of Roam can be miles wide, and
many dozens of miles long. When encamped, the wagons can spread
out to cover a hundred square miles. In their numbers, the people of
Roam are virtually invincible. They have no standing army or militia,
no police beyond a loose collection of distant cousins and demi-
brothers that regulate interaction between familia and kumpania.

"The arrival of Roam is invariably seen by the more permanent
inhabitants of a region as the advent of the greatest circus imaginable,
combined with the opening of the world's largest shopping emporium,
leavened with the news that a nearby prison for the criminally insane
has suddenly and without warning thrown wide its door, releasing all
patients and prisoners. The people of the Sakrian plains have a saying:
'When Roam is in view, take the good with the bad, and win what bargains you may.'"

✦

They reached the edge of Roam by sunset, which Hieronymus insisted was the best time to arrive at any circus or fair.

It was everything Benu had said, and more. Innumerable wagons and caravans, arranged in haphazard patterns of streets or aisles, stretching as far as the eye could see. Lanterns swayed on strands overhead, and firelight danced from bonfires and cooking pits, suffusing everything with a warm, welcoming orange glow. Dogs and children were everywhere underfoot, and the lanes between lines of wagons were thronged with Roamish, the women in swirling skirts that reached to their ankles, their tops often covered with little more than knotted handkerchiefs, while the men wore blousy shirts bound up with broad leather belts over baggy trousers tucked into knee-high boots. And in amongst the Roamish were outsiders, some of them local farmers by their looks, others merchants or travelers from nearby Sakrian villages and townships, all of them with the same slightly bewildered look in their eyes that Leena knew she could not keep from her own expression.

These makeshift lanes of arranged wagons were lined with vendors of every imaginable stripe, peddling everything from weapons, to comestibles, to spirits, to exotic fauna for use either as pets or meat. The vendors worked from the doorways of their own wagons, or from stalls or tents, or even from rugs spread out along the thoroughfare. Some accepted the coins of the nearby communities or the larger Sakrian city-states, some accepted barter or trade in kind, but many followed the traditions of Roam, and accepted only secrets and knowledge. The Roaming Empire was an information-based economy, and with the right hermetic wisdom in hand, anything was available for the asking.

"We'll split up here," Benu said when they came to the juncture between several aisles. "The Whisper Market, if this incarnation of Roam follows traditional patterns, will be found in that direction"—

he pointed to the north—"and it is there that I am likely to get our best bargains. Here on the periphery the merchants trade primarily in local gossip and trade secrets, but in the Market itself can be found the serious information traders. I should be able to procure both clothing for myself, as well as suitable transportation to bear us further east. Is there anything else I should seek after?"

"The knowledge of how to move between the worlds," Leena said simply.

Benu sighed wearily, a very natural-seeming gesture for an unnatural being, and shook his head slightly. "I will ask, but I have no confidence in a favorable response. You might busy yourself, in the interval before my return, by seeking the answer to that question yourself, which may serve if nothing else to help establish in your mind the rarity of the information you seek." He turned to Hieronymus and Balam. "Would either of you care to accompany me? I can carry out my tasks without assistance, but should either of you find that you doubt my abilities to select suitable transport . . ." He fell silent, leaving the trailing sentence hanging in the air as a question.

"No," Balam said eagerly, long tongue playing about his fierce incisors. "I'm for the food tents, to see if I can't locate some clay-baked hedgehog." He shivered slightly at the thought, eyelids closing in remembrance of past raptures. "Oh, or meat pudding!" he hastened to add. "Oh, gods, I'm hungry."

"Nor I," Hieronymus said, stepping over to stand beside Leena. "As much as I trust Akilina to look after herself in adverse situations, my experience is that things in Roam are not always as they seem, and it is an unwise visitor who goes about unescorted, their first trip to the Roaming Empire."

"Likely a wise precaution," Benu said. "Farewell for the moment, then. Meet me back at this juncture by sunrise, and we will see where we stand."

Without another word, the artificial man turned on his heel and headed towards the north, drawing stares as he went. Balam gave Hieronymus and Leena a little wave, and then turned to head off down the broadest aisle, following his nose to the nearest food tents.

"Well, little sister," Hieronymus said, laying an arm across her shoulder, "it looks like it's just you and me. What would you like to do first?"

Leena looked around them, taking in the maddening crush of the mobile metropolis, the vendors and the peddlers, the tourists and locals ready to be fleeced. She gave a little shrug.

"I think," she said matter-of-factly, "that I could use a drink."

✦

Hieronymus was able to locate a *piav*, a drinking tent, a few aisles to the west, and in short order he and Leena were sitting on either side of a rough-hewn wooden table, tankards of some sort of fortified wine in hand, their packs in the hard-packed dirt at their feet.

"Cheers," Hieronymus said, raising his tankard in a toast.

"Za vawe zdorov'e," Leena answered in Russian, clinking her tankard with his. *To your health.*

The wine was both sour and cloyingly sweet on the tongue, but it warmed Leena from the inside out as it coursed down her throat, and she could feel her extremities tingle minutely as the spirits did their work.

Leena let out a ragged sigh, and felt herself relax by centimeters, her shoulders slowly slumping, the tension in her neck slowly easing.

"This is such an odd world," she said, "this Paragaea of yours. So much of it familiar, so much of it strange. Men and beasts such as we knew on Earth, walking side by side with creatures from prehistory, and beings who might exist only in nightmares. How is it possible?"

"That's a question that's puzzled me many a long night, little sister," Hieronymus answered. "When I first arrived here, washed up like flotsam on the shores of Drift, I thought myself in a wholly alien land, where I would find nothing like what I had known on Earth. Over the years, though, learning what I have of the gates between the worlds, I've come to understand that countless others have fallen here from Earth. Not just men and women, but animals, plants, and machines. What I still fail to grasp, though, and what no sage of Paragaea has yet been able to answer, is why our two worlds are so connected. It is a mystery that still plagues my thoughts, in quiet hours."

"I wonder sometimes, Hero, if I'll ever return to Earth and discharge my duty."

"Why ever would you wonder that?" Hieronymus sipped his wine, looking genuinely confused.

"Well, I suppose because it seems a very real possibility, if not even probability. These long weeks—months, I suppose I should say—that I have been traipsing around this strange world, and I've yet to come near a glimmer of hope that anyone knows the way between the worlds. Lots of hints and opinions, lots of myth and legend, but nothing concrete, nothing substantive. My duty as a cosmonaut and a loyal Soviet requires that I return and report what I have learned about this strange world, but I have begun to fear that that duty will go forever undischarged."

Hieronymus shrugged. "In the years that I have wandered across this circle of lands, I have had to accept one simple truth of life on Paragaea: Nothing is impossible. Improbable, perhaps, but not without the realms of possibility. I have seen such sights in these years as to beggar the imagination, and been forced time and time again to accept the reality of the most unreal situations. And if nothing is impossible, then given enough time and opportunity, anything can and will happen . . . including your finding a safe passage back home to Mother Russia."

"I don't need to be pacified or patronized," Leena said, scowling, finishing off the rest of her tankard in one long pull.

"Nor do I mean to patronize or pacify." Hieronymus motioned for the *piav* vendor to bring them another round. "I speak only the unvarnished truth. From what I have been able to determine, through personal experience and the testimony of others, gates between this world and our own occur at very regular intervals, and open onto all points from the Earth's earliest prehistory to the farthest futurity. That means, in all likelihood, that the door to your own home, place, and time, is opening at this very moment, in some hidden corner of Paragaea. We just need to search long enough that we might locate it."

Leena fell silent as the vendor refilled their tankards, and then regarded Hieronymus for a long moment before answering. "And this is your honest opinion?"

Hieronymus nodded.

"Then I will do my best to maintain hope as well, Hero." Leena smiled, and took another long draw off her tankard. "How could I not, in the face of such optimism?"

Morning found the company reunited at the juncture between the aisles, somewhat worse for wear. Only Benu, in his new suit of clothes, finely cobbled shoes, and slouch hat, seemed to have gotten the better end of the bargain. Leena and Hieronymus were bleary-eyed and dehydrated, passing a large skin of water back and forth between them as quickly as their somewhat enfeebled reactions would allow, while Balam groaned softly, clutching his distended belly, trying not to let his gaze land on any greasy foodstuffs in the nearby stalls.

"Any luck finding the way between the worlds, Akilina?" Benu slung his new pack across his shoulder, having returned to each of them their loaned items of clothing.

"No," Leena answered, stuffing her returned shirt unceremoniously into her pack, wrinkles and all. Her temples pounding, she couldn't help but smile when she glanced over at Hieronymus, who was splashing water from the skin into his eyes. "But I'm confident that we'll find the answer, in time."

CHAPTER 19

Horseback

Benu led the company through the twisted lanes of Roam to the far eastern extremity of the mobile metropolis, where the animal pens and stables could be found. A nomadic community the size of the Roaming Empire required thousands of horses to keep in motion, as well as an equal number of sheep and goats, cattle, and innumerable dogs.

"In addition to my new accoutrements and raiment," Benu explained, leading them to a stall at the stables' edge, "I was able to trade sufficient secrets on the Whisper Market to procure for us a string of horses, including a pair of large draft horses of sufficient size to accommodate the Sinaa."

Balam, in light of his intestinal discomfort, growled uneasily at the idea of going horseback in short order.

"I had considered the option of not securing horses for my own use," Benu went on, "as my capacities are such that I could locomote at speeds sufficient to keep abreast of a galloping horse, but to do so would potentially expend my reserves of energy faster than I could replenish them, leaving me incapable of physical exertions at the end of a day's travel. Considering the fact that we are never certain what obstacles or challenges we might encounter, I decided against that option, preferring instead to conserve my energies until they could be put to their best use."

Benu handed a marker to the Roamish within the stall, and in a few moments a dozen horses were brought out to them.

"Two each for riding, in turns," Benu explained, "and a third each for packs and supplies. Our current supply situation being what it is, I also took the liberty of procuring dried beans, salted and jerked meats, cornmeal, and flasks of fresh water, along with cooking utensils and the like." Benu pointed to the parcels being hauled over by the Roamish and loaded onto the packhorses. "On the high plains of Sakria, grass for the horses will be plentiful, but we might not find food for humans and jaguar men quite so readily, and while my own bodily processes can continue at some length without replenishing my material input, the same cannot be said for you organics." He paused, and then said in all sincerity, "I hope I have not overstepped the bounds of our relationship."

Hieronymus waved a hand hastily, squinting in the bright morning sun. "Not in the least, friend Benu. If you find us . . . less than enthused, you may mark it down to the price of our overindulgence last night, in food"—he gestured to Balam—"and drink"—he motioned to Leena and himself—"and not in our lack of appreciation." He paused, made an urping noise, and swallowed hard as bile rose in his throat. "'Cuse me."

"It's . . . great!" Leena said between painful hiccups, trying to sound enthusiastic.

"I think I'm going to be sick," Balam said, hand to his mouth.

"Splendid," Benu replied, clapping his hands together, then tightening the cinch on his horse's saddle. "Shall we be off, then?"

By midmorning, following an unpleasantly jostling ride through the eastern reaches of Roam and out onto the plains, the company had more or less regained their composure, having sweated out the last of the alcohol, or passed the bulk of their meals, whichever was the case. Feeling somewhat refreshed, they paused for a brief meal—flatcakes, fried bacon, and tea, expertly prepared by Balam, who was regaining his appetite by leaps and bounds—and consulted Hieronymus's maps and charts.

"The fastest route to Keir-Leystall," Hieronymus said, "is via the Inner Sea. The closest port is Bacharia, at the mouth of the river Pison."

"Hmm," Balam said, sipping at his tea, "but in recent decades the Bacharian Polity has taken a dim view of outsiders, closing off the port and forbidding entrance into the city walls by land and sea to any but fully accredited citizens."

"A pity," Benu said. "In centuries past, Bacharia was a most progressive and enlightened culture. But it is an inevitable cycle, I have found, and while it is tragic they have turned away from the world in this era, in time the forces of change will grind away and Bacharia will open up once again."

"It is a historical imperative," Leena said, nodding, "that oppressive oligarchies and capitalist empires will in the end fall to the will of the proletariat. That some cultures retrograde in the face of counter-revolutionary forces is unfortunate, but just as inevitable."

"Be that as it may, we find ourselves living in *this* era." Hieronymus pointed along the coast of the Inner Sea, some distance to the east of Bacharia. "And in this day and age—assuming we don't want to wait for the cycle of civilization to turn, and Bacharia to become a flower of culture and openness once again—our best option is to travel

overland to Masjid Empor, the port city, and book passage on a southbound ship. We can ford the river Pison here"—he indicated a point
upriver from where the Pison emptied into the Inner Sea—"where the
ferry lines run, and reach Masjid Empor no more than a week later."

"I've visited Masjid Kirkos in the south, years ago," Balam said
thoughtfully, "but I don't think I've ever seen the walls of Masjid
Empor."

"I was there once, years ago," Hieronymus said, a cloud passing
momentarily across his face, "but I had to leave in a hurry." He glanced
to Leena, and then to Benu. "But with any luck, that cycle of history
of yours has turned once again," he said with a smile that didn't quite
reach his eyes, "and they've forgotten all about me."

According to Hieronymus's maps and Benu's recollections, the company had more than a thousand kilometers to cover before they reached
the river Pison, and another few hundred beyond that before they
arrived at Masjid Empor. Even switching horses at midday, traveling
an average of ten hours a day, they could cover no more than thirty or
forty kilometers a day. As a result, the journey from Roam to the ferry
on the Pison would take them well over a month.

Having walked on foot through rain forest ever since the crash of
the *Rukh*, Leena would have thought that traveling by horseback
would prove a relief, but was surprised to find herself, if anything, even
more fatigued at the end of a day of riding than she had been after a
full day's slog through the undergrowth. Different muscles were sore,
and bruises were found in new and sometimes surprising locations, but
the fact that the horse was the one expending all the energy of locomotion appeared to do little to conserve the rider's strength.

As exhausted as their bodies might be at day's end, though, their minds were hungry for activity and exercise. With only the unbroken expanses of the high plains to look at, and nothing but the endless days of riding ahead of them, they passed the time in near-endless conversation—morning, day, and evening—leaving off only while sleeping, and sometimes not even then, as on frequent occasions one or the other of them would be found talking in their sleep, carrying on the conversations of the day.

Having traveled with Balam and Hieronymus since the day she first arrived on Paragaea, Leena felt that she knew them well enough, though the stories, jokes, and anecdotes they shared on those long days on the high Sakrian plains let her know just how little any one being could truly know another. But while there were occasional surprises, little character flaws or past indiscretions, that she found surprising, on the whole nothing was not in keeping with what she could have guessed about her two longtime companions.

Benu, though, was another matter entirely. Though they'd traveled at his side for a period of weeks, now, Leena felt that they'd hardly come to know the artificial man at all. He seemed so different than the frail, ancient creature he'd been when first they'd met, and his hairless, perfect skin and large opalescent eyes only served to remind her at every turn that he was not human like Hieronymus and she. That he never complained of aches and pains, never hungered, never tired, served to remind her that he was not even a living nonhuman sentient like Balam. But neither was he a creature of pure artifice, merely a machine. A kind of soul seemed to lurk behind those opalescent eyes, and a personality bubbled up during his often strange pronouncements and lectures. Here was a being who had walked this circle of lands for countless millennia, had seen things that no other living being had ever seen, and who knew more than any single being she'd ever met.

But what kind of being was he, at the core?

"Benu," Leena began one morning, as they cantered across the grass-lands, side by side, their string of horses following on a lead. "In the days past, the topic of family has arisen from time to time. We have heard about Balam's sisters Sakhmet and Bastet, and Hero has told us of his parents—the scholar and the cartographer's daughter—and I have even made mention of my own parents, Mikhail Andreyevich and Irina Ivanovna."

"Yes," Benu said contemplatively. "And I've been struck by how often your stories seem to end in tragedy of one sort or another, whether death, or betrayal, or both."

On her other side, Balam began to growl, a low rumbling thunder deep in his chest.

"Perhaps," Hieronymus hastened to interrupt, trying for a light tone, "what Benu means to say is that each of us, in our own way, has experienced the travails of life firsthand."

"No," Benu answered, shaking his head and glancing casually over at Hieronymus. "I mean to say that you, Hieronymus, betrayed your father's wishes for your life by running away to sea, rather than pur-suing an academic course as he had intended for you. And you did so shortly after your mother's death, only further linking the two con-cepts." He turned to Leena, twisting expertly in the saddle, casually leaning against his saddle's pommel. "And you, Akilina, lost your par-ents when only five years old, and were forced to survive a feral exis-tence in the remaining months of a siege, a hardscrabble life that left you little more than a reactionary beast by the process's end." Leena stiffened, but before she could respond, Benu had moved his attentions on to Balam. "And you, friend Sinaa, were betrayed by your cousin Gerjis, who turned your sisters away from you, and led your nation into a close alliance with the leader of the Black Sun Genesis cult, one

Per, an individual of rather dubious qualities, or so your report would suggest."

The jaguar man's fingers tightened on the reins, and his black lips curled back over saberlike incisors. "I prefer not to discuss Per, if you please," he said between clenched teeth. "So make your point, homunculus, if you have one."

Benu raised a hand in halfhearted apology.

"I mean no offense," he said, turning from one to another. "I just observe that the concept of family so often is tied up inextricably with the more negative aspects of culture, whether the betrayal of personal confidences, or the end of existence. Though, to be fair, since all existence ends sooner or later, I suppose one could argue that data point isn't particularly relevant." He turned to Leena, his expression open and confused. "I apologize, Akilina, is that not the point you intended to make?"

Leena was still caught in a wash of emotion thinking of her lost parents, and couldn't help but wish that she hadn't mentioned them a few nights before, in the late hours of the evening, when Hieronymus had left off talking about his own parents, and their loss.

"No," Leena finally said, fighting to remain calm and collected. "My *point*, had I been allowed to make it, would have been that in all this talk of family, we have yet to discuss your own origins, Benu."

"Oh." Benu paused for a moment, lids sliding slowly over opalescent eyes, as he looked past Leena at Balam, and then over to Hieronymus. "My apologies. I mistook your meaning. My own origins are fairly inconsequential. I was constructed by the wizard-kings of Atla, as I may have indicated before. I was designed to be a reconnaissance probe, my original charter to walk the planet, making a complete circuit every few centuries, and to report back what I had learned to my creators. Millennia ago, though, the way to Atla was sealed off, the citadel city hidden behind an energetic barrier wall, when the wizard-kings scorched the steppes of Eschar with cold fire, thus ending the Genos Wars."

"And the age of the Metamankind Empires began," Balam said thoughtfully.

"Exactly so. It was an interesting time, though as the old saw holds, one does not always find it enjoyable to live through interesting times. Though, in their way, the metamen did not prove any better or worse as stewards of civilization than the Nonae or the Black Sun Empire had before them, or than the human cultures appear to be proving today. Civilization is, in many ways, an emergent phenomenon, and it seems to matter little to history what species of being steers the ship of state, so long as the ship is steered somewhere or other. And like families and individuals, death seems to claim all civilizations in the end."

Hieronymus drew in a long breath through his nose, his mouth clamped shut, and seemed to marshal his reserves of patience before answering. "You speak cavalierly of families and deaths," he said, his tone level, "for a being who seems to have known nothing of either."

Benu regarded him for a moment, something like sadness creeping around his eyes, and shook his head slowly.

"I'm afraid I've given you a mistaken impression, my friends, if you have come to think I know nothing of family or of loss."

"What could you, undying and sexless," Balam shot back, "know of either?"

"Because I have almost died, many times, and once at the hands of the one I came to know as Ikaru."

"Ikaru?" Leena asked.

"My son."

CHAPTER 20

The Story of Benu

"**T**hough my outer form appears little different than that of a human," Benu said as they gathered around a campfire at day's end, their horses grazing on a line in the near distance, "it must not be forgotten that I am an artificial being. My bodies are able to walk unscathed through fire, stay underwater for long periods of time, run fast for days on end, and lift huge weights. I have a weakness, though, which I am understandably reluctant to share. However, since you have bared such personal moments of your pasts with me, it seems only right that I unburden myself to you, to a degree. And awareness of my limitations is crucial in the tale which I now relate."

I am fueled primarily by the sun, *Benu went on.* I can draw energy and sustenance through consuming and metabolizing matter, but such

processes are time-consuming, and the resultant energy yields are com-
paratively low; as a result, I am designed to draw my energy chiefly
from the sun's rays. And though I am able to store a certain amount of
energy in my body's cells, if I overexert my reserves can burn through
quickly. Whether quickly or slowly, though, as energy is consumed it
must be replenished. If my stores run low in the daylight hours, I can
recharge fairly quickly, just by absorbing the sun's rays, and after a
brief respite I can be fully replenished. If my reserves are depleted at
night, however, I can be left in a weakened state until sunrise, forced
to subsist on the reflected light of the moon.

When at my full strength, I can go without rest for days, can hear
sounds undetectable to the most sensitive of organic creatures, and my
eyes can perceive every band of the electromagnetic spectrum from
radio waves to gamma radiation. In time, though, my systems can
become corrupted, decayed, or damaged, and must be repaired.

My makers imbued me with the ability to repair myself, even to
the extent of manufacturing new parts and components to replace
worn and defective ones. I assume that my original parameters were set
such that, when wear and tear reached systemic proportions, I would
return to Atla to be decommissioned. Perhaps another probe unit
would be sent in my place, or my personality core would be transferred
to a new body. I'm afraid that I don't recall. That knowledge is among
that which was lost to me, over the course of the events I now recount.

In any event, whatever my original conditioning, it is clear that I
have adapted over time, so that I now can construct an entire replacement body. Only my central personality core, seat of consciousness and
storehouse of memory, cannot be replaced. Once in every millennium,
I construct a new body, and when it is complete, simply move the core
from the old body to the new. This is the time I am at my most vulnerable, as you three should well know.

If the process goes correctly, there is a continuance of perception
from one body to the next. Though the physical bodies may differ

somewhat, one to another, so long as the personality core is transferred as the new body is coming online and the old body is shutting down, "Benu" remains.

Once, though, this did not happen. A discontinuity was introduced, and crucial data was lost.

Ultimately, the blame is solely mine. I had waited too long to construct my new body. Having become attached to a small group of humans, I traveled with a young girl and boy, exploring the far reaches of the Paragaean continent. I'd delayed for years returning to the temple to construct my new body in safety, and when I finally had the body nearly complete, my old body gave out suddenly. Before I was able to transfer my personality core from my aged form to the new, I lost first motor control, and then consciousness.

I collapsed, insensate. When next I opened my eyes, my systems nearly completely failed, my perceptions only taking in a fraction of the data they typically collected, I found that my new body was no longer on the slab. My first thought was that the body had been stolen, but by whom, and for what purpose, I did not know.

I was forced to construct a new self, my systems overtaxed to support an already decaying body for another year beyond its expected termination. Much data was lost in the intervening months, corrupted and irretrievably overwritten, as the personality core took on more and more of the maintenance and upkeep of the body, normally run by the secondary control system located in the skull.

At the end of the year, the new body was complete, and with its final ergs of energy the old body transferred the personality core to the new form before shutting down forever.

When I opened my eyes, I had trouble adjusting to this new form. I'd gotten so used to the limited motion and prescribed perceptions of my dying body that it took many long weeks before I was able to move comfortably in the new body. My handiwork, too, had been hampered somewhat by my previous sorry state, and it was not until I was able to construct a new body, only recently, that I am able to walk without a slight limp, or to express a full range of emotions with my face. And for a millennium, I had trouble hearing the shorter wave bands of radio transmissions, but since most were naturally occurring, the result of plate tectonics and not artificially created communication signals, I didn't consider it a major loss.

If I wondered what had become of my purloined body, who had stolen it and why, it was only infrequently, and never for long. With more pressing concerns, I just chalked it up to a mystery, and resolved to increase the efficacy of the temple guardians (for all the good that seems to have done) before constructing another replacement body.

Had I been in better control of my faculties, had I incarnated in a new form with all my memories, senses, and capacities intact, would I have displayed greater curiosity, and bothered to check whether there was any sign of entry or invasion, to search the surrounding environs for any sign where the body might have been taken? Perhaps. But perhaps, too, in my many millennia of wandering, I had grown complacent. When a being lives as long as I have, it is very easy to dismiss perils and threats, no matter how clear and present.

I would have occasion to regret this lack of curiosity in later centuries. Perhaps if I'd known earlier, even a few years or decades after the fact, I could have intervened, and things would have gone differently. But as it was, almost a half-dozen centuries passed before I learned what had become of the missing body, and by then it was far, far too late.

It was on the island of Pentexoire, one in the archipelago that stretches out into the northern reaches of the Outer Ocean, off the coast of Taured, that I finally learned how much had been lost.

I had not been in the region in long millennia, and had resolved to visit each of the cultures in the island chain, to record what changes the intervening centuries might have wrought. I passed through Mistorak, and Bragman, and came at last to Pentexoire. On my previous visit to Pentexoire, I had found it a placid and contemplative society, largely agrarian, that deeply prized the study of natural processes. A rich but sparsely populated principality, it was ruled over by a council of elders. Pentexoire had no standing army, no navy, and its principal export was scholars and thinkers. For a time, to have a Pentexoirean tutor was the distinguishing mark of quality for any wealthy scion's upbringing.

Now, on my return to the island after so long an absence, I was surprised to see everything I had once admired about the culture stripped away. Militant, aggressive, anti-intellectual, Pentexoire was now a culture perpetually preparing for armed conflict. The centers of learning and natural study had all been shuttered and closed, replaced with temples and places of religious instruction. The locals I questioned were all fearful of outsiders, having been convinced by their religious and political leaders that all non-Pentexoire were in league with dark forces, intent only on their enslavement. Worse, some feared that I was an agent of the secret police, trying to ferret out dissidents to join the other malcontents on gibbets strung up along the thoroughfares, dying by fractions. Near the cities, the posts from which the decaying corpses swung were as thick as the trees in the forest of Altrusia, the victims numbering in the hundreds, if not thousands.

Analyzing what I knew of the culture's history, I could not recall any societal trends that might account for such a remarkable shift. I questioned as many of the locals as would speak to me, and most of the respondents attributed their culture's movement away from learning and towards dogma—which all averred was a positive move—as the work of their tireless leader, an absolute dictator who carried the title "presbyter." Remarkably, most of them could not recall how long the presbyter had held the throne, saying only that he had been their ruler all their lives. Considering that the oldest of the respondents was nearly in their first century in age, that meant a considerably long-lived ruler.

I resolved to go to see this ruler for myself. When I arrived at the capital city, though, I found that the presbyter and the rest of the government had only recently departed. The court had relocated from the main residence at Nyse, to spend the warm months behind the sardonyx gates and ivory bars of the summer palace at Susa.

After a journey of several days, I reached Susa, which was no longer the contemplative city I remembered from prior visits, once devoted exclusively to the pursuit of intellection. Now, it was a city at war, more a military encampment than a township.

I was taken prisoner immediately on entering the city, charged with traveling without the appropriate accreditation, and taken before a military official. My physiognomy, which usually went unremarked in my travels, was a subject of considerable discussion among my captors. Of particular interest were my opalescent eyes and pale, hairless skin. My strength, even in that slipshod body, was such that I could have escaped at any moment, but I was curious to observe the Pentexoireans under their natural conditions, and this provided a perfect opportunity. One of the military officials left for some brief time, evidently consulting with some superior, and then returned, to escort me elsewhere.

I assumed initially that I was being led to some audience or interrogation, surprised that I had not been shackled hands and feet, as prisoners typically are. Instead, I was led down a long flight of stairs to the sunless depths of the palace, to a well-appointed room lined with tapestries. I was asked to take a seat, and told that someone would be along shortly.

I had become too reliant on my physical capacities, and once again failed to recognize potential threats. When the door to the small room closed with a clanking sound of finality, I realized I had been tricked. The lights went out, and I was plunged into darkness. It took no more than a few minutes' investigation to reveal that behind the delicate tapestries were stone walls, unimaginably thick, and that the door through which I'd entered was of reinforced metals as thick as I was tall, an incalculable fortune in ore, here spent on keeping me imprisoned.

Long days passed, blurring into weeks. Even without expending any energy on fruitless attempts to escape, which I knew could only fail, as the weeks passed my reserves of energy slowly leached away, and I weakened fractionally with every hour. Out of sight of the sun, in this dark pit, I gradually lost all but my final reserves of strength.

When the door finally opened again, I could do little more than lift up my head.

"Presbyter Ikaru will see you now," said the uniformed man who stood at the door.

Dragged to my feet unceremoniously, I was taken through dimly lit halls, up a winding flight of stairs, to an audience chamber of some kind. Through the open windows I could see a clear, moonless night sky.

Sitting on a throne at the front of the room was a figure dressed in elaborate robes of jet black and blood red. He was pale and hairless, and regarded me coolly with opalescent eyes.

CHAPTER 21

The Story of Ikaru

"This Ikaru, then, was your purloined body?" Leena asked as they broke camp in the morning, setting out for another day's ride across the plains.

"So I immediately surmised," Benu answered, climbing into the saddle.

"And yet you said Ikaru was your son?" Balam asked, cinching up the saddle on his lead draft horse.

"Though I lack the generative capacity, in all regards I have come to look upon Ikaru as a kind of offspring, so the term is correct. From the first words we exchanged, though, I knew I had failed my son."

Weakened and hardly able to move, *Benu said*, I was deposited at the feet of the presbyter, who was seated on the throne. The uniformed man who had escorted me from my cell departed through a side door, and the presbyter and I were left alone in the audience chamber. I had energy enough to speak, but could not have taken a step unaided without depleting the last of my reserves.

"Who are you?" Presbyter Ikaru asked imperiously. "There is some connection between the two of us—that much is obvious. With your lack of body hair, your alabaster skin, and unusual eyes . . . we could be brothers. I had thought I was the only one of my kind, having seen only one other like me in all my long years, and that one already dead."

I understood at once the reason for my long imprisonment. This Ikaru was aware of the weakness of our artificial form, and when he received word that a being who resembled himself so nearly had been discovered in the streets of Susa, he ordered me captured, and kept imprisoned out of reach of the sun's rays.

"Answer me," Ikaru repeated, growing agitated. I could tell he was impatient, having waited now long months for me to weaken to the point where I could be safely interrogated.

"I am an artificial being," I explained, though he doubtless knew. "I was forged to act as a probe for the wizard-kings of Atla, a culture that has long since sealed itself off from any congress with the outside world, millennia ago."

Ikaru regarded me for a long moment, scratching his chin. Though his skin was as pale as mine, it bore the scars and abrasions of many injuries, and the years hung on him more heavily than on me.

"Am I a probe, too, then?" Ikaru asked at length. "But my memory stretches back little more than six centuries, not over millennia. Why was I constructed, and by whom?"

"I may be able to answer those questions," I told him, "but I must first know what you remember of your earliest moments. And how did you come to rule this island nation, so changed since last I saw it?"

"Very well," Ikaru answered, as though he were granting me some magnanimous boon. "My first memories are of waking up, confused and alone, in a ruined temple some centuries ago. On the floor at my feet lay an ancient man, with unseeing eyes like glittering opals, who appeared to all indications to be dead. On reflection, I quickly came to realize that while I had some basic knowledge—familiarity with language, knowledge of geography, and so forth—I had no notion who I was. I staggered out of the temple, past strange rows of statues, past small biting creatures who gnashed their teeth at my feet and ankles but caused no injury, out into the jungle."

He paused, and his hand drifted across his forehead dreamily, as though he were brushing away a spider's web.

"I've had so little occasion to recall those early days in the last few centuries that I find a strangely . . . emotional response to my now recounting them." Ikaru paused, and straightened on the throne. "In any event, not knowing where I should go, nor what I should do, I found myself traveling north, wandering aimlessly, searching for some idea who I was. I came upon a settlement of the Pakunari of Ogansa Valley, and passed some years among them. It was the Pakunari who named me Ikaru, which means 'ageless' in their tongue."

A faint smile played on his lips, and then faded, as a shadow seemed to pass over him.

"In time, though, the hairy creatures came to view me with suspicion. While they aged and died, I remained young and unmarred, and when a particularly cruel season saw a large number of their young and old killed by plague, I was blamed. But they could not harm me, and were forced instead to settle for driving me out. I traveled south, skirting the western edge of the Rim Mountains, moving from fishing village to fishing village. I passed a few years on a whaling vessel, and eventually jumped ship on the island of Croatoan. But the strange habits of the island's distributed consciousness unsettled me, and I soon moved on. I traveled through the Eastern Desert, spent a few years as the prisoner of a cohort of the Nonae, who had the good fortune to catch me in a weakened state and to bind my hands and feet with bonds that were proof even against my great strength.

The Nonae kept me as a kind of pet, a toy for their amusement. I eventually escaped, killing the entire cohort in the process, and made my way to Masjid Logos, where I found work illuminating manuscripts at a scholarium.

"From my time among the Nonae, I had learned the possible uses of a strong warrior caste, and to what ends a nation dedicated to warfare could be directed. While illuminating religious texts in Masjid Logos, I learned the powerful effects that doctrine could have, even when not founded on experiential data of any kind. Were one to establish a warrior caste motivated by religious doctrine, I reasoned, great things could be accomplished."

Ikaru waved a hand around the audience chamber, indicating the map of the island on the far wall.

"Pentexoire is my second attempt to put this theory into practice. My previous attempt was in a Sakrian township a few days' travel outside of Azuria. The presence of surrounding cultures, though, proved too much a contaminating influence, and within a few generations the populace rejected my temporal and spiritual authority, and I was forced to flee ahead of an angry mob. For my next and latest experiment in social controls, then, I selected an island culture, isolated both by geography and circumstance from outside contamination."

"What is the purpose of these . . . 'experiments'?" I asked.

"I have seen organic culture at its best and worst, and I have come to question whether organics, with their short-lived vantage, are best suited to govern their own destinies. It seems to me that organic culture would be better served to look to a superior intellect for governance, one with a longer view of history."

"And yours, naturally, is the superior intellect in question?"

"Naturally," Ikaru said, without a hint of irony. "And given that it is my responsibility to govern, it is in my subjects' best interests that I devise the means of social controls that will result in the most effective organization and structure of culture."

The presbyter leaned forward, regarding me closely.

"Now," he said, "I believe you owe me some answers. Having heard what you have of my earliest memories, and my activities since, are you now in a position to address my origins?"

"You were never intended to develop an independent consciousness. The knowledge you possessed on first waking was the basic programming incorporated into the secondary control system housed in your skull. The cavity on your chest is intended to house the personality core of Benu, which is now incorporated instead into this body." Benu indicated the gem on his chest. "Herein reside the thoughts and memories which should have been yours on wakening."

"So you hold the mind that was intended to be mine?" Ikaru said. "But who constructed you, then?"

"The same hand that constructed you," Benu answered. "My earlier self, the former Benu, whom you mistook for a corpse on the temple floor upon awakening. I was not dead, but only momentarily deactivated, having failed to transfer the personality core in time. Had all gone as planned, when your eyes opened, you would have had my memories. Instead, I was forced to build this new form."

"And that is why we look as alike as brothers?"

"Yes. We share the same basic design, though the minute details differ from iteration to iteration."

"Fascinating," Ikaru said. "And how is it that our internal processes function? I have, of course, surmised the need for direct sunlight, but the mechanisms through which our bodies collect and store energy elude me."

I had little desire to engage in lengthy discourse about my systemic processes at that juncture. I was at the disadvantage, in my weakened state, and had begun to suspect that my "offspring's" motives were not the purest. I could allow that he had, in first learning of my arrival, wanted to take all precaution before our initial meeting, but having spent some time in his company, I had come to the conclusion that his every attention was bent on the domination of his subjected nation, and that he had no intention of us ever meeting one another on equal footing.

I answered his further questions, though, my answers as lengthy and circuitous as possible. It seemed that Ikaru, having learned of his origins for the first time, was so distracted that he had not noticed the passage of time, nor the fact that the first light of dawn had already begun to pink the eastern sky. Even the feeble rays of this early gloaming were enough to begin slowly to replenish my long-discharged stores of energy.

When I had explained the rudiments of our bodies' internal processes, Ikaru held up a hand to silence me, and looked at the gem on my chest contemplatively.

"I wonder what would eventuate," he said, "if I removed the personality core from your body and installed it in myself?" He pulled apart his jet-and-crimson robes, revealing the cavity at the center of his chest. "Would I merely gain your memories and knowledge, all that you possess and have learned? Or would my personality be subsumed by the personality of Benu?"

"I don't know," I told him, and while I honestly didn't, I had no desire to find out.

"Perhaps, then," Ikaru said at length, "I will just keep you imprisoned in the oubliette. Then I could interrogate you at my leisure, to take from you what knowledge I might find of utility. I would very much like to learn more about our original designers, these wizard-kings of Atla, who seem so cavalierly to have discarded their probes into the world."

"Ikaru," I said, looking upon him with genuine sympathy, "if I have learned anything in my long years of wandering this circle of lands, it is that the best use of power seldom ever lies in its exercise. My fear for you is that, having set yourself up as master of this nation of people, you have lost all perspective. I have, in my time, been subject to many of the same temptations which now drive you. I would help you, if you'd let me, avoid the mistakes which I have made, and which I have seen others make, so that you can make the best use of your time on this globe."

"Nonsense," Ikaru replied, dismissing my words with a wave of his hand. "My perspective is my own, thank you, and what lessons I'll learn from you will be of my own choosing, not your soporific platitudes. Power exists to be used. In the potential it is meaningless; only when made actual is it of any utility."

"In that case," I said, "I will not remain your prisoner any longer than I already have. And I have no desire whatsoever to help advance your plans."

Before Ikaru could respond, I made my move.

My strength still at perilously low levels, in a single motion I rose to my feet and launched myself bodily at the nearest window. I sailed out into the sunrise and plunged down dozens of stories, my landing creating a small impact crater. I climbed unsteadily to my feet, and made my way into the twisting streets of Susa, managing to keep a few steps ahead of the presbyter's guards. Within a matter of days, I was on a ship bound for Taured, my strength regained, putting Pentexoire forever behind me.

I had considered staying on the island, remaining in hiding while locating pockets of dissidents, and helping to mount a resistance to the presbyter's rule. Cleaning up Ikaru's mess. But the historical processes involved were inevitable, and eventually the Pentexoireans would rid themselves of Ikaru on their own. Perhaps not in the present generation, perhaps even not for centuries, but eventually. And when they did, when Ikaru saw that organic cultures will not suffer a dictator interminably, then perhaps my son would learn that he had chosen the wrong path.

There would always be other cultures, though, increasingly remote, wherein he could perform his "experiments," so perhaps he would not.

CHAPTER 22

Crossing the River Pison

After more than a full month of riding, they came in sight of the river Pison.

"Finally," Balam said, breathing a sigh of relief. "Some variety after all the damned endless grasslands."

Leena could not help but agree. "Even so," she said, "it is perhaps not the most beautiful river I've ever seen."

In the distance, still some kilometers before them, the river looked like a murky, brown scar on the land, winding slowly from southeast to northwest.

"We've wasted enough time," Hieronymus said, spurring his horse into a gallop. "Let's not waste more in idle chatter."

Leena watched Hieronymus ride ahead for a moment, and then glanced over at Balam, but when their eyes met, he just shrugged, shaking his head sadly. The jaguar man seemed to have no better idea of what vexed Hieronymus than she did. Their friend had been in a dark mood for long days, since Benu had related to the company the story of his "son." Perhaps there was something to Benu's tale that cast a shadow over Hieronymus's thoughts, but what it might be, Leena could not begin to guess.

"Come on, Benu," Leena said, goading her horse to speed while calling back over her shoulder to the artificial man. "I'm tired of this damned saddle, and I'm looking forward to our brief respite."

✦

The plains gave way to scrub brush, which gave way to a stretch of gravel leading down to the shores of the river. But the river was edged not by sand or by rocks, but by an ancient and pitted quay that ran along the river's shores for as far as the eye could see, up- and down-river. The whole river was paved with some sort of concrete, as though it had once been a massive spillway.

A short ride downriver, they found the ferry station. The city-state of Bacharia was another day's journey south, following the river's course, but considerable traffic took this more northern route, avoiding the city and its Polity's strictures altogether.

The ferry station was little more than a ramshackle building, long and low, that housed both the offices and residence of the ferry owner, as well as a rough canteen providing food and drink for ferry customers waiting for passage. There were stables and pens set up out back, with a half-dozen horses and an equal number of domesticated animals milling about aimlessly. The ferry owner was a heavyset woman of advanced years who seemed to have started life as human but con-sumed such enormous quantities of food in the succeeding decades that she had evolved into a species of her own. She seemed to weigh as much as the four of them combined, lumbering with surprising grace out of the offices as they arrived.

"You needing to cross, I take it?" she said, without preamble or preface.

"Yes, indeed," Balam said, bowing in the saddle. "Now, as to your fees . . ."

"It'll cost you," the owner said, cutting him off. She took a step forward, crossing her massive arms over her prodigious chest, her forearms barely touching. "Now," she said, a hungry look in her eyes, "what have you got that's worth a tinker's damn?"

The toll was steep, and they had little currency with which to pay. And the ferry owner was not interested in trading secrets or knowledge, as the Roamish had been. So the company traded six of the horses for their passage, leaving each of them one to ride, with two packhorses to carry their remaining supplies. It was a steep price to pay, little more than bald-faced extortion, but they would reach their destination in a matter of days anyway, after which the horses would no longer be of any use to them. They'd sell the rest once they reached Masjid Empor, to fund their passage on a southbound ship.

"You'll have to wait until tomorrow for the ferry to arrive," the owner explained as a small brown-skinned girl appeared from within the residence to lead the six horses around the building to the stables. "The journey t'other side takes most of a day, and it's a two-day round trip."

She pointed a finger the size of a sausage at the far end of the ramshackle building.

"Your cost of passage includes a meal at the canteen. There ain't no rooms, as such, but you can bunk along the wall at no extra cost, providing you don't bother any of the other passengers with snoring, excessive flatulence, or noisy bundling."

"We shall endeavor not to offend," Hieronymus said, a dark edge to his words.

✦

That night, they sat in the canteen, their feet propped on the rough-hewn table, relaxing as best they were able. Having eaten the meager fare available on the board, they now busied themselves drinking the marginally passable spirits available to passengers at a small upcharge, some manner of oily liquor served in clay jars. They were alone in the canteen, the owner and her minion—the small, brown-skinned girl—coming in on occasion to ensure their needs were met, at least as well as they could be.

When the company had worked their way through several rounds of clay jars, even Benu making an effort to metabolize the sour stuff, in an effort better to fit in, two newcomers appeared at the door.

It was a pair of humans. They entered the canteen, giving the company a wide berth while staring at the four of them openly, expressions of disgust on their faces. The pair crossed to the far side of the room and, when the brown-skinned girl had filled their orders, sat huddled together, whispering and casting fierce glances at the company.

"What ails those men?" Leena said, her brows knitted in annoyance. She had little liking for the scorn with which the two men regarded their quartet.

"They are Bacharian, I would guess, as evidenced by their clothes and manner," Benu said.

"What is that to me?" Leena asked. "I understand their laws make travel to their city inadvisable, but why should they look upon us with such scorn, who have not darkened their door?"

"It is not merely their laws that are unpleasant," Balam said. "Their cultural character in general leaves much to be desired."

"The Bacharian Polity holds that the various races and species should not intermingle, and the sight of humans and a metaman traveling together—in addition to whatever type of creature they take Benu to be—must seem anathema to them. What Bacharians would be doing beyond their city walls is unclear, but I would lay odds that they are agents of the Polity sent out on scouting missions into the wider world."

Leena wondered whether they should fear that the pair might mean some mischief, but before she could voice her concerns one of the Bacharians answered the question for her.

"Hey," the taller of the two said, lifting his chin imperiously and calling out to them in heavily accented Sakrian. "You." He pointed at Hieronymus, whom they evidently took to be the leader of the company, as he was both human and male. "We in Bacharia have had trouble with the mongrel metamen in recent years, prowling around our borders. In particular those zealots who adhere to the calling of the Black Sun Genesis. Is your . . . jaguar"—he spat the word, an insult—"such a one?"

"I can answer for myself, thank you," Balam growled. He stood, taking a few steps forward, towering over the seated Bacharians. "I have no more love for the followers of Per than I have for the mewling humans found in Bacharia. Both cultures, exclusionary and pig-ignorant, represent the worst tendencies of Paragaean history."

The Bacharians jumped to their feet, eyes flashing, and reached for bulky pneumatic blunderbusses hanging at their belts. Cumbersome firearms, they were inaccurate and low-yield over a distance, but dangerous in close quarters.

Leena and Hieronymus were just as quick to jump to their feet, but even quicker to draw their pistols.

"Might everyone relax for a moment," Benu said calmly, still in his seat, "before matters escalate out of control?"

The five of them stood frozen in a tableau, pistols and blunderbusses aimed and cocked, but not yet fired—the two Bacharians on one side, Balam in the middle, and Hieronymus and Leena on the other.

"Don't point those things at me, Bacharian." Balam bared his fangs, his claws extending.

Leena saw the two Bacharians' eyes flick to her Makarov and Hieronymus's Mauser.

"You have not seen firearms like these before, I'd wager," Hieronymus said, his tone level and cool.

The Bacharians did not answer, but their aims drifted slightly, so that their barrels were pointed at Leena and Hieronymus, and not at Balam between them.

"We'll not breathe the same air as you mongrel trash," the shorter of the two Bacharians said.

"We can arrange that," Balam growled, rising up on the balls of his feet.

Leena glanced to her right at Hieronymus, who nodded silently without taking his eyes off the two Bacharians.

"Now!" Hieronymus shouted.

In the crowded moment that followed, three things happened:

Balam lunged forward, claws slashing at either side;

Leena ducked to the left, and Hieronymus dove to the right, each firing a single round at one of the Bacharians;

And the Bacharians, finally, emptied their blunderbusses, their buckshot of compressed carbon pellets sailing through the empty space Leena and Hieronymus had occupied the second before.

In the next moment, it was over. The two Bacharians tottered for an instant, their spent blunderbusses dropping to the floor, each of them gored on one side by the passage of the enraged Sinaa, each with a single gunshot wound in his chest. They blinked, and looked at one another confusedly before finally collapsing in a heap on the floor.

"You're cleaning that mess up," the owner said from the door, pointing one of her sausage-fingers at the two bodies on the floor, "or I'm charging you extra for my trouble."

Leena climbed to her feet, holstering her Makarov. She glanced at Benu, still sitting calmly in his seat. "Were you planning on helping?" she asked.

"You three seemed to have things well in hand," he said, smiling slightly. "And besides, I thought it might have seemed disrespectful to the Bacharians' beliefs, if they were to be dispatched by an artificial being. As it eventuated, it was likely the bullets which proved fatal, as much as I must admire the artistry of the Sinaa's attack, and so these two humans go to their maker—if they believe in such—having been felled by one of their own kind, which one hopes would serve as some endorsement."

"You are a strange being, Benu," Balam said, cleaning his claws on the shirtfront of one of the fallen Bacharians.

"For this observation, I thank you," the artificial man said with a gallows smile.

The next morning, the ferry, having arrived in the night, was ready to depart. The company and their reduced number of horses were waiting on the quay to board.

The ferry was an ancient craft of burled wood, with chrome fittings dulled to the color of ash by age and lack of attention. This had been a pleasure barge at some point in the distant past, though its provenance was now difficult to determine, given its decayed state.

"It was likely constructed during the interregnum between the fall of the Black Sun and the rise of the Metamankind Empires," Benu lectured at Leena, while she tried to rub the sleep out of her eyes, "when human cultures were allowed briefly to flourish on the north shore of Parousia. These mayfly societies were brief-lived, going through the inevitable stages of historical development quickly, reaching a decadent, hedonistic stage within only a few generations. Their pleasure craft plied the waters of the Inner Sea, the lords and ladies carrying on opulent parties that lasted for weeks and months at a time. Obsessed with pleasures of the flesh, and prurient license, they had no interest in preserving their own history, or in the pursuit of knowledge, or exploration. When the metamen expanded their respective spheres of influence from the south and east, these mayfly cultures were extinguished almost overnight."

Leena, for her part, was more interested in the ship's design and locomotion than in the fate of the decadent culture that had constructed it. At one time, evidently, the barge had been propelled by some variety of internal combustion, using some explosive material as fuel. The gears and pistons, though, had long since rusted solid, and now the ferry was propelled across the river by sheer strength of arms. A long cable ran from one shore to the other, woven fibers as big around as a man's waist secured at either shore and threaded through a clamp on the port side of the barge. The deckhands' sole responsibility in transit, having either loaded or unloaded cargo and vehicles at either end, was to haul on this massive cable, advancing the barge by centimeters. But since the cable was not stretched taut, but had to be allowed to trail a few meters underwater so as not to ensnare any vessels sailing up or downriver, the weight of the cable was trebled or more by the brackish river water, and the cable itself was slick and black with algae.

The barge hands were a motley mix of all races and species: humans of all stripes, from those like Leena and Hieronymus to the half-sized Sheeog, from the barrel-chested, thick-nosed Kobolt to the towering Rephaim; and metamen of all varieties—Sinaa, Struthio, Canid, Arcas, and Tapiri.

The ferry's captain, a slight, frail-looking man with a fringe of dirty-gray hair that ringed his head, his skin a deep walnut brown, was introduced to them as the owner's husband. The mind boggled at the two of them in any kind of congress, but when it was revealed that the small brown-skinned girl was their daughter, it was almost too much to believe.

Frail as he looked, though, he drove the deckhands with an iron will, shouting at them to be about their duties, his voice alarmingly loud and booming.

"Pull, you dogs! Pull, or I'll lash the life from you!"

The barge slowly crossed the murky, slow-moving river, through waters sluggish and brown.

✦

It took the better part of a day to cross to the other shore, and then the company was once more on its way.

Unable to change horses at midday, their progress was not as swift as it had been on the earlier leg of the journey, but they were still able to travel for eight or nine hours a day, covering more than thirty kilometers at a stretch. East of the Pison, the terrain was much different than that through which they'd been riding. The scrub brush lowlands that abutted the eastern shore of the Pison quickly gave way to arid stretches, dry and grassless, with the only trees small, twisted husks that rose like gnarled claws from the bone-dry ground. When the winds blew, sand and dust gritted in their eyes, noses, and mouths; and with the exception of Benu, who was not perturbed by such things, the company took to wrapping stretches of cloth around their heads, covering their mouths, ears, and noses, leaving only thin slits through which they could see. The sun beat down on them mercilessly, and after the second day they took to traveling by moonlight, and sleeping as best they could under the shade of their makeshift tents during the brightest hours of daylight. When Leena was informed that they had entered the edge of the Eastern Desert, she was hardly surprised.

By the end of their fourth day of traveling, they came within sight of the coast, and Leena got her first glimpse of Masjid Empor.

CHAPTER 23

Masjid Empor

Masjid Empor was a city of contrasts, a gateway, a place of the borderlands. Not only did it straddle the border between the scorching deserts to the north and the crystal-blue waters of the Inner Sea to the south, but between the young Sakrian cultures to the west, and the older cultures to the east—the Nonae, and the scattered remains of the Parousian Dynasty, and the Sabaean culture of which Masjid Empor was the northernmost outpost. Even the ancient culture of Keir-Leystall, toward which they were bound, lay beyond Masjid Empor to the east.

Unlike the cities of the Sakrian plains, with their multistory buildings, Masjid Empor was low and wide, with only the calif's palace and the minarets of the temples rising up above the skyline. The rest of the city rose little more than two stories tall, with canopies hanging out over every door and window to increase the available shade, and wide thoroughfares that radiated out from the shore like spokes, to extend the cool breezes off the waves as far as they would travel. Only the poorest dwelt in the quarter farthest from the seashore, on the desert side of the city, where the heat seemed to rise up off the sands like air from an open oven.

It was in this quarter that the company found lodging.

"I've seen enough of deserts," Balam complained. He stood on the balcony, beneath the sheltering shade of the canopy, looking out on the endless desert stretching before them. They were on the second floor of a building at the far edge of the city, with nothing between them and the desert but a low wall. Evidently, the city builders had not feared invasion from the land side, and fortifications were negligible. "Couldn't we spend a little more for a seafront view? It's just for a few nights, at most."

They had rented out a suite of rooms that shared a common area and a bathing room. The common area opened onto the balcony, through which nothing but sand was visible.

"If it's only for a few nights, you can stand the heat a while longer," Hieronymus replied, stretched out lengthwise on a settee. "We need the money for our passage and, besides, we'll be on the waves soon enough."

"More's the pity," Balam said, shaking his head. "I much prefer watching waves to riding them." He looked with deep apprehension over at Benu and Leena, who sat on matched chairs at the far side of the common area, their packs at their feet. "Are you sure we can't just ride on to Parousia, and the oracular forests beyond?"

"You were right, Hero." Leena's mouth curled in a mocking smile. "He *is* afraid of the water."

Benu looked at Balam, curious, and in all seriousness said, "Is this the result of some childhood trauma, perhaps? Phobias are typically the result of early imprinting, of incidents that occur in adolescence and which the psyche is not developed sufficiently to process."

"It's not a phobia!" Balam shouted. "I just . . . I just don't like the water, all right? I just really don't like the water. I don't need a reason, do I?"

"In point of fact," Benu said, "an irrational fear or dislike is the very definition of a phobia."

"I'm going to take a bath," Balam said dismissively, crossing to the entrance to the bathing chamber. "You lot can keep your amusements to yourselves."

"I'm just glad he's not afraid of the water in *there*," Leena said.

"Though from the smell of him, you wouldn't know it," Hieronymus said, waving a hand before his face, his nose crinkling comically.

"I wouldn't be so quick to point out the Sinaa's odorous qualities, Hieronymus," Benu said. "You have yourself been emitting a somewhat pungent aroma these past weeks."

Hieronymus sniffed experimentally under his arm, and then jerked back his head in alarm.

"Dear god, what a stench. Baths for everyone before we take another step."

"But I'm next up," Leena said, jumping out of her chair and snatching up her pack. "Bad enough I'm forced to clean jaguar fur out of the tub before cleaning myself, I'll not contend with your grime as well."

✦

Within the hour, once the sopping jaguar man had been driven from the bathing chamber, Leena luxuriated in the tiled tub. She'd not had a proper bath in ages. The best she'd managed since leaving Laxaria had been a few moments to sponge herself off in the privacy of the water closet aboard the *Rukh*. Thereafter, she'd been forced to make do with quick dips into rivers, ponds, and streams, having to keep a sharp lookout for snakes, leeches, or any other aquatic or amphibious predators—reptile, mammal, dinosaur, or otherwise—and usually in full view of the men. This was the first time she'd been able to shut a door behind her, strip out of her well-traveled clothes, and soak in a hot tub in long months.

Leena rested her head on a cushion at the tub's edge, her eyes closed. She breathed slowly in and out through her nose, her mouth curled in a contented smile. She felt better than she had in a longer time than she could recall. The hot water of the tub, laced with oils and perfumes, soothed her aching muscles, and the fact that they would soon board a ship that would carry them to the one place that might hold the answer to her return home helped calm her thoughts.

Leena was teetering on the edge of sleep when the door opened. Too relaxed to be startled, Leena rolled her head to the side and languorously opened her eyes. Hieronymus stood at the threshold, a clean set of clothing folded in his arms, his eyes wide.

"Ex-excuse me." Hieronymus blushed, and averted his eyes. "I—I thought you were done in here, and already in your room."

He turned to leave, his shoulders hunched and head low.

"Hold a moment, Hero," Leena called after him. "There's something I wanted to ask you. But first . . ."

She stood up from the tub, the water sluicing off her bare skin. Suddenly exposed to the cooler air, her nipples stood erect, the areolas dark against the smooth white skin of her breasts. Leena put her hands on her hips, and cocked her head to one side.

"Why are you so embarrassed to see my nakedness? I've been disrobed in your company any number of times in our travels together."

Hieronymus tried to keep his gaze fixed on the ceiling, but his eyes kept flicking to her chest, to the curve of her hips, to the thatch of hair between her legs. His face flushing red, he shifted uncomfortably. "Well, that is . . . You see, when we are in the wilds, and circumstances demand, your nudity seems functionary, merely a practical concern. Here, though . . ." He gestured around them. The inn was inexpensive, but the bathing chamber was no less opulent for its affordability. "Within doors, such a state seems terribly intimate, and I can't help but feel as though I am intruding on your privacy."

Leena stepped dripping out of the tub and, wrapping a thick linen towel around herself, perched on the edge of the tub. "If I should live to be a hundred years old, I'll never understand the opposite sex."

"Then we have that in common," Hieronymus said with a weary sigh. He turned back towards the door. "I'll leave you to it."

"No," Leena called after him, "that wasn't the question which I wanted to ask."

Hieronymus set his clothes down on a low table, and leaned against the wall, his arms crossed over his chest.

"I wanted to ask you about . . . well . . . I couldn't help but notice that your mood has been rather dark this past week or more. It is as though some nightmare of tortured sleep has clung to you throughout the daylight hours. You seem often sullen and withdrawn, and when you do smile or jest, it seems almost forced, as though you are trying to compensate for something. What is troubling you?"

Hieronymus took a deep breath, and paused before answering. "Perhaps some elements of Benu's story, related to us en route, reminded me of things in my own past of which I am not proud."

"I thought as much." Leena nodded. "All of us have done things which we later have cause to regret. But circumstances force our hand, and we do what we must to survive."

"Perhaps," Hieronymus said. "Or perhaps some of us are merely weak, and given to succumbing to our darker natures, without the influence of others to keep our feet on the appropriate path."

Hieronymus crossed to the shuttered window, and looked down through the slats to the street and the desert beyond. He seemed pained, as though haunted by some memory he could not escape.

"What happened to you, when last you were in Masjid Empor?" Leena asked.

Hieronymus grimaced, and turned his back on her. "It was simply a . . . business opportunity that went awry. I would imagine the locals might not look back too fondly on that time, as indeed I don't myself."

Leena stood and took a step forward, reaching out a tentative hand to touch his shoulder. But in the instant before her fingers made contact, Hieronymus whirled, a smile forced onto his face.

"But enough of the gloomy past," he said. "Masjid Empor is a marvelous metropolis, the jewel of the Inner Sea's eastern shore, and we've nothing to gain from staying indoors and moping. Let's see a bit of the town before we set sail for Parousia, and beyond that the forests of Keir-Leystall."

"And beyond that, Earth?"

"And beyond that, Earth," Hieronymus said, taking Leena's hands in his. "With any luck, we'll have you home in a trice."

With her hands in Hieronymus's, her arms lifted and her towel slipped off, falling to the ground. Hieronymus looked down, standing only centimeters away from her naked form, and his face flushed even redder than before. After a long, awkward pause, he dropped Leena's hands as though they were hot rocks, rushed to the door, gathered up his clothes, and scuttled out into the common area.

"I'll just get dressed, then, shall I?" Leena called through the open door, a smile on her lips.

The company, at last refreshed, bathed, and dressed in clean clothing, set out into the streets of Masjid Empor. It was late afternoon, and the sun had just begun to set over the Inner Sea.

"We'll find the most likely vessels this way, I believe." Benu walked up the street quickly, with a purpose.

"What is your rush, Benu?" Hieronymus called after him.

Benu paused in his tracks, and turned around, a confused expression on his unmarred features. "Are we not bound for the waterfront, to seek passage on a southbound ship?"

"We are bound for the waterfront, perhaps," Hieronymus

answered, "but not yet to seek passage. In time we will. But first, we've needs to fulfill, even if you don't. I was anxious about returning to Masjid Empor, but I find now that having arrived, and walked once more these welcoming streets, I worried needlessly."

"I'm hungry," Balam said.

"You are always hungry," Benu answered.

"No, I'm *frequently* hungry. I could always *eat*, but I am not always hungry. Now, however, I am hungry."

"And I could use a drink," Leena said.

"As could I," Hieronymus answered with a will. "And I believe I recall just the place in which we can fulfill all of our purposes. This way." With that, he took Leena by the elbow and strode down the avenue, leaving Balam and Benu to follow behind.

Hieronymus led the company through the wide avenues of the city, and as they progressed they felt the heat of the desert at their backs slacking, and the cool breeze off the waves slowly building, cool caresses on their sun-scorched faces. The avenues ran straight down to the sea, and through the milling crowds and overhanging awnings, Leena could catch postage-stamp glimpses of brilliant blue. Above the babble of voices she could hear the slow susurration of the waves lapping against the shore, and the distant call of seabirds.

When they were a few blocks away from the waterfront, Hieronymus stopped short in front of an unimposing structure. The canopy over the low doorway was tattered and bleached with age, and the room beyond the entrance was dark and gloomy.

"This has all the earmarks of a dive," Balam said guardedly.

"Right you are, my furry friend," Hieronymus said with a smile. "And this particular dive serves the best dinner you'll find in all Masjid Empor. And Leena will be happy to know that they've got the finest selection of spirits I've seen this side of Elvera."

"So what are we waiting for?" Leena said, heading towards the door. Balam followed close behind, licking his black lips.

"Benu, will you join us for some refreshment, or will you hurry yourself on to the waterfront in search of transport?" Hieronymus laid a comradely hand on the artificial man's shoulder.

"I suppose, if you don't feel there's any especial hurry," Benu said, following the others inside, "that there is no reason I can't rest myself with you."

Leena had located the company a table near the center of the room, and as Hieronymus joined them, there came a shout from across the room.

"You!" A man dressed in the fine robes of a merchant, his beard oiled and trimmed, pointed directly at Hieronymus. His eyes wide, he jumped to his feet, almost overturning his table, and rushed frantically out the open door.

"What was the matter with *him?*" Leena said, turning towards Hieronymus.

Hieronymus did not answer, but shifted uncomfortably, his expression dark.

"He seemed to recognize you," Benu said unnecessarily.

"Just what *did* happen the last time you were in Masjid Empor, Hero?" Balam asked, arching an eyebrow.

At that moment, nearly a dozen of the local constabulary rushed in through the open door, scimitars drawn and expressions fierce. They ringed the table in steel, shouting in thickly accented Sakrian for the company to remain seated and immobile.

Hieronymus scowled. "Something bad," he answered.

CHAPTER 24

Imprisoned

Balam started to rise to his feet, his claws extending.

"Hold," Leena said in a harsh whisper. "In such close quarters, with the numbers so far out of our favor, our chances of escaping without injury are slim. Besides, where are we to go, back into the desert?"

"Not the desert," Balam growled under his breath. "I just had to wash sand out of holes I didn't know I had."

"Perhaps we'd best go along with the gendarmes," Benu said, "and see what the fuss is about."

Balam and Leena nodded. Hieronymus didn't make a sound, immobile in his chair.

✦

"Where are you staying in the city?" one of the constables asked Leena as he bound her hands behind her with a stout cord. The gem affixed to the front of his turban, and the deference with which the other constables treated him, picked him out as the leader.

Leena gave him the location of the inn, and the names under which they were registered, and the constable sent one of his subordinates to fetch their things.

"What is this about, anyway?" Leena asked, craning her head around. With his dark features and trim beard and mustaches, the constable presented a dashing figure, and Leena was surprised and a little ashamed that she found him considerably attractive.

"The magistrate will explain the charges against you and the punishment to be meted out when you appear before the tribunal." The constable checked her bonds, and then moved on to secure Benu's hands behind his back.

"Don't you mean if we are found guilty?" Leena said.

The constable looked over at Leena, a confused expression on his face. "What do you mean, *if*? Your trial was held nearly a decade ago, and the ruling and sentencing phase concluded soon after."

"But we've never even been to your city before," Balam objected, his fangs bared.

"Perhaps not. But *he* has"—the constable pointed at Hieronymus —"and the verdict carries to any who travel in his company."

$$\maltese$$

The company was led through the city streets, through milling crowds that parted reluctantly for the constables, but who whispered eagerly behind their hands when they were passed word of who the four prisoners were. Leena could not pick out any words from the babel of voices, none of them speaking any language she knew. Whatever their meaning, it was clear that the crime of which Hieronymus was accused, and which they all now stood guilty, was infamous.

Up the avenues, away from the waterfront, and across town to the city's center, where they came to a stout building that squatted like a predator amongst the less-imposing structures around it. Its crenellated battlements rose like stone teeth, and as they passed through the archway into its dark interior, Leena felt as though she were being swallowed whole.

$$\bigstar$$

The cell was small, no more than four meters on a side, with three walls of stone and one of ancient ironwood bars. A low shelf ran along the three stone walls, and a small window high overhead offered the only illumination. There was a drainage hole in the center of the floor, apparently the only concession to plumbing and biological requirements, to judge from the rank smell emanating from it.

"Paris of the Inner Sea's eastern shore, eh?" Leena said, wrinkling her nose and trying to find a comfortable sitting position on the shelf.

Across a narrow passageway was another identical cell, which held two prisoners. One was an indistinct figure wrapped from head to toe in damp robes, with only black eyes peering out between folds of cloth. The other was a fierce-looking, muscular woman, her light hair cropped short, with a smoldering gaze and a symbol carved into her left cheek, a figure X framed on three sides. Her skin was the color of wet sand, and her eyes were light beneath knitted brows. Her clothing consisted of hardened leather and straps, with a kind of cuirass of shaped leather, a heavy apron, and greaves on her shins and bracers on her forearms.

"Are you awaiting trial, too?" Leena called to the woman opposite, her tone enraged. She slammed a fist against the wall, and shot a sharp glance at Hieronymus. "Or are you already judged unfairly in absentia and awaiting punishment?"

"Relax yourself, little sister," Balam said soothingly. "You've nothing to gain from injuring yourself."

"Is this what passes for justice in Masjid Empor?!" Leena leapt to her feet and began to pace. "Grabbing innocents off the street and locking them away in some gulag, awaiting who knows what tortures?"

"Silentio!" shouted the woman in the opposite cell in some foreign tongue, rubbing her temples. "Caput meum doleo."

Hieronymus stood, and crossed to stand beside Leena, his expression unreadable. "Justice," he said in a harsh whisper, taking Leena's hand and leading her back to the shelf, "in Masjid Empor, is a severe thing. A man caught stealing a fish has his hands cut off at the wrists. A man caught with another man's wife has his generative organs cut off. A man caught trading in forbidden knowledge has his ears cut off." He paused, and with his eyes lowered, answered, "A convicted murder is publicly executed in the square."

"What, then," Leena asked, her eyes narrowed, "is the crime of which you are accused, the blame for which appears to extend to the rest of our company?"

"It had better not be adultery with another's mate," Balam growled, cupping his groin protectively, "or you and I will have words, Hero."

"No." Hieronymus shook his head, and turned his back to his companions, looking up at the small window overhead. "Your organs will remain intact, of that I am sure."

Balam breathed a sigh of relief, and patted his groin appreciatively.

"When they bury you," Hieronymus went on, "I'm sure none of your constituent elements will be missing."

Hieronymus turned, and Leena could see tears pooling in his eyes.

"The charge, I am ashamed to say, is murder."

CHAPTER 25
The Story of William Greenslade

Leena, Balam, and Benu sat in stunned silence, regarding their weeping companion. Hieronymus, his shoulders hunched, collapsed onto the shelf at the far corner of the cell and leaned to one side, resting his head on the ironwood bars.

"Hero, I . . ." Balam left off, unsure how to continue.

"I'm not sure I understand," Benu said, filling up the silence. "I take it the charge is a valid one, and that you feel some remorse over the incident. Which would be understandable, if I'd not seen you on previous occasions end another being's life without suffering the slightest effects. Those two in the canteen on the river Pison, for example. Did you shed a tear over them?"

"They deserved what came to them," Hieronymus said in a ragged voice, "as do any who raise their hands in violence. I've killed many others in my days, and none that didn't deserve killing, in one form or fashion. You could argue that, when my number is up and someone gets the better of me, I'll deserve it just as much, considering how many I've sent to their graves. But this one of whose murder I stand convicted deserved no such thing. It was no righteous killing, but murder, pure and simple. And for my sins, the blood is on my hands still."

His name was William Greenslade, *Hieronymus said*, and he was an Englishman, like me. He was also a sailing man, though a marine and not a naval officer, as I'd been. He'd sailed from Plymouth in 1768 aboard Captain James Cook's HMS *Endeavour*, thirteen years before I first squalled bloody on my mother's sheets. But with the vagaries of the passage of time between Earth and this world, he was but a boy of twenty-one years when first he set foot on Paragaea, while I was already approaching the end of my third decade when we met.

The way Greenslade told the story, the *Endeavour* was three months out of Tierra del Fuego, in the southern seas in search of the mythical *Terra Australis Incognita*. Holding the rank of private, it was Greenslade's turn on sentry duty rotation, and so he stood guard outside one of the ship's cabins, keeping watch over the ship's supplies. A sailor was working amongst the supplies that night, cutting pieces of sealskin to make tobacco pouches. Greenslade asked the sailor if he could have one of the pouches for himself, and the sailor refused. With the weakness of character that one often finds in the young, Greenslade resolved that he would have one of the pouches, come hell or high water, and when the sailor's back was turned, he stole a piece of the sealskin. The theft was discovered shortly after Greenslade went off duty, and came quickly to the attention of his superior, a Sergeant Edgecombe. While the sergeant conferred with the captain, Greenslade began to reconsider his decision to purloin the sealskin, and slunk off to the forecastle to try to think a way clear of his fix.

When first I heard Greenslade's story, I wasn't sure how much of it to credit, and in later days, I was given cause to reconsider my assessment of the man. But I think, in retrospect, that my first impressions of him had been correct, and that he was, at heart, a decent man, led astray by impulses which his strength of character was not sufficient to suppress.

In any event, it is impossible to say whether Greenslade would have stood before the mast like a man and taken his punishment, for circumstances contrived to keep him from that fate. Standing in the forecastle, the South Seas stretching out before him and the starry sky arching overhead, Greenslade was startled to discover that a star seemed to have fallen from the sky, and hovered just before him. It was a small, silvery sphere, like a mirror curved into a ball, that hung in midair just a few feet in front of him.

All of us, of course, know precisely the import of this mirrored sphere, but young Greenslade had no conception, any more than Leena or I did when first we saw one. So he reached out a tremulous hand, touched the surface of the sphere, and was immediately translated to a world not his own.

I was, at that point, living amongst the people of Drift, the floating city of the Inner Sea. This was some time before Balam and I met, and I had been in Paragaea but a short number of years. I had learned enough of the local dialects to make myself understood in Sakrian, Sabaean, and the language of Drift, and had seen much of the shores of the Inner Sea at all points of the compass. I was eager to see what the land had to offer, and so bid my farewells to my adopted kin of Drift, and went ashore in Bacharia. That proved as disastrous a choice as you might expect, but it was fortuitous in at least one regard, for it was during the unpleasantness with the Bacharian Polity that I first encountered Greenslade.

He'd arrived in Paragaea only a few days previous, and had not weathered the experience well. Knowing nothing of the local language or customs, with no currency in his purse, and no earthly notion where he might be, he was literally at wit's end. He was like a crazed thing, more mad animal than man, and had I not chanced upon him, he'd have ended his days as a gibbering lunatic, haunting the back alleys of Bacharia until starvation or violence took him, whichever did first.

As it was, I heard his maddened cries, and recognized immediately the sound of a fellow Englishman in distress. I ran to his aid, and with my saber fended off the locals with whom he was embroiled. Greenslade was understandably relieved to meet a countryman, and when I suggested we make a hasty retreat from the city-state into more hospitable climes, he quickly assented.

We stowed away on a freighter bound for Masjid Kirkos, and managed to remain undetected until we reached the southern port. Hidden there in the hold, I told Greenslade what I knew of Paragaea, and instructed him in the rudiments of the local languages and customs, while he familiarized me with his origins, relating to me the story I've just retold.

Jumping ship in Masjid Kirkos, Greenslade and I clasped hands and resolved to travel together, seeking adventure where we might. In the months that followed, more than a year all told, we ranged across the eastern reaches of the Paragaean continent, from Parousia to far Croatoan, until our journeys led us finally to Masjid Empor.

Not to put too fine a point on it, Greenslade and I had plied the trade of the thief, working our way through desert emirates and the coastal cities and towns, stealing gems and crowns and scepters, fencing them, and then carousing on the proceeds. Even at the time, I knew it was wrong, but it was an exciting, adventure-filled pursuit, and so suited my cast of mind in those days. Besides, Greenslade and I never stole anything from anyone who could not afford the loss, and so in that regard we were more involved in the redistribution of wealth than in anything that might properly be termed thievery.

All that changed one hot night in Masjid Empor, when we stole from the local calif something that could never be repaid. Greenslade had always been of a somewhat vicious temperament, I had found, and for my sins I was not much of a role model. We had come to Masjid

Empor for what I then considered one last big score. The calif's signet of authority was an emerald the size of a man's fist, and Greenslade and I concocted a plan to sneak into the calif's palace and steal the gem. We had performed similar burglaries dozens of times, if not more, sneak-thieving our way into sleeping houses and making off with valuables without anyone in the residence being the wiser until morning came and we pair of thieves were far away. On rare occasions, we were forced to contend with guards and gendarmes, but those ended up concussed at worst, most of the time; and if from time to time one of the fallen guards was injured fatally, at least they had been hired for the purpose, and when their faces and dying screams haunted my restless slumber, I could at least take small comfort in that.

On this particular occasion, though, Greenslade and I were caught in the process of stealing away by the calif's eight-year-old daughter. We were at a high window, on the verge of slipping out and over the sill, when the little girl, still rubbing the sleep from her eyes, chanced upon us in her sleeping gown. Greenslade at once snatched up the girl and stifled her cries before she was able to call for help.

"We should leave the girl," I told him in hushed tones, "and make good our escape."

"We wouldn't make it a dozen steps if the bitch raises the alarm," Greenslade answered, his eyes flashing. "We throw the girl from the window, dash her brains out on the flagstones, and *then* we escape."

The calif's palace is the tallest building in all of Masjid Empor, standing four stories tall. Diminutive compared to the towering structures of Laxaria or Hausr, but certainly tall enough that a fall from its height would do grievous injury to an eight-year-old skull.

"Let the girl go," I told him, bristling.

"Have you gone mad, Bonaventure?" Greenslade spat. "It's her life or ours."

"I'd sooner kill you myself than let you bring harm to that child," I said.

"You *have* lost your senses!" Greenslade hissed.

"I may only be regaining them, William," I told him, my grip tightening on the hilt of the scabbarded saber at my side.

Greenslade did not waste another moment in conversation, but made his move towards the window.

I lunged forward, whipping my blade free of its scabbard and driving it into Greenslade's chest in one smooth movement, the point piercing his breast just centimeters from the girl's right ear. He was fatally wounded, my saber slicked with his blood, but it was too late. As Greenslade tumbled backwards, he dragged the doomed girl with him, and they plummeted together through the open window, the girl screaming and Greenslade's last breath rattling in his throat.

I stood at the open window, looking down on the red ruin on the flagstones below me. I didn't think, just sheathed my sword, raced to the opposite window, and leapt from the window onto the top of a sheltering canopy only two stories below. From there I made it intact to the ground, and ran, numbly scrambling away into the hot night.

I found myself the next morning miles outside the city, standing at the shores of the Inner Sea, tempted to throw myself into the waves. But I realized that would be the coward's way out. Nor could I conscience returning to Masjid Empor, where the executioner's blade would too quickly release me from my torment. The only just punishment for me would be to live and bear the guilt of that poor girl's death.

I held in my hand the fabled emerald of Masjid Empor, cutting red lines into my palm. I scarcely remembered carrying it with me from the calif's palace, much less holding it all this while. With contempt, I hurled it into the surf, and it sank without a trace.

CHAPTER 26

Escape

"It was shortly afterwards, when I left the east behind and first traveled the Western Jungle, that I met you, Balam." Hieronymus glanced at the jaguar man, a bittersweet smile playing across his lips. "I tried to look upon saving you as an act of penitence, but that didn't make the guilt any easier to bear."

"And you never told me," Balam said.

"Have you told me all the shameful secrets in your past, friend?" Hieronymus asked.

The jaguar man averted his eyes.

"Can you possibly be surprised that I would choose not to share the fact that my avarice and greed led an impressionable young man to a life of crime, eventuating in his death and that of a blameless girl? Having sunk to the level of a common criminal, I now had innocent blood on my hands."

"And then you saved Balam's life," Leena said, crossing the floor in long strides and standing before Hieronymus. "And then you saved my life. How many more must you save before you feel you've atoned? That girl's death is an unfortunate tragedy, but you can't let it haunt you for the rest of your days." Leena's eyes fluttered closed for the briefest instant, pain flashing across her face. "It is like I told you. We all have done things of which we're not proud"—she tried not to think back to Stalingrad, but could not escape the memory, the confused expression of the young soldier looking up at her, the Mauser still smoking in her hands—"but the fact that we live now should be sufficient. It is within us to improve ourselves—"

"'But that was in another country,'" Hieronymus interrupted, in a mocking singsong voice, "'and besides, the wench is dead.'"

Leena shook her head, exasperated, and stomped to the far side of the cell.

"All of this is beside the point," Balam said, scratching behind his notched ear with an outstretched claw.

"And what is the point then?" Hieronymus glared at him from across the cell.

"The point is that we stand accused of murder, *Hero*, and will no doubt be executed in short order."

"Is there any chance for appeal?" Leena asked.

"There is a definite finality to the judicial system of Masjid Empor," Hieronymus said, shaking his head. "And besides, even if the magistrate was inclined to consider overturning the ruling, the man who recognized me in the restaurant was one of the locals whom Greenslade and I plied for information while planning the robbery. His testimony, given a decade ago or again today, would identify me as the accomplice of the dead man found with the calif's murdered daughter. So I feel quite certain any call for appeal would fall on deaf ears."

"So all that remains is for your sentence and punishment to be pronounced," Benu said, "which punishment will doubtless be execution?" The artificial man had remained silent since their arrest, speaking only to question Hieronymus's tears.

"Doubtless," Hieronymus said.

"In that case," Benu answered, climbing to his feet, "for your sakes, if not for my own, might I suggest that we make a hasty retreat?"

Hieronymus leaned over and, grabbing hold of the ironwood posts that barred their cell, rattled the gate. "And how are we to accomplish that?"

Benu walked calmly to the cell door, placed his hands on two bars, and ripped the door off its hinges, reducing the adamantine ironwood to splinters and kindling.

"My bodies are designed to last long centuries, remember," Benu explained with a slight smile, "and this is not the first time I've been jailed for another man's crimes."

"Why didn't you do that *before?*" Balam's eyes goggled.

"I wanted to see what eventuated." Benu shrugged. "And besides, your behavior at the restaurant indicated a desire not to evade capture, and I thought it a prudent course to follow your example."

"Your guilt will have to continue to be punishment enough, Hero," Leena said, rushing to the corridor, "as I've no intention of watching any of us be executed in the public square."

"And I want to remain alive to enjoy my constituent elements as long as I'm able." Balam followed Leena into the passageway, his claws bared but with a leonine smile on his face.

"Very well," Hieronymus said, leaping to his feet. He and Benu joined the other two in the corridor. "We must first retrieve our weapons and provisions."

Before they could take another step, they were brought up short by an angry voice from the opposite cell.

"Attend!" shouted the fierce woman, rattling the bars of her cell. "Free me at once!"

"Why should we?" Balam asked.

"Because thou can." Her brows narrowed, and her gaze burned into Benu.

"That hardly seems a compelling argument," Balam answered with a shrug.

"Then mayhap thou will be compelled by the fact that I know the master of a ship currently riding at anchor in the harbor. He owes me a favor, and could bear us quickly away from the city." She paused, sneering, as if daring Balam to dismiss her now. "Or wouldst thou prefer to flee into the deserts?"

"Free her." Hieronymus snapped his fingers at Benu. "And hurry."

The artificial man bowed slightly, miming a subservient attitude with a sardonic smile, and demolished the ironwood bars with a single swipe of his arm.

"Follow," the woman barked, leaping through the gap and rushing past the company. "Our arms and effects are kept in a storage locker this way."

Leena turned to her companions. "This does not appear the first time our new friend has run afoul of the authorities in Masjid Empor."

"Are you coming, or do you wait for the guards to return you to your cell?" The woman paused at the end of the corner, shouting back at them, before racing around the curve and out of sight.

"Come on," Balam said, following after her. "The sooner we're away from here, the happier I'll be."

Hieronymus glanced back at their former cell, his expression pained. Leena could see that, having come so close to being brought to account for his past misdeeds, there was a part of him that was reluctant again to escape punishment.

"Go on, Hero," she said, laying a hand on his shoulder. "There are many others out there in the world who need saving, if you've more atoning to do."

Hieronymus looked back at her with a weary smile, and took to his heels, racing down the corridor after the jaguar man.

"Benu, are you coming?" Leena looked back at the artificial man, who still stood in the opened doorway of the opposite cell, his attention on the figure in damp robes huddled in the corner.

"Will you not accompany us?" Benu asked the indistinct figure.

The figure shrugged, the movement mostly hidden beneath the folds of cloth, and climbed unsteadily to its feet.

From around the curve of the corridor came shouts of alarm, and the sickening thud of bone hitting flesh.

"Come on, then," Leena urged, hurrying towards the tumult. "We've wasted enough time as it is."

CHAPTER 27

Pursuit

By the time Leena reached the locker room, Balam was already in the process of strapping on his harnesses and knives, and a pair of guards lay insensate and moaning on the floor.

"Did I miss the excitement, then?" Leena asked.

"I suspect there'll be enough to go around in a moment," Hieronymus answered, strapping on his belt, arranging his sheathed saber on one side and his holstered pistol on the other.

Balam handed Leena her short sword and Makarov.

"Where's our new friend?" Leena asked.

Just then, the woman appeared at the doorway. "The guards must be changing shifts. There don't appear to be any more about. But it won't be long before more arrive."

"Then we'd best be on our way, and quickly," Leena said.

"Thou!" the woman shouted at Hieronymus, who stood by the weapons locker. She pointed to a short sword, hanging from a peg. "Hand me yon gladius."

Hieronymus snatched the sword from the peg, and tossed it end over end across the room. He nodded with satisfaction when the woman snatched it handily out of midair by the hilt. Balam's eyes, too, widened fractionally at the display of martial prowess.

Benu and the figure in the robes joined them, both moving at a leisurely pace.

"Why didst thou bring the drunken fish along?" the woman asked, scowling with distaste. "It snores unpleasantly in its sleep, and smells of seaweed, cheap spirits, and week-dead eel."

"It made little sense for five detainees to leave a sixth behind," Benu answered, "who might be punished for their escape."

Hieronymus handed Leena his pack, and slung his own onto his back. "What's your name?" he asked the woman, who had slid the gladius into a sheath of leather and brass and fixed it to a baldric slung across her chest.

"I am Spatha Sekundus," the woman said.

"I am Hieronymus Bonaventure," he answered. "These are my companions, Balam, prince of the Sinaa; Akilina Mikhailovna Chirikova; and Benu."

The woman named Spatha Sekundus nodded curtly to each of them in turn.

"And you, friend?" Hieronymus said to the robed figure, checking the straps of his pack and making for the door.

"Kakere," came the slurred, burbling voice from within the robes.

Whether that was the robed figure's name, or another response in some unknown tongue, Leena was not to learn for some time, as at that moment, shouts echoed down the corridor from the demolished cells.

"Time to go," Spatha said, and raced out the doorway, heading towards the exit.

Balam shrugged, and turned to his companions. "Well, you heard what the lady said. Let's go!"

The company, now six, made it to the exit of the jailhouse without encountering the guards, but on reaching the street their luck ran out.

"You!" The captain of the constables, who had arrested them in the restaurant, stood now in the street before them, three guardsmen at his side. They were evidently returning to their headquarters after making their appointed round through the city, and were shocked to see prisoners at their liberty.

"I knew this was too easy," Balam growled, drawing a pair of knives and baring his fangs.

Hieronymus whipped his sword from its sheath, and drew his Mauser.

The lead constable pointed his scimitar at Hieronymus's chest, his eyes narrowed. "I don't suppose you would just return to your cell, and avoid this unpleasantness, would you?"

Hieronymus smiled slightly. "And I don't suppose you could just step aside?"

The constable shook his head.

"Pity," Hieronymus said, and lunged forward.

The constable deflected Hieronymus's thrust with an effective parry, and the two closed with a ringing clatter of steel on steel.

Leena drew her short sword just in time to swat aside a blow from the largest of the constables. A hulking, powerful brute, he swung his scimitar in a wide arc, treating it more like a club than a blade. Leena's teeth buzzed with the impact of his blow on her sword, but her grip on the sword's hilt didn't falter, and she kept to her feet.

On the other side of Hieronymus, Balam and Spatha each closed with the remaining constables.

"We would probably be best served to be on our way," Benu calmly said, standing in the open doorway. "Reinforcements are sure to arrive quickly."

"A fine idea," Balam said through gritted teeth, his knives cutting
red rills on the forearms of his opponent. "Why didn't *we* think of that?"

Leena's opponent roared, and swung his scimitar again in a wide
arc, with redoubled ferocity. She danced out of the way, spinning to the
side, but the tip of the brute's blade nicked her shoulder, blood
streaming out in a red ribbon.

From behind them, voices shouted from within the jailhouse, the
guards inside evidently having located them.

"I'll take care of this," Benu said.

Leena chanced a glance over her shoulder as she brought her sword
into ready position, and watched as Benu dispassionately knocked the
heads of two armed guards together, making a comical noise like
coconuts striking one another.

Leena's opponent, too, had been momentarily distracted by the
sight, and his attention was diverted from her for a split second. Leena
seized the opportunity, diving forward towards her opponent's unpro-
tected abdomen. Her sword's sharp point pierced his chest just below
the sternum, the blade thrusting into him up to the hilt.

"Urm?" her opponent said, looking down in confusion at the red
bloom blossoming on his shirtfront as Leena pulled her blade free. His
scimitar slipped from his fingers into the sand, and he tottered for a
moment on his feet, unsteadily, before falling backwards lengthwise
like a felled tree.

Leena had not blinked or breathed in long seconds, and now as she
caught her breath she turned to see how the rest of the company was faring.

Balam had made relatively short work of his opponent, who
moaned in the dust at his feet, red gashes running in parallel lines
across his cheek and arms. The woman Spatha Sekundus stood with
one foot resting on the chest of her fallen foe, who now seemed to have
fewer fingers on each hand than he'd had a moment before.

Only the captain of the constables remained on his feet, his lithe form
darting back and forth as his blade danced with Hieronymus's saber.

"You're a fine swordsman," Hieronymus said admiringly, his breath ragged. "It'd be a shame to kill you. Like spoiling a piece of art."

"I appreciate your concern," the constable replied through a tight smile, thrusting towards Hieronymus's head, his scimitar knocked away by Hieronymus's saber at the final instant. "When you are dead, I will speak fondly of your skill with the blade."

Without warning, Balam struck the constable a thunderous blow to the back of his head, and the constable collapsed in a heap, insensate.

"Whatever did you do *that* for?" Hieronymus asked, eyes wide. "I was very nearly about to deliver the final blow."

The jaguar man shrugged. "You'd have killed him, he'd have killed you, or the two of you would have settled down in a cottage somewhere and raised a family. I was getting bored with your reciprocal flattery, and, besides, we're in a hurry, remember?"

"Hey!" came a shouted voice from a short distance away. Another contingent of constables had just rounded the corner, more than half-a-dozen strong. Seeing their fallen comrades, they drew their scimitars and rushed forward.

✦

The company raced through the streets of Masjid Empor, the scimitar-wielding constables following at their heels.

"This way!" Spatha shouted, and dove down an alleyway. The rest followed close behind.

The alley emptied out onto a bazaar crowded with market stalls and thronged with shoppers and vendors raising their voices in a confusing babel of tongues.

"Sheathe your weapons," Hieronymus ordered before stepping out of the sheltering shadows of the alleyway. He glanced behind and saw that the constables had just rounded the corner into the alley. "If we mix in with the crowds, we'll be harder to find."

"Make for the southwestern corner," Spatha said to Hieronymus, sheathing her gladius in her baldric and slipping into the crowd without another word.

"Separate, and make for that corner," Hieronymus relayed to the others in a harsh whisper, and then plunged into the throng.

Leena nodded, sliding her sword into its scabbard and walking briskly away from the alley's mouth. At her side, Balam, Benu, and the robed figure hurried into the crowd, trying to rush without drawing attention.

Leena was a few dozen strides into the throng when the constables reached the end of the alley, raising their voices in calls of alarm. But the crowd was too closely packed and noisy for their calls to have much effect, and her heart pounding in her chest, she continued to swim through the masses of men, women, and metamen to the far corner.

Having regrouped at the market's edge, the company reached the waterfront without incident.

"There," Spatha said, pointing to a dhow riding at anchor at the dock. "That's the ship of which I spoke." She raced across the board-walk and up the gangplank, vaulting onto the ship's deck.

The rest of the company followed close behind, with Leena and Hieronymus setting foot on the deck just as the shipmaster came up from the hold.

"What's the meaning of this?" the man barked. His head was shaved clean, and he had waxed mustaches over his full lips, with a large hoop earring in one ear, the other cropped off at the lobe. He wore silk pantaloons over leather boots, a sash around his ample midriff, and a loose-fitting blouse open to the waist. "Spatha Sekundus! What do you mean by this intrusion? And who is this motley band of reprobates?!"

"List, Tyrel." Spatha strode up to the well-fed shipmaster and snapped her fingers under his bulbous nose. "If thou would sail immediately, with me and my companions on board, I will consider thy debt to me repaid in full."

The man named Tyrel drew up short, his eyes widening. "Repaid in full?" he repeated, scratching his chin.

"In full," Spatha answered with a curt nod.

"Well, then," he said amiably, slapping Spatha on the shoulder, an avuncular grin on his wide face. "Why didn't you say so?"

He turned to the deckhands, who hung back uneasily, eyeing the newcomers.

"Cast off, you swabs!" he said. "We've cargo to deliver, and paying passengers to transport!" Tyrel turned back to the company. "If you've been embroiled in any . . . local difficulties, shall we say, it might be best if you went below until we were out of sight of land."

The shipmaster gestured with his double chin to the dock, where a trio of scimitar-wielding constables had just skidded into view.

"A fine idea," Leena said, hunching low. "Lead the way."

"Welcome to the good ship *Acoetes Zephyrus*, my lady," Tyrel said with an oily smile, and pointed towards the hatch. "Your cabin awaits."

CHAPTER 28
Aboard the 'Arcoetes zephyrus'

Some time later, the shipmaster joined the company down in the hold, where they sat amongst casks and crates, tending to their wounds.

"We got clear of the waters of Masjid Empor without coming to the attention of the barques and corvettes of the harbor patrol. We're making for the open sea, so it should be safe for you to come topside now, if you like."

"Our thanks for your pains," Hieronymus said.

"Oh, I've suffered no pains for your sake yet, and I don't intend to start." The shipmaster gestured at the hold around them. "My hold was already full of cargo, and I was just waiting for my ne'er-do-well nephew of a first mate, who is no doubt away carousing on the town, to return from shore leave. But I'll pick him up on the return trip, if he should survive that long. It'll break my sister's heart if I have to tell her that her wee lad has come to a bad end, but into every life a little rain must fall, after all. And besides, if he survives it might help to strengthen the boy's character a bit. Of course, come to think of it, I'm now left a bit shorthanded. I don't suppose any of you lot have any sailing experience, do you?"

Hieronymus smiled broadly. "I spent better than fourteen years before the mast," he said, "working my way up through the ranks of my nation's navy from the position of midshipman to first lieutenant, and it's been too many years since I felt the roll of the waves beneath my feet."

"Well, I don't know I have such a dire necessity for a first lieu-tenant," Tyrel answered guardedly. "What I really need is help with the more, shall we say, taxing tasks of a deckhand. This is a fairly green crew, most of them come aboard in the last months, and I've always a need for a skilled pair of hands in the rigging, or working the bilge bumps, or even swabbing out the deck."

If anything, hearing a list of the onerous tasks of a common sailor only caused the smile on Hieronymus's face to widen. "I'm your man, Captain," he said with a gleam in his eye.

✦

By the time Leena and the others came topside once more, they were out of sight of land, the clear blue waters of the Inner Sea stretching out to the horizon in all directions. The sky overhead was clear and bright, with only a few low clouds to the north, hugging the coastline.

Leena heard a rumbling she initially took to be distant thunder, but which she quickly discovered was the growling of Balam's stomach. She realized that they'd not eaten before they arrived in Masjid Empor, considering that their last attempt to break their fast had been interrupted by their unexpected arrest.

"Have you anything to eat?" Leena asked the shipmaster as he joined them on the deck.

"And I wouldn't say no to a drink, myself," Hieronymus put in, licking his dry lips.

"Ooooh," burbled the voice beneath the damp robes. "A dram of spirits would *so* ease my jangled nerves."

"Afraid not, all," Tyrel said with a shake of his head. "I'm a strict adherent to the doctrine of the Meliorists, and I'll not allow any intoxicants on my ship, no matter how much my crew . . . or my inadvertent passengers . . . might grumble."

"Wha-at?" said the voice beneath the robes, and a webbed hand appeared from between the folds of cloth, grasping at the shipmaster. "But I'm *thirsty*!"

"If you're thirsty, mate," Tyrel answered, not without compassion, "it's not spirits you'll be needing, now is it?"

The robed figure gave a howl of disconsolate pain, and slumped off to sulk in the shadow of the wheelhouse.

"What kind of creature *is* that?" Leena asked.

"I thought you knew," Balam answered.

"It is an Ichthyandaro," Spatha said, saying the word like it was a curse.

Leena glanced at the robed figure, a confused expression on her face.

"That there, lassie," Tyrel explained, "is a genuine fish man. Their kind tends to have a weakness for alcoholic spirits, though their bodies tolerate the stuff not at all. Tends to dry them out, you see, which is bad for the gills."

"Gills?" Leena looked closer at the sulking figure, and at last understood the need for the dampened robes.

✦

That night, while the others enjoyed their evening meal under a cloudless sky, Leena spent her time studying the constellations. Many of the arrangements of stars seemed somewhat familiar, similar to those she knew from Earth's night sky, but subtly altered, their positions in the heavens and their relation one to another changed.

When the others went below, to hang hammocks between the bulkheads and swing off to sleep, Leena stayed topside, her eyes on the heavens. In the strangeness of the past months, it was sometimes easy to forget that she'd so recently slipped the bonds of gravity, and traveled beyond the horizon. That she'd traveled so far beyond the horizon, she now reflected, and found herself on an alien world, however, was a fact she could never escape.

Perhaps, then, this oracular forest towards which they sailed would hold the answers to the riddle of Paragaea, and the key to her safe return home. If she'd deserved a promotion to senior lieutenant for the successful completion of the Vostok 7 mission, surely she'd merit a commander's star for discovering a whole new world.

Commander Akilina Mikhailovna Chirikova. It was a long distance to travel from the dirty-faced urchin who'd nearly died in a hail of incendiaries during the Great Patriotic War. A long distance, indeed.

The next morning, Leena came on deck to find the robed figure huddled in the lee of the wheelhouse. The cloth of its robes had dried out in the night, and the fabric covering its head, chest, and left arm had been shrugged off. Its skin was ashen and gray, and while it appeared to be unconscious, its extremities trembled uncontrollably.

"You there," Leena said, turning and pointing to a sailor swabbing the deck with a bucket and mop. "Get me a bucket of water, if you would."

The sailor looked at his mop and his bucket in turn, shrugged, and dropping the mop to the deck carried the bucket over to Leena.

"Thank you." Leena took the bucket from the sailor's hands and, without preamble, upended it over the trembling figure on the deck. The brackish water splashed over the fish man, partially soaking the robes.

Leena turned, and handed the bucket back to the sailor. "More, please," she said firmly, and then turned her attention back to the trembling figure.

After a half-dozen buckets, at which point the sailor's rather slow-witted patience seemed to have been mostly exhausted, the fish man began to sputter, and rose up on its elbow.

"Wh-where am I?" the fish man said, voice tremulous.

"You're on board the *Acoetes*," Leena replied soothingly. "A dhow sailing on the Inner Sea. Do you remember how you came to be here?"

With Leena's help, the fish man rose into a sitting position, and then stood up on unsteady feet. On rising, the robes slid down off his slight frame, and standing unclothed, it was clear that he was a male of the species. Also, she could now see that fins ran along the back of his calves, and behind his scalloped ears were gills, swollen and reddish-raw. His skin was all over mottled and ashen, looking sickly and gray.

"I was arrested? Wasn't it?" the fish man said uncertainly. He swayed unsteadily with the rocking of the ship, squinting his dark eyes at the sea all around them. "In some city or other?"

"Masjid Empor," Leena said, nodding. She gave the fish man an arm to steady him. "My name is Leena. My friends and I escaped from imprisonment, and you joined us."

The fish man's head swung around on his thin neck like a balloon in a high wind, and he regarded Leena with one eye squeezed nearly shut and the other one opened wide. "Did I now? That sounds like it must have been exciting."

Leena smiled. "Perhaps a bit. And what is your name, if you don't mind me asking?"

"Kakere." The fish man paused for a moment, as though considering whether that was true or not, and then nodded. "Yes. Kakere."

"It's a pleasure to meet you, Kakere."

"Likewise, I'm sure." The fish man tried to take a step forward, and nearly pitched face-first onto the deck, saved from falling only by Leena's quick intervention. "Thank you kindly," he said, nodding languorously. "Now, do you know where I might find a drink on this tub?"

That night, Leena sat in the forecastle, her eyes once more on the heavens. Benu was busy talking with the crewmen, while Balam grumbled about the quality of the ship's food and Spatha sharpened her gladius's edge on a whetstone. The fish man Kakere huddled against the railing, moaning for a sip of alcohol, clutching his head in pain.

Leena glanced over at Kakere, a pained expression on her own face.

"He'll dry out in time." Hieronymus appeared out of the shadows, and dropped to a seated position at her side.

"It's his drying out I'm worried about," Leena answered, sounding more cross than she'd intended.

"You know what I meant."

Leena shook her head, as though to knock loose dark thoughts. "I'm sorry, Hero," she said with a slight smile. "It's just that I know how difficult these next days will be for him. Some cannot handle their drink, and should they attempt to turn their back on it, the thirst brings them to account in the hours and days that follow."

Hieronymus narrowed his eyes and looked at her thoughtfully. "It sounds as though you're speaking from experience."

"Oh, not me." Leena rubbed her hands together, glancing at the stars overhead. "The bottle and I have never been anything but boon companions. But I've known one or two who could not master their thirst before their thirst mastered them, I'm afraid. One of them . . ." She broke off, her eyes on the middle distance.

"Someone close to you?" Hieronymus leaned in, his voice dropping.

"His name was Sergei Vasilevich Tabanov," Leena answered after a lengthy pause. "We met in East Berlin, when . . ."

"*East* Berlin?" Hieronymus interrupted, puzzled. "Some cognate metropolis in the Orient, perhaps, named after the Germanic original?"

"No, merely the half of the original city which was given over to the rightful control of the Soviet after the Great Patriotic War, along with the east half of the German state, while the rest was divided up like slices of a fattened calf among the imperialist powers of the decadent West."

"Yes," Hieronymus said, nodding sagely, "I remember well the imperial tendencies of nations. But Russia, too, had its empire, in my day."

Leena shrugged off the comment. "In any event, when I was old enough to leave the state-run orphanage into whose care I had been entrusted after the Battle of Stalingrad, I enlisted immediately in the Red Army. I excelled at hand-to-hand combat and languages, and was assigned to a radio listening post in East Berlin." She paused, shaking her head slowly. "I was bored beyond comprehension almost immediately. Spending all day listening to static punctuated only occasionally by banal chattering, I quickly decided that I might better serve the Soviet in some other, more engaging capacity. It was during this tenure that I first met Sergei. He was twenty years old to my eighteen, and was a technician at the post, who kept all the electrics and equipment in working order. A genius of the first order, at least when his hands didn't shake too violently for him to manipulate his tools."

Leena glanced over at the shuddering Kakere, her eyes half-lidded.

"Sergei and I, working in such close quarters, became naturally acquainted, and in short order our relationship progressed, as relations between young people in such circumstances always do." She paused, and her eyes met Hieronymus's. "Have you ever been in love, Hero?"

Hieronymus smiled, briefly, and then a cloud drifted across his face. "Once, perhaps." He took a deep breath. "I've known women, if that's what you mean, but I've never felt the all-encompassing, all-consuming passion that the poets speak about. Never but once. Her name was Pelani, and she might have been the mother of my child. But it was not to be."

"Why? What came between you?"

"Her family. Her culture. My duty." He sighed. "It just wasn't in our stars, I suppose you could say."

"Duty," Leena repeated, nodding. "Well, whatever was between us, me and Sergei, I don't know that I can say it was love. But it was as near as I have ever come, and it felt real enough to me." She folded her arms over her chest, hugging herself tightly. "Sergei wanted to work on planes and rockets. He talked of nothing else. And he applied as often as he could to the Air Defense Forces of the VVS. He'd only been called to take the entrance exam once, though, and he'd had so much to drink in the days prior, to soothe his nerves, that he swore he'd not touch a drop just prior to the exam, and so when he went to complete the practical elements of the testing, his hands trembled so violently that he couldn't hold a screwdriver between thumb and index finger without dropping it. He passed it off as an ailment, some stomach flu, but it would be months before he could retake the examination and qualify for the transfer.

"Sergei, laying beside me in my cot at night, made me swear to help him overcome his thirst for drink. I so swore, and the next night we began to sweat the spirits from his body." Leena shuddered, and held herself tighter. "I cannot say they were the most unpleasant days of my life, having lived through the days following my parents' immolation during the Battle of Stalingrad, but they ranked high on the list, nonetheless. He vomited everything in his system, and was still racked with dry heaves. He convulsed. He hallucinated, and carried on conversations with those long dead. He sweated profusely, and stank of sickly sour desperation for days."

Leena's gaze drifted over to the suffering Ichthyandaro, and then looked back at the stars overhead.

"In all, it took the passage of weeks before he would wake up in the morning and not beg me for a drink. It was a test of wills in the months that passed for Sergei not to return to the bottle, and I did what I could to assist by abstaining from drink myself in those long days and nights. But when the time came for him again to take the practical examination, he passed with flying colors, and was transferred in short order, not to the VVS as he'd thought, but to the technical facilities at Star City, to work on the new generation of rockets. I stayed behind in East Berlin, for a time, getting reacquainted with my boon companion the bottle."

"Did you see him again?"

"Only once," Leena answered. "Inspired by Sergei's drive, I applied for and was accepted into the pilot training program of the Air Defense Forces. Women had served as pilots since the days of the Great Patriotic War, but our numbers were still small compared to the percentage of men fliers. As a result, though I scored highest marks on all examinations, and executed my test flights perfectly, after being fully certified as a pilot and parachutist I was given a desk assignment in the offices of the Air Defense Forces, tracking materiel requests and personnel movements. On leave, I traveled once to Moscow, where Sergei and I met, and spent a glorious week together, as though we'd never been apart. We swore that we'd meet again soon, and when we parted, he asked for my hand in marriage. Already a jaded woman of twenty-three years, I still felt a flush of thrill as I accepted."

Leena's eyes dropped to the deck, and her mouth drew into a tight line.

"Only a few months later, Sergei was working on a rocket launch when the unthinkable happened. There was a leak in the fuel tanks, or so the rumors go, and the launch team, of which Sergei was a senior member, was ordered to attempt repairs. They climbed the scaffolding, and attempted to weld closed the opened seam in the fuel tank." Leena scowled, and twisted her hands into white-knuckled fists. "Though the official report placed no personal blame, in the corridors of Star City it is widely held that the fault lay with Field Marshal Mitrofan Nedelin, for violating all standards of safety by ordering technicians to weld shut a leaky fuel tank. But blame is for courts and historians. What matters is that the second-stage engine ignited, causing a cascade effect as the fuel tanks of the first stage burst and covered the launchpad in a tidal wave of flames. Seventy-four people were killed immediately, and forty-eight more died in the ensuing weeks from burns or contacts with the toxic and corrosive propellants." Leena bit her lip, her eyes glistening. "Sergei was one of the lucky ones, I suppose, and was consumed by the flames in the initial instants, probably not ever knowing what had happened."

In the protracted silence that followed, Hieronymus reached out a hand, laying it gently on Leena's knee. They sat quietly like that for a long time after.

CHAPTER 29

Shipboard Life

As the days blended slowly into weeks, the ship moving ever southward, the fish man Kakere was slowly transformed. Shedding his robes altogether, he began to spend hours every day in the water in an effort to keep hydrated, coursing along beside the dhow, slowly bringing a healthy blue-green pallor back to his cheeks, the gills behind his ears becoming less swollen and reddish-raw. The paunch and flab that had hung from his belly began to shrink, and he made friends among the crew by bringing up fresh fish and seaweed by the armload for their meals.

Balam and Spatha spent the days sparring on the deck, honing their martial skills. Each was the product of a warrior society, now traveling abroad, and they grudgingly saw in one another a kindred spirit.

During a break in one of their sparring sessions, Balam busied himself over a collection of urchins and fish that Kakere had brought up from the deep. Leena watched as the jaguar man, with a surgeon's skill and patience, carefully cut the fish and urchin into cubes and strips, marinated them in spices and oils, and laid them out on boards polished to a mirror sheen.

"Behold," Balam said triumphantly, beaming at his handiwork. "The bounty of the sea, prepared for you in the style of Drift."

"It looks like raw fish," Leena said, wrinkling her nose.

"It *is* raw fish," Spatha Sekundus said, squatting on her haunches at her side.

"In actual fact," Balam said haughtily, "they are delicacies, and masterfully prepared delicacies, at that."

"Your humility is boundless." Leena smirked across the polished boards at him, her arms crossed.

"And I think thy sense of smell is impaired," Spatha said, pinching the bridge of her nose. "Is it *supposed* to smell like that?"

"Savages." The jaguar man craned his neck, shading his eyes with his hand as he peered up at the crow's-nest atop the mast. "Hero! I've prepared a masterpiece of Driftian cuisine. Come and pay proper homage, to provide an example for these uncivilized women!"

Hieronymus peeked his eyes over the edge of the crow's-nest, and shook his head. "Can't eat!" he shouted back, cupping his hands around his mouth like a megaphone. "Working!"

Balam shook his head, tsk-tsking under his breath. "I think our Hero has quite forgotten how to relax."

"Maybe he just doesn't have a taste for raw fish?" Leena put forth.

"He can probably smell the foul stuff from up there," Spatha said.

The fish man, who'd been underwater for most of the morning, clambered over the side of the dhow, and dumped a net full of seaweed, urchin, and strange deep-sea fish onto the deck, to the delight of the crewmen.

"Kakere's transformation these past days has been nothing short of remarkable," Leena said admiringly.

"They are a strange race, the Ichthyandaro," Balam said, popping a cube of urchin into his mouth and humming appreciatively before continuing. "They have rarely interacted with the other races of metamen, even during the days of the Metamankind Empires. They keep to their submarine existence, and are seen above water most often in port cities, rarely out of sight of the sea."

"And yet they fester in places like Masjid Empor." Spatha spat on the deck planking at her feet. "Spirits are their principal vice. The tolerance for it is not bred in the bone as it is in other species, where a weakness for alcohol makes one more apt to die early and less fit to produce progeny, thus weakening the species. The only Ichthyandaro who imbibe spirits are the drifters and outcasts who leave their people behind, drinking their lives away in port cities as they slowly desiccate their bodies from the inside out."

"Perhaps everyone deserves a chance at redemption," Leena observed. "Even Kakere."

At the mention of his name, the fish man's eyes turned towards them, and he approached them across the deck.

"It is those damned seashell ears," Spatha hissed.

"They're intended to hear underwater calls from leagues away," Kakere said, drawing near. "My hearing is more than sufficient to pick out your words from across this little boat."

"I offer no apology." Spatha looked up at the fish man from beneath knitted brows.

"Nor do I ask for one," Kakere answered. "Nothing you've said was untrue. Drink had nearly killed me before I found myself trapped on this abstemious craft. But I know full well that, were a bottle before my eyes at this very instant, I'd not be able to keep my hands from reaching for it. That I've fallen from grace I cannot contest, but my own life carries little weight." He paused, glancing at the open seas around them. "The heaviest burden to bear is the knowledge that I've disappointed my people, whose numbers dwindle in the deep with every passing generation."

Spatha's eyes had opened wide when Kakere had mentioned disappointing his own people, Leena had noted, and now her face flushed angry and red.

"Enough of this prattle!" Spatha shouted, leaping to her feet. "Come, Sinaa! Spar with me!"

Balam slipped another sliver of fish wrapped in seaweed into his mouth, and shook his head. "I'm eating," he mumbled around a mouthful.

"Spar with me, or be damned!" Spatha shouted back, stomping away across the desk.

Balam shrugged, and shoveled another handful of urchin into his mouth. He dusted off his hands, and climbed slowly to his feet.

"You'll excuse me?" he said to Leena and Kakere, giving a courtly bow from the waist before turning and following Spatha across the deck.

Leena looked to Kakere, an awkward smile on her face.

The fish man watched Spatha's retreating back for a long moment, and then he glanced at Leena with a sorrowful look on his face. Without another word, he took two long strides towards the prow, vaulted over the railing in a smooth arc, and sliced into the water with scarcely a splash.

Leena shrugged, and reached for some of the raw fish on the board. She was hungry enough that she could ill afford to be particular.

High in the rigging overhead, Hieronymus noticed none of it.

Leena sat in the forecastle with Hieronymus, as she did most evenings now, watching clouds roll across the moon. He'd spent his day hard at work, turning his hand to the noisome tasks of the lowly sailor as though he had won some contest, and this was his prized sweepstakes. She'd not seen him happier during all their travels together, and his smile was often infectious. At the end of his long day's labors, his scent was laced with the sweat of his exertions, but Leena found it strangely appealing: an honest, earthy musk.

"The moon . . ." Leena said, and then paused. They'd sat side by side for some time, not speaking, just gazing at the heavens, the only sound the creaking of the rigging and the muffled voices and laughter of the crew belowdecks. In speaking suddenly, Leena felt that she'd shattered some reverie; in silence, the crystalline moment could have lingered on indefinitely, but speaking only dragged them back into the flow of time.

"Yes?" Hieronymus finally said at length, casually.

"It's just . . . ," Leena smiled awkwardly. "It just seems to me that Paragaea's moon is so much smaller than that of Earth. And I fancy that I can see bands of green across its body, punctuated by areas of pale blue."

"Hmmm." Hieronymus nodded thoughtfully. "I've heard legends about the moon. It's said that the wizard-kings of Atla, in unimaginable antiquity, traveled to the moon and transformed it into a living world. I'd always dismissed the stories as stuff and nonsense, sure that living beings could never pierce the vault of heaven. But, having met you . . ." His voice trailed off, and he gestured deferentially towards her.

"We race for the moon, in my own era. Conquering space is only the first stage in a lengthy struggle. Having been first to launch unmanned satellites, then first to launch animals, and then first to launch first men and then women into orbit, the Soviet Union which is my proud home is the most likely to reach the moon before all others. But it is not a certainty. I worry, should the decadent West with whom we vie reach the lunar surface, that they will simply make a giant billboard of the celestial sphere, to better sell products to their spoiled citizenry." She shook her head, an expression of distaste twisting her features. "The American pursues his own arrogant pride and vanity, while the Soviet pursues knowledge."

"And yet you seem quite prideful of your nation's achievements," Hieronymus observed with a slight smile. "But I mean no offense," he hastened to add, seeing her scowl in the low moonlight. He sighed deeply, and turned his gaze back to the moon hanging overhead. "I just cannot fathom the idea of sailing into space, much less the notion that men of my own kind have accomplished such things back on Earth. And so soon after my own age."

Hieronymus turned back to Leena, and their eyes met.

"I envy you the sights you have seen, little sister. The vantage of Earth from so high above, the stars laid out before you like a Persian carpet."

Leena drew a heavy breath, and nodded. "I remember the Earth spinning slowly below me, the mountains and deserts and gray hillocks of ocean swells. The lands all one, the seas all one. And the realization that all boundaries between nations are the artificial constructs of cartographers, and that though imperialist governments keep peoples separated for their own gain, all the Earth's people are one, and that someday we will all be joined together in a single collective with the coming of the Soviet man. It was . . . it was indescribable."

"No," Hieronymus said, drawing near, "I think you describe it quite well."

Their hands brushed against one another, and they drew back fractionally, their fingertips almost touching. Without another word between them, they looked overhead, side by side, and watched the heavens wheel on in silence.

One morning, Leena was on deck, her gaze drifting across the horizon purposelessly. Balam lay a short distance away, stretched out lengthwise on the deck, sunning himself in the bright midday sun.

Spatha came up from below, wearing a linen loincloth and a strophium, a kind of soft leather belt wrapped around her chest holding her breasts in place. She was otherwise unclothed, and likewise unarmed.

"Arise, thou lazy beast," Spatha said, kicking at Balam's head with her bare foot. The jaguar man rolled out of the way just before her kick connected, and growled sleepily. "Rouse thyself."

"What do you want, demon woman?" The Sinaa shaded his eyes with an outstretched hand and regarded Spatha warily.

"To spar, naturally. If we don't keep our wits honed to a razor's edge, how can we possibly be prepared for the travails which life may place in our path?" Spatha crouched down beside him, sitting back on her heels.

"We sparred yesterday, and the day before," Balam moaned. "And besides, I'm quite certain my wits are honed just as sharply as they're going to be. Any sharpness beyond this point would be a needless indulgence."

Spatha's hand snaked forward, quick as lightning, and snatched the emerald pendant hanging from Balam's ear.

"Thy wits could use some sharpening still, it appears." Spatha leapt to her feet, dangling the emerald between her fingers, a sly smile on her face.

In a heartbeat, Balam surged off the deck, lunging forward and grabbing Spatha by the neck with one hand, pincering the hand that held his emerald with the other. His lips curved back over saber-teeth, his eyes flashing, Balam lifted her bodily off the ground, trembling with rage.

"Give. That. Back." The words seethed through the jaguar man's clenched teeth.

Leena jumped to her feet, and watched helplessly as the warrior woman blinked slowly, smiling a broad, incongruous smile.

"Certainly," Spatha managed to hiss through her constricted larynx, and released her hold on the emerald.

As the pendant dropped towards the deck, Balam immediately released his hold on Spatha, and snatched the emerald out of midair.

"I'm . . . sorry." Balam began slowly to regain his composure, and cradled the emerald in his two hands for a moment, looking at it lovingly, before slipping it back into place on his ear.

"I seem to have struck a nerve," Spatha said, rubbing her throat, the marks of Balam's grip standing out like red welts against her dark skin.

"Balam?" Leena stepped forward and laid a tenuous hand on his tensed shoulder. "Are you all right?"

"Yes," Balam answered, with some difficulty. "It is merely . . ." He took a heavy breath. "This gem was once worn by my late wife, Ailuros. When she died, all I had left as proof of our love and time together was this emerald, and our daughter, Menchit. When my cousin Gerjis forced me from the throne of the Sinaa, and drove me from our lands, my daughter was taken from me, to be raised by my sisters, Sakhmet and Bastet. I attempted to take Menchit with me, of course, to prize her from the hands of my scheming cousin and deluded sisters, but the numbers of the faithful Sinaa at their backs were too great, and I was forced to abandon her to their care. My only consolation is the knowledge that my sisters, as misguided as they are, truly love their niece, my daughter, and that among them, at least, she will know safety." He paused, and tapped the emerald at his ear with an outstretched claw. "Were I to lose this gem, though, I would sever my last connection to my lost wife. And that," he said, his gaze darting angrily towards Spatha, "I will not allow."

"My sincere apologies for giving offense," Spatha said, bowing, a smile on her face, "but my compliments on thy attack. Strong, swift, and unexpected. A praiseworthy assault." She dropped into a martial stance and raised her hands before her, in a ready position. "Wouldst thou care to give it another try?"

Balam's lips split in a toothy grin, and without another word he lunged for her. As Spatha parried his attack, using his own momentum to throw Balam to the deck, Leena hurriedly stepped out of the way, and when Balam leapt back to his feet for another attack, Leena was already safely on the other side of the deck.

CHAPTER 30

The Story of Spatha Sekundus

One night at sunset, the company gathered in the captain's cabin for the evening meal. The menu consisted of fish and seaweed, as had all their meals for some weeks, all of them prepared from foodstuffs brought up from the depths by Kakere. On this evening, though, the fish was not prepared in the manner of Drift, but breaded and fried in oils.

"I apologize for the somewhat meager fare aboard the *Acoetes Zephyrus*," Tyrel said expressively, "but we had not yet taken on all our supplies when your arrival forced our somewhat premature departure from Masjid Empor. We've stores enough of necessities to last until our next landfall at Masjid Logos, particularly when supplemented by the daily haulings of our Ichthyandaro here, but we've been forced to do without some delicacies."

"Fortunate, then, that we have a cook of Balam's caliber in our company," Hieronymus said.

Leena mumbled appreciatively in agreement, around a mouthful of fish.

"But you've cooked the taste right out of it," Kakere said, wrinkling his nose in displeasure. His head and hands were bare, but he wore soaked robes wrapped around his torso, arms, and legs.

Balam nodded. "Though I prefer my meat fully cooked, I allow that fish is invariably better served as nature intended, cold and raw, lightly seasoned with oils at best. But I'm afraid our companions don't share our opinions, and so we're forced to make do." Balam gestured with a bandaged hand at the tureen sitting at the middle of the table. "Though perhaps you'd find the seaweed stew more to your liking."

"You've cut yourself?" Benu pointed to Balam's hand. "Is it something that you'd like me to look at? My knowledge of physiology is unparalleled, if you'll excuse the lack of false humility, and perhaps I could help to mend your injury."

"No, it's nothing." Balam shook his head. "Spatha and I were doing a bit of fencing on deck this afternoon, and I was a bit too slow in the riposte, and paid the price for it. It's a minor wound at best, though, and the bandage—and the scar that will no doubt linger—serves only to remind me not to become complacent."

"Thou hast left me a scar or two of my own," Spatha said from across the table, raising her mug in salute. "Those are lessons I'll not soon forget, either."

"That reminds me," Leena said casually, leaning forward with her elbows on the table, her chin propped on her hands. "I've been meaning to ask you about your unusual facial scars." Leena pointed to the symbol carved into Spatha's left cheek. "Does it have some significance? And is there meaning in the fact that your right cheek is unmarred?"

Spatha bristled, eyes narrowed, and her hand tightened on her cutlery in a white-knuckled grip. She opened her mouth and emitted a wordless bellow of rage, and made to lunge across the table at Leena.

"Hold!" Balam shouted, grabbing Spatha's arm and dragging her back into her seat.

Spatha's eyes flashed, and she turned on the jaguar man, her ceramic dinner knife sweeping in a wide arc. The jaguar man's grip on her arm remained firm, and the knife drew no nearer to his chest.

"She is a stranger to our land," Balam said calmly, indicating Leena with a nod of his head. "She doesn't know about the Nonae, nor what your cheek suggests."

"Intent or no, thy companion has given grievous offense," Spatha snarled.

"That is as may be," Hieronymus said from Spatha's other side, on his lips a smile that didn't reach his eyes, "but if you bring harm to any of my friends, I'll be forced to revenge. And no one wants that." He laid a hand on Spatha's shoulder, in a manner far from comradely.

"What *does* her cheek suggest, anyway?" Kakere said with a shrug.

Reluctantly, Spatha nodded, and through gritted teeth said, "Pax." She released her grip on the dinner knife, and it clattered harmlessly to the table.

"My apologies," Spatha said as Balam released his hold on her arm and Hieronymus drew back his hand. "I forget, from time to time, that I travel among barbarous savages, who often know little about my culture." She reached up and touched the unmarred skin of her right cheek. "Thy question," she said, gaze darting grimly to Leena, "touches upon the very reason for my exile from my own people, and the situation that leaves me with no option but to wander the wide world, a warrior without a nation to defend."

Dozens of centuries ago, *Spatha Sekundus said*, after the metamen had broken the back of the Black Sun Empire, but before they rose up and divided the world between the empires of Metamankind, the whole of Paragaea was brought together beneath the banner of the Nonae. The rule of the Nonae, though, lasted no more than a millennium, a brief flickering instant of order and stability, before collapsing under pressure from without and corruption from within.

We Nonae, though, did not fade gracefully into the pages of history like the forgotten nations of the past, nor seal ourselves away like the Black Sun Empire of Atla before us. Pulling back from the farthest reaches of our influence's sphere, we retreated into our arid home in the Eastern Desert, there to train and wait for the next turn of fortune's wheel. We were a nation always mobilized for war, divided into our family cohorts, meeting together only once every turn of the seasons for the Convocation and the exchange of cadets.

Among the Nonae, men and women play an equal role in every aspect of society, whether military, or hunting duties, or the rearing of children. Our offspring are raised in common by elders selected for the task, each child knowing no parent but the cohort itself. The elders, drill paters and drill maters, are responsible for a child's upbringing from infancy until the trials at the end of adolescence, when the child becomes an adult and a full member of a cohort.

Cadets, as all Nonae children are known, are not considered full citizens of the Nonae nation. Only when the cadet has taken and passed the maturation trials at the end of their sixteenth summer can they be accepted as members of the nation. It is at this time that their left cheek is emblazoned with the ix, the sigil of the Nonae. Until the new-made citizen is accepted by a cohort other than the one into which they were born, though, they are not yet adults. These citizen cadets must wait for the Convocation, which tradition demands be held every summer.

Cadets are forbidden from joining the cohort in which they are born, to prevent inbreeding and to ensure that the blood is distributed throughout the Nonae nation. For a man and woman born into the same cohort to lay together and beget a child is the rankest offense to the Nonae sensibility, our gravest taboo.

When I was a child, our drill mater told us about the Convocations of her youth, in which dozens of cohorts would gather together out on the high deserts. The tents of the gathered families would spread as far as thy eye could see, and when the martial trials were held—in which the caputs of each cohort could evaluate the latest crop of cadets, and determine which to invite into their families—the numbers of cadets in the ring numbered in the hundreds, if not even thousands. At the end of the martial trials, the cohorts would barter to exchange the cadets, and at the close of the Convocation the citizen cadets would have the insignia of their new cohort branded onto their right cheeks, signifying that they were now full adults.

When I reached my sixteenth summer, and had the ix burned onto my left cheek, I was the last cadet in my cohort. Our caputs were a pair of ancient men, so enfeebled they could scarcely stand, and aside from them and my drill mater, there were just a handful of men and women, rapidly approaching senescence. The other cadets of my childhood had either fallen to injury or disease, been snatched away by raiders, or had already graduated from cadets to adults when they joined other cohorts.

I was eager to leave the old ones of my birth cohort behind, and find a place for myself in a fresh, virile cohort. But as the months turned into seasons, turned into years, our cohort found no sign of any others in our roaming through the desert wastes. There had not been a Convocation since I'd been just eight summers old, and even then it had been just three cohorts, who exchanged a half-dozen cadets after halfhearted martial trials before disappearing back into the arid wilds.

My drill mater died when I was twenty summers old. One of the caputs when I was twenty-one. By the time I was twenty-three summers old, only three old women and two old men constituted the members of our cohort, not counting myself. And since my right cheek was still unmarred, I did not count, after all. I was not an adult, and not a true member of the Nonae, but was still a citizen cadet at my advanced age. There had not been a Convocation in fifteen summers, and we'd not seen another family of Nonae in almost half that long.

I left my birth cohort before I'd reached twenty-four summers, and made my way to the west. I've traveled around the circumference of the Inner Sea, from the mouth of the river Pison to the shadow of the Lathe Mountains, hiring out my good right arm to whomever can spare the coin. I've soldiered, guarded, bullied, assassinated, and stolen. Whatever ends my employers would have me turn my talents towards, so long as they exercise the martial skills with which I was raised.

The last of my birth cohort may have died in my absence and, for all I know, I might well be the last of the Nonae. A once-great nation, that gathered together all the lands of Paragaea under its banner in the distant reaches of memory, now degraded to one sword for hire, eking out a meager existence at the fringes of barbarous cultures, still a child in the eyes of her vanished people. And when I die, the final indignity will be that I was never a true adult, never a full member of the people who may well live on only as long as I myself do.

CHAPTER 31

Landfall

A t last, their course turned again towards the east, and they approached the southern inlet of the Parousian peninsula. They sailed along with the Parousian coast at their port side for some days, until they reached the point where the shore curved before them before continuing back to the south and west.

"This is the nearest landfall to Keir-Leystall," Tyrel explained to Leena and Hieronymus, who had joined him in the wheelhouse, maps and charts spread before them.

"And if what our companion Benu says is correct," Hieronymus said, pointing to a crosshatched patch of darkness a few finger widths from their current position on the map, "the oracular forest itself can be found there, many days' journey overland to the east."

"Then what are we waiting for?" Leena said, straightening. "I'm ready to be off this tub and on our way."

"You've no time to waste on pleasantries, lassie, which I respect." Tyrel flashed an easy smile, but a scowl lurked at the corners of his mouth. "You're on my ship still, though, and I'll thank you kindly not to impugn the good name of the good ship *Acoetes Zephyrus*."

"She meant no offense, Captain," Hieronymus said, stepping between them and clapping an arm around Tyrel's shoulder. "Your dhow is one of the worthiest vessels upon which I've sailed, and I count it a privilege to have served, if only briefly and by half measures, as one of her crew." Hieronymus skillfully steered Tyrel away from the maps, towards the cabin door, and out onto the deck.

"You're a rank flatterer, lad," Tyrel said with a grin, "but I'll do you the favor of believing every lie. If I was to be forced to smuggle unfortunates from the clutches of the Masjid Emporean constabulary, I consider it my good fortune that one of you, at least, had sea legs beneath you, and did not shrink from a bit of honest work."

Balam and Spatha were resting on the deck, having passed another morning sparring, while Kakere sat looking on in the shadow of the wheelhouse, and Benu calmly studied the horizon.

"Drop anchor," Tyrel called to his crewmen. "And ready my gig, to take our passengers ashore." He turned to the company, and shrugged apologetically. "The draw in these waters is much too shallow for even the *Acoetes Zephyrus*, I'm afraid, so you'll need to go ashore in my gig"—he pointed to a small, clinker-built boat being lowered over the side—"but my crewmen will be at the oars to do the pulling, so you'll need only enjoy the ride until you're on solid ground again."

"Gather up your things, friends," Hieronymus said to the company, motioning them to hurry. "We need waste no more of the good captain's time than we already have."

Balam climbed to his feet, and made for the hatchway, following Benu and Hieronymus, who'd already gone below. He stopped halfway across the deck, and glanced back at Spatha, who still lounged on the deck.

"Sekundus?" Balam called back, waving her to follow. "Are you planning on leaving your armor and arms behind?"

"Hardly," Spatha said. "The answer is simpler. I'm not coming with thee."

"But why?" Leena asked, halfway through the hatch.

"I've no desire to go traipsing through the underbrush, looking for some mythical forest of metal with you lot." Spatha turned her gaze from Leena to Balam. "If thou was to come with me, Sinaa, I'm sure thou would find work as a sword for hire. There are many as would pay handsomely for thy skills."

"I'll not abandon my friends, Sekundus," Balam said darkly, and turned to the hatchway.

"I think I'll just stay onboard, too, if it's all the same to you," Kakere said from the shadows of the wheelhouse.

"I'm afraid, friend Ichthyandaro," Tyrel said, raising his hand, "that whether it is the same to them or not is irrelevant, as what matters in this instance are my desires alone. And my desire is that you all, every one of you, leave my ship at this landfall. And further, I desire that I never see a one of you again, meaning no offense."

"What?" Spatha climbed to her feet and advanced menacingly on the captain. "What is thy meaning, Tyrel?"

"After we stop at Masjid Logos and Masjid Kirkis in the south, our course will carry us eventually northward again, back to Masjid Empor." Tyrel gave a shrug, an unapologetic expression on his face. "I won't have you onboard when I arrive again in a port. I've stuck my neck out far enough as it is, and I won't take on any more trouble on your account, or on account of any of your company." He crossed his arms over his chest, resting them on his ample belly. "You and yours have been the perfect passengers, Spatha Sekundus, and I know there are those in my crew who will be sorry to see you go, friend Kakere, and the bounty of the sea with you, but I've got to do what is in the ship's and the crew's best interests, and sailing any farther with escaped felons on board is in no one's interest."

Leena turned, and climbed belowdecks. The gig was nearly lowered all the way to the water, and it would soon be time for them to leave.

✦

The company rode to the shore in silence, the crewmen pulling at their oars, bearing them ever farther away from the dhow that had been the only refuge they'd known for long weeks. Hieronymus and Leena were in the prow, Balam and Benu in the middle, and Spatha sat in the stern next to Kakere, who was once more wrapped head to toe in his dampened robes. The Nonae muttered excoriations back at Tyrel, while Kakere peered over the gig's side at the blue waters beneath, his expression hidden in folds of damp cloth.

The gig reached a sandy spar, and two of the crewmen jumped out, to haul the gig ashore. Then, they unceremoniously tossed the company's baggage out onto the sands, and stepped aside to stand in the shade and smoke illicit weeds in clay pipes, safely out of the sight of their Meliorist captain. The company climbed gracelessly over the side, and gathered up their packs and bags, tightening their sword belts and holsters, readying themselves for their trek.

"The land seems to swell and rise," Balam said, swaying uneasily.

"You're used to the pitch and yaw of the waves, friend," Hieronymus said with a smile, reaching out a hand to steady the jaguar man. "Your balance has become accustomed to the sea, and it'll take a short while for you to get your land legs back beneath you."

"If you think *this* is bad," Leena said, grimacing, "you should try walking after being in orbit for a few hours, and see how bad your balance is *then*."

✦

When they'd finished smoking through their bowls, the crewmen returned to the gig, pushed off into the waves, and rowed back to the waiting dhow.

"Let's push ahead," Hieronymus said, making for the tree line.

The green of the canopy, after the unbroken blue of the ocean and the sky above, was shocking to Leena's eyes. These trees, with their twisting, branching trunks, were shorter than those of the jungles and forests to the west, rising no more than ten meters from the sandy ground. The ground beneath the trees was damp, and Leena's boots squelched in the thin layer of sandy mud.

"These are mangroves," Hieronymus said as he climbed through a gnarled twist of branches and trunks. "I saw similar in the equatorial regions of Earth, in my days in His Majesty's Navy. There'll be tidal channels and waterways throughout, making the going that much slower."

"The sooner we get through this mess and onto solid ground," Balam said, "the better."

They came through a copse of trees and stood at the shores of a wide waterway that ran inland from the sea.

"I'm tired already," moaned Kakere, his voice muffled by his damp robes.

"Thou could leave at any moment," Spatha spat, "and save us all the burden of thy company."

"Would that I could," the Ichthyandaro answered, and pointed at a shadow beneath the sapphire-blue waters of the tidal channel.

"What is that?" Leena asked, coming to stand beside him.

"I'm not sure," Kakere answered, "but it's big, and I'm willing to lay odds it would like nothing more than to eat a tasty Ichthyandaro like me. I saw a school of them coursing along beside the boat that rowed us from the ship. These waters must be teeming with them. I couldn't return to the seas here if I wanted to." His shoulders seemed to move beneath the robes, which Leena read as a shrug. "So I've no choice but to come along, it appears."

"Oh, blessed joy," Spatha said, rolling her eyes. She turned to the east, and began to walk along the edge of the waterway. "Well, come along," she called back to the company over her shoulder, her hand resting on her baldric. "The sooner we get through this mess the better, right?"

Leena glanced over at Balam and Hieronymus, who only shrugged, and then turned to follow the Nonae deeper into the mangrove swamp.

By nightfall, they'd still not reached the edge of the mangrove swamp, though they'd forded a number of narrower streams and waterways since that morning. With the light dimming to the east, they sought out the highest land they could find to make camp for the night.

"We'll just have to hope that the tide doesn't reach this high," Hieronymus said when they'd found a likely spot, a high plateau at the end of a narrow isthmus, separated from the mainland by waterways only a meter or so across, "or at least that it comes in late enough in the day that we'll already be up and on our way when it arrives."

"Don't the tides come in regularly with the morning light?" Leena asked. "I thought Tyrel had mentioned that."

"Perhaps," Benu said thoughtfully. "Though the Paragaean tides have become somewhat erratic in recent millennia. I've often thought it a result of the slow recess of the moon from the planet, and the attendant irregularity in the lunar tidal forces." He glanced around them, where driftwood and creeping vines dotted the sandy ground beneath the twisted mangrove trees. "It might be a mistake to count on the regularity of duration or extent of the tides in this region."

"As for me," Balam said, yawning, "I just want to get some food in my belly, and a few hours' sleep behind my eyes. Anything else is of secondary concern."

"So long as thou cook it," Spatha said, dropping into a crouch, "whatever meat it is, that is fine with me."

✦

Leena slept fitfully, if at all, kept awake by the sounds of the mangrove swamps. Strange birds called from the near distance, an endless cacophony of sounds, and in the small hours of the morning a symphony of chattering began to issue from the canopy above them, which in the firelight proved to come from a band of small, lemurlike creatures that hooted and jeered at one another throughout the hours of the night.

She felt as though she had just fallen asleep when she felt herself being shaken forcefully awake. She opened her eyes on the gray predawn light, and saw Balam standing over her, a worried look on his leonine face.

"We've got a problem," he said, fangs bared. "Several, in fact."

✦

Leena joined the others standing at the water's edge. The spar of land over which they'd walked the night before to reach their campground was now completely submerged, the tide rising higher as the waves lapped at the trunks of the mangrove trees.

"We're surrounded," Spatha said, like a soldier reporting battle-front conditions to an officer. "The rising tide has cut off access to the isthmus, and the waterways surrounding us are now too wide to cross without swimming."

"Our isthmus of yesterday is our island of this morning," Hieronymus said philosophically.

"I *hate* swimming," Balam said, snarling.

"I wouldn't worry too much about it," Kakere said, and pointed to shadows prowling the waterway before them, dimly visible in the low light. The waterways, only a meter across the night before, now spanned three meters and more. "There's more of those . . . things . . .

whatever they are. You wouldn't make it more than a few lengths before they started nibbling on you."

"Okay," Leena said calmly. "So we can't leave by land, and we can't leave by water." She glanced around, her gaze taking in all of her companions, looking for consent. When she didn't get it, she went on anyway. "So we just wait it out here, until the tide recedes. Worst-case scenario we could always climb into the trees, right?"

"Except," Balam said, pointing back towards the center of their new island, "I think they are able to climb, too." Leena looked the way he indicated, and then glanced back at the jaguar man, horrified. "Remember," Balam continued, "that I said 'several' problems."

Pouring from burrows all around them, which had gone unnoticed in the dark of the previous night, came giant ants the size of overfed hummingbirds, clacking vicious mandibles, driven from their homes by the rising tide.

"Der'mo," Leena swore, reverting to Russian.

✦

Overhead, the lemur-creatures chattered, hurling abuse down at them, while around their feet swarmed the giant ants, which they fended off with burning brands lit from their campfire. But most of the wood in reach was damp, and only sparked and smoked weakly before extinguishing, so they could not count on the heat of the torches for long.

"We need to think of something soon," Leena said, waving her torch at the hundreds of ants who crowded at her feet.

"Do you have any suggestions?" Hieronymus asked over his shoulder, warding off the ants with a torch in one hand, swiping off their heads with his saber in the other.

It was near full daylight now, the sun glowing ruddy gold through the branches to the east.

"Not being eaten would be a good start," Leena said.

At that moment, there came from across the waterway the sound of voices raised, and Leena looked up to see a collection of crocodile men atop enormous flightless birds, who milled on the opposite bank. Before she'd had time to register this unexpected sight, a number of the crocodile men spurred their mounts, who crouched low momentarily and then leapt into the air, propelled across the rising waters by massive legs, their tiny wings used only for balance. The enormous birds landed squarely among the company, beaks snapping.

"I think our odds of that just worsened," Hieronymus replied, eyeing the bird riders darkly.

Standing more than three meters tall, the enormous birds whipped their vicious, snapping beaks from side to side, trampling the giant ants underfoot, while in their saddles the crocodile men's long snouts split in toothy grins as they eyed the company hungrily.

CHAPTER 32

The Tannim

Balam and Spatha did not wait to exchange words with the interlopers, but sprang immediately into action. Balam leapt high in the air, claws out and fangs bared, tackling one of the crocodile men around his waist and dragging him from his mount, while Spatha drew her gladius and lay about her with its blade, scoring wicked cuts at the arms and legs of the two crocodile men nearest her, taking out hunks of the bird mount's flesh as she went.

Hieronymus drew his saber, and Leena her short sword, but they hung back, watchful, as Benu and Kakere lingered behind them, their attentions still on the giant ants underfoot.

Balam grappled with one of the crocodile men, rolling back and forth across the sandy ground, the crocodile man's teeth gnashing as he bit at Balam's head and hands, Balam's claws cutting red rills into the crocodile man's warty flesh.

Spatha, meanwhile, contended with two of the crocodile men, both scored by her blade, who had climbed from their mounts and now menaced her with long spears tipped with points of chipped black glass. One of the crocodile men thrust forward with his spear, and Spatha handily batted it to one side with her gladius; but when the other lunged forward shortly after, his own spear tip grazed Spatha's arm, glancing off the bracer covering her forearm, but drawing a wicked line from her elbow up to her shoulder, where it caught on the edge of her cuirass. Spatha swung about, but with the force of the spear thrust throwing her shoulder back, she spun out of true, and her gladius whistled harmlessly through the air, striking nothing. As the first crocodile man stepped forward, though, hands grasping and teeth snapping ferociously, Spatha quickly riposted, swinging her blade backhanded in a wide arc, and opened the crocodile man's belly from side to side.

Spatha turned from the crocodile man who now clutched his belly, endeavoring to hold blood and viscera in, and directed her attention at the other crocodile man, who advanced on her warily, with his glass-tipped spear raised. Balam, only a short distance away, still rolled in the bloodied sand with another of the crocodile men. Throughout the brief melee, another of the crocodile men, larger than any of these, had remained in the saddle, watching the proceedings with interest.

"Why aren't the others attacking?" Leena said to Hieronymus, indicating the half-dozen or so other mounted crocodile men who milled at the far side of the growing waterway. "They could cross the distance as easily as these four, and make short work of us."

"Has it escaped your notice that Balam and Spatha Sekundus attacked first?" Hieronymus asked, raising an eyebrow.

Before Leena could respond, the air was split by the sound of bellowing laughter as the mounted crocodile man before them rumbled with amusement.

"Stand down!" the laughing crocodile man shouted in accented Sakrian, waving towards his three fellows who faced off against Balam and Spatha. "You, too, outlanders," the crocodile man went on, an imperious tone in his gravelly voice. "Belay your attacks. No harm will come to you, if you do no more harm to my Tannim."

The two crocodile men before Spatha stepped back, the one lowering his spear and the other still clutching his sliced belly, while the one rolling with Balam in the sand scuttled away, to climb to his feet and go stand beside his fellows.

Balam and Spatha, uncertainly, moved to stand beside the others of their company.

"We come not to attack you," the vicious-looking crocodile man said from atop his mount, "but to rescue you!"

He laughed again, his barrel chest shaking with the booming noise.

"Mount up, Tannim," he ordered the three crocodile men standing before him. "Nuga, help Cheti into the saddle"—he pointed to the crocodile man holding his belly—"and we'll be away."

The crocodile man turned to the company, and his snout split in an unsettling expression that vaguely resembled a smile.

"Climb aboard our terror birds, and we shall bear you to safety." He pointed a talon across the waterway, where more of the mounted crocodile men waited. "When we are safely away from this shrinking sandbar, we'll introduce ourselves more properly. Yes?"

The company looked at one another, warily, and finally Hieronymus shrugged.

"I don't suppose we have much choice," he said with a faint smile. Then he turned and in a low voice said to Leena, "Out of the frying pan, at least?"

$$\star$$

Once they were safely on dry land, introductions were made all around. Hieronymus introduced all of the company in turn, pausing only when attempting to explain how it was that the six of them had come to travel together. The lead crocodile man greeted them as warmly as one with such a fearsome appearance could manage.

"It is a pleasure to meet you all," he said, "and allow me to welcome you to the lands of the Tannim. We were on a hunting expedition, to bring fresh meat home to our township for a celebration this evening, when we chanced to see your distress across the way. It is not uncommon that travelers and wayfarers will find themselves trapped by the rising or the falling of the Parousian tides, which seem often to have a mind of their own."

"Falling tides?" Leena asked, confused. "How could one be trapped by receding water?"

"If you lived in the water," Kakere said at her side, "you could well be trapped on a sandbar as the water beneath you rushed out unexpectedly to sea."

"Just so, Ichthyandaro," the leader of the Tannim said, dipping his long snout in a show of respect. "It is not uncommon to find seadwellers cast up on the shores of the swamps as the tide rolls out, and from time to time, we Tannim make a nice meal of them."

The Tannim behind their leader snickered from atop their mounts, but if Kakere took offense at the comment, his reaction was hidden beneath the folds of his robes.

"In any event, I am Sebek, and these here with me are the elite riders of the terror birds, handpicked from my township to join me on this hunt."

The company looked around them uneasily, as on their mounts the ferocious-looking Tannim towered full meters above them.

"You look stricken, my friends," Sebek said, chuckling. "You act as though you have never seen a Tannim before." He turned to Balam, waving his arm expansively. "Come, my metaman brother, surely you are familiar with your crocodile cousins?"

"I know of your people, Sebek," Balam said guardedly, "but I have never met one of the Tannim in person."

"I visited the townships of the Tannim," Benu said, raising his hand, "if that's of any assistance. But that was many centuries ago, and then only briefly."

"Well," Sebek said, clapping his hands. "Whatever your feelings at our initial meeting, know that we Tannim are no threat to you. We are always glad to see outlanders, as our remote townships so seldom get visitors. And I was so impressed by the martial displays of your Sinaa and his woman on the sandbar that I would like to welcome you to our township as honored guests at our fete this very evening."

"I am *no* one's woman," Spatha said, glowering beneath her knitted brows.

"Charming," Sebek said, teeth bared in a crocodilian smile.

The morning journey through the mangrove swamp was almost like a strange, fevered dream. Each of the company rode pillion behind one of the Tannim, atop the massive terror birds. With their long necks and powerful legs, the birds were able to cover distance with an alarming speed, even over such difficult and irregular terrain as that found in the mangrove swamp. The long strides of the terror birds produced a kind of rocking motion that lulled the riders into a torpor, but when combined with the heat of the morning and the piquant smell of the fresh kill strapped before each rider's saddle, the result was a kind of unsettling miasma that clouded the thoughts and left one feeling uneasy.

They came upon the Tannim township where the mangrove swamp met the dry land of the coastal plains. It was a small village of low, round-topped structures, none standing more than four or five meters tall, arranged in a semicircular arc around a central clearing, in which the preparations for the night's festivities were already under way. The townspeople were surprised to see their hunters arrive with visitors as well as fresh meat, but not alarmed, and they welcomed the company with open arms.

Once they had recovered from the torpor of their morning ride, the company quickly found their footing, and soon discovered that their hosts were not nearly so alarming as their ferocious mien might suggest. For all their terrifying appearance, they were a boisterous, affable people, and the company was quickly put at their ease. Soon even Spatha was lounging in the plaza, sipping on fermented fruit juices and laughing at the hunting stories of their Tannim hosts. Kakere, for his part, eyed the spirits with obvious thirst, but managed to forbear.

Leena had cause to doubt their good fortune. There had been, in her experiences traveling across the face of Paragaea, no unalloyed joys, and she found that she invariably expected some adversity to follow close on the heels of any fortuitous turn. With the fall of night, though, the fete began, and still the sky had not fallen in on them, and Leena began to relax. Perhaps this night would be an exception to the rule, and they would pass a few relaxing hours in the company of these pleasant folks, and then continue on to their goal rested and rejuvenated.

Then, when the main course had been served and consumed— some kind of large river rodent, similar to a capybara—Sebek called for the night's entertainment to be brought forth, and a pair of Tannim rushed into the darkness, to return a short while later with a wheeled platform, on which rested a dolphin. Its fins and flukes were cropped back, and its back was covered in crisscrossed white scar tissue, and only the buckets of water its handlers dumped onto it from time to time kept it from dehydrating completely.

The dolphin, it transpired, had been trained to perform tricks on command. And so, in response to orders from its handlers, the dolphin rose up on its belly, or jabbed its snout comically in the air in a mock duel with one of its handlers, or else barked out a rough semblance to a popular Tannim folk tune through its blowhole. The performance lasted for the better part of an hour, while the dolphin quietly whimpered between each trick, moaning piteously.

The Tannim clattered their teeth—their form of applause—uproariously at every cavorting move of the dolphin, while the company looked on somewhat uncomfortably, whispering to one another behind their hands, except for Kakere, who sat in stock silence, eyes smoldering behind the folds of his damp robes.

CHAPTER 33
A Prisoner's Reprieve

With the conclusion of the fete, the company was escorted to apartments in one of the round-topped structures that ringed the clearing.

"Consider these apartments yours for as long as you need them," Sebek said as one of his Tannim started a fire in a pit at the center of the common room. The room was ringed by five doors leading to small chambers, separated by hanging curtains of beads.

"Your hospitality is most appreciated," Hieronymus said, bowing slightly. "We'll most likely be on our way with the morning's first light, but the prospect of sleeping indoors tonight is an appealing one."

"Particularly if we don't have to worry about rising tides or advancing armies of giant ants," Balam added, grimacing.

"Is there anything else you require?" the fire-lighting Tannim asked deferentially.

"No, I think we should have everything we need," Leena answered.

"In that case," Sebek said, clacking his teeth together with a note of finality, "we'll leave you to your rest." With that, he and the other Tannim turned, and strode back into the night.

"Mannerly for such fearsome-seeming creatures, aren't they?" Benu observed, pacing the circumference of the room.

"Thou shouldn't be fooled." Spatha watched the doorway through narrowed eyes. "Our hosts may be properly schooled in manners, but they also have been quite well trained in the arts martial. The two I fought in the mangrove might have done for me, had they their better wits about them." She paused, and turned to look at Benu with an accusing glare. "To speak of which, why didst thou not come to our aid, artificial man? I saw proof of thy strength in Masjid Empor, when thou clunked two constables insensate to the ground. Were thy attentions better served elsewhere while the Sinaa and I earned our new wounds?"

Benu shrugged. "You seemed to have matters well in hand. I suppose if things had taken a fatal turn, I could have intervened. But as it was, I was fascinated by the giant ants which swarmed out of their burrows. I found their level of organization and coordination remarkable. I've long known that ants communicate not only by brushing antennae, but by secreting pheromones that drift on the air, but I'd never before seen such a coordinated attack on such a large scale, over such a short span of time. It was almost as if—"

"I'm sure this is fascinating to someone," Balam said, stretching his arms to either side as his face split with an enormous yawn, "but I for one am for bed."

"As am I," Hieronymus said, unbuckling his sword belt and swinging his pack off his back. He parted one of the beaded curtains with his hand, and glanced over his shoulder as he ducked through into the chamber. "Pleasant sleep, all. And may the only giant ants we encounter tonight be in our dreams, at worst."

Benu shrugged, and took a seat near the fire pit. "I needn't occupy one of the rooms to rest my systems," he said, "so the rest of you may take a sleeping chamber apiece."

Spatha did not respond, but slipped her baldric off her shoulders and disappeared through one of the curtains. Balam made for another, and Leena paused for a moment, glancing over at Kakere.

The Ichthyandaro had not spoken since the fete, not since the night's "entertainment" had been wheeled out. Now he lingered by the open door, glancing out into the night.

"Kakere?" Leena asked. "Is there anything the matter?"

The fish man turned around, his expression unreadable through the folds of his robes. "No, nothing," he said, his voice muffled. "Just . . . just going for a walk."

Leena shrugged. "Suit yourself," she said, and stepped into the remaining sleeping chamber as Kakere slipped out into the darkness.

Leena lay on a woven mat within the sleeping chamber, firelight filtered through the beaded curtain playing on the ceiling and walls. Her arms, legs, and neck ached, as they seemed to always do these days. Since they had left Laxaria, long months before, she had been in constant motion, whether by foot, or airship, or horseback, or ship. Always moving, but in her darker moments, she feared that she was only running in place, and that all of her exertions were not bringing her any closer to home. Would she wander the wide world of Paragaea for endless years, as Hieronymus seemed content to do, never returning to fulfill her duty?

The firelight danced on the ceiling overhead, and when Leena finally closed her eyes and drifted off to sleep, she dreamt of flames.

Leena awoke to shouts of alarm, out in the township. She leapt to her feet and, grabbing her sword belt and holstered Makarov, raced out into the common room. She had been asleep for only a few hours, and through the open door she could see that it was still full dark outside.

Benu was on his feet, standing near the entrance and peering out into the darkness intently, and as Leena rushed to stand beside him, Balam, Hieronymus, and Spatha issued forth from their sleeping chambers to join them. All of them, Leena included, were barefoot and in various stages of undress, but all were armed and ready for action.

"What are we looking at, Benu?" Hieronymus asked, hand on his saber's hilt.

"I'm not certain," Benu answered, glancing over his shoulder, his opalescent eyes glittering like gems in the firelight. "First came a single voice, shouting for someone to stop, and then sounds of violence, and shortly after a half-dozen or so voices calling out for assistance."

Spatha glanced around the common room, her gladius drawn and in her hand. "Where is the fish?"

Leena looked from Spatha back to the open door. "He stepped out when we all went off to sleep. He said he wanted to take a walk."

"Well, his walk hasn't yet brought him back here," Benu said.

"That is an unpleasant sign," Balam grumbled, popping the claws of his hands, retracting them, and then extending them again nervously.

"Thou hast said a mouthful." Spatha scowled, tightening her grip on the gladius.

"Come on." Hieronymus pushed past them, hurrying into the night, leaving his saber sheathed but with his hand still resting on the hilt.

They followed the shouts, and came upon a crowd of Tannim gathered a few meters beyond the arc of buildings, a short distance from the pens where the terror birds were kept. Flickering torchlight lit the scene, casting dancing shadows on the ferocious countenances of the crocodile men.

At the center of the jostling crowd, they found Kakere, standing unrobed and naked in front of a glassed-in case. At the fish man's feet lay the fallen form of a young Tannim, while in the case the still form of the dolphin floated in blood-clouded waters.

Kakere looked about him, his black eyes wide and frightened, as the Tannim called for his blood.

"What is the meaning of this?" Sebek called out, joining the throng. His hungry gaze took in the scene in an instant, and then his eyes settled on the face of the Tannim lying lifeless in the dirt at Kakere's feet. "Sobek," he said in a quiet voice, his toothy mouth clenched tight.

"Kakere!" Hieronymus said, stepping forward and interposing himself between the Ichthyandaro and the mob pressing ever closer. "What transpired here?"

Kakere looked from Hieronymus, to the lifeless dolphin in the red-stained water, to the jostling mob of crocodile men, and back.

"He told me to do it, you see?" the fish man began. "I came to speak with him, to join him in the water and exchange sounds as his kind and mine have done beneath the waves since time immemorial. He told me he'd been captured in his youth, beached on a sidebar by the retreating tide, and found by a company of Tannim hunters."

Kakere's eyes flashed angrily for a moment, and he looked around him at the gathered throng, kept from attacking the fish man only by reproachful glances from their leader, Sebek, who it appeared wanted to hear Kakere's testimony before proceeding.

"The Tannim kept him in bondage all the years since," Kakere went on, looking back sorrowfully at the state of the dolphin in the tank. "His fluke and fins crippled by his cruel handlers, he knew he could never survive again on the open seas, and that escape was not an option. So he begged me to release him from his torments."

Kakere held up a bone-handled knife, of the type used by the crewmen aboard the *Acoetes Zephyrus*, its blade slicked with blood.

"And Sobek?" the leader of the Tannim said in a faraway voice, pointing to the dead crocodile man on the ground.

"Oh," Kakere said absently, and looked at the bloody form at his feet. "It was . . . I didn't mean to hurt . . . He came upon me as I was carrying out my grisly task, and . . . Well, I *had* to kill him, in order to finish matters with the dolphin."

"You . . ." Sebek began, and his words choked off in his throat. "You killed my nephew Sobek in order to euthanize a dumb beast?"

At this, the Tannim whose numbers swelled by the moment began to howl for Kakere's blood. One of them, bolder or more impetuous than the rest, pushed past Leena and Balam, rushing towards Kakere with murder in his black eyes.

"No!" Spatha leapt in front of the charging Tannim, taking out a slice of his shoulder with her gladius as she moved past him.

Spatha landed in the dirt before Kakere, the point of her gladius held high, crouching in a martial stance.

The Tannim whom she'd nicked gripped his wounded shoulder and bellowed with rage as two more rushed forward from the crowd, talons out and grasping. Spatha dealt one of the two newcomers a ringing blow to the head with the flat of her blade as the other tackled her to the ground.

"Spatha!" Leena shouted as Balam and Hieronymus charged forward. But before either of them could reach Spatha's side, the Tannim with whom she wrestled had clamped his vicious jaws on her shoulder and neck, and when he pulled away, her side was left a red ruin from her jawline to her upper arm.

Balam hauled the Tannim to his feet, his jaws dripping red with gore from Spatha's wound, while Hieronymus stood astride Spatha's supine form, turning his blade's point to the other two Tannim, who even now were regaining their footing.

"Cease fighting!" Sebek called out, his voice booming. "Stand down."

The Tannim immediately backed away, stepping back into the circle of Tannim who thronged about the scene. Balam kept in a ready stance, his eyes wary and watchful, while Hieronymus knelt at Spatha's side to check on the extent of her wounds.

"Your woman's wounds are doubtless fatal," Sebek said to Hieronymus, stepping forward, "and she will not live to see another nightfall. And so the blood debt of Sobek, my own nephew, has been paid." He turned to Spatha, who lay bleeding into the sandy ground. "The Tannim that you marked will survive, and will carry their scars as a lesson never to underestimate an opponent." He took a step back, his gaze encompassing the whole company. "You are free to go. But know this. The hospitality of the Tannim is at an end, and if any of you are seen again in the vicinity, our next meeting will not be as cordial."

CHAPTER 34

Triage

Leena and Benu were sent to retrieve the company's articles from the apartments, and by the time they returned, Hieronymus and Balam had constructed a rough stretcher upon which to carry the moaning form of Spatha Sekundus. Kakere, meanwhile, had retrieved his robes from the ground beside the glassed-in case, and dressed himself, the robes now stained faint red by the blood-soaked waters of the tank.

Leena checked her pack while Hieronymus pulled on his boots, and Balam strapped on his harness and secured his pack on his back. The crowd of Tannim had thinned, most of them following Sebek as he carried the lifeless body of his departed nephew away from the scene, but some still lingered on, casting angry glances at the company. If they were not away quickly, there might still be additional bloodshed, despite Sebek's orders to the contrary.

"I'm ready to go as soon as you are," Leena said impatiently as Hieronymus and Balam positioned themselves at the head and the foot of Spatha's stretcher. As they lifted her slowly into the air, Spatha coughed, a sick, sputtering sound racking her chest as blood-flecked foam collected at the corners of a mouth twisted in agony. The rough compress of shirts and blankets Benu had wrapped around her ruined shoulder and neck was already soaked through, glistening black with blood in the flickering firelight.

"Let's go," Balam said urgently.

"You'll get no argument from me." Hieronymus glanced over at Kakere, who stood now clad in his robes, but with his head and neck bare. The fish man's expression was confused, disoriented, his eyes lingering on the mangled corpse of the dolphin in the tank, and on the bloodstained sand at his feet. "Kakere," Hieronymus went on gently. "Let's be away from here, shall we?"

Kakere nodded absently, and followed along as Leena led the company out into the humid night, away from the township and into the wilderness.

✦

Once they had journeyed far enough from the township that they felt comfortable stopping for a brief span, the company took the opportunity to check on the full extent of Spatha's injuries. Benu was motioned over to inspect her wounds by firelight, after Hieronymus had lit a fire in a small clearing.

"The news is bad," Benu said after a few moments, "but not quite so grim as the Tannim leader seemed to believe. Spatha's injuries are fatal, no doubt, but her remaining lifespan can be measured in days, not in hours."

As he spoke, Spatha seemed to rouse, murmuring through twisted lips. The company gathered around as she slowly opened one eye.

"Not . . ." the Nonae said, her voice straining. "Not dead . . . yet."

Kakere stepped forward, and bent low over Spatha.

"Why?" the Ichthyandaro asked. "Why suffer these wounds for my sake?"

"Because . . ." Spatha began, before she was cut off by another coughing fit. Pink spittle foamed at the corners of her mouth, but when Kakere began to pull away, she reached out and grabbed the hem of his robe, dragging him back down to her level. "I was . . . ashamed . . . not to have acted as thou had done. I know"—she coughed again, her whole body trembling, and her nose began to bleed—"what it is like . . . to be imprisoned by circumstance, kept apart from . . . one's own kind."

Spatha's eyes closed, and her head lolled to one side.

"Is she . . . ?" Kakere said in a reverential voice, looking up at Benu. "Is she . . . dead?"

"Do you doubt my diagnostic skills so readily?" Benu shook his head. "No, of course she's not dead. I just said she had days left to live. She's just lost consciousness again. No doubt her system is in shock, due to trauma and loss of blood. However, there's little to nothing we can do about her injuries in the wilderness, and we must find some civilization if we're to prevent her inevitable death."

"We press on to Keir-Leystall," Hieronymus said, straightening. "As the oracular forest is said to hold all knowledge, perhaps it will know the secret of healing Spatha's wounds."

Hieronymus looked from one to another of his companions, as if seeking consent or disagreement, but if anyone had a better idea, they kept it to themselves.

The company continued on, leaving behind the mangrove swamps, tidal channels, and alluvial plains of the coastal regions and moving into a lightly forested zone. By midday, though, they'd traveled no more than a few hundred meters, progress made difficult due to the

preponderance of boiling pools of mud scattered through the landscape.

"What is that stench?" Balam said as he lowered Spatha's stretcher
to the ground, once they'd found a dry spot to exchange positions. He
and Benu stepped away from the stretcher as Hieronymus and Kakere
stepped forward to take their shifts.

Leena sniffed the air, and wrinkled her nose in disgust. The air
stank of rotten eggs, or flatulence.

"Sulfur, if I'm not mistaken," Benu answered, "and I'm not. These
hot pools of mud must be evidence of volcanic activity, not far below
the surface, the bubbling we see the product of escaping volcanic gases."

"Well, *I* think it's disgusting," Balam said, pinching his nose shut
with a thumb and forefinger.

"It could well be worse than disgusting," Benu said, following
Leena as she led the company deeper into the forest. "If the gas levels
grow sufficient to drive out the breathable oxygen, the smell of the
gases which asphyxiate you will be the least of your concerns."

✦

They had gone another few kilometers through the burbling pools of
mud, and had just passed a small lake of brackish water, when from
behind them came a loud popping noise. Balam suddenly stopped
short, sniffed the air, and shouted.

"Run!"

Without another word, the jaguar man took to his heels, sprinting
up the forest track ahead of them as fast as his legs would carry him.

The company didn't waste any time in discussion, but followed as
quickly as they could, Hieronymus and Kakere struggling with the
awkward load of the stretcher, Leena sprinting full out, and Benu following at the speed of a brisk walk, taking his time.

Leena chanced a glance back over her shoulder and saw the multi-form denizens of the forest racing after them: birds, small lizardlike dinosaurs, and large mice the size of capybaras. Leena raced a few more dozen meters, then glanced back again and saw Benu calmly studying the fallen forms of the small creatures, scattered around him and lying unmoving on the ground.

✦

Dizzy and lightheaded, the company gathered at the shores of a narrow, paved stream. They'd run flat out for several kilometers, and all of them were out of breath. Only Benu had lagged behind, and as they fought to catch their breath, chests burning and leg muscles aching, he casually strolled out of the forest, whistling tunelessly.

"It is nice to see proof that the olfactory capacities of the Sinaa are not overestimated," Benu said, smiling at Balam, who wheezed on the ground, tongue lolling.

"What . . ." Hieronymus began, panting. "What was that?"

"A cloud of poisonous gas," Benu answered simply, kneeling in the dust before them, "issuing from beneath that small lake we passed. If Balam hadn't given us early warning, I'm afraid all of you would have asphyxiated as quickly as the smaller organisms who fell in the cloud's wake. As it was, you were able to keep just ahead of the cloud as it spread and, now that it's been dissipated, you should be in no further danger."

"You didn't appear to be in any hurry," Leena said, rubbing her inflamed calf muscles.

"Why should I have been?" Benu answered. "After all, *I* don't have to breathe, now do I?"

The company, once rested, forded the paved stream, and as they continued on, the volcanic pools and small copses of trees gave way to wide
plains of stone. It was as if an entire prairie had been paved over in
cement, untold millennia before. No blade of grass nor flower nor scrub
brush grew here, only the ancient stone rising in slight waves and val-
leys, broken into archipelagos of shattered rock by the passage of time.

They moved through the desert of stone for two nights and two
days, eating and drinking only what they carried in their packs, seeing
nothing but gray sky and gray stone ground, until at last, they reached
the periphery of the forest of Keir-Leystall.

CHAPTER 35

The Oracular Forest of Keir-Leystall

"**W**hat *are* they?" Leena said in a low voice. Less than half a kilometer from them, across the final stretch of broken pavement, stood what appeared to be a hedge of large metal bushes.

"Little sister," Hieronymus said, wonderstruck, "your guess is as good as mine."

"Benu," Balam said from his position at the foot of Spatha's stretcher. "You have been here before. What, exactly, are we looking at?"

As they drew nearer, the strange metal objects came slowly into focus.

"They are the trees of Keir-Leystall, of course," the artificial man answered simply. "Once, in ancient days, the long-forgotten culture of Keir-Leystall was a satellite of Atla in the far south, as was Hele in the Lethe Mountains to our south, and Scere beyond the Rim Mountains to the west. In days of unimaginable antiquity, the people of Keir-Leystall mastered the art of duplicating a man's mind, and recreating it in a machine. Similar skills were used in my own forging, I hasten to point out. And the ancients of Keir-Leystall further mastered the art

267

of fashioning mechanical devices so fine that they could manipulate the
very particles that make up matter itself. At some point, as their culture aged to senescence, these two arts were combined in the creation
of the oracular forest. History has forgotten whether the men and
women whose minds were uploaded into the fractal robots were prisoners, patients, or priests, and whether they were being imprisoned,
cured, or saved."

Balam sneered, regarding the metal structures as the company
drew nearer their goal. "Why doesn't someone just ask the trees which
it was? Don't they hold all knowledge?"

"Well, you could try," Benu replied thoughtfully, "but the answers
could not be trusted. The trees, you see—at least those who have not
retreated from all interaction with the outside world, about whom
nothing can be known—are all quite mad."

"And we come here to find the way to Earth?" Leena asked. "To ask
these insane beings for answers?"

"I never said you were certain to find the knowledge you seek,
Akilina," Benu said. "I merely said that the answers you seek, if they
are to be found anywhere in Paragaea, are to be found here."

They had, by this point, neared the forest close enough that they
could begin to make out details of the "trees" before them. They did
indeed look like large metal bushes that grew upwards from the
ground, branching into three branches at intervals, standing about
four meters tall. At the tips of the branches, the air seemed hazy and
indistinct, as though the branches continued to exfoliate smaller than
the eye could see.

Without warning, when they were within a few meters of the
nearest tree, the air around them buzzed with a sound like the voice of
a swarm of bees. The nearest tree vibrated in time with each syllable.
"What do you want?"

Hieronymus stepped forward, and opened his mouth to speak, but
before he could answer, the strange voice buzzed again.

"One of you is damaged." There came a pause, and the metal tree shimmered slightly. *"Would the damaged one be repaired? It is within our power to effect this change."*

"Yes," several of the company quickly said in unison. Balam and Kakere stepped forward, set the stretcher down on the ground at the base of the tree, and then retreated to the rear of the group.

"Very well."

The branches of the metal tree twitched, and then began to ripple slowly as if plied by a slight wind. Leena felt a whisper on her cheek, like someone had just run past her.

The company looked down at the supine form of Spatha, but she still lay broken and bloodied on the stretcher, unchanged.

"Um, guys?" came the voice of Kakere from behind them.

Leena turned, and saw Kakere standing naked, his robe reduced to powder that dusted the pavement at his feet. He held his hands out at arm's length to either side, his expression bewildered. His skin had a bluer cast to it than normal, though he seemed otherwise unchanged.

"This one had an unnecessary dependence on hydration, a faulty design. We have improved the model, and this one will be much more efficient hereafter."

"No," Kakere said, stepping forward, pleading. "Not me! Repair her!" The fish man stabbed a finger at the dying Nonae on the ground at the tree's base.

The voice buzzed, wordlessly, with a distracted air.

"This one's phenotype appears to be operant."

"Your pardon," Benu said, stepping in, "but I hasten to point out the systemic imbalances, caused by trauma, which are preventing this one from operating at peak efficiency."

The tree shimmered again.

"We have had intercourse with you before, though you are now housed in a new shell."

"Yes, both statements are true," Benu said, his voice laced with impatience.

"Has much time has passed since our last encounter? The days pass so strangely, here."

"By my reckoning, nearly two thousand, five hundred and seventy-three solar years."

"That short a span? I thought it would have been longer."

The tree rustled, its hazy branches moving as if in a slight breeze, and it seemed to Leena that the mind within was contemplative.

"You will have to visit again. This has been most engaging. Good-bye."

"No," Benu said forcefully, as if scolding a recalcitrant child. "You must repair this one"—he pointed at Spatha Sekundus—"and then you will answer our questions."

"Oh. Really?" There followed a long pause, and Leena could feel her pulse sounding in her ears. *"Very well."*

The tree shimmered once more, and again the wind kissed Leena's cheek, and in the next instant Spatha was lying naked on the ground, her wounds healed. But not only her most recent injuries had vanished, but ancient injuries, too, were gone. Even the ix, the Nonae ensign on her cheek, was gone.

Kakere rushed forward, and helped Spatha climb to her feet. They stood side by side, looking up uneasily at the metal tree above them, too stunned to speak.

Hieronymus whistled low. "They are as naked and unblemished as the day they were born. They might be some Adam and Eve from the pages of myth, facing a newborn world."

"The world is newborn every day, and when one's perceptions cycle through a dormant phase, it dies again."

Benu glanced over at Leena. "If you're going to ask your question, you might want to do it quickly. I'm not sure how long the trees will remain this lucid."

"This is lucid?" Balam asked, eyes rolling.

"Trees of Keir-Leystall," Leena said, not wasting a moment. She stepped nearer the tree, coming almost within arm's reach of the smooth, cool surface of its metal trunk. "Do you know of Earth, and the way between the worlds?"

"*Yes,*" buzzed the tree's answer.

Leena's heart skipped a beat, and she held her breath.

"*And no.*"

Leena's breath expelled in a defeated sigh.

"*We indeed know of Earth. Passage between that plane and our own is through transient gates. Predicting the appearance, duration, and characteristics of these gates is beyond our knowledge.*"

"So no one knows the way?" Leena cursed, her shoulders slumped.

"*No. The answer to your question can be found in Atla, and nowhere else.*"

"But no one may approach Atla," Benu objected, stepping forward to stand at Leena's side. "Not since the citadel city burned the steppes of Eschar with cold fire and sealed the south away from the rest of the world."

"*Not true, little machine. You forget, if you ever knew, about the Carneol of Hele.*"

Hieronymus and Balam exchanged glances with Leena, and they all looked to Benu, who only shrugged.

"*The Carneol is a gem used as the sign of office by the coregents of the Hele, but what even the rulers of the hidden city themselves do not know is that it is actually an ancient Atlan device. Hele was first settled as an outpost of the Black Sun Empire, long millennia ago, established to investigate certain*"— the voice paused, its branches rustling for a moment—"*peculiar characteristics of the region. The Carneol could grant its bearer free passage into Atla, a key to unlock the barrier long enough for entry, just as it did in ancient days, when the barrier was used only for defense, and not concealment.*"

Leena drew a ragged sigh. "So, if we steal the crown jewel of this place—Hele—then we can use that to sneak into the one place in all the world where the knowledge I seek can be found?"

"*Yes.*"

"Oh, delightful," Hieronymus said, crossing his arms over his chest.

Kakere and Spatha edged away from the tree, moving to stand beside Balam, while Benu strode up and rapped the tree's trunk with his knuckles.

"What do you know of Atla, since the barrier raised?" Benu asked, an urgent tone in his voice. "Do the wizard-kings still rule their citadel city, or have they all fallen to dust, long ago?"

The tree was silent for a long moment, rustling slightly.

"We have had intercourse with you before, haven't we? How long ago was it?"

"We spoke only seconds ago," Benu answered, exasperated.

"That short a time? It seemed so much longer."

"Answer my question," Benu demanded.

"Good-bye."

The tree fell silent, and nothing they could do or say would make it buzz again.

CHAPTER 36

Departures

None of the company had any desire to traipse into the thick of the metal trees, especially considering that the branches could remake their constituent elements with the barest touch, and that the collective intelligence with whom they'd spoken had been, according to Benu, the most rational and sympathetic of all the intelligences uploaded into the forest. The minds they might encounter in the metal forest's dark interior, were they to enter, might well remold their bodies in horrific, irreversible ways, and death would be the least of their worries. Without dissent, then, the company skirted the forest to the south, and then made for the southeast.

It was hoped that they could reach the trade routes, the main trunk of which ran from northeast to southwest in this region before turning back to the northwest once it passed the Lathe Mountains. Traffic along the main trunk was fairly frequent, and with some luck, they'd manage to catch up with a caravan of one kind or another that might be willing to give them transport.

The first night out from Keir-Leystall, Spatha Sekundus and Kakere sat apart from the others, some distance from the campfire, and spoke together in low tones. With his robes demolished by the manipulators in the branches' tips, the uncharacteristically quiet Kakere now clothed himself only in a makeshift kilt, his torso, head, arms, and legs exposed to the air; but after a full day of walking through the dry heat, he seemed none the worse for wear, displaying none of the symptoms of an Ichthyandaro in the throes of dehydration. Spatha, for her part, had seen her leather armor reduced to molecular dust, and now wore only a linen shift, belted at the waist with a length of cord. Her gladius and baldric, which had been on Balam's back when she'd been "repaired," was all that remained of her former armory, and she now laid the sheathed sword across her legs, thoughtfully, as she and Kakere whispered together.

Leena rubbed the bridge of her nose, and then ran her fingers through her hair. It was matted and greasy, and longer than she'd worn it in years. She realized, glaring disconsolately at the campfire before her, that some part of her had just assumed she'd be home by now. During their long trek through the mangrove swamp, their flight from the Tannim township, the slog through the bubbling mud pits and volcanic gases . . . every step since she'd come ashore, more than a week before, she'd been convinced was carrying her closer to home. The miraculous trees of which Benu had spoken would surely have the knowledge of how to traverse the gulf between the worlds, and she could bathe, and shampoo and cut her hair, and all the thousands of things she'd done in her former life, when she returned home to the Soviet Union.

Now, her only prospect for ever leaving Paragaea behind was to travel another span of weeks or months, infiltrate a hidden city deep within a mountain range, steal the monarchs' crown jewel, exfiltrate, journey another span of weeks or months, circumvent a barrier that had kept out all intruders for long millennia, and find someone willing to show her the way to Earth. Assuming, as Benu evidently did not, that anyone within the walls of the citadel city of Atla still lived.

Leena felt at times that the world contrived to make her path difficult for its own amusement. This was most definitely one of those times.

Two days later, they reached the main trunk of the trade route.

"Our destination lies some distance in that direction"— Hieronymus pointed along the road, such as it was, to the south—"and we'll be lucky to reach it before the autumnal rains begin, but we're on the path, at least, and that should be counted as a minor victory." His maps were spread out across his knees as he crouched by the roadside.

"And how many more kilometers beyond that before we reach Atla?" Leena asked sullenly.

Hieronymus rolled up his maps once more, and returned them to his pack. "Trust me," he said apologetically, "you don't want to know."

Leena joined Balam, who stood at the center of the road. It was pitted and gouged, with great ruts dug irregularly into the hard ground, looking almost like widely spaced blast craters from mortar explosions.

"What are those?" Leena said, pointing to the nearest pit, which was easily as wide as she was tall.

"Tracks," Balam said.

Leena whistled low. "What could have made such tracks? Some sort of large machine? A tank's tread of some kind?"

"No." Balam shook his head, glancing up and down the road nervously, as though worried something might be coming. "Not a machine, but a beast. A very, very large beast."

"Well, come on," Hieronymus said, hitching his pack onto his back. "Let's not waste daylight, shall we?" He turned towards the south and started to walk along the roadway, taking care to skirt around the huge craters.

Benu followed close behind, and Balam went to join them. Leena took a few steps along the road before glancing back to see Kakere and Spatha lingering by the side of the road, looking northward with guilty expressions on their faces.

"Aren't you coming?" Leena called back to them, her thumbs tucked through the shoulder straps of her pack.

Kakere and Spatha looked at each other, nodded, and then turned back to Leena.

"No," Spatha said with a shake of her head.

"Where would you go, then?"

"North." Spatha pointed up the road with her sheathed gladius.

"Um, sorry?" Kakere smiled sheepishly at Leena, and shrugged.

Hieronymus and Balam came to stand beside Leena, while Benu lingered down the road, impatient to press on.

"Why?" Balam asked, idly tapping the emerald hanging from his ear.

The Nonae and the Ichthyandaro looked to each other again, and Spatha drew a heavy breath before answering.

"When the oracular tree healed my wounded body, it seems also to have mended my broken spirit. I find that I miss my people, and want nothing more than once more to hear the sound of my mother tongue. I may be the last of the Nonae, as I fear, but if I am wrong, and any more of my nation still wander the desert wastes, I would find them, and set about rebuilding. We were a proud people once, with good reason, and there is nothing to say that we could not be so again."

"And you, Kakere?" Hieronymus asked, crossing his arms over his chest. "Do you intend to head into the north, as well?"

Kakere nodded, and smiled.

"But water is difficult to find as you head north from Parousia, and near impossible once you reach the Eastern Desert. How would you survive?"

"That tree really did a number on me," Kakere answered, gesturing to his bare, blue skin. "I've had barely a sip of water in the last two days, and I still feel perfectly fine. And on top of that, I've not had a single craving for alcohol since the tree touched me. I'm not quite sure what I am now, but I don't think I'm exactly an Ichthyandaro anymore."

"That is as it should be," Spatha said. She reached up and touched her left cheek, now smooth and unmarred. "Thou are no longer the fish man of thy earlier days, and I am no longer the citizen cadet I have been these many years. Perhaps we are each the first of a new model, each a new type of our species."

Spatha reached out, and her hand found Kakere's. Their fingers laced together, and they turned to Leena and the others, hand in hand.

"I can't really explain it, but it's like some bond has developed between us, these past few days," Kakere said.

"Since the trees of Keir-Leystall changed you?" Leena asked. She wondered what changes the strange machines might have wrought to their minds, as well as their bodies.

"Perhaps." Spatha nodded.

"Or maybe even earlier, when you saved me from those Tannim," Kakere said, looking lovingly at the woman at his side.

"Perhaps," Spatha said, and smiled.

With that, the pair turned and started to walk towards the north. When they had gone but a few steps, Kakere glanced back over his shoulder, smiling broadly.

"Good-bye, everybody! It was really nice meeting you." Kakere waved eagerly.

Spatha turned back, too, and nodded. "Best of fortune, Akilina, and may thou find the object of thy quest."

Leena waved, awkwardly, and turned to Hieronymus and Balam, who watched the retreating pair with expressions intermingling confusion and amusement. Kakere and Spatha were by now dozens of meters away, making good time across the uneven ground.

"Well, *that* was unexpected," she said.

"It's like they say, I suppose," Hieronymus answered, shaking his head. "The heart finds comfort where it may."

"What?" Balam said. "You believe that this is of their own choosing, and not some desire implanted by the twisted trees of Keir-Leystall?"

Hieronymus shrugged. "Who can say? But I've seen stranger love matches in my time, both here and on Earth, and who am I to judge?"

Balam sighed, and his eyes followed the pair as they walked into the distance. "Pity. She was a magnificent woman, despite her sundry flaws."

"Ah, take heart, old friend." Hieronymus clapped the jaguar man on the shoulder. "She was much too dainty for the likes of you. I'm sure we'll find someone more to your tastes when we reach Hele."

From behind them came the voice of Benu. They turned and saw him standing in the middle of the road a few meters away, tapping his toes impatiently.

"Should I begin work on constructing my next body now?" the artificial man called. "I won't need it for another thousand solar years, but at the pace we're going, we may not have moved from this spot by then."

Leena, Hieronymus, and Bonaventure joined him, laughing, and the company, now once more a quartet, made their way towards the south.

CHAPTER 37

On the Road

The area through which the company moved now was broad savannah, dotted here and there with copses of trees, pampas grasslands stretching out to either horizon with only the gray scar of the main trunk road interrupting the waves of silvery stalks.

The sun pounded down on them from above, and the only respite they found was the meager shade from the gnarled trees found irregularly spaced, but the trees were often too far from the road to make the side trip for a brief midday rest worth the time, and they made due with taking tarpaulins from their packs and setting up makeshift awnings propped up with their swords and scabbards, stretching out at full length in the minuscule amounts of shade provided.

Nights, they slept by the side of the road, making surprisingly comfortable beds for themselves by gathering up stalks of grass cut down with Hieronymus's saber and piling them into nests. Their meals were simple: dried, salted fish that Balam had brought with them from the *Acoetes Zephyrus*, supplemented by the occasional bird or small rodent caught along the way.

As they moved farther south, day by day, it became clear that they were following close on the heels of some large convoy, a caravan of enormous beasts that had churned up the road in their wake. Leena could scarcely imagine how these massive creatures must appear.

$$\star$$

The days passed mostly in silence, the company's energy and attentions focused more on locomotion than on communication, but when night fell, and they had eaten their humble meals, they sat around the flickering firelight in their makeshift nests of piled grasses, the heavens wheeling overhead, and passed the hours in quiet conversation.

To Leena, these nights seemed of a piece with the weeks she had spent with the three men traveling across the Sakrian plains. Though different muscle groups now ached, since she walked instead of sitting astride a trotting horse all day, the pains were familiar, as were the jokes and jests shared across the flickering firelight.

Benu's stories were, typically, the most wide-ranging, since he had a much larger store of experience from which to draw. And Balam knew hundreds of ribald jokes, handed down by generations of Sinaa princes, each more toe-curlingly hilarious than the last. But it was Hieronymus's tales that Leena found the most engaging. Whether he was relating one of the Greek myths his mother had taught him as a child, or recounting one of his own adventures as a naval officer on the oceans of Earth, just the sound of his voice was often enough to keep Leena's rapt attention.

As she sat and listened to Hieronymus speak, she couldn't help but be reminded of Sergei. The two men resembled one another not at all—not in appearance, manner, or habits—but nonetheless when she looked at Hieronymus, of late, there was something that brought her former love immediately to mind.

Nights, when the conversation drifted off to silence and the company settled down to rest, Leena would look up at the stars overhead, unable to sleep, inescapably aware of the nearness of Hieronymus's sleeping form.

It was midmorning when Hieronymus cried out, slipped, and promptly fell flat on his back. "Ugh," he spat, lying lengthwise in a deep pile of greenish mud, which had splattered onto his chest and face as he fell. "What is that stench?"

Balam rushed over, but when he saw that his friend was unhurt, just stood back, pinching his nostrils shut and shaking with laughter.

"What?" Hieronymus said, his tone annoyed as he tried unsuccessfully to stand, the green mud seeming to have cemented him in place. "I tripped!"

Leena and Benu came to stand beside the jaguar man, and immediately saw what he found so amusing.

"Oh, Hero." Leena tried to retain her composure, but her sympathetic noises were laced through with barely controlled laughter. "You seem to have taken a bit"—she ineffectively stifled a laugh—"of a spill."

"What am I lying in?" Hieronymus tried to lift his arm, but it took effort to pull away from the murky green stuff in which he had fallen, and his arm came away with an unpleasantly loud squelching noise.

"I had no idea, Hieronymus, that you had coprophilic tendencies." Benu rarely laughed, but even he now grinned broadly, amused at their companion's predicament.

"What?" Hieronymus struggled into a sitting position.

"Dung, Hero," Balam called out, doubled over with laughter. "You're lying in dung."

Hieronymus scrambled, trying to climb to his feet, but instead slipped again, this time pitching face-first into the greenish mound.

"Arrgh!" He pushed to his knees, and launched himself forward, clearing the mound and landing in the pitted road. He spat out clumps of the foul stuff, which coated his cheeks and clung to his hair.

"Fresh, too, by the looks of it," Benu observed, peering at the mound without getting a step closer than was necessary.

"Blast!" Hieronymus climbed unsteadily to his feet, and then reached out to Balam and Leena. "For god's sake, help me get this mess off of me."

"Oh, no," Leena said, raising her hands to ward him off as she and Balam danced out of reach.

"Go roll in the grass," Balam ordered, still pinching his nose shut. "It won't be as good as a proper bath, but it'll have to do."

Hieronymus staggered into the high grasses, stripping off his soiled clothes and doing his best to rid himself of the clinging clumps of dung. While he did, Leena and Balam stepped as near to the dung heap as they dared, their eyes wide.

"How big must be the monster that laid *that?*" Leena said, disbelieving.

"Too big," Balam said warily. "Much, much too big."

✦

That night, as the sun dipped below the horizon to the west, and the company prepared to make camp for the night, they spied an orange glow to the south.

"The convoy?" Leena asked.

"Quite likely," Hieronymus said. He'd managed to wash most of the dung from his clothes, face, and hair in a little puddle of brackish water they'd passed that afternoon, but the smell of the foul stuff still clung to him like a shroud.

"Well, shall we go and make our introductions?" Balam said. "If we're lucky, maybe they'll have something besides dried fish or prairie mice to eat, eh?"

A short while later, they approached the firelight of an encampment. As they drew nearer, they could hear the lowing of giant beasts, and saw large shadows hulking on the horizon.

"Approach carefully," Hieronymus warned, his voice low. "We don't want to startle them."

Suddenly, above the sounds of the beasts there rose the voices of men and women shouting calls of alarm.

"It wasn't me!" Balam said quickly, raising his hands in protest.

"Hsst!" Hieronymus raised a finger to silence him, and cocked his ear to listen closer. His eyes widened, and his hand flew to the hilt of his saber. "They're under attack!"

Hieronymus didn't hesitate, but charged forward, saber in one hand and Mauser pistol in the other. The others followed close behind, Balam with a knife in either hand and Leena bearing her short sword and Makarov.

In a span of heartbeats, they came upon the encampment, and in the flickering light of the campfire found a dozen men and women fending off a pack of carnivores. Each of the creatures was as tall as a horse, and looked somewhat doglike, but with hooves instead of claws, and a long snout, with meter-long jaws that looked like they were strong enough to crush a human skull in a single bite.

"Fenrir!" Hieronymus spat.

Already men and women lay wounded and bleeding on the ground, and the number of defenders standing against the pack of fenrir seemed to be dwindling.

"Come on," Balam shouted, racing for the nearest of the huge carnivores, fangs bared and knives out. "This looks like fun!"

CHAPTER 38

The Master of the Indriks

By the time morning arrived, the last of the ferocious fenrir had been killed or driven away, and Leena felt that she could not hold her sword point up for an instant longer. Balam's knives, claws, and fangs were slicked with gore from the necks and flanks of the fenrir, and even Benu looked in disarray, the simple tunic and trousers he wore ripped to shreds by the incisors of the creatures, leaving him standing unclothed and naked in the morning light. The defenders of the camp, seeing his odd, sexless parts, shied away from the artificial man, even after Leena insisted that he clothe himself once more with spares from his pack.

Hieronymus cleaned his saber on the pelt of one of the fallen fenrir, and grimly regarded the ruins of the encampment. From the looks of things, several of the men and women who had fallen before the carnivores had since died from their wounds in the night.

"What *were* those beasts?" Leena asked, coming to stand beside him, holstering her Makarov, from which she'd fired two shots in the intervening hours of the engagement. Her sword she cleaned on the grass, and with it sheathed, she collapsed into a sitting position on the ground.

"Fenrir," Hieronymus said, his mouth drawn into a line.

"I gathered that much," Leena said, scarcely amused. "But what manner of beast is a fenrir? They seemed something like enormous wolves, but I found their cloven hooves to be . . . unsettling."

"You know as much as I, little sister. I've had a run-in or two with them in my travels, but never a pack that size. These people are lucky to have survived the night."

"Those of us that did survive, that is."

Leena and Hieronymus looked up into the face of a man nearly as tall as Balam. His skin was the color of ebony, his head completely hairless. Dressed in a suit of dark blue linens with scuffed brown leather boots that came to his knees, he was built like a prize-fighter gone to seed, still muscled but with ample layers of fat for padding.

"Yasen Kai-Mustaf at your service," the man said, extending a massive hand. He spoke Sakrian with an Elveran accent. "Bondsman of the Six Brothers Consolidated Shipping Concern, and master of beasts on this caravan. And you?"

Hieronymus took the man's hand in a firm grip.

"Hieronymus Bonaventure, honest traveler. And this is my companion—"

"Akilina Mikhailovna Chirikova," Leena said, taking the man's hand and introducing herself. "The Sinaa is Balam, and the newly clad man with the unusual eyes is Benu."

"You are welcome," Yasen said as the other two joined them. "And our thanks for your assistance against the dread creatures last night. Had you not joined the fray when you did, I'm not sure that any of us would have survived till morning came."

"It was nothing," Hieronymus said with a shrug.

"It was fun," Balam said.

"Not so fun for those who perished from their wounds," Leena said, scolding.

"Now, now, my dear lady," Yasen said, resting a comradely hand on Balam's shoulder. "Do not berate our friend Sinaa, for taking joy in the fact that he still lives. The dead do not envy us, nor should we pity them. Besides, the men who died did so in fulfilling their contracted duty to the Six Brothers Consolidated Shipping Concern. They were bonded guards, they guarded, and their untimely extinction was merely the price of doing business." He clapped his huge hands together and grinned, ivory teeth showing in his dark face. "Now, is there anything I can do to repay you? Our generosity is limited only by our means, which are meager to say the least."

"We seek passage to Hele," Hieronymus said. "Are you taking on passengers?"

"Well, now, that is a sticky question," Yasen said, chewing his lip. "You see, my employers at the Six Brothers Consolidated prohibit us from taking on any passengers, wayfarers, or stowaways in the course of our route. To do otherwise would be to risk offending my employers, which could mean censure at best, and elimination at worst."

"Elimination of your contract?" Benu asked.

"No, elimination of *me*!" Yasen drew a finger across his neck, and stuck out his tongue. "My employers take contracts very seriously, and I'm sorry to say that renegotiation of terms is rarely an option."

The master of beasts began to pace in front of them, clasping his hands behind his back. "However," he went on, talking at breakneck speed, "it occurs to me that there might be another alternative. While neither I nor the freight master are permitted to allow passengers, we are either of us empowered to hire on new labor, circumstances demanding. And considering that we lost the lion's share of our guard contingent to those bloody fenrir, I think that circumstances are quite demanding at the moment, don't you? Yes?"

Leena and Hieronymus glanced at each other, having trouble parsing out his meaning.

"Are you offering us a job?" Balam said, squinting his amber eyes at the figure pacing faster and faster before them.

"Precisely. I can't pay you much, if anything, beyond two square meals a day, but our course will bear us southwards, and Hele is one of the stops along our route."

The four companions looked to one another, and shrugged.

"Why not?" Hieronymus said. "Count us in."

"Splendid." Yasen said. "We've four new guards, which puts us at three-quarters strength at best, but you'll not hear me complain. Now, come along with me, and I'll introduce you to the beasts, and show you the burdens you'll be guarding."

✦

The company followed Yasen Kai-Mustaf around a line of tents, past a copse of gnarled trees, and came at last to the beasts. These were the shapes they'd glimpsed shadows of in the night, but nothing could have prepared Leena for the sight of them in the broad daylight.

There were some dozen of the creatures in all, each standing nearly seven meters tall, so huge that even Balam came only up to their knees. They had long, giraffelike necks, surmounted by narrow heads looking almost like that of a sheep, and were covered in a rough gray hide, like that of a rhinoceros.

"What *are* they?" Leena breathed, barely above a whisper.

"These, dear lady," Yasen said, indicating the enormous creatures with a grand gesture, "are my babies, my only friends, the finest indriks you will find anywhere on the Paragaean continent."

"Big, aren't they?" Hieronymus said, leaning over and whispering into Leena's ear.

"Too big," Balam said, looking up at the giant creatures uneasily.

"No," Benu said, shaking his head slightly, "that is the normal size and proportion for an indrik."

"Well, I say they're too blasted big," Balam sneered.

"What?" Yasen said, overhearing the whispered conference. "Do you fear these gentle giants? Nonsense! They're as tender as a babe in arms, and wouldn't hurt a fly. Provided, of course, the fly wasn't in their path as they walked by, but then, that would really be the fly's lookout, and not the fault of the indrik, now wouldn't it? They are nature's perfect engines, my friends the indriks. They can go without food and water for days, thanks to their prodigious size, and can live into their eighties, so that once you teach them a route, they'll remember it for as long as you're likely to require. Some of these beasts have been walking the trade routes of the east since my grandsire first plied the cargo trade, back when there were only four brothers in the Consolidated Shipping Concern. And some of them will be walking these pitted roads long after you and I have moldered to dust."

"I wouldn't be so sure of that," Benu said with a slight smile.

The indrik, having fed and watered, were driven back to the road. The indriks in the lead and in the rear carried howdahs upon their backs— large platforms the size of a boat's deck, ringed with railings that rose a meter above the planks, and covered by a sheltering canopy. The other indriks in the train were each loaded down with crates and bales strapped to their broad backs.

When the indriks had all been led back onto the road, everyone clambered up rope ladders and climbed aboard the howdahs, with the freight master and his able landsmen in the rear, and the master of beasts and the guards in the front.

"Count yourself lucky you ride fore with me, and not abaft with the others," Yasen explained as the indriks began to lumber forward. "If you were in that end of the train"—he jerked a thumb behind him—"you'd have nothing but the back end of an indrik to look at, all the livelong day. Never a pleasant sight, to say nothing of the occasional smell."

"Yes," Hieronymus said through gritted teeth. "We've encountered it before."

"Have you now?" Yasen said, smiling broadly. "I knew I was right to think you a group of worldly individuals, well traveled and the like. I'm glad to have you aboard, and no question."

From what Yasen had said, their role as guards on the convoy was fairly simple. The guards' primary role appeared to be as deterrent, with little call for action. Aside from the tussle with the fenrir the night before, the guards on this journey had done little more than sit atop the howdah day and night, watching the scenery roll by.

Aside from the four of them, there were only two other guards, one a heavy-browed, barrel-chested Kobolt with a broken nose, who stood only to Leena's shoulder; and the other a Rephaim who towered over even Balam, with rippling muscles and huge hands that could wrap twice around Leena's waist. Neither spoke much, keeping each to himself, and so it was almost as if the company traveled alone with the master of beasts.

Days passed, blending into weeks. The indriks could travel long hours during the day, stopping only during the hours between sunset and sunrise to rest.

The landscape changed around them as they moved farther south. Grasslands gave way to wide, dry plains, with high mesas on the far horizons. In the rainy season, Yasen explained, this route would become almost impassable, the plains turned to squelching quagmire, and in that season the shipping routes—and shipping schedules—doubled, tripled, or sometimes quadrupled. Most shipping occurred during the summer and winter months, with spring and fall being either very slow, or very, very difficult. It was late in the season, near the full rains, but in recent years the Six Brothers had come under new management that tried to milk every possible profit from the operation. As a result, they had been asked to squeeze in one more regular shipment before the rains, to keep from having to pay their employees the increased wages of an off-season journey.

✦

The master of beasts pointed out interesting bits of geography as they went along. The other guards paid him no mind, and it was clear that Yasen was grateful for a fresh—and more or less captive—audience. One afternoon, on the horizon ahead, a strange cloud roiled, where before there had been only blue sky. Their path took them underneath, and they were surprised when they were pelted by salty drops of rain, and flapping, gawking, live fish.

"Think nothing of it," the master of beasts said in response to their startled looks. "It happens in this spot, from time to time. But have no fear; it doesn't signal the coming of the raining season. Instead it just means we'll have a bit of variety in our diet, yes?"

Leena slid close to Hieronymus and Benu, leaning against the forward railing and looking up at the unearthly cloud overhead.

"There must be a gate to Earth at the cloud's center," Leena said guardedly.

"Undoubtedly," Benu said.

"If only I could reach it." Leena smacked a fist into the palm of her other hand.

"What would that accomplish?" Hieronymus asked. "If you were somehow able to get hundreds of feet up in midair, you have no way of knowing when or where the other end of the gate opens. It could be into the distant past of Earth, or its far future. In fact, the only thing you would know for certain traversing the gate is that you will likely find yourself somewhere far beneath the ocean's surface, and you'd likely drown before you made it through."

"Cheer up," Balam called, holding a flapping sea bass in his hands, still slick with brine. "Look what we're having for dinner."

"Delightful," Hieronymus grumbled. "More fish."

CHAPTER 39
The Approach to the Hidden City

Finally, after weeks on the trunk road, their route led them to the foothills of the Lathe Mountains.

"There," Benu said, pointing to the snowcapped mountains rising in purple majesty above the lowlands. "Deep within the greatest of the Lathes, we will find the hidden city of Hele."

"I hope you find what you seek," Yasen said, "but I don't envy you going down into that benighted hole. I've never been myself, but my scant dealings with the Heleans who come to the surface to do trade with outsiders have convinced me my time would be better spent in other pursuits."

"If it brings us one step nearer to our goal," Leena said, resolute, "then I would walk through the gates of hell itself."

"You might just, my dear," Yasen said, his tone guarded. "You might just."

✦

The trade route wound up into foothills a short span, reaching a depot of some sort at the base of the largest mountain before turning back and angling towards the lowlands.

At the depot there was a wide loading dock, cantilevered out from the mountainside, so that one side was flush with the living rock while the other rose some seven meters off the ground. Where the dock met the mountain, there was a slant-roofed structure, beside which was parked some manner of tram on a track, its cargo bins empty and waiting.

As the indrik convoy approached, a motley collection of stevedores emerged from the slant-roofed structure, went to stand at the end of the dock, and waited patiently for the indriks to pull up, one by one. After they had arranged themselves in their lines, the foreman stepped from the structure to survey their progress.

The stevedores of Hele began to unload the indriks, loading up the spring-driven trams, which ran on tracks running back and forth up the gentle mountain slope before finally disappearing into a tunnel entrance high overhead. Most of the stevedores were metamen of various races—Canid, Arcas, Struthio, even Sinaa—though their foreman was a slight human with green skin who huddled under a broad parasol, shielding his eyes against the faint afternoon sun.

Yasen Kai-Mustaf climbed from the howdah, and went to speak with the foreman, while Leena and the other guards milled around the dock, stretching their legs and marveling at the bulk of the mountain rising above them.

Once the foreman had finished transacting his business with Yasen, Hieronymus, Leena, and Balam stepped forward, waving for the green-skinned man's attention.

"Yaas?" the foreman drawled daintily, motioning distractedly for them to speak.

"We require admittance to Hele," Balam said.

"Oh, *do* you?" the foreman blinked at them slowly, his expression unreadable. He turned to Hieronymus and Leena, and said, with a slight tinge of disgust in his voice, "Am I to take it that the . . . jaguar . . . speaks for you all?"

"Yes," Balam said, becoming annoyed, "I do."

The foreman glanced over his shoulder at Balam, and wrinkled his nose in distate.

"We-ell, I'm afraid that Hele does not welcome visitors, only workers."

"We can work," Leena said, straightening.

"Oh, *can* you?"

"We're honest travelers in search of employment, sir," Hieronymus said, managing to sound surprisingly deferential.

"Well." The foreman sighed deeply. "We *are* somewhat short-handed at the present instant, and this current load *is* a large one. We've had . . . labor difficulties, I suppose you could say . . . recently, and have had to work at half-strength." He sighed again, and looked them up and down appraisingly. Benu came to stand beside his companions, and the green-skinned man sneered slightly. "Well, I *suppose* if you are willing to hire on as stevedores and help get this shipment into the city in one trip, I can take you on provisionally, and see about getting you temporary access chits once we reach the city."

"Agreed," Balam said, and stuck out his hand.

The foreman looked down at the jaguar man's hand as though it were a dead fish, and shuddered. Then he waved them towards the other side of the dock. "Well, go *to*, go to."

✦

The four bid farewell to the master of beasts, and were surprised when even the Kobolt and Rephaim grunted their good-byes. Once they had retrieved their things from the howdah, they joined the stevedores in loading up the tram.

When the last of the freight had been loaded onto the tram, the four joined the rest of the stevedores in the rear car, and the tram began to inch its slow way up the mountain.

From the ground, it had looked as though the distance was short, the tunnel entrance just a short ride from the bottom. As the tram inched along, though, it seemed to Leena as though time slowed and distance elongated; they moved farther and farther from the bottom, but the top still seemed so far away.

Balam caught the eye of one of the Sinaa stevedores, and tried to engage him in conversation.

"Mat'? Mat'ata'das'ul?"

The Sinaa averted his eyes, and would not meet Balam's gaze.

"Mat'uk'odat?" Balam said, leaning forward, glancing at another of the Sinaa.

This jaguar man, too, turned away, covering his eyes.

"Mat'tar'let Per," Balam said, glowering.

The Sinaa all turned away from him, their expressions hard, but one of them nodded faintly.

"What is it?" Leena whispered, leaning in close.

"They are Black Sun Genesis," Balam hissed through clenched teeth. "They consider any metaman who does not follow the 'teachings' of Per to be unclean, and will not respond." He sneered, baring his teeth. "I lost my throne, my kingdom, and my daughter to nonsense like this. I didn't think I'd have to face it here."

"Courage, friend," Hieronymus said, laying a hand on Balam's knee. "We'll be on our way in no time, you watch, and all of this far behind us."

✦

Finally, the tram reached the tunnel mouth, and they began to descend once again, this time down into the cool heart of the mountains. The tunnel was darkened, lit only by a faint glow from up ahead.

The tram rattled and clanked out of the darkness, and there before them was the hidden city, now revealed. Down in the sunless caverns, in a perpetual twilight illuminated by bioluminescence from lichens that grew on the damp walls, crouched the hidden city of Hele.

The city was constructed in nine rings, concentric circles rising one atop another, with a spire rising up from the innermost ring. It looked to Leena like a series of Matrioshka nesting dolls, all with their top halves removed. Water ran in a gentle fall from a fissure in a high wall, and became a slow-moving, murky green river running around the outermost ring, the river Dys.

"The water," explained Benu, who had been in Hele in ancient days, "is suffused with a strain of algae which, when consumed over the span of years, imparts to the skin a greenish tint, which accounts for the unusual skin tones of our friend the foreman. Hele is a wealthy city, made so by the minerals dug up from its deep mines, and the fine porcelains and ceramics manufactured from the clay found in the lower reaches. Still, the city has reportedly fallen from its earlier grandeur, become decadent in its old age. Most of the hard labor in the city is now performed by immigrants, many of them metamen who have come to Hele in search of a better life." Benu nodded to their fellow stevedores, who sat on the tram's benches with slumped shoulders. "The native Heleans spend much of their time in recreation, their favorite game a type of bowling sport using stone pins and a fired-clay ball, leaving the industry which maintains their culture to the hands of outsiders."

Opening off of the central cavern were innumerable caves, tunnels, and channels, snaking in and out like the passage of termites through rotten wood.

"There," Hieronymus said, pointing to the spire rising from the highest ring, his voice lowered in a whisper pitched so only the companions could hear. "There must be the palace of the coregents of Hele. There we will find the object of our quest."

Leena's hands tightened into fists, and in a voice barely above a breath, she whispered, "The Carneol."

CHAPTER 40

Hele

The tram reached the terminus, and the company and the rest of the stevedores busied themselves unloading the freight. The work was grueling, the air in the terminus building stifling and close. Leena could not say how long they labored, so far from the light of the sun. In the eerie twilit gloom of the cavern, it was difficult to mark the passage of time, and when their work was complete, it seemed to Leena that it might have taken them a quarter of an hour, or the better part of a day. Either seemed as likely.

With the tram fully unloaded, the green-skinned foreman appeared, his parasol collapsed and propped at a jaunty angle on his shoulder. He paid the stevedores a few small, squared-off ceramic coins apiece, all except for the four newcomers, whom he also presented with a small ceramic disc apiece, emblazoned with nine concentric rings.

"These are temporary worker's chits," he said, not entirely unkindly, "along with a few coins for your labors. Remember, though, if you *can*, that these chits are only for a short span, and you must

298

appear tomorrow morning by no later than four bells at the offices of
the Ministry of Foreign Labor to apply for more permanent employment. If the Ministry is *unable* to find appropriate placement for you
by the end of this cycle, you will be expelled from the city, your rights
of access revoked."

"Where might we find food and lodging, until tomorrow?" Hieronymus asked, slipping the coins and the ceramic disc into a pocket.

"*Well*," the foreman said, sighing a belabored sigh. "You will want
to proceed to the Immigrant Quarter in the ninth ring." He waved
absently towards the exit of the terminus, and the walls of the city
beyond. "You might find it difficult to find accommodations, particularly with the coronation drawing so near. Many hoteliers and tavern
owners will no doubt prefer to keep empty rooms on their registers
than take on unknown lodgers so soon after the recent troubles. But so
long as you steer clear of *agitators*, you should not encounter any especial difficulty."

With that, their audience with the foreman was apparently at an
end. Without another word, he turned and sauntered off towards his
offices.

"He was certainly helpful," Benu said, "I shouldn't think."

"No doubt," Balam said, his eyes narrowed as he watched the
foreman's retreating back. "I can't say that I care for his patently con-
descending attitudes towards metamen."

"To say nothing for his penchant for emphasizing random words in
his speech," Hieronymus said. "Most unpleasant."

"Well," Leena said, slinging her pack onto her shoulders. "I'm pretty
sure I heard the word 'tavern' in there somewhere, which suggests to me
that we might find something to drink, if we look hard enough."

"Little sister," Hieronymus said with a smile, hooking his arm
through hers, "I believe you've just said the magic word."

✦

Beyond the entrance to the terminus, they found a path that led to the main gates of the city. The stevedores with whom they'd labored on the tram were now lined up at the gate in an orderly queue, identification chits in hand, each being inspected by the city guards in turn. At random intervals, one of the stevedores, invariably a metaman of one kind or another, was taken out of the line to a fenced-off area a short distance away, stripped naked, and thoroughly searched.

"What are they looking for?" Leena asked, whispering behind her hand as the company joined the end of the queue.

"The foreman said something about agitators, and a coronation," Hieronymus answered, watching the guards and their motions carefully, "but I didn't follow his whole meaning."

"They should take care not to drag me out for such an examination," Balam growled, eyes flashing as a Canid was led to the enclosure. Once the dog man's clothes had been stripped from his body, he was bent over a low table, and his snout twisted in a grimace of pain as one of the guards used a short, wicked-looking ceramic instrument to probe his nether regions, doubtless searching for some type of contraband.

"Strange that they don't object to such treatment," Hieronymus said.

"I have found, over my long years," Benu observed, "that there are no indignities which beings will not suffer, if they believe the ends are justified. These metamen have traveled great distances and at considerable risk, hoping to claim a small portion of the riches of Hele for their own. That few if any immigrants are ever granted full Helean citizenship is apparently not a deterrent, and so with visions of mineral wealth and luxury dancing before their eyes, they allow themselves to suffer privations they would otherwise find abhorrent."

"Such is the way in decadent capitalist societies," Leena said scornfully.

"Perhaps." Benu nodded thoughtfully. "But I have seen similar in cultures which have rejected monetary exchange for other economic structures. The Bacharian Polity, for example, ostensibly shares all property in common, and yet I've seen hungry mothers and starving children lined up for days on end for their dole of bread and weak soup. Is that really so different?"

Leena shot a hard glance at the artificial man, her mouth drawn into a line. "That is hardly the same thing. Such shortages are invariably the result of interference from without, a burden shared among all the populace when the state stands against the capitalist oligarchies of decadent empires."

"So you would hold a system like the Polity's unaccountable for its own shortcomings?" Hieronymus asked. "A government that sends spies against its neighbors, brigands who think nothing of raising a hand against honest wayfarers who happen to differ in species from their genetic purity?"

Before Leena could respond, they reached the head of the queue.

"Next!" The guard snapped his fingers, motioning impatiently for them to approach. His green skin stood in stark contrast to the bright reds and blues of his uniform, a cuirass of polished ceramic across his chest, and beneath his helmet his hair was the same light blond as his mustache and beard.

Hieronymus went first, presenting the ceramic badge the foreman had issued him. After regarding it closely, the guard asked Hieronymus a few questions about his country of origin, his reasons for coming to Hele, and so forth. Hieronymus answered as simply as possible, saying simply that he came from an island far away, and that he came in search of work to which his hands could be turned.

The guard looked Hieronymus up and down, appraisingly, and then handed him back the ceramic badge.

"Next."

The others of the company were each in turn interviewed, their temporary access chits inspected closely. Leena and Hieronymus both sighed with relief when Balam was waved through without being taken to the enclosure for further examination, and when Benu was passed through, the company was on their way.

They passed under the high gate and, crossing the threshold, found themselves in Hele.

✦

They were in the ninth and lowest of the nine rings of the city. It was constructed as one broad avenue that curved back on itself to their left and right, lined on both sides with buildings. Behind the buildings on the inner curve rose the retaining wall of the eighth ring, beyond which they could just glimpse the other rings, while the spire of the coregents' palace towered above all.

Directly before them, opposite the entrance through which they'd passed, rose a wide ramp that zigzagged in switchbacks up the steep slope of the inner wall, terminating at the edge of the eighth ring above them. Men and metamen, vehicles and beasts, moved slowly up and down this winding ramp, about the business of the city.

The majority of beings that passed them on the avenue, or that jostled up and down the ramp, were metamen, but what humans the company did see had skin that ranged from the pale white of Leena's own to the dark ebony of Yasen Kai-Mustaf, with only a scattered handful whose pigmentation was the dark green of the foreman and the city guards.

"So few green faces," Leena observed.

"There will be few Heleans found here in the lower rings, I would imagine," Benu answered. "As one ascends the rings of the city, one also ascends the social strata. Down here at the bottom are the poorest of the city dwellers, most of whom, like us, are immigrants to the hidden city."

"I'm fairly certain someone mentioned something about getting a bite to eat," Balam interrupted, becoming impatient with the conversation. "I've been on my feet hauling crates for who knows how long, and I want a bed, a meal, and a drink, though not necessarily in that order."

"I would take any and all of the three, in *any* order," Hieronymus agreed.

"This way, then," Benu said, starting to walk towards the right around the avenue's curve. "If I read the signage correctly, and I do, then the Immigrant's Quarter will be found a short distance ahead."

The first three establishments they tried refused them admittance, with one tavern even refusing to open its doors to them. At an overpriced hotel along the avenue, they were told that there were no vacancies, though the corridors echoed empty and dark. A restaurant shuttered its windows as they approached, only a bare handful of green-skinned patrons glimpsed momentarily through the panes of glass. And as they walked on, the avenue seemed to become more and more vacated, fewer pedestrians and vehicles passing them by the moment.

"You there," shouted one of a pair of green-skinned guards, approaching them from across the avenue, each with a half-meter long trident in hand. There was, by now, no one else in sight, only shuttered windows and barred doors lining the way. "What are you about?"

"We're just looking for food and lodging," Hieronymus answered casually.

"Not past curfew you aren't," replied the other of the guards.

"Curfew?" Leena said.

"We were told about no curfew on our entry." Benu glanced at his companions and shrugged.

"Ignorance of the law is no defense." The guard tightened his grip on the trident, menacingly. "Get indoors, and there won't be any trouble."

"But we can't find anywhere that will take us," Leena objected.

"Try the House of Mama Jahannam," the other guard said, not without a slight trace of compassion. He pointed up the road, to a red lantern swinging above an open doorway. "They'll take *anybody*."

"Well, we are most definitely anybody," Hieronymus said, on his face a smile that didn't quite reach his eyes. "I suppose we'll be on our way."

"Watch yourselves," warned the first guard, pointing to the company with his three-pronged trident.

"We will," Balam growled ominously.

"Come along, friend," Hieronymus said, taking the jaguar man by the elbow and dragging him down the avenue. "Let's get indoors, shall we?"

When they had gone a few dozen steps, Leena glanced back over her shoulder and saw that the two guards were still standing in place, watching them. "What does it mean," she asked in a low voice, "to have a curfew when no one can say what the hour is with any certainty?"

"Curfews are never about the hours of a clock," Benu said, his opalescent eyes glinting dully in the gloomy twilight, "but are only about control. It would seem that the Heleans are afraid of something, but that they are not precisely sure what that something is."

As they drew near the red lantern, they could hear voices raised in laughter, and saw a warm glow spilling out from the open doorway.

"Ah," Hieronymus said, his chest swelling with a deep breath. "Signs of life, at last."

Mama Jahannam's proved to be a tavern such as could be found near wharfs or warehouses or loading docks in any city, Earthly or Paragaean. It had a low ceiling, hung with lanterns that produced a ruddy glow, and was crowded with pitted tables and wobbly chairs, nearly all of them occupied. The laughing, singing, boisterous crowd included every species and variety of sentient being imaginable: human, Kobolt, Sheeog, Rephaim, Struthio, Canid, Arcas, Sinaa, Tapiri, even a handful of Ichthyandaro in damp robes in a far corner, and a pair of Nagas playing bone flutes while sitting cross-legged on a table. Only a few of the patrons seemed dour and sullen, metamen who invariably sat in small groups apart from everyone else.

The company found an open table, and ordered food and drink from a waiter who drifted by with a tray of beverages, all of which he seemed to be sampling before serving, which left his speech and his locomotion notably impaired. After a brief delay, though, their order arrived, more or less correct, and they fell to sating their appetites.

Once they had worked their way through the rough meal, and had a couple of drinks in them, Hieronymus and Balam began to scan the tavern patrons studiously.

"What are you doing?" Leena asked, noting their careful attention.

"In every establishment of this sort," Hieronymus explained, "one is likely to find individuals who have a willingness to answer questions when suitably inspired."

Leena drew a sharp breath. "You're not going to torture someone for information, are you?"

Balam looked at her with a shocked expression on his face, while Hieronymus just chuckled.

"What do you think we are, Leena?" Balam asked, horrified. "Savages?"

"No, of course not, little sister." Hieronymus took a sip from his mug, and licked his lips appreciatively. "We'll just get them drunk, and then start asking questions."

✦

In short order, they found their mark. A human, his skin a pale white with a slight tinge of green that indicated, Benu explained, that he had been in Hele for some time, but was not a native-born citizen. He introduced himself as Alfe, and was apparently desperate for conversation, as he started answering the company's questions before his first drink had even been poured.

"What's this coronation business all about, anyway?" Balam asked.

Alfe looked at the jaguar man askance. "Blind me, did you just fall off the tram today, or what?"

"Yes," Hieronymus said, nodding, "as a matter of fact, we did."

Alfe shrugged, and reached for his mug of lager. "Fair enough. So it's the coronation you're wanting to hear about, is it? Well, you see, Underlord Akeronh has recently died, and his coregent, Underlady Persefonh, now holds the throne only as steward, waiting for a pair of worthies to pass the rites of coronation. Already, though, two pair of green-skinned children, boy and girl, have marched into the cave tunnels, the juice of the royal pomegranates still staining their chins. It remains to be seen if they come back out again, but if they don't, another pair'll go in after them, and another after them, and so on, until Hele's got itself a new set of monarchs, and things can get back to normal for a while."

"What about these agitators we've heard about?" Leena asked, leaning forward.

"Oh, them," Alfe said with a sneer. "There's a mess of foreigners being held for trial, metamen arrested for fomenting revolution among the others of their kind in the city. Their trial has been postponed until a new underlord and underlady take up the Carneol and mount the throne, but it's all over but the shouting, at this point. Those agitators are as dead as dead, and have no doubt."

"Where do they come from, these agitators?" Benu asked. "Whence do they come?"

"They're from among the numbers of the Black Sun Genesis," Alfe said, "or so I'm told. There's more of them arriving every day, agitating for their captive brethren to be released." He took a long sip of his lager, and then pointed past Hieronymus at the open door. "There's some of them newly arrived ones now, who've no doubt been off pestering the upper-ring nabobs about their fellows' release."

The company glanced over, and saw a small group of metamen: a

Canid, a Struthio, and an Arcas, with a young Sinaa female at their vanguard.

"It can't be!" Balam shouted, leaping to his feet. "Menchit!"

Balam rushed forward, his arms wide, but when he was within a meter of the young Sinaa, she held her hands up, claws out, warding him off.

"But Menchit," Balam said, eyes wide and confused. "Don't you know me?"

Balam drew nearer, and the young female swiped her claws at his face, forcing him to pull back or lose an eye.

"Menchit, I'm your father!"

The young Sinaa regarded him coolly. "I know no father but Per."

Balam took a step backwards, stunned, and the young Sinaa swept past him, the other Per-followers in her wake.

CHAPTER 41

Industry

The following morning, in the same unending twilight, the company set out for the Ministry of Foreign Labor, as instructed.

Balam had scarcely spoken since his encounter with his long-lost daughter the night before, and when Leena suggested they make for the Ministry building, he objected, saying that he preferred to stay in the tavern, in the hopes of meeting again with his daughter.

"Come on, friend," Hieronymus said, placing an arm around his shoulders. "It would do no good to be deported for lack of proper identification before we even came near the palace."

"Very well," Balam grumbled, arms crossed over his chest. "But I'm back here at my earliest opportunity."

The company made their way through the thronged avenue of the ninth ring, back to the long ramp they'd seen the night before. The Ministry of Foreign Labor, a helpful patron of Mama Jahannam's had explained after Hieronymus had bought him a dram of lager, could be found in the first quarter of the eighth ring. The building, once they located it, proved to be an unimposing structure of white stone that looked dilapidated and aged.

"One assumes that, despite its evident value to their culture, the Heleans place little stock in Foreign Labor," Benu observed.

In the vestibule of the Ministry building, they found an ancient Helean sitting in a stall, his white hair like wisps of cloud against his dark green skin, his uniform stained and threadbare.

"Yes?" the official asked disinterestedly.

"We were given these," Leena held out her ceramic badge, "and told to come here to find work."

The official reached out a wrinkled hand, covered in dark viridian liver spots, and took the ceramic badge from Leena. "Well, you won't be able to get work with *these*. This is just a temporary access chit. In order for anyone in Hele to hire you on, you'd need a provisional employment chit."

"And where might we get one of those?" Hieronymus asked.

"You'd need to go to the Ministry of Immigration Control," the official said. He pointed back towards the open door, and handed Leena back her ceramic badge. "Sixth ring, second quarter, you can't miss it."

"And with this employment chit, we don't run the risk of deportation?" Leena asked.

"No," the official answered with a sigh, "any nonproductive immigrant is liable to be expelled from the city, whether they have a provisional employment chit or not. The temporary access chit gives you free passage throughout the unrestricted areas of the city, until such time as you are able to find employment. The provisional employment chit, however, merely indicates that you are *eligible* to be employed, but does not guarantee employment. That determination is made by the Ministry of Foreign Labor on a case-by-case basis."

"So can you tell us whether you have work for us, then?" Hieronymus asked.

"Not with just a temporary access chit, I can't." The official waved them once more towards the door, and then turned his attention away, their audience evidently at an end.

"I don't have time for this nonsense," Balam growled as they stepped back out into the eighth-ring avenue. He began to pace, extending and retracting his claws anxiously. "I've not seen my daughter since she was a bare cub, and now she's grown, and refuses to recognize me. I'll not waste any more time dallying with the unnecessarily complex bureaucracies of this stagnant culture, when we're on some damned idiotic quest, resident here only temporarily to steal the crown jewel!"

"Hsst!" Hieronymus grabbed his arm and dragged him to a halt. He leaned in close to the jaguar man's ear, and in a harsh whisper, said, "A little more circumspect in future, if you wouldn't mind. I've no desire to spend the rest of my days rotting in a Helean prison cell, thank you."

Balam took a deep breath and relaxed fractionally, but his posture and manner still made his tension evident. "I'm sorry, all. Honestly. But as important as I know it is to you to return home"—he glanced imploringly at Leena—"you must understand how weighty this moment is for me."

Leena stepped forward and laid a hand on Balam's arm. "Of course you must go to your daughter," she said. "Leave the Carneol to me, Benu, and Hero."

"Actually," Benu said, raising his hand, "if this access chit will give me passage in and out of the city for a few days, as the official indicated, I may well forgo the employment process myself, and pass the time instead exploring the surrounding caves."

"Why?" Hieronymus asked.

"I have been in Hele on occasion, over the long numberless centuries of my existence, but I now find myself puzzled over what it was about these sunless caverns that the wizard-kings of Atla investigated, all those millennia ago. I would find that answer for myself."

Hieronymus looked from Benu to Leena.

"Well, little sister, you've released Balam from his labors. Do you now absolve Benu of any responsibility, as well?"

Leena shrugged. "What can six hands do that four hands cannot, in these circumstances?"

"Fair enough," Hieronymus said, and responded with a shrug of his own. "Balam, you go mend bridges with your estranged daughter, and Benu, you go solve the riddle of the sunless caverns. Leena and I, meanwhile, will work on penetrating the defenses of the first ring, infiltrating the royal residence, and making off with the most valuable gem in Hele." He smiled broadly and winked at Leena. "What could be easier?"

It took the better part of a day for Hieronymus and Leena to make their way through the labyrinthine bureaucracy of the Ministry of Immigration Control, but after swearing out affidavits and signing countless forms, averring that they had no desire to topple the rightful government of Hele, they were presented with their provisional employment chits. It was nearly curfew by the time they returned to the Ministry of Foreign Labor on the eighth ring, and neither of them had eaten since early that morning.

"Well," the bald-headed Ministry official said after examining their employment chits and looking over their papers. "I think we *may* have work for you, after all. There are vacancies in the municipal laundry facilities on the second ring. Non-Heleans have not *tradition-ally* been employed above the fourth ring, but circumstances in recent decades have forced us to accept the notion of foreigners taking on the less-desirable posts in the upper rings. That being the case, one still cannot conscience having nonhumans in those positions, and so when suitable human candidates come forward, they tend to find employment fairly quickly."

"The laundry?" Hieronymus wrinkled his nose distastefully.

"Yes," the official drawled. "The municipal laundry handles the washing for all of the ministry branches, but its primary responsibility is to the palace spire."

"Oh, really?" Leena said. "That sounds very . . . engaging."

"Quite." The official waved his hand absently. "And who knows? If you work out in the laundry, and please your overseers, I suppose there's always the possibility that you might someday be able to work within the walls of the palace spire itself. What do you think of that?"

Leena and Hieronymus exchanged glances and smiled.

"I think that sounds just splendid," Leena said.

CHAPTER 42

The Best-Laid Plans

Hieronymus and Leena reported the next morning for their first day of work at the municipal laundry. Their overseer was a Helean woman of advanced years and considerable girth named Shafan, who pointed them towards vats of lye, powdered borax, and grease, explained the rudiments of making laundry soap, and then left them to their labors.

The pair of them were, for all intents and purposes, invisible. The other laundry workers were mostly low-ranking Heleans—their green skin marred by scars and burns on their hands, arms, and faces, the result of carelessness with hot dryers, irons, and acidic compounds—for whom any immigrants, human or otherwise, were beneath notice.

There were few in the laundry who did not bear the marks of their employment somewhere on their exposed skin, and Leena knew that if she and Hieronymus remained there too long, they would prove no exception. But Leena had no desire to remain there for long.

In the days that followed, the pair of them cycled though a number of different responsibilities. When they had manufactured a sufficient amount of detergent for the cycle, they were assigned to cleaning out the traps on the enormous steam-driven dryers, and when that was done, were put to work unclogging the drains beneath the huge tubs. When the traps were all clean, though, and the drains all unclogged, Shafan felt that they had proved their aptitude sufficiently that she put them to work on sorting the incoming laundry into piles. The combinations and permutations were near endless—white linens, white linens with red highlights, red linens with white accent, blue linens, blue wool, white wool with blue linen trim, and so on, and so on—but Leena could scarcely complain. This was the position they had wanted, the reason they had decided to accept the posting at the laundry in the first place. Now, it was just a matter of time before the right articles came through their hands, and in the meantime, they had planning to do.

$$\LARGE \diamondsuit$$

Once Leena and Hieronymus had proven themselves dutiful, diligent workers, Shafan warmed to them, slightly. When Leena started bringing in little baked treats for the overseer, and Hieronymus flattered her shamelessly at every opportunity, in short order Shafan was the best friend they'd ever had. They'd already learned what they needed to know about the schedules and processes of the laundry. What they needed to know now were the habits of the palace staff and, most importantly, the security protocols employed in the palace spire itself.

Shafan had worked in the municipal laundry for most of her life, starting as a rug beater when she was not yet nine summers old. Now, with her wrinkled hands greedily unwrapping the sweets and confections that Leena plied her with, Shafan happily explained to her two young friends all about the guards in the palace spire, to which she had once been invited for a dinner, a few years before, when she'd been awarded a special merit for productivity. Shafan stared wistfully into the middle distance when recounting the grand ballrooms, and the fine lords and ladies, and the guards with their tridents and ceramic cuirasses, and pointed with pride to the yellowed parchment tacked up to the wall over the overseer's desk.

Hieronymus took careful note, while Leena prompted the old woman with questions about how a visitor's identity was verified, about how many guards patrolled the grounds, and so forth.

Within a week, their plan was nearly ready.

The plan, considering how much effort went into researching it, was fairly straightforward. Leena and Hieronymus would keep working at their posts as laundry sorters, waiting until they came across the uniforms of members of the palace household staff. They would purloin a set of the appropriate size and rank for each of them, and once they could both be outfitted in the livery of the palace staff, they would sneak into the coregents' palace.

The plan was simple. Timing was everything. They'd found that the southern entrance to the palace spire was manned by only a single guard, who periodically slipped away for romantic dalliance with one of the younger women from the laundry. When they saw the young lover leave her position at the dryers, they'd dress themselves in their purloined livery, dash up the steps to the first ring, and then slip through the unguarded entrance. Once inside, they'd stick to the less-trafficked routes, behaving just like two members of the palace staff about their business, and with any luck could reach the royal throne room without anyone asking them for identification.

"But what if someone *does* ask us for identification?" Leena asked as they reviewed the plan late one night, in whispered conference in their rooms at the tavern.

A cloud passed across Hieronymus's features. "Then we will do what is necessary," he said darkly.

Leena knew he was remembering the calif's daughter, that long-ago night in Masjid Empor.

"I shouldn't worry," Leena said, reaching out and taking his hand in hers. "Once we're inside, no one will give us a second look."

Hieronymus smiled, but it didn't quite reach to his eyes, and Leena knew that he was no more convinced than she was.

✦

"Good news, Balam," Leena said, sliding onto the bench across from the jaguar man while Hieronymus sat down beside him. "Yesterday we found a woman's uniform in the laundry from the palace, which we've secreted behind a loose brick in a corner of the laundry."

"Yes, indeed," Hieronymus said, thumping the Sinaa on the back. "As soon as a uniform for me comes along, we'll be ready to make our move, and then we can be away from here."

"I'm not going," Balam said, eyes still on his plate.

"What?" Hieronymus asked, pulling back his hand in disbelief.

"I've scarcely been able to exchange three words with Menchit," the jaguar man explained. "Whenever I draw near her, she runs away, and has her followers block my path. I'll not leave her here—not until I've made things right."

"Then you might just have to bring her along, my friend," Hieronymus said, "because once we've got that little rock in our hands, we're not going to be sticking around for long."

"Don't worry, Balam," Leena said, poking at her bowl of cold porridge with a ceramic spoon. "It'll be a few days before we can locate a uniform for Hero, after all, so you'll have time yet. Today is a citywide rest day, so there'll be no laundry today."

"Speaking of which," Hieronymus said, glancing around the room. "Where is everyone?"

The tavern was strangely empty, especially considering that it was time for the morning meal on a rest day. What was more, of the few patrons that were there, none of them were metamen.

"No doubt the same place Benu is." Leena tried not to grimace as she ate a spoonful from her bowl. "Missing."

"Yes, I've seen nothing of Benu in days. Balam, how about you, have you seen our wandering friend?"

Balam just shook his head, his attention on his untouched plate.

A waiter drifted by, hoisting a tray of clean mugs and plates.

"Ahoy," Hieronymus called out, motioning the waiter over. "Where has all your custom gone today? Is everyone ill?"

"No," the waiter said, shifting the tray to his shoulder, balanced on one hand, "there's some sort of big protest in the offing up on the second ring, at the Ministry of Justice. Those bunch of Black Sun fanatics are going to be agitating for their coreligionists' release, and if they don't get what they want, there's going to be blood spilled on both sides."

"What?!" Balam jumped to his feet, knocking the bench clattering to the floor. "If there's a protest, it's a surety that Menchit is involved. And if there's to be bloodshed, I need to be there to stop it."

Without another word to his companions, Balam raced to the door, pushing past the waiter, who staggered comically and dropped the loaded tray to the ground with a resounding crash.

Hieronymus, climbing to his feet after being toppled backwards by the falling bench, dusted himself off. "Well, we better follow him. If we don't, he's bound to get himself into a considerable mess."

"I suppose you're right," Leena answered, sighing. She dropped her spoon into the cold porridge with a dull thwacking. "I've no appetite for this muck, anyway."

Leena and Hieronymus did not catch up with Balam until he had almost reached the steps of the Ministry of Justice, high on the second ring of the city. Above the stalwart arches of the building rose an enormous ceramic representation of the trident, Helean symbol of justice, which was also carried as badge of office as well as weapon by the green-skinned constabulary gathered around the building's entrance in their dozens.

There were hundreds of metamen in attendance, swarming over the steps, held back only by the serried ranks of the city guard, who clutched their tridents in white-knuckled fists, waiting for their orders.

"Release our brothers and sisters," rose a voice above the tumult, "or face the dire consequences! The children of the Black Sun Genesis will not be caged, and the word of Per the Holy will not be mocked!"

Leena and Hieronymus stood on either side of Balam, just beyond the edge of the crowd, and could see the jaguar man immediately stiffen.

"Menchit," Balam said, his eyes pleading, his voice as wrought as only a parent's can be.

Leena followed his gaze, and saw the young Sinaa woman standing at the head of the assembled throng, standing just a spear's-thrust from the ranks of the city guards.

"I've got to stop this," Balam said, and rushed forward, swimming through the crush of protestors, trying to reach the front.

Leena took a step forward, as though to follow, but Hieronymus took hold of her elbow, pulling her up short.

"No," he said. "Look at their eyes, these followers of the Black Sun Genesis. They're maddened, enraged. They don't like humans in the best of circumstances, but if you got in the middle of that mix, you'd come out the worse for it."

Leena started to object, but then nodded slowly, relaxing. "I just hope he knows what he's getting into. The last thing we need is trouble with the authorities when we're so close to our goal."

Hieronymus pointed to the entrance to the building, where a well-fed green-skinned man wearing the necklace of a high-ranking ministry official stepped into view, securely protected by a ring of oversized city guards.

"Return to your appropriate places in the lower quarters," the official ordered, raising his voice, but still only barely audible over the shouts of the protestors. His green face was tinged with red, and he trembled with barely controlled emotion. "Those still in custody will face trial as soon as the coronation is complete, and I assure you that our new underlord and underlady will give the matter its due attention. But under no circumstances are we prepared to release prisoners to meet the demand of an uncouth rabble."

"Rabble?!" shouted Menchit, her fangs bared. She turned her head over her shoulder and addressed her followers. "*This* is the level of respect which the Black Sun Genesis receives in these benighted lands. Our brothers and sisters traveled here as missionaries, to bring to all the metamen living here the good word of Per, and to help them stand up to the corrupt Helean authorities, to demand better living and working conditions, as is their natural right!"

Leena leaned over and whispered to Hieronymus behind her hand. "I can't say that I blame them. You know I've no patience for religious zealots, but you can't deny that conditions for immigrants here are appalling, and I don't envy the metamen here for an instant."

"True enough," Hieronymus said warily, "but I'm not sure *this* is the way to go about it."

Hieronymus pointed to one of the Struthio towards the front of the assemblage, who had produced a large chuck of flagstone from somewhere, and was waving it menacingly above his head.

"Free our brothers and sisters!" Menchit shouted.

"Never!" the official shouted back, losing all composure. "I would sooner die than disgrace my high office by capitulating to the demands of an unruly mob!"

"Then die!" shouted the Struthio, and hurled the stone overhand at the official.

The official tried to duck, but too late, as the stone careened off his skull, drawing a nasty gash along his wide forehead.

"Der'mo," Leena spat, as the trident-wielding guards swarmed into the protestors without warning.

More protestors produced broken flagstones, which they hurled at the approaching guards.

Menchit turned towards her followers, exhorting them to charge the entrance, when one of the guards swung his trident in a long, wicked arc, smacking her solidly in the back of the head and knocking her to the ground. From their vantage, Leena and Hieronymus could not immediately see what became of her, but they had little time to wonder, as a heartbeat later Balam surged out of the crowd. The enraged jaguar man clawed the guard viciously, from navel to neck, and as the guard fell bleeding to the ground, screaming in agony, Balam ducked down, slung his daughter over his shoulder, and ran away from the melee.

Leena and Hieronymus watched Balam fleeing into the twilit gloom, making for the stairs to the lower rings. The guards were mostly engaged with battering the protestors, or were forced to deal with their own wounds, and none appeared to be giving Balam pursuit. It hardly mattered.

"We can't wait any longer," Leena said, grabbing Hieronymus by the arm and leading him from the crowd. "We have no choice but to make our move *now*."

"What?"

"If we stay in the city much longer, we run the serious risk that Balam will only end up arrested along with his daughter, and perhaps the rest of us, as well."

"But we have only the one uniform," Hieronymus objected as Leena steered them towards the municipal laundry building. "If we make our move now, then you will have to go alone."

"Like I said," Leena answered, her mouth drawn into a thin line, "we have no choice."

CHAPTER 43

The Underlady of Hele

Leena and Hieronymus raced round the curve of the second ring, in short order reaching the entrance to the municipal laundry. The door was locked but unguarded—who would waste manpower guarding dirty linens when there were riots in the streets?—and Hieronymus was able to make short work of the lock. Once they were within, the smell of lye strong in the air, they made their way to the far corner, and the loose bricks behind which they'd secreted the purloined uniform.

"I'm not sure of this plan, little sister," Hieronymus said as Leena climbed into the purple-and-jet livery of the palace household staff. "Our plan hinges on the southern entrance to the palace spire going unwatched while the guard dallies with the laundry girl. We've no assurances that you'll even be able to make it through the door, without that gap to exploit."

"Possibly," Leena answered, unconvinced. "But it seems likely to me that, with so many of the city's guards redirected to the steps of the

Ministry of Justice, other areas of the city will be left less well
defended."

Hieronymus nodded, his expression no less grave. "Perhaps. But I
still don't like it."

"We have no choice, Hero." Leena fastened the gold sash around
her waist, and then regarded herself in a silvered glass on a nearby wall.
The uniform fit her well enough, though the extra bunches of fabric at
the bosom and thighs suggested that its rightful owner was considerably more curvaceous than she. She spun on her heel, her arms out to
her sides, turning to face Hieronymus. "Well, how do I look?"

Hieronymus took a step towards her, his brows knitted. "You have
your knife, and your pistol?"

"Naturally." Leena patted the deep pockets stitched into either pants
leg, the hard outline of the Makarov visible through the dark fabric.

"Don't hesitate to use the latter, should circumstances require."

Leena raised an eyebrow. "And waste precious ammunition?"

"Just . . ." Hieronymus said, and then paused. He chewed his lip,
and regarded Leena closely. "Just be safe, understand? Do what you
must to complete your task and to leave the tower in one piece."

Leena nodded slowly. "I understand," she said. "But don't worry.
I'll be fine."

Hieronymus managed a weak smile, but didn't speak.

As Leena had suspected, the southern entrance to the palace spire was
vacant and unguarded. She passed through the high arch, walking
swiftly and with purpose, like a dutiful minion about her daily chores,
and was not accosted.

Leena and Hieronymus had been able to wheedle from Shafan the
information that the Carneol was always kept in the throne room. When

the underlord and underlady were in attendance, the Carneol was held by one or the other of them personally, ensign of their authority, but when they were in their private quarters or otherwise engaged, the gem was kept on display in a crystal case. The plan called for Leena to scale the spiraling stairs of the palace to the throne room, which occupied its highest peak, and once there take the Carneol from the case.

Unfortunately, Shafan had not been able to say with certainty what sort of protection was provided the Carneol, when in the case. Were there guards? Beasts of some variety? Elaborate traps and baffles? Leena did not know. But as she stepped across the threshold and made her way towards the interior stair, her imagination conjured up dreadful possibilities.

As she walked through the opulent corridors of the palace, festooned with tapestries and ceramic statues, Leena passed household servants about their business, but few guards, only a handful standing watch or walking on patrol, their ceramic cuirasses polished to a mirror shine. When she reached the interior stair, and mounted the steps, she found that she was alone, with no one ascending or descending above her. In a few minutes' time, she would reach the top, and the throne room.

It seemed that Leena's surmise about the effect of the protest on the other areas of the city was proving correct. Perhaps, then, this inconvenient acceleration of their schedule would prove a blessing in disguise. Assuming, of course, that something horrible did not await her in the throne room above, for which their plans had no contingent.

✦

The creature beyond the door to the throne room, ancient and bent, was the last sight Leena expected to see. An ancient woman, dressed in the vermilion whose use was taboo for all but the Helean monarchs themselves, stood near a wide window, looking down at the rings of

Hele below, and the innumerable caves beyond, distant and indistinct in the twilit gloom. A brazier burned between a pair of thrones on a dais, casting a faint yellow glow across the room, and set into the wall above was a crystal case, sitting open and empty.

"Underlady Persefonh," Leena said, breathless both from mounting the countless steps of the interior stair, and from running headlong into the monarch of the hidden city unexpectedly.

The old woman turned slightly, her watery eyes glancing Leena's way. In her gnarled hands was a multifaceted gem the size of a man's fist, scarlet and seeming to glow with an inner light.

"The Carneol," Leena said in a whisper.

The underlady's green skin was wrinkled, and parchment-thin, veins standing like blue cords beneath the surface.

"They have not returned yet, you know," Persefonh said in a care-worn, husky voice. "If they had survived, we'd have seen some sign of them by now. So Hele is not to have a new underlord and underlady just yet, and I will have to continue to carry my burden alone." She lifted the red gem until it was only centimeters from her nose, a strange expression on her wrinkled features. "And my burden has become so heavy, of late."

Leena, hesitantly, took a step forward, playing the part of the dutiful household servant. "Your Majesty, is there . . . is there anything you require?"

The underlady shook her head, absently, and turned back towards the window.

"I was just a child of seven summers when Akerohn and I were selected from the royal crèches, you know," she said, glancing momentarily at the empty throne across the floor. "Before we even fully understood what was happening, we'd been fed the sacred pomegranates, and sent out into the tunnels, the final tests of the coronation rituals. The future rulers of Hele, after all, have always had to prove their worth by going into the consecrated tunnels, passing a full day and night, and returning with the gemstones which the ancient religion of our foreparents holds sacred." She paused, and then turned back to Leena with a rueful smile on her narrow mouth. "Just rocks, really. Don't tell anyone, my dear, but the sacred gemstones were really just rocks, pebbles found down in the caves. Perhaps in ancient days children who returned without the proper gems were denied the throne of Hele, but in recent centuries, we'll crown anyone who returns from the caves half-alive."

Leena drew closer, her hands held behind her back, her eyes respectfully on the floor. "Yes, Your Majesty."

"There is danger in the caves; there is no doubt of that. Even if the children survive, they can be crippled by falling rocks and the like. Most that fail in the attempt are lost forever to the caves, their bodies never found. So if a pair of children return with a bit of gravel, they ascend to the throne of Hele and are given the Carneol, and no one thinks twice about it." The underlady sighed, and cradled the scarlet gem in her withered hands. "As history records, in some eras the trials seem to go without incident, the first pair of children who are sent out returning unharmed at the end of the appointed term. In other eras, though, wave after wave of children are sent into the dark caves, two by two, with none returning after the long days and weeks." She looked back to Leena, her expression weary. "Leaving the surviving regent to occupy the throne, all the while. Alone."

Leena was now little more than a meter away, her head still bowed deferentially.

"I just want to step down and hand over the signet of office." Persefonh closed her eyes, and her chin fell to her chest. "I am just so very tired, and I miss my Akerohn, and I just want to sleep." She opened her eyes again, looking down angrily at the gem in her hands. "And the Carneol is such a heavy burden to bear."

Leena's hand drifted to her pocket, and closed around the hilt of her knife.

"Is there no one who can take this burden from me?"

Leena lunged forward, and struck the underlady with the butt of her knife's hilt, clouting a blow to the back of the old woman's skull where it met the neck.

The underlady collapsed to the ground in a heap, vermilion gowns swirling around her, and the Carneol clattered noisily to the floor.

"I'm sorry." Leena sighed, stepping over the still form of the underlady and snatching up the Carneol.

The narrow chest of the underlady rose and fell. Leena had struck hard enough to knock her unconscious, but not hard enough to kill, or so Leena hoped. She slipped the Carneol and the knife back into her pocket, and slipped away to the interior stair.

CHAPTER 44

The Caves of Hele

Hieronymus was waiting in the municipal laundry for Leena when she returned.

"What happened?" Hieronymus said, jumping to his feet and rushing towards her. "Are you all right?"

"More than all right," Leena said grimly, and held the Carneol out for his inspection. "Now, hand me my clothes so we can be away from here."

✦

As they had hoped, they found Balam at their rooms at the tavern, his unconscious daughter stretched out on a cot. Her head was bandaged, swaddled with turns of linen, but she seemed to be breathing regularly.

"How is she . . . ?" Hieronymus began, then broke off when he saw his friend's tearstained cheeks.

"She has . . . She has yet to regain her senses," Balam said, wiping his face dry on the back of his hand, smoothing out his fur. "But her injuries don't seem serious, and I think that she should be fine. Given time, she should be fine."

The jaguar man knelt by the side of the cot, and took his insensate daughter's hand in his own.

"We need to be away, and quickly," Leena said, gathering up her things, secreting the scarlet gem in her pack.

"Yes, the authorities are busy with the rabble for the moment," Hieronymus said, stuffing his clothes and supplies into his own pack, "but they will begin searching for the agitators' ringleader before long"—he pointed at the unconscious Menchit—"and too many have seen her comings and goings for their search not to lead them straight here."

"Agreed." Balam took a deep breath, and rose to his feet. He began fastening the buckles of his harness, slipping his knives back into their sheaths.

"But what of Benu?" Leena said. "I should hate to abandon him here, without any word from us."

"I won't risk my daughter's safety by waiting," Balam said sternly.

"That won't be necessary," said a voice from the door, and Hieronymus and Leena spun around, their swords drawn.

Benu stood in the open doorway, a strange expression on his face, his opalescent eyes unreadable.

"And now our company is complete," Hieronymus said with a sigh of relief, sliding his saber back into its scabbard.

"No." Benu shook his head, and smiled slightly. "I won't be going with you."

Leena stopped short, and looked at the artificial man, confused. "Why ever not?"

Benu looked at the unconscious form of the Sinaa on the cot. "There isn't time to explain now. You must follow me into the caverns, and quickly. I know a way out of the city by which you can avoid the city guards, and I have something to show you."

With that, the artificial man turned, and hurried away down the corridor. Leena glanced at Hieronymus, who shrugged, as Balam carefully slung his daughter across his shoulder.

"Let's go, then," Leena said, and followed Benu into the corridor.

They reached the city gates in the outer wall of the ninth ring without incident, and found only one guard on duty. Seeing the unconscious Sinaa female draped over Balam's shoulder, though, the guard was immediately brought on the defensive, raising his trident and shouting for them to halt immediately.

"I'm sorry, but we don't have time for this," Benu said, and in an eyeblink, struck a lightning-fast blow with the heel of his palm to the guard's chin. The guard's head snapped back, violently, and he fell to the flagstones, his trident clattering to the ground beside him.

"Come along," Benu called back impatiently over his shoulder, hurrying away from the gate at speed. "It wouldn't do to be apprehended so close to freedom."

Benu's course carried him away from the city, towards the cave mouths that pocked the walls of the immense cavern, heading out into the eternal twilight.

Benu led them to the mouth of a wide tunnel, dimly lit and mysterious.

"I have discovered," he explained, "why the wizard-kings of Atla were interested in the Lathe Mountains, and how Hele came to be."

"This is fascinating trivia, I'm sure," Hieronymus said as the artificial man stepped into the gloom of the cave mouth, motioning them to follow, "but I fail to see its relevance to our present circumstances. I thought you knew of some passage out of these caverns, and yet you lead us now to a cave which to all appearances will lead us even further from daylight."

"You will see," Benu said, disappearing into the darkness beyond the tunnel mouth. "All answers are revealed within."

Hieronymus, Leena, and Balam were left standing in the twilight, peering into the darkened cave tunnel. On his shoulder, Balam's daughter stirred, moaning piteously in her sleep.

"Well," Leena said, glancing back at the walls of the city, and the tram tracks that mounted the opposite wall of the cavern. "I don't see that we have much choice, at this point."

"The tram is too closely guarded," Balam said. "We'd have to fight our way to the surface, and I question how effective I would be in combat with Menchit across my back."

"Agreed," Hieronymus said. "Well, let's hope our strange artificial friend has discovered something miraculous, indeed."

As they moved deeper into the tunnel, Leena's eyes adjusted to the gloom, and she could see faintly in grays and blacks, a monochromatic world. If the cavern of Hele was a perpetual twilight, the tunnel was a moonless night.

Benu was in the lead, directing them with the sound of his voice, while the others followed close behind, trying to stay within arm's reach of one another. Periodically they reached a juncture between two tunnels, and Benu would pause for them to catch up before starting down a branch.

"Regard the snaking character of the tunnels, my friends," Benu said. "And your eyes may not have the sensitivity to see them in fine detail, but the shadows you see on the tunnel walls are other, smaller veins, some no wider than a finger's breadth, which intersect the larger passages at intervals."

"We seem no closer to the surface," Balam growled. "The only sight I wish to see is clear blue skies overhead. I've had enough of these damned caverns to last two lifetimes."

"But what engenders such strange ducts in living rock?" Benu went on. "There's no evidence of volcanism here, and even if there were, the passage of molten rock or volcanic gases does not produce artifacts such as these. So whence came they?"

"I detect a rhetorical tone to your words," Hieronymus said impatiently, "and suspect that you already have an answer to your questions."

"Quite so," Benu said, and turned down a branching corridor.

As Leena came around the bend, she saw a faint light glowing up ahead. "What . . . is that?"

"I would tell you now," Benu said with a smile, "but I do so hate to spoil the surprise."

The company continued down the tunnel, the light around them intensifying as they drew near the juncture up ahead.

Benu stopped at the juncture, and gestured beyond the curve of the tunnel wall, glancing back eagerly at the company. "There," he said proudly. "There are all your answers."

Leena and Hieronymus rounded the corner, Balam following close behind, and found themselves in a wide chamber, lit bright as day. To their left, a passage branched off, climbing at a steep angle, while to their right, against a far wall, hovered a silver sphere, twin to the one that had brought Leena to Paragaea.

"A gate!" Leena said in an urgent whisper.

"Yes," Benu said, taking a few steps towards the silver sphere. "Gates seem to appear with startling regularity within the Lathe

Mountains, but they are transient, lasting sometimes for moments, sometimes more than a century. But, short-lived as they are, they migrate, moving from one point to another before disappearing. It was these wandering gates that carved out the tunnel complexes of Hele." Benu pointed to the passage branching to the left. "That corridor leads to the surface, and will take you to the southern foothills of Lathe."

"So why aren't you coming with us?" Hieronymus said, his eyes on the silvery sphere.

"Because I intend to traverse the gate," Benu said, "and see what lies on the other side."

"What?" Balam said, drawing back.

"And why wouldn't I? When I first joined your company, in the forests of Altrusia, I indicated my desire to travel to Earth. It will be an entire world of new information to gather. I'd have purpose once more, with an unwritten book of knowledge to fill."

Leena stepped forward, mesmerized by the floating sphere. "I'm going with you," she said breathlessly.

"You'll do no such thing!" Hieronymus said, grabbing hold of her arm. "You have no way of knowing when or where the gate will take you. Benu may be willing to take that risk, but I thought that you wanted to return to your own time and place, not just any chance point in Earth's history."

Leena looked from Hieronymus to the silvery sphere, and nodded reluctantly. "You're right, of course," she said at length. "I just . . . I just don't know how close I'll come again."

"Have faith, little sister," Hieronymus said, smiling. "We'll press on to Atla. If the wizard-kings know how to predict or map gates of particular characteristics, I promise you we'll squeeze the knowledge from them."

Balam's daughter, slung over his shoulder like a sack of potatoes, stirred. The light from the silvery sphere seemed to flicker, inconstant for a moment, and then stabilized.

"I don't want to delay much longer," Benu said, stepping nearer the sphere. "With no way of predicting the movements of these gates, I've no way of knowing whether it will last for another millennium or another heartbeat, but I don't want to take the chance of it disappearing." He turned to the company and smiled fondly. "Farewell, my friends. These last months you have given me something which I thought I'd never find again. Companionship. And for that, you have my thanks."

Leena raised her hand in a wave, and Hieronymus snapped off a little salute, but Balam just nodded thoughtfully.

"Good-bye." Benu reached out, and touched the surface of the gate with his fingertips.

For a split second, Leena thought that they'd been wrong, thought that nothing would happen. But then Benu seemed to shrink before their eyes, as though he were receding quickly without moving any farther away, and then he was gone.

CHAPTER 45

Southwards

By the time they reached the surface, it was morning, and Leena felt the sun on her face for the first time in days.

"I'd almost forgotten what fresh air smells like," Hieronymus said, breathing deeply through his nostrils. "After a few days down in that pit, I no longer noticed the smell."

"I don't think air quality is high on the Heleans' list of concerns," Leena answered absently, glancing around her.

They were standing on a treacherous scree, a slope of gravel that ran at a steep grade for more than half a kilometer, ending at a wide plateau below. The bulk of the Lathe Mountains rose above them, while to the south ambled rolling foothills, sparsely forested. Somewhere far beyond, over the curve of the horizon, lay the final destination in Leena's journey, the last place on Paragaea in which they might find the answers she sought.

Leena could not help but wonder whether she'd made a mistake. Had she gone through the gate with Benu, down in the cavern, she'd at least be back on Earth, though whenever and wherever she might find herself remained a mystery. Now, having passed up that opportunity, she ran the risk that her quest would prove fruitless, should the Atlans prove either to be entirely extinct, or failed to measure up to their mythic reputation. If she were to return here, to the Helean caverns beneath the Lathe Mountains, she might find that gate now closed, and another might not open again in her lifetime. At this stage, her only hope to return to Earth lay atop Mount Ignis to the south, in the citadel city of Atla.

A short distance away, Menchit struggled to regain consciousness, stretched out on the gravelly slope. Balam checked the dressing on her head wound, his expression that of concerned fathers in all times and places.

"Well," Hieronymus said, taking a drink of water from a flask in his pack, and handing it to Leena. "Shall we be away? We've a long day's travel before nightfall, and I, for one, would like to be miles and miles away from here before we sleep."

Leena took a deep draught of the water, and handed it back to Hieronymus, wiping her mouth dry on her sleeve. "Lead on, Hero," she said, hitching her pack up on her shoulders.

Balam carefully picked Menchit up in his arms, and the company started down the mountain.

At midday, passing through rolling hills, they were forced to stop when Menchit regained consciousness. Her last memories those of leading a crowd of the faithful against the oppressive Helean guard, she was less than pleased to discover her present circumstances.

"Unhand me!" she shouted, clawing at Balam's face, writhing in his arms.

"Daughter!" Balam cried, yanking his head back, the black fur of his cheek bloodied.

The young Sinaa fell to the ground snarling. She was on her feet in an instant, but wavered unsteadily, her eyes rolling.

"You've got a nasty head wound, Daughter," Balam said, his tone calm as he reached out his hands to steady her. "No one is going to do you any further harm. You're safe now."

"Where am I?" Menchit said, baring her fangs, and then collapsed to the ground, her eyes rolling up in her head.

Balam rushed to her side, and Leena and Hieronymus came back to offer what assistance they could.

Hieronymus dug the water flask from his pack, and when Balam had helped his daughter into a sitting position, forced her to drink a few sips from it.

"You lost a fair amount of blood in the night, Menchit," Balam said calmly, "but your wound appears to be healing as well as could be expected, and so long as you don't make any more sudden or violent movements— say, viciously attacking your father, unprovoked—then you should be fine."

"I said, where am I?" Menchit demanded, knocking away the water flask, her amber eyes flashing. "I had business in Hele, freeing my imprisoned brethren, and now a crystal-blue sky stretches above my head. Where have you brought me?!"

"The Helean guards knocked you unconscious, and quickly broke the back of your protest. If I had not brought you with us when we fled the city, you'd be imprisoned, or worse."

"If I was to die, it was because it was fated," Menchit said. "The Holy Per tells us that the universe has a design for each of us, and that it is importunate for us to attempt to circumvent our destinies. Just as our fates are mapped out by the demiurges of Atla, whom the ignorant call wizard-kings, so too are the skeins of their destinies woven by the universe itself. None of us should attempt to disrupt the natural order, or the whole world suffers thereby."

"So the world suffers now that you did not die needlessly in a Helean gaol?" Balam snapped.

"If that was the will of Atla," Menchit said defiantly, "then yes, it does."

"Well," Balam answered, climbing to his feet. "Our journeys carry us to Atla, so perhaps you'll have a chance to ask your *demiurges* what they think about your continued existence, yourself."

The young Sinaa's eyes widened. "You travel to Atla? But even if you could cross the burned steppes of Eschar, none can pass the sacred barrier."

"Oh," Leena said with a smile, tightening her grip on her pack's shoulder straps, "I don't think we'll have a problem on that count."

"Atla?" Menchit said, shaking her head in disbelief. "But it is blasphemy to think that mortals can approach the abode of the demiurges."

Hieronymus smiled, and helped Balam to his feet. "You'll find, I think, that blasphemy comes easily to such as we."

The company continued to the south. The rolling hills slowly gave way to broad steppes, and the farther they traveled, the colder and drier the air grew.

Menchit proved to be a very reluctant addition to their band. It became clear very early that if she had the opportunity, she would attempt to return straightaway to Hele, to complete her holy mission. Balam would have none of it, and in short order bound her hands to a length of stout cord, which he carried like a leash. As the company marched to the south, then, Menchit would be dragged behind her father like a stubborn pet, hands bound all day, and then fixed to a tree or the like by night. Leena felt that this treatment was degrading, even for one as recalcitrant as Menchit, but Balam refused to release his daughter until he had made her see reason. Balam felt, understandably, that she had been poisoned against him by his sisters—her aunts—and by his cousin, Gerjis. Menchit remained silent, for the most part, and when she did speak, it was to throw the words of "Holy" Per in Balam's face. In her eyes, he was a heretic, one who had heard the good word but refused to listen, and for that he was damned.

Menchit was most vocal in the hours after sunset. All during the evening meal, she hailed abuse down on her father, pelting him with quotations from scripture, damning him as a disgrace to his people and to all the races of metamankind, hurling invective in a steady torrent. Balam took her abuse with a quiet stoicism while preparing the evening meal, and when he had finished eating and cleared things away, he sat down just beyond Menchit's reach, and tried calmly to reason with her. He tried to explain that her perceptions of events and individuals had been distorted by the lens of Per's Black Sun Genesis, and that her memories of childhood did not correspond with reality. Menchit accused Balam of abandoning her and her mother, preferring to carouse and drink and whore his way across Paragaea, and said that when her mother had died, she had been fortunate that her cousin and aunts were there to look after her. With the patience of a saint, Balam told Menchit again and again how her account of events differed in nearly every particular from reality, and that they were both the victims of her Uncle Gerjis's conniving, not Menchit the victim of her father's philandering. But Menchit would have none of it, rained further abuse on him, and the cycle continued.

By the second night of this theater, Hieronymus and Leena decided to make camp farther up the path from Balam and Menchit, leaving the two Sinaa to work out their familial difficulties in private. They journeyed a farther kilometer due south, found a suitable spot to set up camp, and then enjoyed their simple evening meal in glorious, uninterrupted silence.

When the meal was through, Leena and Hieronymus sat side by side, looking up at the stars above. The southern skies differed somewhat from those they'd watched wheeling above the deck of the *Acoetes Zephyrus*, and it felt, too, as if they themselves had changed in the interim.

"I always find," Hieronymus said, breaking the silence that had lingered over their little camp since the evening meal, "that the more I am around the devoutly religious, the less tolerant of religion I become." He smiled wanly and glanced over at Leena. "In the absence of the devout, I tend to feel that anyone can believe whatever they bloody well like, and what business is it of mine? But after a few hours spent in the company of one who lives and breathes nothing but dogma, I find my palms itching for my saber's hilt."

"She is difficult to take for long stretches, isn't she?" Leena looked over her shoulder to the north, and shuddered slightly.

"*That* is putting it mildly."

"Still," Leena said, lying back on the soft grass, pillowing her head on her hands, "it is not only the religious who become so enamored of dogma that they do nothing but regurgitate platitudes." Leena closed her eyes, lost in memory for a moment. "I was the second woman of my country to launch into space. The first was Valentina Vladimirovna Tereshkova, a woman from the Yaroslavl region, born just a few months before me. But by all rights, the first should have been Valentina Leonidovna Ponomaryova, a woman from Ukraine. Ponomaryova is the most technically astute of any in the Female Cosmonaut Group, and truth be told, could fly rings around any of us. But Ponomaryova is not 'ideologically pure.' She says that a woman can smoke cigarettes and still be a decent person; she took unescorted trips into Feodosiya while the rest of us were busy training. She is a free spirit. But, sadly for her, the Soviet Union does not much care for free spirits. When it came time to give our final interviews to the board, to determine who would be the first woman into space, we were asked, 'What do you want from life?' When I answered, I said simply, 'I want to fly.' Ponomaryova, for her part, smiled and said, 'I want to take everything it can offer.' This was *not* the answer the board wished to hear. It was no surprise that they picked Tereshkova. Do you know what she answered, to that same question? She said, 'I want to support irrevocably the Komsomol and Communist Party.' Can you believe that? As though she were a handbook of proper behavior for party membership. I placed third, in the end, not quite as technically astute as Ponomaryova and not quite as ideologically pure as Tereshkova. Tereshkova, though, the only one of us who did not receive the highest marks in the academic tests, was selected to be the first woman in space."

Leena sighed deeply, and stared in silence for a moment up at the stars.

"They told Ponomaryova that she was next, that Tereshkova was the most political choice for the first launch, but that her chance would come. When the crew for Vostok 7 was announced, though, it was my name on the list, and not hers. I am not the pilot she is, but I suppose I am more ideologically pure, for all of that, and so it was me in the module and not her."

Leena shook her head, and her eyes moistened.

"Poor Ponomaryova. In a more honest culture, it would have been her."

"You know," Hieronymus said, leaning in close, "I think that may be the first criticism I've heard you utter about your native land."

Leena dried her eyes on her sleeve, and looked at him.

"I am honest," she said. "My nation is not perfect, I'm the first to admit, but I maintain that our system is better for the largest percentage of the population than any other history has yet produced."

Hieronymus smiled. "That's exactly what I used to say, in my school days, about the British system, too."

"Well, that's what sets us apart from the zealots, I suppose. We recognize the dogma for what it is."

"Yes," Hieronymus said, and inched closer.

They were bare centimeters apart, now.

"You know," Leena said, her voice low, "this may be the first time in all our journeys together that you and I are actually alone."

Hieronymus pursed his lips, thinking back. "I believe you're right.

Even on the dhow, there was always someone within a few meters' distance."

Leena had not been with another man since Sergei had died, all those years ago, and though she'd never before realized it, she may have abstained since then out of respect for his memory. Even his shade, though, should it still linger, could find no fault in two people seeking warmth and comfort in one another's arms.

"Alone," Leena said, their noses nearly touching. "Interesting."

"Hmmm. Isn't it?"

Hieronymus's mouth was on hers, and her arms were snaked around his back before Leena quite knew what was happening. There, beneath the stars, they shed their clothes and their inhibitions, and found something like peace in one another's arms, if only for a brief span.

CHAPTER 46

The Burned Steppes of Eschar

They traveled on, the steppes changing, become permafrost, with a light hoar of frosted grass growing atop a deep level of frozen ground. They had reached Eschar, the boundary between the southern peninsula and the rest of the Paragaean continent. Strange objects and machines jutted out of the landscape, rusted steel and viridescent bronze and alloys Leena could not name.

"These are the remnants of the Genos Wars, millennia ago," Hieronymus explained as they passed beneath the shadow of a towering spire whose purpose they could not begin to guess. "When the races of metamen rose up against the Black Sun Empire."

"When I was a child," Balam said, "my tutors told me that there were . . . things buried beneath the frozen steppes of Eschar—men, metamen, machines, and monsters. It is said that, in ancient days, the races of metamankind were the servitors of the wizard-kings of Atla, and that tiring of their oppression, they rose up, and did battle against their former masters."

Menchit laughed mirthlessly. She walked freely now, too far distant from Hele or any other settlement for the leash to be of any need, and stared up at the towering structures with reverential awe. "Ignorant fool. We did not rebel against our masters. We were cast out, for our weaknesses. The Holy Per writes that the demiurges of Atla came to believe that the races of metamankind had become enfeebled, overly dependent on the good graces of their creators, and to strengthen us, the metamen were cast out. The demiurges of Atla burned the steppes of Eschar with cold fire, leaving the dead landscape a sign for future generations, and sealed themselves behind the sacred barrier. One day, when we have purified ourselves, we will be welcomed back into the loving arms of our creators, joining them once more in the paradise of Atla."

Leena and Hieronymus exchanged meaningful glances, while Balam sighed a long-suffering sigh.

✦

Several days across the burned, lifeless steppes, as they prepared to make camp, they saw a glow up ahead, far over the southern horizon.

"Is that Mount Ignis?" Leena asked. "Isn't the citadel city of Atla built atop a volcano?"

Hieronymus consulted his maps by firelight, noting the additions and corrections Benu had made to his cartography while they sailed aboard the dhow.

"No," he said at length, shaking his head. "It is far too close to be Atla. Besides, we should be able to see Mount Ignis by day long before we could see its lights by night."

"There is someone out on the burned steppes ahead of us," Balam said simply.

Menchit, who seemed to have become more of a reluctant fellow traveler than a prisoner, for all of her vocal disagreements with her

father, looked nervously to the southern skies, and drifted uncon-
sciously nearer her father.

Leena shivered.

That night, she and Hieronymus kept camp close by Balam and his
daughter, suffering through their row, rather than separating and
risking discovery by beings unknown out in the darkness. She ached to
be at his side, this the first night in many long days that they did not
lie together under the stars, but she clutched her blankets close around
her in the cold air, and shivered until dawn.

✦

The next day, in late afternoon, they came upon a large encampment. Not
a fraction the size of Roam, there was still to this tent city something of
that flavor. Thousands of temporary dwellings gathered together, forming
a metropolis out on the bare permafrost. They decided to exercise caution,
and kept hidden behind a towering spar of oxidized steel until nightfall.

✦

Under cover of darkness, they stole into the encampment.

"Take care," Hieronymus whispered as they slipped between the
pickets into the confusion of tents. Overhead, clouds drifted across a
moonless sky, and the night was nearly as dim as the caves of Hele. "I
would prefer to avoid discovery, if possible, until we learn with whom
we are dealing."

"Agreed," Balam said in a quiet voice, and at his side Menchit
seemed as worried as any about what they might find.

Leena kept a hand near the hilt of her short sword, her other hovering over her holstered Makarov.

Keeping out of sight behind tents and tarpaulins, the company made their silent way into the makeshift metropolis. Unlike Roam, with its ordered rows and avenues, this assemblage of tents was arranged in no discernible pattern, clustered haphazardly across the flat plains of the steppes.

"There," Balam whispered, and pointed ahead.

A group of metamen, nearly two dozen strong, were moving together through the tents, making for the center of the encampment. Male and female, they were of every conceivable strain and variety of metaman.

"Who are they?" Leena whispered, drawing near Hieronymus.

"A more pertinent question," Hieronymus answered, "might be, What are they doing?"

"Let's follow and see, shall we?" Balam said. He glanced to his daughter. "Stay with me, Menchit. Do you understand? I want no harm to come to you."

Menchit did not speak, but only nodded, her jaw clenched.

"Come on," Leena said, and followed the party of metamen, keeping to the shadows.

Near the center of the tent city, they found a large excavation under way. Hieronymus found them a place to hide beneath a large pile of excavated dirt and rubble, and they regarded the scene before them.

Scores of metamen of all races worked together under bright lanterns, with picks, axes, and shovels, unearthing some massive, ancient engine of war. On the far side of the pit, they saw a collection of metamen dressed in finery, standing with what looked to be a withered old human, ancient and hairless, wearing shimmering robes.

"Gerjis!" Balam cursed spitefully, his eyes on a Sinaa who was standing amongst the dignitaries and had a royal harness crisscrossing his chest.

Menchit's eyes opened wide, and she leapt to her feet and cried out with joy, "Per!"

The jaguar man reached up to drag his daughter back out of sight, but it was too late. Menchit broke away from him, and began racing around the perimeter of the pit.

"Who is that?" Hieronymus hissed.

"My cousin, and my foul sisters," Balam replied sharply, jumping to his feet and taking a few long strides after his daughter. "And the old human is the twice-damned Per!"

"Balam, wait!" Leena said, reaching out to take his arm. "Look!"

Menchit's joyous cry had drawn the attention of the metamen, and as she raced around the pit's edge to where her aunts, cousin, and spiritual leader stood, Hieronymus, Leena, and Balam were subjected to the angry stares of the workers in the pit, who now advanced on them, hefting pick and axe menacingly.

CHAPTER 47

The Barrier

The mass of the metamen in the pit drew nearer, their eyes flashing angrily in the lantern light.

Hieronymus took to his feet, sprinting back the way they'd come, and called back needlessly to Leena and Balam, "Run!"

Leena made to follow, but glancing back saw that Balam had extended his claws, and was actually moving *towards* the advancing mob.

"No!" Leena cried, grabbing the jaguar man's arm and dragging him after her. "Now is *not* the time."

Balam looked across the pit to where his daughter even now was embracing his reviled cousin, and then glanced back at Leena, agony etched on his face.

"We must go," Leena said urgently, sparing a glance at the advancing mob, now no more than a dozen meters away.

Balam bared his fangs, but nodded angrily. Turning his back on the pit, and those who stood beyond it, he turned and raced after Hieronymus, Leena following close behind.

The trio reached the northern edge of the encampment just ahead of their pursuers. Returning the way they had come, they raced out into the dark night, momentarily losing the metamen in the jutting spars of ancient engines of war to the north.

"Here," Hieronymus said in a harsh whisper, pointing to a rusted shell of metal that rose just over a meter from the ground before bending back on itself, leaving a small cavity within accessible by a narrow fissure.

Leena slid through the fissure, crouching in the cavity beneath the curving shell. Hieronymus followed, his shoulders barely fitting through, and then Balam, who was scored front and back by the ragged edge of the metal, though he bore the pain of it stoically, his thoughts running in tight circles.

"Damn them!" Balam snarled, pounding a fist into the burned ground. "Damn Gerjis, damn Sakhmet, damn Bastet, and damn me!" His breath caught in his throat, and he sobbed, "My poor, deluded girl."

Hieronymus inched over, and laid a hand on the Sinaa's knee. "My friend," he said, barely above a whisper, "you must calm yourself. Our pursuers still search these wastes for us, and our numbers are too few to fend them off. If you cannot keep silent, they are sure to find us."

As if in answer to Hieronymus's words, through the fissure they could see a group of metamen approaching from the south, bearing torches. The Canid and Sinaa among their number sniffed the air, but it seemed that the trio's scents did not travel far in the cold night, and they were hidden from view within the sheltering wreckage. The pursuers passed by, and the trio remained undetected.

Long after the pursuit had gone by, the trio drew close together in a whispered conference, trying to work out what to do next.

Balam, for his part, was all for storming the encampment and seizing his daughter, and damn the consequences.

"I'm sorry, Balam," Leena said reluctantly, "but Menchit *did* seem to be overjoyed to be reunited with her family.

"*I* am her family," Balam snarled.

"However," Hieronymus whispered, "though it pains me to say, she does not accept you. In an ideal situation, perhaps, you might in time force her to recognize you, but in present circumstances, it seems hardly likely. Her heart and mind are turned against you, and now there stands between you and her this massed army of the Black Sun Genesis."

"Coming to that," Leena said, "why *is* there an army of religionists in these burned wastes, anyway?"

Hieronymus shrugged. "That's a question we'll have to ponder at a later hour, when we've put more miles between us and that angry mob. For now, I think our only choice is to continue on towards Atla, and leave Menchit for the moment with her people."

Balam bared his fangs in an angry sneer, but slowly nodded.

"Agreed," the jaguar man said at length.

"But go quietly," Leena said as the trio crept on hands and knees out from the sheltering cover of the spar. "The last time I faced a horde of angry metamen it did not go well for me, and I've little desire to repeat the experience."

✦

The company edged around the encampment without further incident, moving farther south.

The next morning found them many kilometers to the south, the encampment of the Per followers only dimly visible on the northern horizon. To the west, east, and south were nothing but the burned steppes, dotted here and there with the rusting promontories that stood as silent memorial to the lives lost in the Genos Wars.

They stopped to rest and feed themselves. Hieronymus passed

around a flask of water, while they munched unenthusiastically on strips of dried meat and salty hunks of hard bread.

Balam had not spoken since the night before, glowering in silence as they marched to the south, extending and retracting his claws with a fire burning in his amber eyes.

Finally, the silence was more than Leena could bear. "I had understood the Black Sun Genesis to be a religion of the metamen. Why, then, was there a human among their leaders?"

Hieronymus said, "Yes, I puzzled over that, too, in the brief moment I had to consider it. You are sure, Balam, that the old human was the spiritual patriarch Per?"

Balam's eyes flashed, momentarily, but then he sighed, and visibly forced himself to relax. "Yes, I've seen him before, once, when I was a child. That was Per, no question about it."

"Who is he?" Leena asked. She was beginning to form a theory, but was reluctant to voice it until she had more evidence. "Where did he come from?"

"I'm not certain. All I know is that Per appeared first among the metamen decades ago. It was said he could work miracles, and that he held secret wisdom. He taught that the wizard-kings of Atla had created the races of metamen in ancient days, and that the time would come for the metamen to return home, in the final test that Per called the Reckoning. No one knew where he had come from, though some whispered that he was one of the wizard-kings himself, cursed with immortality and forced to wander the circle of lands until the wizard-kings and their metamen creations were finally brought together."

Leena nodded, and rubbed her chin thoughtfully.

✦

Days later, the trio reached the southern boundary of the burned steppes of Eschar, and saw shimmering on the horizon before them a translucent curtain of green light extending as far as the eye could see to either horizon, seeming to rise up endlessly into the heavens above.

"The Barrier of Atla," Hieronymus said wonderingly.

"It seems to curve away in the distance," Leena said, looking to one side and the other, and then craning her head back as far as it would go. "Is it a dome of some kind, perhaps, curving back on itself?"

"Perhaps." Balam stood in place, regarding the energetic barrier with an unreadable expression on his face. "I've heard stories of this since I was a cub, but never expected to see it."

"And none have passed through this barrier since it was erected?" Leena asked.

"So Benu said," Hieronymus answered. "Or if any have passed through, then they have not returned to tell the tale."

"And how is this"—Leena held aloft the scarlet Carneol, which she'd drawn from her pack—"going to grant us passage?"

In the gray light of the late afternoon, the red gem seemed to glow faintly with an inner light.

"I suppose we'll just have to see, won't we?" Hieronymus said with a smile, and continued marching to the south.

It was near sunset when they reached the base of the barrier and, in the fading light, the green curtain seemed to shimmer and dance like the Aurora Borealis, casting off a faint green glow. What little they could see of the terrain beyond the barrier was hazy and indistinct.

"Regard the gemstone," Hieronymus said, awestruck.

Leena looked at the Carneol, still held in her hands, and saw that it was now indeed glowing with an inner light, bright as a lantern, that strobed and pulsated as she watched.

"Look!" Balam pointed at the barrier before them.

A section of the curtain directly in front of them, a roughly circular patch approximately three meters in diameter, had changed from shimmering pale green to a rich, vibrant crimson.

"It resonates somehow with the gem," Hieronymus said. He turned to Leena. "Draw nearer the barrier, little sister."

Leena took a few steps closer, and the Carneol glowed even brighter. The scarlet circle became a fissure in the barrier, opening slowly like a hand parting the curtain, just broad enough for the three of them to pass through.

"Hurry," Leena said, frozen in place. "I've no idea how to control this thing, and I don't much care to see what happens if we should be standing in the aperture when this thing chooses to close."

After exchanging a brief, nervous glance, Balam and Hieronymus slipped through the opening, and Leena followed close behind.

As soon as the Carneol had passed through to the other side, the barrier immediately sealed shut behind them, becoming once more a uniform, shimmering green.

"There," Hieronymus said, pointing to the south.

Atla was still a full day's journey before them, but already they could spy Mount Ignis looming on the near horizon, the red diamond of the citadel city dimly visible at its peak.

CHAPTER 48
The Approach to Atla

Beyond the Barrier, the terrain and climate changed markedly. The landscape through which they now moved was a barren waste of ice and snow, the air so cruelly frigid that it stung their lungs to breathe deeply. Leena and Hieronymus swaddled themselves in multiple layers of clothing, shirts, trousers, and jackets, but still felt the bite of the cold wind as it blew over the frigid plain. Balam, who never wore anything but his loincloth and harness, shivered as snowflakes matted his black fur, hugging himself to try to keep warm.

Their day's journey became two, the passage through the frozen wasteland so hampered by the thick snowbanks and the refusal of their own muscles to work at normal speeds. They slogged through the first night and most of the following day without stopping, finally forced to make camp near nightfall. They found a sheltering outcropping of rock, meager protection against the fierce winds, and huddled together around a small fire, trying to conserve their warmth.

After they'd finished a simple meal of hot broth and hard bread, warmed over the fire, they sat in a sullen silence, trying to keep their teeth from chattering.

"I believe," Leena said at length, shivering in the cold, her voice quavering, "that I know whence this Per comes."

Hieronymus merely raised an eyebrow, his hands tucked beneath his arms for warmth, but Balam turned to her and said, through chattering teeth, "What?"

"I believe he is Ikaru, the 'offspring' about whom Benu told us."

Hieronymus nodded, licking chapped lips. "That would account for his reportedly long life."

"That was my thinking, too," Leena said. "And I think I even saw a hint of opalescence to his eye color."

"But why," Hieronymus asked, "would this Ikaru want to start a religion among the metamen, spend decades building its following, and then mass the faithful at the gates of Atla?"

"Perhaps," Balam said, "Per, whatever his real name, may have darker motives than his followers suspect."

✦

It was past midday on the second day past the Barrier that they reached the foot of Mount Ignis. Since passing through the shimmering green curtain, they had seen no sign of life, and nothing to indicate that the southern peninsula was anything but a lifeless, frozen tomb.

It was at the base of the mountain that they saw the first indication that there had ever been any civilization here at all, discounting the incomprehensible energy barrier.

"What is it?" Leena said, in her awe forgetting the unforgiving cold.

Running straight up the side of the mountain was a narrow channel, ribbed with steps.

"The fabled Stair of Ignis," Balam said admiringly.

They drew nearer, and approached the first step of the stair.

"Look," Hieronymus said, pointing to the edge of the channel.

The stair was some four meters across, the steps themselves no deeper or taller than one would find in any human household. What was remarkable about the stair, though, were the sides of the channel. These railings were cut into the rock of the mountain itself, with delicate curves and intricate bas-relief throughout. Leena took a few short strides nearer the railing to the right, and saw intricately carved representations of men, animals, and machines crowding the channel's sides.

"Well, I don't see any reason to delay," Leena said, hiking her pack higher on her back and mounting the first step.

Hieronymus paused for a moment, his fingertips brushing against the shapes of the figures carved in the railings, and then reluctantly turned to follow Leena up the stair. Balam hung back for a moment, looking up the steep pitch of the steps to the summit of the mountain, high overhead, before finally placing a foot on the first step.

✦

Hours later, having climbed hundreds of meters, the company stopped to rest. The winds were fierce, battering into the side of the mountain, but strangely the higher they climbed, the warmer the air seemed. Warmth began to bleed back into their extremities, and Leena could not say that it was only the exertion of the climb that was responsible.

The trio passed a water flask from hand to hand, and munched what remained of their dried meat and hard bread. After they had eaten, they paused for a few moments longer, collecting their strength and wits about them.

"I simply cannot move my thoughts past contemplation of these railings," Hieronymus said. He sat on the far side of the step, his nose just centimeters from the carved relief. "I don't know how closely you two have been able to look at them during our climb, but they are simply remarkable." He reached out, and followed the shape of strange machines, carved in relief, with his fingertips. "These railings are not just functional, nor even just decorative, but must have originally been intended to likewise serve an instructive purpose. Every square foot of them is covered in these minute carvings showing the history of the Black Sun Empire. And the closer one looks, the more detail is revealed."

"Fascinating," Leena said without feeling, rubbing her aching calves.

"I know," Hieronymus said without a hint of irony. "It is surely a sign of the age and power of the Black Sun Empire in former days that they would expend so much effort on the back steps."

"Be that as it may," Balam said, drawing a knife and sighting down its blade, "I find myself a little more concerned not with what was, but with what *is*. Namely, what is waiting for us at the top of this stair."

With the knife's point, Balam pointed up the stairs, to the summit of the mountain above, where the red diamond of the citadel city could just be glimpsed.

$$\Large \diamond\!\!\!\!\!+$$

Hundreds of meters, blending into kilometers, Hieronymus, Leena, and Balam followed the stair as it ran straight up the mountainside.

They reached the top, swords and pistols drawn.

Leena was not sure whether to be surprised or not when, mounting the final steps, they found no one and nothing there to bar their way. Only plants, and mechanized gardeners, and the walls of the citadel city.

The stair ended at a wide, open plaza above which the many-faceted walls of Atla rose. The air in the plaza was surprisingly warm and still, and in the wide open space beneath the cantilevered city walls spread a well-tended garden, close-trimmed grass beneath man-icured trees, flowers and bushes arranged with geometric precision, spelling out strange sigils and formulas in their dazzling hues. Small machines scuttled to and fro, looking like wide-bodied spiders of metal and crystal, tending to the grass, clearing away fallen leaves from beneath the manicured trees, and sweeping away drifts of dirt, keeping the plaza looking fresh-minted and new.

"It looks like one enormous gemstone," Leena said, looking up with awe at the citadel rising above her.

"Any culture capable of generating that barrier," Hieronymus said, "must have had science we can scarcely guess at. Perhaps the city *is* an immense gem, a cultured diamond grown into this enormous size and strange configuration."

The dazzling walls of the multifaceted citadel seemed to glow from within, the same shade of vivid scarlet as the Carneol in Leena's pack.

"Look there," Balam said, pointing. Set into one of the lower facets was an immense doorway, standing open and unguarded.

Warily, the trio crossed the plaza, while small machines went about their business, paying them no mind. The trio entered the door, passing into the forbidden city of the wizard-kings.

CHAPTER 49
The Citadel City

Beyond the doorway, the trio found themselves in the city proper. It was like nothing Leena had ever seen, like nothing she'd ever imagined.

Past a small vestibule that led to the plaza garden, they entered a large space whose crystalline walls rose to vertiginous heights overhead. The floor was like the surface of a diamond, slick and unmarred, decorated with intricate swirls of color and light that seemed to shift beneath their gaze, as though living things moved beneath the surface, though Leena was sure it was a trick of the strange light, a reddish glow that seemed to emanate from the very walls themselves.

Strange shapes rose from the floor at intervals, constructed of the same crystalline material as the walls and floor, though whether these were furniture, or sculpture, or something stranger, Leena could not guess. There were also small pillars of polished metal, rising a meter or so off the floor, surmounted by square tabletop-like structures, on which were arranged crystals of all shapes and colors, in intricate geometric patterns, which for Leena called to mind the switches and dials of the Vostok module.

The air within the city was clean and sweet-smelling, not nearly so thin as Leena would have expected for such a lofty height. And on occasion, they could hear distant tinkling sounds, like water falling or metal striking gently against metal, but whether this was music or the sound of hidden machinery, none of the trio could say.

It took the trio several minutes to walk across the wide space to the doorways on the far side, and they passed the distance in silence, gripping swords, knives, and pistols warily, watchful for any sign of life. But the only movement that greeted their eyes was that of the scuttling crystal-and-metal machines, in their various sizes and configurations, that crawled over the floor and up the walls and over the ceiling, about their strange work.

"They must be some sort of autonomic maintenance system," Hieronymus said, pointing to the machines as they scuttled back and forth, polishing the crystalline protuberances, mending minute cracks in the walls and floor, and rearranging the crystals atop the metal pillars.

"But where are their builders?" Leena said guardedly.

"This place has the funereal air of a tomb," Balam grumbled, tightening his grip on his knives.

"Come along," Hieronymus said, striding towards the doorway. "Let's see what other strange wonders the citadel city holds, shall we?"

✦

They passed through massive galleries filled with sculptures and art that defied understanding; through huge arcades filled with stuffed and mounted creatures of all imaginable types, even a massive indrik. In another huge chamber they found machines and vehicles, airships at full size dangling from impossibly high ceilings, ground cars, tram-engines driven by coal, or spring, or oil. But still they had no sign of any living creatures.

After an hour of searching, having found no sign of life, the trio relaxed their vigil, and knives and swords were slid back into their scabbards, pistols returned to holsters.

"This is madness," Leena snapped, growing increasingly impatient. "We've traversed the length and breadth of the Paragaean continent, sent from one far-flung location to another, to reach the one place in this whole, misbegotten world where the answers we seek are rumored to be known, and we find no one here even to answer our questions!"

"Perhaps the Atlans *are* all gone, as Benu surmised," Balam said thoughtfully.

"Don't lose hope, friends," Hieronymus said, continuing on. "By my reckoning, we've still only explored a small fraction of the city's structure. There may yet be Atlans to be found."

"Suppose, though," Balam said, "that they don't *want* to be found." He glanced around them nervously.

Hieronymus smiled, and threw an arm around the jaguar man's shoulders. "If there are Atlans still living, my friend, they are but beings like you or I, not the semidivine demiurges of the Black Sun Genesis's imaginings."

Balam straightened, and nodded curtly. "Lead on, Hero," he said, his voice level. "I'll follow."

✦

Finally, they entered a large, sunlit chamber in which dozens of men and women lounged, eyes open but unmoving, on couches and beds arranged haphazardly around the room. All of the unmoving figures had deep red skin, white hair, and long, thin skulls, with small gems of various opalescent shades set into the flesh of their foreheads. They wore loose robes of silvery white and pale greens and reds, draped over them like burial gowns.

"The Atlans," Balam said, unable to keep a reverential tone from creeping into his voice.

"Are they dead?" Leena said, reaching out a tentative hand towards a woman on a nearby couch.

Hieronymus crouched beside a man stretched out on a divan, and touched a fingertip to the unmoving figure's neck.

"No," he said, shaking his head, "this one's pulse still beats. Slowly, but beating. They yet live."

"So do they slumber?" Balam asked, peering into the face of one of the unmoving women, her eyes wide and sightless.

Leena, Hieronymus, and Balam moved from one to another, trying to rouse them, but while they seemed healthy and whole, none even blinked in response.

Balam, frustrated, lifted one man off his bench, shaking him violently. "Wake, damn you!"

"Balam," Leena called out from the far side of the room. "Put that man down!"

"Very well," Balam said, shrugging angrily, and dropped the unmoving body unceremoniously to the floor.

As soon as the man hit the ground, more of the many-legged machines scuttled out of a low alcove, lifted the still form back onto the couch, and carefully arranged its clothes.

"I wish you wouldn't do that," came a liquid voice from behind them. "It can't possibly disturb their repose, but I can't help but feel that it is in poor taste."

A man stood beneath a high archway, smiling but weary. He was of average height, dressed in a loose-fitting robe that seemed to be made of spun moonlight, and like all of the still figures in the room he had white hair that stood in stark contrast to his deep red skin; a long, thin skull; and a small gem set on his forehead.

"Who are you?" Hieronymus demanded, hand flying to his saber's hilt.

The strange figure gave a slight curtsy.

"My nomen is Edurovrahtrelarnivast-$(\Psi/b)^2(\Theta_e)$ж-Descending-Viridian-Prime, but you may address me as Eduro."

CHAPTER 50

Paragaea

"You are welcome to Atla," the man called Eduro said, gliding across the floor to stop just before the trio, moving effortlessly and with an impossible grace, "as we have not had any visitors in long centuries, if not longer."

"You might entertain more often," Hieronymus said warily, moving nearer to Leena, "if the Barrier wall did not still prevent all approach to the mountain."

"Oh," Eduro asked distractedly, "is that old thing still on?" He tilted his head momentarily to one side, stared into empty space, and blinked. "There. We'd simply forgotten it had been left on, all those years ago."

He held his arms wide, and regarded the trio with a thin smile.

"Now," he asked, "why have you come to Atla?"

Hieronymus and Balam both looked to Leena, who stepped forward, shuffling her feet sheepishly like a recalcitrant student summoned to the front of a classroom, uneasy in the spotlight's glare.

"I am from Earth, an inadvertent traveler to this land," Leena said after a moment's pause, her tone firm and determined. "Tell me. Do the Atlans know of the gates which lead to Earth?"

"But of course," Eduro said with a dismissive wave. "The fissures are simply a side effect of the unfortunate incident which created Paragaea itself."

"Created Paragaea?!" Hieronymus regarded the strange man through narrowed eyes. "What 'incident' do you mean?"

"An experiment involving a singularity, of course, much like the one which now powers Atla itself."

"Singularity?" Leena repeated. "You talk in riddles!" She paused, taking a deep breath, collecting her reserves of patience. "Explain yourself, if you please."

Eduro shook his thin head fractionally from side to side, and his eyelids slid closed and open sleepily. "I'm afraid all of this excitement has quite exhausted me." He turned and started to walk back under the archway. "The servitors will lead you to your rooms"—he waved his hand, and a trio of the metal-and-crystal machines scuttled out of hiding, one stopping before each of them—"where you can make yourselves comfortable. When we have all regained our strength, I'll summon you and we can talk further, yes?"

Eduro passed beneath the archway, and from a hidden recess above, a door slid down into place in an eyeblink, sealing off the passage.

"It would appear," Leena said, her mouth drawn into a line, "that we have no choice."

✦

The scuttling creatures led them to a suite of sumptuous, palatial rooms, the finest Leena had ever seen. Each room had a separate bathing chamber, with a crystal tub the size of a small boat that filled with steaming hot water at the touch of a fingertip, smelling slightly of roses. Trying to quell her mounting impatience, Leena took a long, luxurious soak in the tub, collecting her thoughts.

"This is a remarkable place," came the voice of Hieronymus from the doorway. He had stripped off the bulky layer of clothes he'd worn through the frozen wastes, now barefoot and wearing only a new pair of trousers and a loose-fitting shirt open to the waist. "If anyone has the answers we seek, it must be these people."

"New clothes?" Leena said, leaning her soap-slicked elbows on the edge of the tub and giving him an appraising look.

Hieronymus looked down at his shirt and trousers admiringly. "Yes, it appears our host has thought of everything. When I climbed out of the bath, I found the strange little servitor machines had lain out clean clothes for all of us in the vestibule."

"Oh," Leena said with a disappointed pout, "so you've already bathed, then?" She rolled over and kicked to the far side of the enormous tub, floating lengthwise on the surface, her breasts and belly just cresting the water's edge.

"Well," Hieronymus said with a sly smile, "I suppose I *could* still use a bit of cleaning, at that. Balam will be busy grooming himself in his room for ages, and until this Eduro summons us, we've got nothing to do but wait."

He slipped out of the shirt, which fell to his feet, his tattoos and scars revealed, like a history of his lifetime written in ink and blood.

Leena stood, the water coming just to her navel, her wet hair plastered against her neck. Hieronymus shucked off his trousers and, as he slipped into the tub, she watched him admiringly, and smiled as she took him in her arms.

After a time, the voice of Eduro echoed from the walls, inviting them to dine with him. Hieronymus and Leena smiled sheepishly, entangled in rugs on the floor of the bathing chamber, and dressed quickly in the clothes provided. Leena's options included a floor-length gown, a kilt and blouse, or a pair of trousers and a loose-fitting shirt much like Hieronymus now wore. She opted for the trousers and shirt, though was grateful to find a pair of comfortable slippers in her size laid out on the bed, thankful not to have to put her boots on again for a short while.

When they had dressed, the trio gathered in the vestibule. Having traveled rough for so long a time, they each found it strange to see one another clean-scrubbed and dressed in finery. Each of them, though, had strapped on their holsters and scabbards, just as a precaution.

The servitors, scuttling before them, led the three through the corridors of the citadel city to a small room, modestly appointed with strange paintings and tapestries covering its walls, dominated by a long dining table upon which was piled a confusion of fruits, vegetables, and meats. At the head of the table sat Eduro, a beatific smile on his face, his teeth showing bright white against his red skin.

"Eat, my friends," he said, gesturing broadly to the table. "The city's senses indicate you have not eaten well in many days."

Leena, Hieronymus, and Balam exchanged guarded looks, but then sat around the table, eagerly diving into the proffered food.

"Why have we seen none of your countrymen," Balam asked, fruit juice dribbling down his chin, "none but the living dead in the sunlit room?"

"I am the only Atlan to remain mobile," Eduro explained, taking a sip from a crystal goblet that held some sort of light green liquid, "the rest having opted to impair the functioning of their right temporal lobes, severing their sensory connection to the outside world, preferring instead to live on in silent contemplation in their ageless, near-immortal bodies. Most of the more adventurous Atlans departed millennia ago, off to explore space or time."

"Exploring in ships, you mean?" Hieronymus asked. "Sailing the heavens?"

"Some left in vessels, to the moon, the planets, and the stars beyond," Eduro said. "But others used the fissures to travel back to Earth, in an attempt to save Atla that was, the original island nation that had been their home before the creation of Paragaea; but the fact that Paragaea persists suggests that they failed. Or, if nature prefers diversity to paradox, perhaps their efforts merely created an Earth where the island nation of Atla did not destroy itself in an accidental discharge of energy with the unleashing of a black hole, incredibly small but dissipating so quickly that their whole culture was destroyed."

Leena looked to Balam and Hieronymus, and it was clear they were as confused as she.

"I'm not sure I understand," Leena said. "You said *back* to Earth?"

"Yes," Eduro said, with a heavy sigh. "My people originated on Earth, like you. But at our civilization's peak, we destroyed ourselves, and were very nearly pushed over the brink of extinction. Our civilization had harnessed the power of singularities, such as that found when a star is so massive it collapses under its own gravitational pull. We used the power of controlled singularities to conquer the fundamental forces of the universe, and were the undisputed masters of Earth. In our arrogance, though, we grew lax in our precautions, and as a result, there was . . . an accident." Eduro blinked slowly, deep in thought. "Atla was a highly developed nation, our cities covering the length and breadth of our island continent. We had outposts on the other six continents, and our sphere of influence covered the globe."

Eduro pointed to a painting on a nearby wall, which seemed to depict a stylized map, with an island at its center, roughly circular, with a large inlet on the east, a hump to the west, and a tail of a peninsula to the south, surrounded by oceans ringed by oddly familiar landforms. Leena looked at it for a long moment before realizing that it appeared to be a map of Earth, with the Antarctic continent at the center of the projection.

"We had harnessed the means of creating singularities," Eduro went on, "and then drawing power from the energies that evaporated from them. But the temperature radiated from a singularity is inversely proportionate to its mass, and the smaller the singularity, the faster it evaporates away. Our scientists . . . miscalculated, and created a singularity that produced such a high energetic output over such a short span of time that our machinery was unable to compensate."

Eduro lowered his head for a moment, his eyes shut, but after a pause, resumed.

"We can only speculate what happened to Earth in the days and weeks following the destruction of Atla. It is theorized that one effect of the catastrophic release of energy might have been to shift the Earth's crust around its molten core, creating ecological havoc world-wide. Others object that the crust could not move in such a fashion, and in the absence of empirical evidence, the debate has raged for millennia. But, as I am the only Atlan still communicative, and I hold to the crust migration theory, I suppose that is the history to which we will adhere."

Leena and Hieronymus exchanged a glance, while Balam munched happily on some kind of iced fruit concoction.

"Whatever the extent of the devastation, though, Atla as it was had been destroyed. Only the pocket realm of Paragaea, created by chance in the wake of the explosion, proved our salvation. Two ships full of Atlans, aware of the coming catastrophe, attempted to flee, and found themselves thrown into the maelstrom of gravitational effects, where the very stuff of space-time itself was distorted. One of the ships passed through a fissure into an infant universe, which had been spawned just moments before in the final instant before the singularity released its energy in the final cataclysm. The other ship did not appear, and it was originally believed that it had been destroyed along with the Atlans' island home. In any event, this infant universe in which the Atlans found themselves was like a degraded copy of their home universe, though operating at a different time scale, and by the time the hapless Atlans were through the fissure, a billion years had already passed. Here, they found a twin to Earth, the continents familiar but lifeless."

"Lifeless?" Hieronymus asked.

"Yes, here on Paragaea, life had not taken root. The world which first greeted my forebears' eyes was barren and lifeless. Our history does not record their thoughts of those early days, but they must have been dark days, to say the least. They had only the contents of their ship to sustain them, and meager supplies at best."

Eduro motioned to a tapestry on a far wall, which depicted a few dozen red-skinned men and women standing before a large, crystalline ship, overlooking a wide, barren desert.

"It is conjectured that the microscopic singularity that powered the Atlan craft was responsible for changing the dynamic between the original universe and this sick, lifeless twin. The housing which contained the singularity had a negative energy characteristic, vital to maintain control of the powerful gravitational and energetic effects of the singularity. In any event, when the first Atlan craft passed into the fissure, it emerged into a new universe which was already billions of years old, but which had not yet been contaminated by contact from Earth. When the second Atlan craft attempted to pass into the fissure, at the moment of the cataclysm on Earth, the craft must have been destroyed, and in so doing, its constituent elements were reduced to powder. The negative energy housing of the drive mechanism, it is believed, shot like shrapnel through the fissure. Permeating the environment of this newfound world, the particulate elements periodically intersected with naturally occurring wormholes in the quantum foam, which in one in a billion trillion instances resulted in a transient, traversable wormhole, connecting a point on Paragaea to a point elsewhere. And since the space-time in which this new universe grew was connected by an umbilicus to Earth's universe, from time to time these traversable wormholes create fissures between the worlds, through which matter and energy can pass unharmed. Some of them remain viable only for a picosecond, or open onto the cold vacuum of space, or open deep within the molten crust of the planet, but some bare few allow the opportunity to move from one world to the other."

Leena swallowed hard, listening closely.

"Imagine, then, how surprised those Atlans must have been when new fissures began to open, and things fell through from Earth. Animals, organism-filled showers of seawater, seeds, even human beings. But due to the random nature of the fissures, they led to and from all points in Earth's history, not just the Atlans' own era. Now, with Paragaea slowly becoming stocked with flora and fauna, the Atlans would be able to survive." Eduro took another sip from his crystal goblet, and raised it in salute to the red-skinned men and women woven on the far tapestry. "My forebears, though, were not content merely to survive. Given this new world to inhabit, they sought to improve it, to make a better world than the one they had left behind, sundered forever. And so, the Atlans began to experiment with the animals and people who were transported via the fissures to Paragaea."

"You experimented on people?" Hieronymus asked, drawing back with shock.

"And why not? Isolated on our island home on Earth, we Atlans had developed into a subspecies of humanity ourselves, so we bore no guilt for using other human species in our experiments just as we used animals."

Eduro glanced at Balam, and flashed an avuncular smile.

"The results of these early experiments were the first metamen."

Balam stopped eating, and narrowed his amber eyes at the red-skinned man.

"The metamen were an amusing diversion for a time, grafting human and animal genetic material, manipulating the genes to create advantageous mutations, increased intelligence, improved senses. But after a time, we bored of these games, and released the viable species into the wild."

Leena and Hieronymus looked to Balam, worried about how he might react, but to their surprise, he merely thought for a moment, shrugged, and went back to eating.

"For a long span, we Atlans kept to ourselves, but when we had rebuilt over the generations to the point where it was possible once again to harness the power of a larger-scale singularity, our thoughts turned towards control. This was the beginning of the Black Sun Empire. But even in those days, in which we ruled all of Paragaea, most Atlans stayed atop Ignis, preferring to send out agents to collect information and send it back. Agents either human, or metaman, or even artificial."

"Like Benu," Leena said, nodding.

"Yes," Hieronymus said. Seeing Eduro's confused expression, he explained. "We met an artificial man, who said that he had been constructed for a similar purpose in ancient days by the Atlans."

"Oh, really?" Eduro leaned forward eagerly, eyes wide. "And where is this Benu now?"

"Somewhere, nowhere, who knows?" Balam shrugged.

"He entered one of the gates," Leena said, "and left Paragaea behind."

"That's too bad," Eduro said with a sigh. "I would have liked the chance to meet one of our probes."

"You might still get your wish, if you desire," Balam said darkly.

"Oh?"

"Yes," Hieronymus said, "there is an army of religious fanatics encamped to the north, excavating something from the dead soil of Eschar, for what reason we don't know. And at their head is a being who we believe might be the 'son' of Benu, a replacement body that was allowed to develop a mind of its own."

"Oh, dear," Eduro said, clapping his hands. "That sounds exciting, doesn't it?"

Leena leaned forward nervously, her fingers laced together. "Eduro, you still haven't said. Have your people . . ." She paused, swallowing hard. "Have your people the knowledge of controlling or predicting the gates to Earth?"

"But of course," he said casually. "We can open fissures to whichever point in space-time we desire. Why, did you want to return?"

CHAPTER 51
The Eye of Atla

The next morning, Eduro led the trio to a vast room at the heart of the citadel city. The crystal floor at their feet glowed red and orange as shapes and shadows moved in its depths, while the ceiling rose in a high dome overhead. Arranged in a circle were metallic pedestals, surmounted by flat tables upon which gemstones were arranged in complex patterns. At the center of the circle, hovering several meters off the floor, was a large sphere of complete blackness, around which coruscated red tongues of flame.

"In ancient days," Eduro said, pointing at the floor, "Atla drew its power from the thermal energies of the volcanic Ignis. In time, our energy requirements outstripped the volcano's output, but fortunately by then we had once again mastered the art of creating and maintaining singularities."

Balam took a step forward, as though mesmerized, his eyes on the black sphere overhead. "What is it?"

"Take care," Leena said warily.

"Oh, it's quite safe, I assure you," Eduro said. "At a distance, of course. You don't want to venture too close to the encasement, as it is constructed of matter which, in addition to not registering on the visual spectrum, also has a negative energy density. It would not be wise to come into physical contact with it."

"So that is the singularity of which you spoke?" Hieronymus pointed at the black sphere.

"Yes," Eduro said. "The sphere you see is actually the event horizon of the singularity within. However, though light cannot escape, radiation does bleed from the singularity, evaporating away in an energetic spectrum, which is then directed through channels to fulfill the energy needs of Atla."

"And this energy will allow you to create the gateway to Earth?" Leena said.

Eduro smiled. "I believe so. It's been some time since any of us had a yen to travel, and so the citadel hasn't had to create a traversable wormhole in a considerable while."

Hieronymus paced around the perimeter of the room, regarding the gem-topped pedestals. "The *citadel* creates the wormhole?"

"In a sense." Eduro walked to the nearest of the pedestals, and repositioned one of the gems on its surface. Then he turned back towards the trio, glanced at the ceiling overhead, and said, "Atla?"

"*Atla awaits your instruction, Edurovrahtrelarnivast-$(\Psi/b)^2(\Theta_e)$ж- Descending-Viridian-Prime, best beloved,*" came a musical voice, seeming to echo from the walls themselves.

"Housed within the walls of cultured diamond which make up the citadel city resides the intelligence which is Atla." Eduro reached out, and touched the edge of the pedestal with a gesture that seemed almost affectionate.

"So the city is *alive*?" Balam said, looking warily at the crystalline walls around them.

"In a sense," Eduro said. "As alive as the probe you encountered, at any rate, to which it is close cousin."

Leena crossed her arms over her chest, uneasy at the thought that the city had senses that could have watched them at any moment. She blushed slightly, involuntarily, and hugged her arms to her chest tighter.

"Now, my dear," Eduro said, turning to her, "if you will help me fix your desired point of entry, in terms both spatial and temporal, I can instruct Atla to begin work on the calculations necessary to locate and open a suitable gate. It may take some time, since the city's intelligence will have to sort through a trillion possibilities every fraction of a second, but in time, it should be able to locate a microscopic wormhole occurring naturally within the walls of the city itself which should suit your purpose."

✦

In the end, it took nearly a day of studying ancient Atlan star charts and projections of stellar precession for Eduro and Leena to work out the point in time to which the gateway should lead, and several more hours to work out a desirable geographical location. The destination would not be exact, and so Eduro instructed the crystalline intelligence of Atla to err on the side of caution, preferring to send Leena back to Earth a small number of years after she departed, rather than risking her arriving on Earth before she launched in the Vostok 7 module, which could engender paradox and the violation of causality. Even Eduro and the combined wisdom of the Atlans could not say with certainty what would eventuate, were that to happen.

✦

The afternoon of the company's third day in Atla, while they waited for the crystalline intelligence to complete its computations, their diversions were interrupted by a gonging sound issuing from the walls themselves.

Hieronymus and Leena had been in their quarters, enjoying their solitude while Balam was in a large kitchen a short distance away, making experimental dishes with the strange foodstuffs with which the city's larder was stocked. They paused in the long silence that followed the sound of the gong, expectant.

"Friends, my apologies." The voice of Eduro echoed from the walls, disembodied. "Will you please join me in the refectory? There's something I wish to show you. The servitors will show you the way."

Leena and Hieronymus dressed quickly, but before leaving their quarters, he took her by the hand.

"We have come a considerable distance to reach this point," he said, pulling her close to him. "And it seems that the means to return to Earth is nearly within your grasp. So I must ask you. Are you still bound to return?"

Leena averted her eyes, squeezing his hand tightly. "I must fulfill my duty. I am obligated to return, and report on what I have learned."

"And nothing would convince you to stay?"

Leena looked up at him, their eyes meeting.

"I . . ." she began. "Though I must go, there are things about this world that it pains me to leave behind."

Hieronymus nodded thoughtfully.

"When you go, would you object to a traveling companion?" He smiled slightly. "I've seen much of what Paragaea has to offer, these last years, and it might be interesting to see how Earth has changed since my long-ago departure."

Leena's eyes misted, and she drew Hieronymus to her, wrapping her arms around him.

"Together, then," she said, her face buried in his chest.

"Together."

They stood like that, holding one another, for a long moment, until a servitor appeared at the doorway and began to twitch anxiously.

"Come along, then," Leena said, drying her eyes and striding towards the door. Let's see what our host has to show us."

The pair followed the scuttling spiderlike machine through the corridors of the city, and at last reached a long, high-ceilinged room dominated by a large, curved screen of translucent crystal that rose dozens of meters above the floor. Balam was already there, lounging on a low couch, munching on a pastry of his own concoction.

"Oh, thank you for coming so quickly," Eduro said, gliding into the room, gathering the folds of his spun-moonlight robe around him. "Atla has alerted me to something that I thought you should see."

The Atlan moved to stand below the curved crystal screen.

"This is the Eye of Atla," Eduro explained, motioning Leena and Hieronymus to join Balam on the couches. "With it, we can see whatever the senses of the city can detect."

Leena and Hieronymus sat together on a divan, a short distance from Balam, their eyes on the translucent screen.

"Go ahead, Atla," Eduro said, and sank into an overstuffed chair.

On the screen an image suddenly appeared, with such detail and clarity that it seemed to Leena as though she were looking through an enormous window, not at a projected image.

"Damn," Balam snarled, fangs bared.

The screen showed them the image of hundreds of metamen crowded about a massive machine of some sort, propelled on an enormous wheeled platform. The perspective of the screen was such that it appeared the viewer stood directly in front of the approaching metamen, behind whom a snow-covered plain stretched to the horizon.

"Rotate," Eduro said, and the perspective of the screen shifted dizzyingly, rotating through space around the metamen while spinning one hundred and eighty degrees, so that in a split second it now appeared to the viewers as though they were standing behind the metamen and looking forward.

Towering before the metamen was a wall of rock, into which a channel had been cut, rising straight up at a steep grade.

"That's Ignis," Hieronymus said, jumping to his feet.

"Of course," Eduro said, surprised. "Why else should I be concerned?"

"That looks like the machine Per's followers were excavating in Eschar," Leena said. "What is it?"

"It is an ancient Atlan war engine, last used in the metamen uprising," Eduro explained. "Pulling its power directly from the singularity at Atla's heart, the weapon is capable of destroying a whole continent. Fortunately, the city's senses indicate the machine's reserves are drained to empty, and so the weapon would need to be brought in close proximity to Atla itself to be recharged."

As they watched, the metamen reached the foot of the mountain, and in their hundreds began to struggle the enormous machine onto the Stair of Ignis.

"Look there," Balam said, pointing to a small, pale figure at the corner of the screen.

"Magnify, please," Eduro said, and the perspective of the screen shifted again, zooming in and focusing on the pale figure.

It was Per, standing with the metamen dignitaries, directing the activities of his followers.

"Oh, yes, indeed," Eduro said excitedly. "That is most definitely a degraded example of one of the Atlan probes."

"Then Per's army *was* marching south to Atla," Hieronymus said.

"And Per is Ikaru, after all," Balam said. "Whatever his dark purpose."

"But how did he get past the Barrier?" Leena asked. "Without the Carneol, we'd not have been able to get through, ourselves."

"Well," Eduro said absently, "the war engine, with its power systems, could conceivably have been modified in such a way to drain its charge from the Barrier wall itself. It would have taken a considerable amount of time, but it would have been possible." He paused, and shrugged. "But since I deactivated the Barrier shortly after you arrived, that wasn't necessary."

A contingent of metamen, armed and fearsome, raced up the Stair while their brothers below labored in their hundreds beneath the war engine, moving it slowly but steadily up the mountainside.

CHAPTER 52
Assault

All eyes were on the image of the ancient, wizened creature on the screen, his mouth wide as he shouted at his assembled followers.

"If Per is the offspring of Benu," Balam asked, pacing before the crystal screen, fangs bared, "then what does he have to gain from all of this?"

"Well," Eduro said, distractedly motioning towards the screen, "let's see, shall we?"

Suddenly, the room filled with amplified sound, and they could hear the whistling wind, the murmuring hordes of metamen, and, above it all, the rising voice of Per.

". . . the blood of the Atlans, who have abandoned you, their offspring! The universe has decreed that the demiurges who created you must now be uncreated, so that you can ascend and take their place, as you have always been fated to do. You have proven yourselves worthy, and now, at the time of the Reckoning, you shall be rewarded."

Eduro motioned again, and the room once more fell silent.

"Well, I think that explains it," Hieronymus said dryly.

"He wants revenge," Leena said. "When Benu related the story to us, he told us of Ikaru's madness, and his thirst for control."

"But surely his cognition is not damaged so extensively that he believes he can actually *survive* the war engine being used," Eduro said, disbelieving. "It was intended for remote detonation only, and one would have to be far from the blast radius to escape complete discorporation."

"Maybe he doesn't want to survive," Balam said, looking at the screen beneath lowered brows. "I think he craves death, not just for himself, but for all living creatures. Look at his eyes. He is beyond madness, now."

"Eduro," Hieronymus said, striding over and taking the Atlan by the arm. "Is there any way to disable the war engine before it can be recharged?"

"Our only option would be to allow the energy of the singularity to bleed into the higher dimensions, leaving the war engine without power. It would also, though, leave Atla itself without power."

Leena stepped forward, eyes wide. "But you must finish opening the gate to Earth. If the power is cut off before the calculations are completed, we'll *never* be able to return home."

"We?" Balam said, and looked from Leena to Hieronymus and back.

"We'll explain later," Hieronymus answered, and turned to the Atlan. "Leena is right, Eduro."

"Oh, very well," Eduro said impatiently. "Come with me."

The Atlan spun on his heel, and glided across the floor to a far entrance, the trio following close behind.

✦

After a winding course through the citadel city's corridors, they reached the singularity chamber, where the black sphere still hung in midair, surrounded by coruscating flames.

Eduro went to stand beside one of the metal pedestals, and rearranged the gems on its tabletop surface. "Atla, full display."

The faceted walls of the singularity chamber were immediately illuminated with images, one for each faceted face. One showed the foot of the mountain, where the being called Per spoke blood and thunder to the massed metamen. On another could be seen the Stair, up which the war engine slowly climbed. Another displayed the higher reaches of the Stair, swarmed with armed metamen, intent on destruction. Still others showed views of the plaza garden beyond the citadel walls, and of the chambers and corridors of the city itself.

Eduro picked a small green gem off the pedestal's top, and then turned to face the trio, who watched the scenes playing out on the crystal walls all around them.

"I will leave the processes running," Eduro explained. "When the calculations are complete, Atla will open the wormhole and provide you with its location. As soon as you are done with the wormhole, merely place this onto the center of the control panel"—he handed Hieronymus the green gem—"and the encasement will reconfigure such that the singularity bleeds off into the higher dimensions, and the war engine will be left powerless." He posed, and then sighed wistfully. "I only hope that the wormhole calculations are complete before the war engine is brought near enough to be recharged, or this discussion is plainly moot."

"Won't you be here to do this yourself?" Hieronymus asked, looking with an expression commingling confusion and disgust at the gem in his hand.

"No," Eduro answered, "I must excuse myself now, I'm afraid. It was a distinct pleasure meeting you three, I'm sure."

"Where are you going?" Leena asked.

"I must go and meet this Per, or Ikaru, or whatever he chooses to call himself. I have always wanted to encounter one of the ancient probes, and this may well be my last opportunity."

Eduro turned, and walked back to the doorway. At the threshold, he turned his head over his shoulder, and smiled at the trio. "You know, I will be the first Atlan to leave the citadel city in more than a millennium. How strange."

With that, he passed through the doorway, and was gone.

On one of the faceted walls of the singularity chamber, nearly an hour later, the trio watched as Eduro stepped out into the plaza just as the first wave of armed metamen poured up over the top step of the Stair.

"He'll be killed!" Leena shouted.

"Perhaps," Hieronymus said. "But perhaps not. Watch."

On the projected image, they saw Eduro touch the gem on his forehead, and as the first of the metamen was almost within arm's reach, a faint aura of shimmering green suddenly appeared around the Atlan's form.

"Hmmm." Balam nodded appreciatively as the metaman swung at Eduro's head with a cudgel, only to be buffeted back forcefully by the green aura.

"A kind of personal barrier," Hieronymus said admiringly. "Must come in handy."

Eduro continued across the plaza, the ranks of the metamen dividing before him like a river bending around a promontory, and finally disappeared from view, climbing down the Stair.

"He might have mentioned this barrier to us," Leena said, sighing with relief. "Of course, in short order, we'll have the metamen to contend with, assuming that the city's processes ignore them as they did us, on our first arrival."

The first of the metamen reached the entrance to the citadel city, and the trio watched on the crystal display as they stormed inside. Balam jumped, startled, when a quartet of Sinaa hove into view, a male and three females.

"Gerjis," the jaguar man spat. "And my sisters, with Menchit in tow."
Balam turned to Leena and Hieronymus, his expression imploring.
Hieronymus nodded, solemnly. "I understand, friend. Go ahead."

Balam took a heavy breath, and then stepped forward, taking
Leena in a crushing embrace.

"Should we not meet again, Leena, know that it was a pleasure to
travel at your side."

"You . . . too . . ." Leena managed, scarcely able to breathe.

"Good luck," Balam shouted, releasing his hold on her. Then he
turned, fangs bared and claws out, and raced off into the diamond
citadel, bent on revenge of his own.

CHAPTER 53
A Final Farewell

From their vantage in the singularity chamber, Leena and Hieronymus watched as the metamen, bloodlust and righteous fury driving them, destroyed one gallery after another, the servitors trying in vain to repair the damage in their wake.

It was some time later that Balam finally caught up to the tide of destruction, in the chamber of the sleeping Atlans. The metamen had reached the room only a few moments before him, and had already begun to slaughter the sleeping Altans, mercilessly.

Leena shuddered as she watched the screen overhead. On it, Balam skidded into the room, eyes flashing, just as the quartet of Sinaa led by Gerjis savaged an unconscious, insensate Atlan, pale blood staining their claws and fangs.

"The calculations are nearly complete," came the voice of Atla from the walls of the singularity chamber. *"Only a final million permutations must be examined before the traversable wormhole can be opened."*

On the crystal screen overhead, Hieronymus and Leena saw Balam cut down his cousin Gerjis with a mortal blow, only to receive a vicious cut to his left leg and arm from one of his sisters.

Blood flowing freely from his wounds, Balam faced off against his sisters, a grim smile on his face, a knife in either hand. A short distance away stood Menchit, watching intently but immobile. Leena thought that perhaps the young Sinaa was experiencing some conflicting emotions, watching her aunts and her father locked in a duel to the death.

"The fissure opens."

A few meters from where Leena stood, a gleaming sphere coalesced into existence, hovering two meters off the crystalline floor. In contrast to the larger black sphere high overhead, this one was no larger than a man's fist, and shone mirror bright.

"Verification follows."

From the doorway appeared another of the servitors, but unlike the scuttling spiderlike creatures they'd seen so far, this one was surmounted by a set of metallic, clattering wings. It advanced on four spindly legs, and when it stood directly beneath the shimmering sphere, the servitor's wings began to beat, as invisibly fast as those of a hummingbird, and the little machine lifted gracefully off the floor. It rose straight up towards the gate, and as soon as it touched the sphere's surface, it seemed to recede from view, and then was gone.

"Transmission received."

One of the crystal facets of the chamber, which before had provided a view of a far-off corridor, now changed, and Leena and Hieronymus could see projected a wide wheat field stretching under a clear blue sky, with men and farm machinery in the near distance. A road sign, barely visible towards one side, clearly showed words written in the Cyrillic alphabet.

"It's a farm collective in the Soviet Union," Leena said, almost breathless.

"Confirmed."

"In that case, Leena, I believe it is time for you to leave," Hieronymus said, his mouth drawn into a tight line.

"No!" Leena turned to Hieronymus, her eyes wide. "Come with me! We don't know that Per will reach the summit with the war engine. Perhaps Eduro can stop him, or reason with him, or—"

"No," Hieronymus answered, shaking his head sadly. "I'm sorely tempted, but we can't take that chance. If I'm not here to shut down the city's power before the engine is brought near, Per is liable to destroy most of Paragaea, all for his mindless revenge. Besides"—he flashed a weary smile—"I can't leave Balam to face his mortal enemies alone, now can I?"

The two drew near, and Hieronymus gathered her in his arms.

"I don't . . ." Leena began, and her voice choked off in her throat. She wasn't sure if she'd be able to go through the gate. "Oh, Hieronymus. If I could stay . . ."

"I know." Hieronymus stepped back, and took her face in his hands, staring deep into her eyes. "You have your duty. I understand. I served a flag once, long ago and far away. Now, my only duty is to myself and my friends, and were I to be the cause of you failing in your mission, or my friend Balam's needless death through inaction, I wouldn't deserve to count either of you my friends. So you must pass through the gate, and I must be here to close it."

He pushed her reluctantly away from him, holding her shoulders in his hand.

"If I can," Leena said fervently, "if it is possible, if there's any way at all, once I fulfill my duty I'll return to you."

Hieronymus smiled sadly, and slowly stepped away. "I'll be waiting, then."

Leena could not wait any longer. It took all the will she could muster, but she turned around and walked to stand before the gate hovering silently above the crystal floor.

Leena reached out her hand, but just before her fingers touched the gate, she turned to Hieronymus, her eyes misting. "Good-bye, love."

Afraid to wait a moment longer, for fear that she might lose her resolve, Leena held her breath and leaned forward. Her fingertips brushed the surface of the sphere, finding it surprisingly warm to the touch. Then she felt a strange sensation deep inside her, as though she were weightless and pulling multiple gees, all at once, and there came a blinding moment of darkness.

She fell more than two meters before she hit the ground, landing with a thud that drove the air from her lungs. She pushed herself up on her elbows, and glanced distractedly at the farmers rushing towards her, hoes in hand, shouting in Russian.

She was home.

FIRST EPILOGUE

Moscow

Leena sat on the unforgiving seat of the hardwood bench, the corridor cold and empty. The door to the committee chamber was closed, but through the heavy wood, she could hear the muffled voices from beyond. She shifted uneasily. Her uniform, starched and pressed, seemed confining and restrictive, the jacket too tight across the belly, and the collar itched her neck.

This would be her tenth appearance before the committee, and her last. She would make one last attempt to convince the committee members, and then wash her hands of the whole matter.

When she had appeared in Moscow, weeks before, no one had believed for a second her account of another world, of ancient science and jaguar men and giant beasts. Most of the officers and agents who had interrogated her in the weeks that followed thought that she was mad, that she had crash-landed more than two years before, and then wandered in a haze of delirium in all the long months since, dreaming of her other world. Some few who'd spoken to her were convinced that she was a traitor, having spent the time since her disappearance among the Americans, selling national secrets, and that she was now being sent back among them like a snake slithering back into a bird's nest to steal more eggs.

Whichever view, in the end, held sway, Leena knew she would never be hailed as a returning hero. The committee would likely send her to an asylum, or a prison, or, at best, to a posting well out of the public eye, in Siberia where there would be few to hear her mad tales, and fewer still to believe.

But Leena would give them one more chance. One last opportunity to hear her testimony and be convinced of its truth, and then she would put her plans into motion.

The door to the committee chamber opened, and a young, fresh-faced private peered out into the corridor. He smiled sheepishly and motioned to Leena. "Lejtenant Chirikova?"

Leena drew a heavy breath, and climbed to her feet. She paused for a moment and laid a hand on her swelling belly. It would be a few months still before she would begin to show, and by then she would either have been exonerated by the committee, or she would be somewhere far, far from here.

Leena crossed the corridor, and stepped into the committee chamber for the final time.

SECOND EPILOGUE

London

Leena stood on a London street, holding the little girl's hand and staring intently at the blue door, as snow fell in flurries all around them.

"Mat'," the little girl cried, catching a snowflake in her outstretched hand. "Snezhinka!"

"English, Sinovia," Leena scolded, shaking her head. She looked down at the child who could never have a future in Russia, but might well here in England. "Remember, always English now."

The little girl twisted her mouth into a moue of concentration for a moment, and then said, tentatively, "Snowflake, Mother?"

"Very good, Sinovia." Leena nodded, and leaning down, picked the little girl up. Only two years old, she seemed to be getting heavier by the day. Leena shrugged her shoulders, repositioning the straps of the pack on her back, which held their every worldly possession. "Snowflake."

The little girl held in her arms, Leena crossed the street, walked up to the blue door and, pausing only a moment to collect her thoughts, rang the buzzer.

A young woman opened the door, her stomach slightly swollen in contrast with her slight frame.

"Is this the Bonaventure residence?" Leena asked, having almost lost all trace of her Russian accent.

"Yes," the woman answered.

"Are you . . . are you a Bonaventure, then?"

"Not quite yet," the woman said with a confused smile, cradling her belly, "but I will be by next month." She turned, and called over her shoulder, "Stephen."

An unassuming man with unkempt hair and glasses appeared at the woman's side. "Yes?"

"This woman is looking for a Bonaventure, darling."

"Hello. I knew another Bonaventure, a relative of yours, I believe, somewhere far away."

"Oh?"

"Yes, and when I located your branch of the family in London, I thought . . . I thought I might introduce myself. And I very much wanted my daughter Sinovia to meet you."

"Sinovia, is it?" The man reached out and patted the little girl's cheek, awkwardly but with affection. "You know, I've got a nephew just about your age."

The young woman beside him placed her hand over her stomach, and smiled at him lovingly. "And we've got a little one of our own on the way. Rodger, if it's a boy; Roxanne if it's a girl."

"Well now," the man said, looking from the woman to Leena and the little girl. "We can't very well leave you outside in the cold, can we?"

The man stepped to one side, and motioned to Leena eagerly.

"Come in, come in," he said.

Leena passed through the doorway, out of the cold and into the warmth beyond.

"Where did you say you knew this other Bonaventure, then?" the man asked, closing the door behind them.

Leena smiled. She would find her way back to Paragaea and Hieronymus one day, but until then, at least Hieronymus's daughter would know her family, in some small fashion.